TORPEDO

A GABRIEL WOLFE THRILLER

ANDY MASLEN

TYTON PRESS

For Lorna Baines

"Anybody can become angry – that is easy. But to be angry with the right person and to the right degree and at the right time and for the right purpose, and in the right way – that is not within everybody's power and is not easy."
Aristotle

Torpedo /tɔːpiːdoː/ n. Russian criminal slang: contract killer.

1

ALDEBURGH, SUFFOLK, ENGLAND

My name is Gabriel Wolfe. Death walks in my footsteps. The further I travel in this life, the more Death enjoys himself. Sometimes, if I keep very still, I can hear the soft pad of his stinking, bloody feet as he dogs my trail.

I was a soldier for thirteen years – in the Paras and then the SAS. After a short, peaceful stint in civvy street, I started killing people for a living again. As a government troubleshooter.

My problem is, however much trouble I shoot for the Queen, I always seem to bring down a whole heap more onto my own, uncrowned, head.

I don't begrudge Her Majesty the imbalance in our fortunes. Nobody forced me to accept my former CO Don Webster's offer to join his "jolly band of cutthroats." I re-entered service as an operative for The Department willingly. In fact, I was filled with a sense of excitement. It was good to be back in action. Helping CEOs negotiate takeovers – my former job – was eating away at my soul.

What's consuming me now is my own ability to kill those dearest to me, as surely as a metastasising cancer cell. And I have come to believe that whereas you might dodge the incoming fire from the Big C with a dose of radiation, chemo or plain old luck, contact with me is one hundred percent fatal.

I can sleep. I've always been able to sleep, even when my PTSD was at its worst. But my dreams are populated with people I loved. Love, I mean.

My best friend from Salisbury, Julia Angell. My former comrades in The Regiment: Smudge, Dusty and Daisy. My mentor and the man who raised me after my parents ran out of patience, Master Zhao. All dead. All gone. All because of me.

And now, Britta Falskog. The woman I proposed to just a couple of years ago, who had just told me and Eli that she was engaged again, to a teacher from Uppsala. Britta did a dangerous job, just like I do. Just like Eli does. Counter-terror isn't exactly risk free, even in social democratic Sweden. But she wasn't killed doing her job. She was killed – murdered – because she got between a hitman's bullet and its intended target. Yours truly, once again.

It was a beautiful day. The sun was streaming down onto the beach just south of my home in Aldeburgh on the Suffolk coast. We could smell salt and ozone in the air. One minute she was laughing, the next she was dead. Falling away from me, half of her head missing.

As I sat beside her, I looked down into her sightless eyes. I wondered why my ex-fiancée wouldn't answer me. Shock, obviously. I tried again.

"Britta! Wake up," I said.

Her lips didn't move.

The *whop-whop* of the air ambulance's rotor blades distracted me. I stroked her right cheek with the backs of my fingers. Her head rolled to the left, spilling more brain matter onto the beach pebbles. I shook my head. *That's not good*, is what I thought. I picked up the soft piece of tissue and gently replaced it inside her shattered skull.

From beside me, I heard a voice. A woman's voice. *Eli! That's it,*

2

I thought. I'd gone down to the beach with Eli and Britta. For a walk. They were laughing. Then Britta fell.

Reality was knocking, but I didn't want to meet it. If I opened the door, I'd have to acknowledge the truth. And I wasn't ready for that. I squeezed my eyes shut. I started to hum. That didn't work, so I started singing instead. Louder and louder. The national anthem.

"God save our gracious Queen! Long live our noble Queen! God save the Queen! Send her victorious, happy and glorious, long to reign over us, GOD SAVE THE QUEEN!"

By the end I was shouting. Shouting, and weeping. It didn't work. I knew what had happened. Reality won. It always does.

Eli bent over me and hugged me to her chest. Her scent, of lemon and sandalwood, replaced the smell of the sea.

"The chopper's here," she said.

Her voice so full of compassion I wanted to scream at her.

"No! Leave me here!"

"Come on, get up. We need to let the paramedics take her now," she said. "And you've been shot. You need surgery."

As docile as a newly trained puppy, I stood, hauling myself to my feet on Eli's arm. She drew me back a few paces, and together we watched as the two green-uniformed paramedics, a man and a woman, slid Britta into a black plastic body bag and zipped her in snug. The man brought out a smaller bag and sank to his knees. He began collecting the parts of Britta's skull and brains that the hitman's bullet had splattered over the pebbles.

I remember very little of the helicopter ride to Ipswich Hospital. They gave me some high-octane painkiller – morphine, I assume – and the next thing I recall with any clarity is sitting up in bed the following morning, my shoulder bandaged and hurting like a bastard, with Eli sitting at my bedside, holding my other hand.

"Take me home now, please," I said to Eli.

They discharged me with strict instructions from the trauma surgeon that I should rest the arm for a minimum of six weeks, although it hadn't turned out to be as bad as everyone thought. Then I left with a paper bag full of painkillers and antibiotics.

The next day, we went for a walk. Just down Slaughden Road.

Nowhere near the beach. I saw someone coming, recognised the look. A detective. I pointed at her.

"Tell her to come to the house if she wants to talk to me."

Eli unhooked her arm and went to speak to the cop. She nodded then walked back towards me with Eli. As we neared the house, I found I was struggling to breathe. I closed my eyes. But that didn't help. I saw Britta, my freckled "super-Swede" laughing, revealing her gappy teeth. In happier times.

"Stop!" I hissed to Eli. "I can't breathe."

"Yes, you can. Look at me, Gabriel. Look at me!" she said. Ordered, really.

I complied, focusing on her grey-green eyes, noticing how the very outer rim of each iris was darker. The iron band around my chest released its grip. I gulped down air. The drowning sensation receded like the waves *shushing* in and out over the shingle. I knew what would happen next. I'd been there before. Questions. Statements. More questions. Raised eyebrows when the subject of my profession came up. Trips to a police station. Sour-tasting coffee.

We went inside and the cop began asking questions. Who? What? When? Where? Why? How? Any idea? Can you? Did you? Were you? I gave her the answers I felt able to. Noncommittal, packed full of incontrovertibly true details that would prove utterly useless.

After a while, she left.

And then, from somewhere deep down, way beyond where my conscious mind lives, an ancient, primal emotion gathered itself and forced its way upwards. Like magma racing through a fissure in the earth's crust before erupting and wiping out whole towns.

A desire for vengeance.

* * *

Gabriel Wolfe folded the sheet of paper into three and slid the narrow rectangle inside a thick, ridged envelope. This he placed in the top drawer of the desk in his study overlooking the beach. His teeth were hurting, and it was with a conscious effort that he unclenched his jaws.

He looked at his watch – 7.05 a.m. – then levered himself out of the battered old wood-and-leather swivel chair. He showered and dressed in jeans and a white T-shirt, careful to ease the stretchy fabric over the dressing on his injured shoulder, then padded downstairs in his bare feet.

2

MEDELLÍN, COLOMBIA

Kneeling at the low mahogany table, his python-skin Gucci loafers placed just beyond the edge of the tatami mats, Martin "The Tailor" Ruiz felt his muscular shoulders unlocking. He shook himself like a dog and the day's cares slid all the way off. Running a global business, especially one whose stock in trade was narcotics, really took it out of a man. When that man also had a large and demanding family, the stresses and strains were doubled, tripled even.

Today, he had burnished his reputation. He had slit the throat of a business rival and pulled his entire tongue out through the gash with his fingers, draping it over the man's bloodstained shirtfront. The infamous "Colombian necktie." In a grotesque innovation of his own, which had earned him his nickname, he had proceeded to stitch the thick, twitching length of meat to the writhing man's chest with an industrial staple gun.

Ruiz had discovered Willow Tree Tea House the previous month, and now visited the place at least once a week. Perhaps Colombia was the last place one would expect to find a club dedicated to the Japanese tea ceremony. He didn't care. The girls who served the powdered green tea – matcha – were all slender and beautiful. Or, he supposed, as beautiful as you could be when caked in that oddly erotic white makeup.

His two bodyguards, Yago and Benny, had protested the first time he'd left them on the street. Yes, he'd agreed with Yago, the streets of Medellín *were* dangerous. And for a drug lord, especially so. But within the serene confines of Willow Tree, he was not in danger.

"What?" he'd teased his six-foot-six, two-hundred-fifty-pound minder. "Are you frightened one of the tea girls will stick a chopstick into me?"

Then, laughing at his own wit, he'd entered, enjoyed an hour of tranquillity in the company of a quiet, respectful and utterly subservient young girl who looked like the genuine oriental article, tipped her five hundred dollars, and rejoined Yago and Benny on the street, free of puncture wounds and feeling spiritually cleansed.

Today, Ruiz had something to celebrate. Yes, he had survived another seven days in a murderous, internecine war between his outfit, El Nuevo Medellín, and a gang of Chinese upstarts who called themselves the White Koi. But, recently, one of the drug squad cops on his payroll had informed him that the White Koi were expecting a huge shipment of heroin. The drugs were coming into Colombia from Afghanistan via Kyrgyzstan and then the Balkans. Ruiz had sent a hit team after the traffickers. Now the heroin was his. The traffickers were floating, or hopefully sinking, in small pieces, in the Caribbean Sea. And, he fervently hoped, the local White Koi underboss was shitting bricks, figuring out how to tell his overboss back East that he'd lost ten million dollars' worth of white-powder heroin.

The table in front of him was set in the precise, ordered, calming way he so enjoyed. A narrow-necked, white-glazed vase held a shell-pink orchid. A bonsai tree, cultivated and pruned so that it appeared to have been blown sideways by some mysterious mountain wind, grew in a white porcelain trough. And, facing each other as if about to do battle, two jade figurines. A sword-wielding warrior and a thickly muscled water buffalo, head lowered, needle-pointed horns aimed at the swordsman's midriff.

The serving girl entered his private room, her white-socked feet hissing as she slid across the rush matting. He looked up at her and smiled briefly before bowing. She returned his bow, though her face remained unreadable behind its thick mask of white makeup. Her lips, painted into a scarlet cupid's bow, did, briefly, curve upwards. He noticed the way the girl touched the groove in the centre of her top lip, just beneath her nose.

She leant over and placed the ancient bronze teapot in front of him. A tiny, bone-china cup followed, its walls so thin that the light from the lanterns on the floor shone through the glaze, making it glow.

Her figure was slender, almost boyish, as far as he could tell, though he noted approvingly the swell of her breasts beneath the stiff silk kimono. Kneeling to his right side, she came a little closer as she poured his first cup of tea. He sat straight, resisting the urge, stronger with each visit, to grab her around the waist and kiss her. That would be an instant ban, and his status within the city's criminal fraternity would count for nothing in here.

When the cup was ready, she sat back on her heels and bowed her head. Ruiz raised the delicate cup to his lips and took a sip, inhaling through his nose as he did so, the better to capture the intense, herbal scent that swirled from its steaming surface.

"Arigato," he said, hesitantly. *Thank you.*

He had been practising his Japanese for a month now, mainly using YouTube, and had, he felt, mastered enough to try out a few basic words at Willow Tree. The girl turned to him and raised her finely arched, painted eyebrows with what he hoped was pleasant surprise.

"Sore wa idesu," she said. *That is good.*

He nodded, feeling unaccountably pleased with this kindergarten conversation. He finished the cup and placed it reverently on the table. The girl smiled, more fully this time, and refilled his cup. He raised it to his lips, then coughed and had to pull the cup away from his mouth. He tried again, managing a sip before a second spasm shivered through his chest wall, making him cough again, harder this time so that he sprayed a fine mist of fragrant tea into the air in front of his face.

The girl frowned and said something in Japanese he couldn't understand. *Are you all right, master?* he supposed she'd asked.

"Estoy bien. No es nada," he said. *I'm fine. It's nothing.*

In fact, he was not fine. The coughing intensified. Tears sprang to his eyes and he fished a fine white cotton display handkerchief from his breast pocket and wiped them dry. He coughed into the handkerchief, and when he withdrew it from his lips he noticed with alarm that its pristine white was speckled with red.

His fingertips were tingling and he thought he could hear the faint ringing of bells. Then the coughing stopped as suddenly as it had begun. He reached for the tea. No. In his *mind*, he reached for the tea. In his body, in the real world, his arms remained motionless at his sides.

And in a flash of most unwelcome insight, he realised. Poison. He moved his eyes to his right. And he watched as the girl got to her feet, unfolding her legs and standing in a single, flowing movement, like a cobra emerging from a fakir's rush basket.

Panicking, he tried once again to move. Although he could sense his legs pushing him upright and his right hand moving inside his jacket towards his pistol, in reality they were just dreams. Wishes, maybe.

She moved around into his sightline and pointed at the two jade figurines. Then, in fluent Spanish, she said, "Míralos. El guerrero y el toro. Yo soy el guerrero, y tú eres el toro." *Look at them. The warrior and the bull. I am the warrior. And you are the bull."*

From a gold silk purse tied to the belt at her waist she brought forth a palm-sized scroll of paper and placed it on the table. She walked to a black-and-gold lacquer cabinet out of his line of vision and returned with a small black pot and a bamboo-handled pen. He could hear the *scritch* of nib on paper. When she had finished, she held it up for him to read. In formal Castilian Spanish it said:

A quien le interese,
Robé del Koi Blanco. Ahora he pagado.
Martín Ruiz.

To whom it may concern,
I stole from the White Koi. Now I have paid.
Martin Ruiz.

Still addressing him in Spanish, she clarified.

"I will put this in your mouth, so your friends will find it easily."

Then she left the room.

Ruiz felt a trickle of sweat run into his left eye. It smarted. He thought of his wife and children, and realised he would never see them again. He prayed for his soul to be freed from sin so that he might be redeemed in the eyes of the Lord and admitted to Heaven.

He heard the room panels slide apart and then together again.

The tea girl was back. In her hands she carried a sword. A long, curved blade that glinted in the lantern light. A gold silken tassel swayed to and fro from the hilt. She tapped the jade bull on the back of its thick neck with the point.

Ruiz waited.

The blade whistled back then forwards.

Ruiz saw it coming. Then it bit cleanly through the tissues and bones of his neck, just below his Adam's apple. As the lights dimmed, he had time for one, final thought.

Sayonara.

* * *

Wei Mei stepped back smartly as the sword reached the end of its swing. But her ceremonial garb hindered her normally athletic movements, and she caught a jet of bright, arterial blood full in the face. Spitting the hot, salty liquid out, she swore, this time in her native tongue. Cantonese.

"Tā mā de!" *Fuck!*

The blood was issuing from the cleanly sliced arteries in thick, ropy jets, spattering the ceiling. She waited until the heart gave out before stepping closer. Swiping a baggy sleeve across her mouth, she pushed her right big toe against the corpse's chest. Slowly – *gracefully*, she thought – the kneeling torso folded backwards over its heels until its shoulder blades met the matting. Blood flowed out from the severed arteries and veins in the neck, sending a lake of crimson across the matting. When its leading edge reached the sliding wall panels, it soaked in and began climbing up the paper infills, turning them from white to red.

She kneeled at the table and rolled the little piece of paper into a tight cylinder. Then she reached for the head, prised the lower jaw open with her left forefinger, and inserted the message between the tongue and the hard palate.

On the way out, she knocked on the manager's door. Three taps, a pause, one, a pause, three. She stopped at a staff locker to grab a long, black trench coat and a broad-brimmed hat, which she settled low over her forehead.

Leaving the building by a rear door, the head bumping against her thigh in a plastic carrier bag, she waited for a count of sixty. Then she followed the narrow lane between Willow Tree and its neighbour, a travel agency, emerging onto Calle 10, a three-lane, one-way street lined with trees. Another left brought her to Willow Tree's front door, sandwiched between a bodega and a nail bar. The heavies had disappeared, called in by the manager who was delivering a pre-agreed message that an assassin had burst in and murdered their boss.

From the pouch at her waist she withdrew a glossy, garnet-coloured plum she had bought from a street vendor earlier that day. She dropped the perfect, unblemished fruit into the carrier bag. She positioned the bag and its oddly mismatched cargo on the bonnet of the black Porsche Cayenne the three gangsters had arrived in. And then she climbed into the rear seat of a waiting Audi with blacked out windows.

As the driver accelerated away from the curb, she called her employer. They spoke in Cantonese.

"Yes, Mei?"

"It is done, Master Fang. The Colombian is dead."

"Thank you. Fly home now. We will celebrate. There is a new restaurant overlooking Victoria Harbour. The best seafood in Hong Kong."

"Yes, Master."

Back inside her room in the nondescript hotel Fang had booked her into, Mei entered the bathroom and closed the door behind her. Standing before the mirror, she untied the broad gold sash at her waist and let it fall to the ground. Next, the stiff kimono, its white and gold embroidery streaked and spattered with the dead drug lord's blood. Beneath the kimono she wore plain white cotton underwear.

Free of the Japanese garb, she leaned closer to the mirror and inspected her face. In clearing her mouth of Ruiz's blood, she'd smeared her perfect cupid's bow, so that it appeared to be racing to her jawline for safety. From her wash kit, she took a tube of makeup remover and squirted a sizeable puddle into a folded white washcloth. Then, with movements like a cat cleaning its face, she pulled and pawed at the white pan stick, revealing, little by little, the olive skin that was her natural complexion. With the lower half of her face cleansed, revealing, beneath the cupid's bow, fuller, wider lips above a pointed chin, she paused.

From the white bandit's mask remaining, her eyes – large, brown and almost round, despite the epicanthal fold at their inner corners – stared back at her. A direct gaze that she knew strangers found hard to read. She applied more cleanser and went to work on her broad, high forehead.

When her face was restored to its natural state, free of makeup and expressionless, she pulled a dozen pins and clips from her hair. She shook it out so that it fell to her shoulders, a deep-brown curtain through which she peered out at herself.

Showered, and dressed in tight jeans, a black vest and a denim jacket, her hair braided into a sleek plait, she packed her bag, dropped to her knees and scanned under the bed, took one final look around the room, and left.

As her taxi took her to José María Córdova International Airport, she noted, without humour or alarm, a convoy of police cars driving at top speed into the centre of the city.

3

ALDEBURGH

Eli was sitting at the kitchen table, reading the news on her laptop. She looked up as Gabriel entered the room. Her forehead crimped with concern as she took in his expression. Then she smiled at him and got to her feet. She embraced him, pulling him close, and kissed him, softly, on the cheeks and then, harder, on the lips.

"Hey," she said, softly. "How are you feeling?"

"Mainly what I'm feeling is angry. She's gone and that's that. And I'm sad, too. Not because she was my ex or anything. I mean, not because we were engaged. But she was one of the few friends I had left. And she was so happy, wasn't she?"

Eli nodded, then sighed.

"Yes, she was. She had that look women get when the pieces click into place."

Gabriel reached for her coffee mug and took a small sip.

"Listen. I've been thinking. You should leave."

"What?"

"Get away from here. From me. I'm bad news, Eli. Every second you spend with me you're putting yourself at risk."

Eli put her fists on her hips and jutted her chin out.

"No! Not, going, to, happen. You need someone watching your six. I'm fine."

He shook his head violently, feeling a sudden flash of anger and finding himself unable to stop it.

"Don't you get it? Were you even actually *there* on the beach two days ago? Some fucking hitman shot her dead. He was aiming at me. You need to get some distance. Some perspective."

Eli reared back. Her eyes blazed.

"No! *You* need to get some perspective. You're in shock, OK? I don't believe in death curses and I'm not leaving you on your own while you're grieving, either. So forget it, soldier, and calm down!"

Something in Eli's tone worked on Gabriel in a way that kind words might not have done. He slumped into a chair. Closed his eyes and rested his head on his folded arms.

"We need, well, I do anyway, to go over for the funeral."

"I want to come with you. You shouldn't have to travel alone. Don will give us both time."

Don was Don Webster. Gabriel's commanding officer in the SAS, and now his and Eli's guvnor at a covert ops unit working to eradicate Britain's enemies. The Department.

"When's the Old Man due?"

"Ten, he said. He called me last night. Tell me, do you remember going to the hospital? Or talking to the detective?"

"Sort of. A woman, wasn't it?"

"Yes. I gave her a statement too. The fact that the shooter was there, dead at her feet, kind of made it an open and shut case."

"We need his phone. His passport. His gun. Everything."

Eli shook her head.

"They warned me off. They bagged the pistol and took it away. To the local copshop, I suppose."

"This is them, isn't it? Kuznitsa."

"That would be my guess, yes. They tried to get you, well, us, before. The mercs in the Merc. When that didn't work, they went for a hitman."

Eli was referring to an encounter they'd had with a group of four tooled-up mercenaries while driving down to the British Army HQ at Marlborough Lines in Andover. The mercenaries were all dead now, one by stabbing with a rusty steel prong from a spring-tined harrow, one from brain injuries caused by his own nasal bones, and two by shooting.

"We need to find out why."

"I know."

"I'm going to find them, Eli. And I'm going to kill them. All of them."

Eli frowned.

"We can talk to the boss about what we do next."

"Have you heard any more from the cops?"

"Yeah, the detective called me this morning. What was her name, Stanwick? No, Strudwick. She's a chief inspector. That's good right?"

"I think so. Pretty senior. Like the woman we had on our side against the Iranians. Stella, remember?"

"Yeah, she was pretty badass. We could have used a few like her in Mossad."

"What did she say? Strudwick, I mean."

"They're trying to find out where the shooter was staying in the UK."

"Don't you think we could do a better job? After all, we're in the same basic line of work."

Eli finished her coffee. She stood, then reached down for his hand.

"Come on."

"Come on, where?"

"Out. I think better when I'm walking. Let's head out of town the other way from the beach, see where we get to."

Gabriel stood, pulling on Eli's hand so that she had to brace herself to avoid tumbling forward. He opened the door onto a bright, sunlit day

They strolled, like any of the other springtime couples, down High

Street, heads inclined towards each other, ignoring the shop windows with their expensive trinkets for the well-heeled trippers who flocked to Aldeburgh every year.

"Did Strudwick say whether the shooter had any ID on him?" Gabriel asked.

"No. That's to say, she did say that he didn't."

Gabriel nodded. It could figure. There were basically two ways to go as a contract killer. You kept everything on you, ready for a quick exit, but risked losing it all if you were captured or arrested. Or you put it somewhere so safe you felt comfortable without it. That way, you were a clean skin if caught. You had your legend and you could stick to it. Or you could until your interrogators put the "pleases" and "thank yous" away and reached for the crocodile clips and the car battery. Gabriel had done both. Worked out of a safe house, carrying only a pistol or a knife, and gone in fully armed and equipped for a rapid IKE – infil-kill-exfil.

"He must have been watching us. Otherwise he wouldn't have known to follow us straight from the house and up the beach," Gabriel said.

"So he was probably here for a few days, maybe before we got back."

"Yes. What would you do in a strange town?"

Striding along, Eli looked up, then straight ahead.

"Place like this? Full of tourists? I wouldn't bother with a hide or a bivvy. Unnecessary, and too much chance you'd have a nice middle-class family on a hike tripping over your washing line. So either a hotel or an Airbnb under a false name."

"Did you get a picture of the shooter?"

Eli nodded.

"I tried to get his good side."

Gabriel nodded, his mouth unsmiling. The man's bad side was very bad indeed, having been mostly removed by a 9mm hollow-point round from Eli's pistol.

"We could show it around some of the pubs and hotels. See if anyone let a room to him."

"What if we come across the cops doing the same thing?"

"I don't care! Fuck them! I've been here before, remember? They're fine with smackheads burgling holiday homes or homegrown murderers, but a pro like that guy? No! Never in a million years!"

Eli reared back at his sudden change of mood.

"Hey, hey, calm down, OK?"

She pushed her left arm through his right and pulled him close.

"Sorry. Sorry. I'm not processing this very well."

"You're doing fine. And anyway," she said, with a smile, "there's no law against asking people questions, is there?"

Gabriel managed a small, tight smile back.

"None at all, last time I checked."

They began by calling in at every pub in Aldeburgh that let rooms, plus the hotels, showing the bar staff and receptionists the photo of the dead hitman.

"Are you police, then?" the young woman keeping bar in The Mill Inn asked. "Only we've had them in already."

"No, we're not police," Eli said with a smile. "But the woman who died, you probably heard about her?"

The young woman nodded, biting at her bottom lip.

"She wasn't local was she? Norwegian is what I heard."

"She was Swedish," Gabriel said. "Her name was Britta. She was a dear friend of mine."

"Oh, God, I'm so sorry," the woman said.

"Yeah, so are we," Eli said, picking up the thread as if she'd never dropped it. "We used to work with Britta as well, and we're just asking around to see if we can get an idea of who might have wanted to kill her. I don't suppose you heard about anyone this guy might have made contact with, only we're sure he must have been renting a place here or maybe in one of the villages outside Aldeburgh."

The woman shook her head, setting the gold hoops in her ear lobes swinging.

"Sorry. But I tell you who might know, 'cause he knows everything that happens here."

"Who's that?" Eli asked, leaning forwards.

"His name's Jack McQuarrie. I went out with him for a few months last year. He's a blogger. I mean, that's not his real job. He works over at the boatyard. But he's got this, like, really cool blog where he reports on all the stuff going on in town. If anyone knows, Jack will."

Gabriel felt the familiar tug in his guts. Action beckoning. A sense of a puzzle box yielding the first of its secrets. A sliding drawer or a joint you push with your thumb to spring the next piece free.

"Did you tell the police about Jack?" he asked.

She shook her head, making the earrings swing again.

"Nope. They only asked if that bloke you just showed me the picture of had booked a room here. I said no and they buggered off."

"How do we get hold of Jack?" he asked.

"Easy. He'll be at work now, or I can give you his number."

"Could you give us his number, please?" Eli said, "That way we can call him and fix up a good time to meet."

"And can you tell us your name, too?" Gabriel asked. "So we can tell Jack we met you."

"Oh, sure. I'm Grace."

With Jack's number saved in both their phones, Eli and Gabriel thanked the young woman and left the bar.

"Call first or turn up unannounced?" Eli asked Gabriel once they were back on the pavement again.

He wrinkled his forehead. Courtesy said call first. Action said get over to the boatyard. And while he didn't think they needed the element of surprise, his instincts always led him to find his man as fast as possible.

"Let's go and see if he's at work," he said. "The boatyard's right next door to my place."

Under a sky the colour of cornflowers, Aldeburgh Boatyard was busy, thrumming to the rasp of electric sanders and table saws, and above it all the jocular tones of a DJ on local radio. A half-built wooden boat occupied the centre of the yard, propped securely so that its clinker-built hull could be finished. Gabriel led Eli past the boat and towards a charcoal-grey Portakabin with a single plate-glass window on the side facing his house.

"The office," he said. "I know the owner. He helped refit *Lin*."

Lin was Gabriel's boat. He and Eli had spent Monday morning sailing her. As he looked back to those few, effortlessly pleasurable hours, it seemed that he was being punished, once again, for daring to enjoy himself. He ground his teeth together. This time, he would be the one dishing out the punishment.

Gabriel strode over to the office door and walked in. Eli followed close behind.

Framed pictures of plans, photos of finished boats, and a variety of certificates adorned the walls. Behind the desk, a middle-aged man with a luxuriant white beard sat leafing through paperwork clipped into a scuffed ring binder. He looked up, frowning, then smiled.

"Hello, Gabriel," he said, getting to his feet with a wince, before limping round the desk to shake hands. "What can I do for you?"

He looked at Eli and smiled, then stuck out his hand.

"Brian Salter."

"Eli Schochat."

"Pleased to meet you, Eli." He turned back to Gabriel. "What's up, chief?"

Gabriel sighed and swiped a hand over his forehead. The day was already warm despite its being only mid-morning.

"Did you see all the action over on the beach the other day?"

Salter nodded.

"Bad business. A young lass got shot is what I heard. You caught up in it, were you?"

Gabriel smiled, but it was a humourless expression.

"You could say that. Eli and I were walking on the beach with a friend. She was the one who died. Britta, her name was. Britta

Falskog." *And if I keep saying her name I can keep a small part of her alive.*

"Well, I'm sorry for you, lad. Can't have been easy. Did they get the guy who did it? A couple of the lads went to have a look but the cops were keeping everyone well back. Bloody phones. Can't pick your nose these days without some idiot trying to film you."

"He's dead," Eli said, in a tone that suggested Salter would be wise to drop the subject.

"Oh is he? Well, good riddance, then. Bastard," he added.

"Have you got a lad working for you called Jack McQuarrie?" Gabriel asked.

"Yes, I have. Why? Is he in trouble?"

Gabriel shook his head and managed a smile.

"No, nothing like that. Eli and I just wanted a quick chat with him, and I thought maybe you could point him out."

"I'll do better than that. Come on, I'll introduce you. He's working on that open gaffer on the yacht stand."

Eli stood aside so that Salter could lead them out of the office.

"What happened to your leg?" she asked. "Was it a sailing accident?"

He turned to her and smiled, slapping the affected thigh.

"This? No. I was Royal Navy before I bought this place. There's a bit of HMS *Ardent* lodged in there, half an inch from my femoral artery. Argentine Air Force bombed us in the Bay of San Carlos during the Falklands War."

Eli nodded, her face serious.

"Hurt much?"

"Sometimes. Mainly in the cold weather. Now, here he is. Jack!" Salter called out. "Couple of folk to see you. Take a break, OK?"

The young man sanding the boat's coamings nodded, and clambered down to ground level, swinging himself down off the galvanised-steel yacht stand.

He pushed his mop of blond hair out of his eyes with a hand furry with sawdust. Muscular beneath his pale-blue T-shirt, he stood several inches taller than Gabriel.

After the introductions were made, Salter retired to his office with a wave over his shoulder and a demand that they call back in for a coffee soon.

"What do you want?" Jack asked.

Not suspicious, Gabriel felt, just frank.

"We met a friend of yours in The Mill Inn," Gabriel said. "Grace?"

"Oh, yeah? What did you want with Grace, then?"

Gabriel smiled.

"We don't want anything with Grace. It's you that we were looking for."

"Me? Why, what have I done?"

"Look, don't worry, you haven't done anything wrong. She just told us that you're a local blogger and you know what's going on and where in Aldeburgh."

Jack seem to relax. Gabriel noticed the way the tension that had lifted his shoulders towards his ears evaporated and the young man's body language said he was willing to help.

"OK, sorry. I've been a bit on edge recently, and things haven't been going too well at work. What is it you wanted to know about the blog?"

"Would you know whether there've been any strangers staying in Aldeburgh over the last week or two?" Gabriel asked.

Jack wrinkled his nose and frowned, a curiously childlike expression, and then he nodded

"Yeah," he said, "that's exactly the sort of thing I look at. I pop into all the pubs and I know everyone in town – all the shops and the restaurants – they just tell me what's going on and whether they see anything interesting and I report it in the blog. Anyway, about a week ago, I heard that there was a guy in town who someone had mentioned because he didn't really look like he fitted in here."

Gabriel felt another spike of adrenaline in his stomach. This was going better than he had any right to expect. He looked at Jack and spoke again.

"I'd love to read your blog post," he said.

"Sure. You just need to look at AldeBugger.com."

"That's brilliant," Gabriel said. He patted the younger man on his left shoulder. "Thanks so much. We'll let you get back to the boat, which looks really good, by the way."

Jack smiled and ran his fingers through his hair.

"Yeah, she's going to look beautiful when she's on the water. I can't wait to see her launched."

Back at his house Gabriel opened his laptop and typed in the URL for Jack's blog. Eli came and sat beside him.

"Here it is," he said.

He started to scroll back through the entries until he came to the one that set his pulse racing even faster than it had been at the boatyard.

Tall, blonde and handsome. Who is the stranger in town?

A little bird tells us that among the DFLs (Down From London) in their Boden tops and cargo shorts, we have a stranger in our midst who definitely doesn't fit the stereotype. He's holed up in a summer house belonging to a local artist (we can't say which one), and she tells us he doesn't seem to know whether he's here for business or pleasure.

"Tall, blonde and handsome," is how she described him, though we can't say anymore as even mysterious tourists deserve their privacy.

Gabriel closed the browser. He turned to Eli.

"This is him, isn't it? It must be."

She nodded.

"Looks that way. If he stood out enough to make his landlady pass on a titbit like that to Jack, he's our man."

"OK." Gabriel checked his watch. "Don's going to be here soon. Can you go next door and use your charms to persuade young Jack to divulge the name of the local artist, please?"

Eli got to her feet and flipped an extra button open on her shirt.

"And if my feminine wiles don't work on him?"

"Then try something else," he said.

She pursed her lips. Then spoke.
"Wiles first."

Ten minutes later, while Eli was negotiating with Jack, Gabriel heard the muted rumble of Don Webster's Jensen Interceptor driving past the window of the sitting room. He knew the boss kept the classic car for high days and holidays. Perhaps his being only a handful of miles up the road from MOD Rothford, the army base where The Department had its headquarters, meant Don thought he could risk taking it out. Gabriel went to the front door. Don climbed out from the moss-green coupe, grunting as he straightened after the drive. Gabriel was about to say hello when the passenger door opened. Don had not come alone.

4

Don's companion was tall, maybe six foot two, and cadaverously thin. He had a shock of white-blonde hair and piercing, pale-blue eyes, which even from across the drive seemed to drill right into Gabriel's skull. Don approached the front door and shook hands with Gabriel before pulling him into an embrace.

"Hello. Old Sport," he said gruffly. "How are you holding up?"

"I'm fine boss, really. I'm doing OK. Who's your friend?" Gabriel asked, nodding at the tall man who was approaching the front door.

"Gabriel, I'd like you to meet Olof Ekström," Don said. "Olof was Britta's boss in Stockholm. I contacted him when the news of Eli's 707 call reached me."

Ekström extended a long arm and shook hands with Gabriel. His grip was dry and firm. He placed his left hand over Gabriel's right and pumped it vigorously up and down before releasing it.

"I am very sorry for your loss," Ekström said.

"And I, yours," Gabriel said. "Britta was one of the best. She'll be hard to replace."

"I know. That is why I have come to see you," Ekström said.

Gabriel stood to one side.

"Come in," he said. "Let me get you some tea, or would you prefer coffee?"

"Coffee would be good," Ekström said.

Mugs of fresh-brewed coffee cradled between their palms, Gabriel, Don and Ekström sat at the kitchen table. Out of the bright sunshine, Gabriel was better able to see, and he took in Ekström's distinctive appearance. If anything, he was taller than Gabriel had originally estimated, perhaps closer to six foot four, but still just rail-thin. His cheekbones were so pronounced that they cast faint shadows onto his cheeks. His teeth, which were visible when he spoke, were large and a horsey, yellowish-ivory colour.

"I'm guessing you want to find out as much as you can about the guy who killed Britta," Gabriel said.

Ekström inclined his head.

"Naturally. We regard her murder as an attack on the Swedish state, and as such, we will leave no stone unturned – I think that is the correct expression – in finding out what happened."

Gabriel opened his mouth to speak, but Don cut him off.

"Perhaps you could start by telling us what happened, Old Sport. In your own words. Leave out the theorising for now and stick to events, if that's OK?"

He sounded friendly enough, but Gabriel had worked for the Old Man long enough to pick up on the coded message. *Play your cards close to your chest, for now.*

Gabriel took a sip of his coffee.

"Britta arrived here on Monday evening. The next morning, the three of us—"

"Three?" Ekström asked, looking around, theatrically, Gabriel thought.

"Yes. Me, Britta and my," he paused. *Close to the chest, Old Sport.* "Partner. She's next door at the moment. She'll be back soon, and then I can introduce you."

Ekström lowered his eyelids, then raised them again.

"I am sorry. I interrupted you. Please, go on."

"We went for a walk on the beach, away from town."

"Whose idea was it, the walk?" Ekström asked,

Gabriel looked up, searching his memory.

"Hers, I think. Britta's, I mean. We'd gone maybe two or three hundred yards, and we were just talking, you know? Bantering. Then Britta stumbled and fell against me and that's when, when—"

Gabriel squeezed his eyes shut and shook his head, trying to dispel the hideous image of Britta's head exploding in his face. He felt a hand on his and opened his eyes, using his free hand to dash away the tears that had gathered at the corners.

It was Don's hand, and he left it in place as Gabriel looked at him.

"You've been through a lot over the last few years, Old Sport, and God knows how you've managed to stay in control. Anything you need, you just let me know, OK?"

"Thanks, Don. I will. I promise."

"Could you continue now, please, do you think?" Ekström asked, seemingly embarrassed by Gabriel's momentary loss of control.

Gabriel found himself fighting down an urge to grab the emotionally distant Swede by his jacket lapels and batter his head against the worn pine top of the kitchen table.

"Britta was killed instantly. Head shot. He got me in the left shoulder. Flesh wound. Nothing serious. I was in shock. On the ground. Eli killed him. We were flown to Ipswich Hospital. They patched up my shoulder, then we came back here. The police interviewed me."

"And do you have any idea why a hitman, if that's what he was, should have wanted to kill Ms Falskog?"

Now what do I say? The boss urged me to stick to the facts. Telling Ekström the hitter was after me would definitely count as opinion at this stage.

Gabriel shook his head. And said nothing. A compromise.

"Olof and I are running a joint operation to discover the identity of the killer and, we hope, his employers. He's staying in the UK for a couple of days, then returning to Stockholm," Don said.

"I'd like to be involved," Gabriel said, looking first at Don and then, more searchingly, at Ekström.

Ekström shook his head.

"Oh, no, I do not think that would be wise, or appropriate. From what I have heard, you and Ms Falskog were at one time romantically involved, so I am afraid I cannot allow it. Your judgement would be impaired. I have enough on my plate trying to replace a valued colleague, as well as finding her murderer, without dealing with her grieving former fiancé."

Gabriel shot to his feet and leaned across the table, sticking his face in Ekström's. The Swede reared back, eyes wide.

"How dare you!" Gabriel said, voice loud in the small kitchen. "You talk about Britta as if she was just an HR problem for you! In case you'd forgotten my story of two minutes ago, she's lying in a mortuary with half her head missing. She was engaged to be married. Did you know that, too? Or were you too busy drafting a fucking recruitment ad?"

Heart pounding, Gabriel remained on his feet, looming over Ekström. His breath was coming in gasps and sparks were shooting around the edge of his vision. Rather than repaying him in kind, Ekström placed his hands together on the table.

"Yes, I did know she was engaged. I may not have quite such ready access to my emotions as you, Gabriel, but I can assure you that she was more, a lot more, than just a colleague. Perhaps I am guilty of taking an over-official approach, but this is not the first time I have lost someone. I have found this is the best way for me to cope. If I offended you, especially as I am a guest in your house, then I apologise."

Before Gabriel could formulate a reply, the back door opened and Eli walked in. He looked across at her as she came into the kitchen. She must have picked up on the tension in the room, he reflected – although it wouldn't have been difficult – because she smiled brightly and turned first to Ekström.

"Hello!" she said. "I'm Eli Schochat, late of Mossad, now working with Gabriel at The Department."

She held her hand out and Ekström got to his feet before shaking, resembling a giraffe unfolding itself from a seated position, his lanky frame dominating the low-ceilinged room.

"Olof Ekström. Deputy-Head of *Säkerhetspolisen*. Oh, no, excuse me. The Swedish Security Service. I'm pleased to meet you," he said. "Please, call me Olof," he added with a smile that displayed those horsey teeth in full, before resuming his seat.

She turned to Don.

"Hello, boss. Everything OK?"

"Fine, thanks, Eli. How are you?"

"I'm fine. It's been pretty hectic here, but, yes, we're good. All good."

She glanced at Gabriel and he saw the minute lowering of her eyelids that he took to mean she'd been successful with Jack McQuarrie.

"I was just explaining to your," a beat, "partner here that I can't have him in the team investigating Britta's murder. He is too involved ... emotionally."

Eli nodded vigorously.

"I completely agree. Gabriel was also wounded, did he tell you that?" Ekström nodded. "Yes, so I think rest and recuperation make a lot more sense than rushing around getting in everyone's way. Don't you agree, boss?" she asked Don.

If Don saw through Eli's playacting for the deception it clearly was, he was too practised a commander to give anything away. He maintained his unruffled composure and merely nodded.

"Quite agree." He turned to Gabriel. "Take some time off, Old Sport."

Don left with Ekström shortly after this instruction, promising to stay in touch and, once again, suggesting that a little travel might take Gabriel's mind off recent events.

5

[Article from Izvestiya, June 2nd]
Saint Petersburg Businessman Dies in 'Suspicious' Car Fire

Genady Garin, 61, Chairman of Garin Group, died early this morning, when his car burst into flames outside a Moscow casino. City police are investigating.

"We are treating Mr Garin's death as suspicious," said Police Major Evgeny Antonov. "Witnesses report hearing an explosion in the seconds before Mr Garin's burning car was discovered."

Mr Garin is survived by his wife, Tatyana, CEO of Garin Group. The couple's only child, Grigori, died in a car accident in London in 2013.

6

Once Don had driven off, the Jensen's exhaust rattling a loose window pane at the front of the house, Gabriel turned to Eli.

"I'm guessing Jack came through?"

"Uh-huh. He was a little reluctant at first, but I managed to persuade him."

"What did you use, wiles or Krav Maga?"

She smiled sweetly.

"My charms, of course! We're looking for a lady called Beverley Watchett. She lives in the last house on Thorpe Road. Apparently, she's hard to miss as she—"

"Always wears turquoise, yes, I've seen her around."

"Well, then? Come on!"

Beverley Watchett's house lay well back from the road, shielded by an unruly tangle of shrubs, one of which, a huge mock-orange, was laying down a heady blanket of sweet-scented perfume. Gabriel pushed open the turquoise-painted wooden gate and led Eli towards the front door. Three cats looked up with suspicious eyes from their resting places on an old tyre swing, a wheelbarrow, and a brick wall festooned with vivid scarlet roses. Presumably sensing no threat from the two humans, they pulled the shutters down and resumed their sleeping.

The sight of the flowers took Gabriel spinning back to his and Eli's recent adventure in Iran. He breathed in deeply and held the musky scent of the roses in his nose for a few seconds. He closed his eyes, then jerked them open again as his inner vision was crowded with the blackened and bloody corpses of Revolutionary Guards killed by a drone swarm strike.

"You OK?" Eli said, looking at him with narrowed eyes.

"Yeah, fine. It's nothing."

"Mm-hmm. Nothing like you were just closing your eyes, nothing? Or nothing like when you woke me up in the night trying to kill me, nothing?"

"It was just the sun, OK? Come on, let's see if Beverley's home."

He strode up to the front door – stripped and waxed wood – and rang the bell.

When, after thirty seconds, nobody came to answer the door, Gabriel leaned harder on the bell push. He stood back and looked up at the first-floor windows, shading his eyes, but the panes merely reflected a few fluffy clouds scudding across the sky. If the lady of the house was at home and observing them, he couldn't tell.

Eli wandered off. A moment or two later she came back.

"There's a little path down the side of the house. Why don't we go round to the back garden? Maybe she's painting or whatever."

Gabriel nodded. More shrubs and thick swags of ivy almost pulling a fence panel over had turned the side passage into little more than a tunnel, one person wide. In single file, Gabriel and Eli pushed through into a huge back garden.

"Wow!" Eli said, "I'd never have thought all this land could fit behind such an ordinary-looking house."

"My grandfather bought it in the twenties! Land was cheap back then," a woman's voice called out. Mature, no trace of the local burr, and an amused tone that suggested its owner enjoyed taking people by surprise. "Stay there, my darling."

Gabriel and Eli turned towards the source of the voice and waited for its owner to appear. Which she did, rounding a clump of bamboo and setting the hard, segmented stems waving and knocking against each other. The woman coming towards them looked to be in her early sixties. She'd caught up her grey-streaked, tawny hair in a messy topknot, speared through by a narrow wooden paintbrush. Her round face was streaked with paint that gave her the look of a genteel savage, marooned unexpectedly in this most English of gardens.

"Hello, I'm Bev Watchett. I won't shake hands; they're covered in paint," she said, holding up multicoloured palms as if they might not believe her.

Silver and turquoise rings on almost every spattered finger clicked against each other at the gesture.

"I'm Gabriel. This is Eli."

Bev smiled at them both then looked back at Gabriel.

"I've seen you around town, haven't I?"

"Probably. I bought the last house on Slaughden Road a year or so ago."

"That's it. And who might you be, my dear? You are extraordinarily pretty. Greek? Lebanese?"

Eli touched the notch between her collarbones and smiled at Bev.

"Israeli. Gabriel and I are," she laughed," OK, wow, I have never said this to anyone before. He's my boyfriend."

Bev widened her eyes, revealing slate-grey irises.

"Oh-ho! So this is a fresh-blooming relationship. How exciting! Now, come through, I can't leave poor Tanis waiting. I know it's a warm day but even so."

They followed Bev as she navigated the bamboo, emerging into a circle of lawn, studded with daisies, delicate blue wood anemones, and buttercups. But it wasn't the wildflowers that held Gabriel's attention. Nor the easel.

Sitting in the crook of a gnarled old apple tree was a naked girl in her early twenties. One foot rested on a low branch, the other was extended in a perfectly straight line so that the toes just touched the grass. Her skin was so pale it looked translucent, and indeed, he could just about discern faint blue-grey veins running across her chest. She made no attempt to cover herself, looking at him with a gaze so direct he felt a blush creeping across his face.

"Hello," she said in a light, amused voice, a younger copy of Bev's.

"Hi," Gabriel and Eli said in unison.

Gabriel was trying hard to avoid looking at the young woman's breasts, which only resulted in his staring intently into her eyes. She laughed, shaking a mane of blonde hair before reaching up and dragging it back behind her ears and into place.

"Now, Tanis, dear, stop teasing our guest. Go and put a robe on. We'll pick this up again in a little while," Bev said.

"Fine," the girl said, before holding out her right hand to Gabriel. "Could you help me down, please? This bark is scraping my bum."

Gabriel hesitated for a second.

"Come on! I won't bite," she said, holding both arms out towards him.

"Yes, go on Gabriel," Eli said from beside him, nudging him in the ribs. "You heard what Tanis said. The tree bark is hurting her bottom."

Feeling cornered by the trio of assertive women, Gabriel stepped forwards and held Tanis under the arms. He lifted her – she weighed virtually nothing, it seemed – and deposited her carefully on the grass. He smelled sun-warmed skin and a musky, sexual perfume that made him even more uneasy.

"Thank you, Sir Galahad," she said, before turning and wandering off towards the house.

Unconsciously, Gabriel followed her progress, noticing the marks left by the rough bark across her milk-white buttocks.

"I must apologise," Bev said, breaking into Gabriel's narrow zone of focus. "Tanis is studying at the Slade." She turned to Eli. "A terribly prestigious art college, Eli, in case you haven't come across it. She models for me during the holidays to earn a little extra cash. No shame. Absolutely none at all. Although I love her for it. Picasso said, 'There are only two types of women – goddesses and doormats.' I've always rather preferred the former to the latter."

"I found her charming," Eli said. "How about you, *darling*?"

Gabriel blinked. Eli never called him "darling" in public. Or much at home, come to that. He panicked for a second, sensing the trap but unable to avoid it.

"I thought she was, er, very confident." *Yes, that'll do. Complimentary but not lecherous.*

"What about her body? They're so fresh at that age, don't you think, Bev?"

The older woman grinned and readjusted the paintbrush in her bun. Clearly enjoying herself.

"As a daisy. It's why I like to paint her. Those beautiful little tits. I'm afraid to say, mine flew south for the winter years ago," she said, lifting her own bosom inside the paint-smeared smock she wore.

"I think you two are being completely unfair, and I refuse to answer on the grounds I might incriminate myself," Gabriel said, having found a diplomatic answer in the few seconds their banter had allowed him.

"Fair enough," Eli said. "Take the Fifth. But you have to admit, she is beautiful."

"Yes. Beautiful, and dangerous. A bit like you." A beat. "Darling."

Bev clapped her hands together.

"Now. I don't suppose you came to visit me just to ogle naked young girls, although there's usually at least one draping herself around the place if you like that sort of thing. How can I help? Is it something to do with that dreadful business on the beach?"

Gabriel explained, briefly, his relationship to Britta, and his and Eli's suspicions that the hitman had been staying in Bev's summerhouse.

"We were wondering whether we could have a look inside," he finished.

Bev put a finger to her chin and pursed her lips. Then she gave Gabriel a frank, appraising look.

"Are you and Eli spies?"

"What? No, absolutely not."

"No? Only I heard that your poor friend was shot. With a pistol. I'm sorry, news travels fast in a little place like Aldeburgh. Especially with inquisitive little pups like Jack McQuarrie on the prowl. It's just that handguns are illegal, as I'm sure you know."

Once again, Gabriel found himself in the delicate position of needing to get people to open up without telling them anything that would land him, and more importantly them, in danger.

"We're not spies. I mean, we'd hardly tell you if we were, but we're not. We, uh—"

"We work alongside the police from time to time," Eli interrupted. "And this is one of those times."

Bev nodded, fiddling with one of her rings, twisting it round and round her knuckle.

"I see. I daresay you'll want to know what name my guest gave."

That's interesting, Gabriel thought. *Not what his name* was, *but what name he* gave.

"Yes, please," he said.

"Moe Asbjørnsen. You needn't write it down, it's fake."

"How do you know?"

"Because Asbjørnsen and Moe were the compilers of a famous series of Norwegian folktales. For some reason, the man wanted his anonymity. He paid me in cash at, I might add, twice what I was asking." Then her hand flew to her mouth. "Oh God, do you suppose the police will want the money he paid me?"

Gabriel shook his head.

"Eli said we work alongside the police. But we *aren't* the police. They don't have to know. Although what I would like to do is buy it from you at one to one. He may have left fingerprints on the notes."

Bev frowned.

"But if there are fingerprints, shouldn't we hand it over anyway? I mean, they *are* trying to solve your friend's murder."

Once again, Gabriel found himself in the position of needing to explain to a civilian that where professional hitmen – and women – were concerned, the police were useless. An impossible position, since to do so would be to reveal just how much of their worlds overlapped. He thought back to Sasha Beck, the woman hired to kill him, twice, and whose body he had left for the bears deep in the countryside in upstate New York. *Poor Sasha*, he thought, before frowning at the incongruous notion of his feeling pity for a woman who'd killed everyone close to him.

"Look, you said yourself, there's no need for you to be involved in all this. You were an innocent bystander. We'll swap the money and I'll take it to the police myself."

Bev twitched her lips to one side. Frowned. Clearly sceptical.

"Who exactly *do* you work for?"

She included Eli in her glance as she asked this, then looked back at the house.

Gabriel made a split-second decision. He wouldn't harm Bev in any way, but she was about to get difficult, and he wanted, more than anything else, to get inside her summerhouse and get a lead to follow.

7

Gabriel moved a couple of inches closer to Bev and fixed his gaze on her left pupil.

"Hold still," he said. "I think you've got an eyelash trapped in there."

And before she could object, he cradled her temples lightly in his fingertips, switching his gaze from left to right eye and back again, bringing his breathing pattern into line with hers. His old mentor, Master Zhao, had long ago taught Gabriel how to hypnotise people. Where Western stage hypnotists and their therapeutic cousins often took minutes to send a subject under, the ancient wisdom Zhao Xi had imparted worked in seconds. It had saved Gabriel's life on more than one occasion. He deployed it now.

"I can't feel anything," she said.

"Just a second," Gabriel said, in a precisely calibrated tone it had taken him three years to perfect under Master Zhao's exacting tutelage.

"*You feel sleepy* – I think I've – *and relaxed* – got it out – *and you want to please me* – oh, no wait – *so you want to* – there it is – *let us search* – I'll just fish it – *the summerhouse* – out – *and exchange the money he paid you*."

"There!" he said, louder than the rest of his hypnotic speech.

He tapped her once, lightly, right between the eyes and she blinked as if she'd been staring into bright sunlight.

She sighed deeply.

"Would you like to search the summerhouse?"

"Yes, please. Where is it?"

"The summerhouse is down the path by the cherry tree there. There's a key safe. Do you want the code?"

"Yes, please."

"The code is one-eight-eight-one."

Someone, Gabriel felt, sent him a flash of insight. He acted on it.

"Picasso's birth year?"

"I'm impressed. Good looking *and* well read."

Gabriel shook his head and looked down for a moment.

"Lucky guess."

Bev snorted.

"No such thing. We get the luck we make."

"And when I tell you how lucky *you* are, you will wake up and remember nothing of this conversation. Why don't you go back to your painting?"

Bev nodded, then turned away, drifted over to her easel, and started dabbing paint on one corner of the canvas.

Gabriel shook his head, smiling at the ease with which he'd been able to put her under and wondering whether the artistic temperament had anything to do with it. Together, he and Eli took the path Bev had indicated. It wound through more fruit trees and flowerbeds before ending at a clapboard summerhouse, maybe thirty feet by fifteen. The walls were a paler, greyer shade of the turquoise that Bev clearly adored, with white window frames. He slid the black plastic cover down on the key safe and entered the code.

Occupying one corner of the space was a saggy, but comfortable-looking sofa covered in a kilim woven in shades of brown, brick red and sage green. A double bed filled most of the remainder, although there was just enough room for a small wooden table with a chair, and a reading lamp. Framed paintings lined the walls, mostly female nudes in the same style Gabriel had glimpsed on Bev's easel.

"You start at the desk end, I'll work in from the bed," Gabriel said.

He began by stripping the bedclothes and lifting the mattress. He didn't really expect to find anything. Only a rank amateur would even dream of hiding his travel documents and cash in so obvious a place. He ran his fingers along the seams on each side of the piping on the edges, though, just in case "Moe Asbjørnsen" had slit one and resewn it. The stitching was uniform and executed with the precision only a machine could manage. He propped the mattress against the wall and began examining the bedstead, a white-painted iron frame. Lying on his back he shuffled beneath it to examine the underside, but discovered nothing.

Upright again, he gripped one of the fleur-de-lys finials on the bed posts and gave it an experimental twist. Nothing. He repeated the move on the other three decorative knobs, but they were welded or screwed on and completely immobile.

"How are you getting on?" He asked over his shoulder.

"Nothing yet," Eli replied.

He looked over at her. She was painstakingly taking one book after another from a small shelf and flipping the pages.

If I wanted to hide my stuff, I'd go under the floor. Gabriel got down onto his hands and knees and began a fingertip examination of the pine floorboards.

Some detail-orientated craftsman had paid a great deal of attention to the flooring; the boards were screwed in place rather than nailed. On the first few boards he looked at, the brass screw heads had oxidised to a matte, greenish-brown. But in a corner under a window to the right of the bed he saw something that gave him hope. The thin film of dust on the floor had been disturbed, and what were clearly finger marks surrounded the screws. Their heads were covered by dust, but when Gabriel blew it away what revealed itself to him was, in his mind, incontrovertible evidence that they had found their target.

Bright scratches cutting through the patina twinkled at him from the screws holding the board in places. He scooted backwards to find the other end of the board. *Yes!* These also had brassy scuffs where the previous tenant's screwdriver had ground against the cross-cut sockets.

"I've got something," he said. "Come and look."

Eli stopped what she was doing and knelt beside him. She peered at the screws, then did what he'd done, in reverse, and checked their counterparts under the window.

"Got a screwdriver?" She asked.

"No. You?"

"Always," she said, grinning, before handing him a translucent-blue Swiss army knife.

The knife's Philips screwdriver wasn't a good fit, but by dint of maintaining steady pressure and taking his time, Gabriel managed to free the screws from the wood. Once all four were out and safe in his pocket, he lifted the board.

And there they were. Just as though the hitman had arranged them for a museum exhibit entitled, "What a torpedo needs on his travels."

In the six-inch-wide trough between the joists lay a small, black semi-automatic pistol, which Gabriel lifted out and identified. A Walther PPS M2. The stubby little gun was chambered for 9mm rounds, which would stop anyone within the gun's admittedly short range. No spare ammunition. That didn't say anything about the man's confidence levels. You would rarely need, or have time for, more than a few shots, and any modern handgun had more than enough magazine capacity to cope with a single assassination. Gabriel couldn't remember what type of weapon the assassin had used on the beach. But this was obviously his backup.

Next to the pistol lay a black-and-chrome flick knife. And beside that, a silver iPhone. A ziplock bag containing a fat passport and a sheaf of banknotes completed the treasure trove.

Gabriel opened the bag and emptied its contents onto the floor. What he had initially taken to be one passport turned out to be five, nested one inside the other: Swedish, German, British, Norwegian,

Israeli. He picked them up and handed the Norwegian and Israeli documents to Eli.

Flipping to the photo page of the Swedish passport, he found himself looking into the eyes of the man who had shot Britta in the head. Nobody looks their best in a passport photo, and some otherwise perfectly respectable people swear they look like wanted criminals, but the man staring out at Gabriel really hadn't even tried. Blond hair cropped short topped a blocky skull, from which deep-set, grey-blue eyes glared, daring the immigration official to deny him entry to their country. The mouth was a thin straight line, as if carved into the man's flesh with a knife. The same ugly face fixed him with that predatory gaze in the other two passports.

He turned to Eli.

"Who have you got?"

"Avram Binyamin Cohen from Israel and Nils Kristersson from Norway. You?"

"Anders Bjorn Carlsson from Sweden, Alan Bernard Chalmers from the UK and Axel Bruno Colbeck from Germany."

Eli snorted.

"ABC? Well, it seems we're looking for Nils Kristersson. You agree?"

"Either that or he was pulling a double bluff. But we can have our friends in the security service check out all five names. They have a database of known assassins and contract killers."

Eli shook her head.

"I'll bet you dinner it's Kristersson. A lot of assassins are very OCD, you know. Rituals, routines, superstitions. It's how they compartmentalise what they do. I knew this one guy, right? Shlomo Mendelssohn. I mean, that sounds like a fake name right there, don't you think? Anyway, he was a kid in the camps. At Buchenwald. He was nine when the Americans liberated it. As soon as he could hold a gun he started training to be a killer. He freelanced for a while, then hooked up with a Nazi-hunting outfit. Not Simon Weisenthal's, another one.

"By the time he made it to Israel in 1965, he had killed thirty-one former Nazis. I met him when I joined Mossad. He was seventy-eight then and retired from the wet work though we retained him as a consultant. So, the thing is, Shlomo always had to sit facing the door in any restaurant and this one time, oh my God it was so funny, we sat down and Director Baruch took the chair facing the door. Poor Shlomo was torn. He just couldn't bear having his back to the door but, you know, asking the Director to swap seats was embarrassing."

"So what happened?"

"What happened? Shlomo excused himself to the men's room and then the fire alarm goes off. We all get up and leave and move to another restaurant. Shlomo is first in and he hustles the manager into setting up a table and sits himself down in his favourite seat."

"And this is relevant, how?"

Eli's jaw dropped and her eyes widened.

"Hey, cheeky! It's relevant because these guys, they do things a certain way. If he used ABC as an alias once, he used it all the time. Four ABCs equals four aliases."

Gabriel smiled and held his hands up in mock-surrender.

"OK, fine. If it's Kristersson, I'll buy you dinner."

Eli shook her head.

"No," she said, drawing out the sound. "You *cook* me dinner. Fresh fish. Now, what else have you got there?"

Gabriel split the colourful notes into piles. Kristersson, if that's who he was, had brought a thousand Norwegian kroner, a thousand euros and a thousand pounds. All the notes looked well used. He pressed the button on the flick knife and nodded with a professional's appreciation as the spring ejected a four-inch blade with a sharp snap. Folding it away again, he slid the knife into his pocket.

He picked up the Walther and dropped out the magazine. Pressing down on the visible round and finding no discernible give, he determined that the mag was full. He removed the magazine and pocketed it, racked the slide to clear the pistol, picked up the ejected round, then slid Walther into a second pocket.

The phone came out last. So much potential to lead him straight to Kristersson's employer. So little chance of discovering its secrets.

He pressed the circular button. As his own did, the phone asked him for a fingerprint or a passcode. He held the phone up to the light and slanted it away from him, looking across the screen.

"Any grease marks?" Eli asked. "If we have the numbers he used, there are only twenty four ways to arrange them."

"Only if he used each of them once. And sorry, but no. That's OCD hitmen for you."

"That still leaves us with touch ID."

Gabriel nodded.

"Fancy breaking into a mortuary in the middle of the night with me?"

She leaned closer and kissed him.

"You're such a romantic. Come on, let's put this place back together, then we should get going. Poor Bev'll probably be clucking like a chicken by now."

"At least we don't have to ask her for her rent money any more.

Gabriel and Eli found Bev where they'd left her. Reassuringly human in her behaviour. Only now, Tanis was back on her perch in the apple tree. She favoured Gabriel with a smile from beneath lowered lashes. He ignored her this time and approached Bev.

He leaned a little closer and when she turned to him, spoke quietly.

"It's a very beautiful painting. You are very *lucky* to have such a talent."

She shivered a little.

"Ooh, I think a goose just walked over my grave," she said.

Gabriel was pleased to see that the brightness in her eyes he had dulled with the hypnosis had returned. They sparked in the sunlight.

"I'm sure it's nothing," he said.

Bev smiled dreamily. She reached out a finger and ran it along the scar on Gabriel's left cheek.

"You have an interesting face. Can I ask you something?"

"Yes, anything."

"Would you pose for me? I'd love to paint you."

49

Eli burst out laughing.

"Oh, God, she's got you."

"I'd love to, but my work is about to get incredibly busy. I'm afraid I can't—"

Bev took a step towards him and placed her palms flat against his chest. She was close enough that he could feel her breath on his face. It smelled of mint.

"When you're less busy, come and see me."

Ignoring the barely suppressed giggles from behind him, Gabriel thanked the artist, who had no idea how helpful she'd been, took Eli's arm, and left, ignoring the grinning Tanis on his way past.

8

Gabriel opened a browser on his laptop and searched "Suffolk mortuaries." Establishing that the nearest to Aldeburgh was at Ipswich Hospital, he looked up the phone number for the mortuary and called. After twenty rings he sighed, and was about to hang up when a tired-sounding male voice answered.

"Mortuary."

The speaker had clearly decided that anyone calling should be left in no doubt as to the purpose, contents or atmosphere of his workplace. Although, Gabriel thought, he sounded like the sort of man who could announce you had reached a petting zoo and make you run, screaming, for somewhere less depressing.

"Hi. Yes, this is DC Hilton, Suffolk Police? My guvnor wants me at the post mortem for that bloke who got shot dead on Aldeburgh beach yesterday. He told me to check you had the body."

"Yeah, we've got him. The woman, too. Apparently her body's being flown back to Sweden, though. No post mortem required, they tell me."

Gabriel's heart stuttered as he heard the man's bored-sounding voice describing Britta. Struggling to stay in character and not lash out verbally, he continued.

"OK, thanks. Listen, how's your security, only the guvnor's pretty paranoid about this case. Says the bloke's some sort of, I don't know, foreign national, or something."

"Security? What do you think this is, the Bank of England? There's nothing here worth nicking. The druggies always go for the pharmacy. We've got household locks on the door to the loading bay, a cardlock on the internal door and that's it."

"What? Not even an alarm?"

"Like I said, it's not as if there's anything worth stealing, is there? With all the cuts, we're lucky we've got a spare set of keys. Look, is there anything else? Only I've got a woman laid out in here and I need to finish up."

"No, that's it. Thanks, mate. Er, who am I talking to?"

"Derek. Gunn."

"Thanks, Derek. Oh, one last thing, mate?"

Gunn sighed.

"Go on then, it's not as if I have anything else to do."

"Cheers. So, I'm new to the area. Where exactly is the mortuary again?"

"Come in via the main gate, take the access road all the way round the hospital to the rear. There's a low brick building with a tall chimney. That's the incinerator room. We're next door. You can't miss it. There're two red skips outside."

Gabriel thanked his impatient but helpful informant and ended the call. He looked at Eli. She nodded.

"Fancy a trip to Ipswich tonight?" he asked.

At 1.00 a.m., they left the house. Gabriel fixed fake plates to the grey Mondeo he'd signed out from The Department's motor pool. He turned left out of the drive and trundled at a sedate twenty-five miles per hour through the town and out towards the A12 and Ipswich. They were dressed in jeans and T-shirts, plus a grey cotton windcheater for Eli and a navy linen blazer for Gabriel. The story, in the unlikely event of a police stop, was that they were driving down to London to stay with friends, preferring to drive at night when the roads were empty. But beneath the boot floor, in a black nylon holdall, a different pair of identities waited for them.

Two all-black outfits including soft-soled boots, gloves with rubber-pimpled fingers and palms, and silk ski masks. And two black nylon daysacks. Distributed between them were a coil of climbing rope, also black, lock picks, black nitrile gloves, torches, a hypodermic of haloperidol, an anti-psychotic drug that would floor the recipient of a dose in seconds, two sheathed tactical knives made by the German firm Böker, and a pack of foot-long, black cable ties. "Going equipped," as the legal term had it. And certainly enough for a very interesting conversation with any cop inquisitive enough to have a poke around.

They'd argued about taking pistols, Eli for, Gabriel against.

"We're not going to go into an NHS hospital tooled up," he said. "It's complete overkill. The worst we're likely to encounter is a security guard working nights to make ends meet. We won't need shooters to persuade someone like that to do what he's told."

Eli threw up her hands.

"OK, fine! I bow to your local knowledge."

"Thank you."

"All I'm saying is, just because we have the firepower doesn't mean we have to use it."

"Look. How many people have you incapacitated, up to and including death, without a firearm?"

She shrugged, then looked up and to the right.

"I don't know. Ten? Eleven? Actually, no. Including the mercs in the Merc, at least twelve. Why, how many have you done?"

Gabriel scragged his fingers through his hair, wishing he hadn't opened this particular cupboard. But now the skeletons were tumbling and he could hear the bones rattling against each other as they fell at his feet.

"I don't know. I've lost count. Enough, anyway. No guns. Please."

Driving at night on back roads that scarcely saw more than ten cars an hour during daylight hours, it took them forty minutes to reach Ipswich.

Tall sodium lamps lit up the hospital, but the amber light they gave out depressed Gabriel. Following Gunn's instructions, he made his way around the vast complex of mostly low, redbrick buildings until he picked up signs for the mortuary. A couple of minutes later, he was parking next to the two skips and leaving the car. The main gate, and the entrance beyond that they glimpsed as they arrived, had been busy with a steady flow of visitors and the odd ambulance. But round here, where the necessary but unexciting business of keeping a complex organisation like an NHS hospital running went on, nothing, and nobody, moved.

The night was warm. Standing at the Mondeo's open boot, they changed from their mufti into their tactical gear and shouldered the daysacks. When the last bootlace was secure, Gabriel jerked his chin in the direction of the back door to the mortuary.

"Shall we?" he asked through the thin silk mask.

"After you," Eli replied.

They walked up to the door. On an impulse Gabriel tried the handle. It moved down but the door was definitely locked.

"Nice try," Eli said.

He shrugged.

"Always worth it. We once walked into a terrorist's compound the same way. Some idiot forgot to lock the gate."

"And after that he never forgot anything ever again."

"Something like that."

He opened the little black leather roll of lock picks, selected two and started work. The lock sprung, he pushed down on the handle again and the door swung inwards. They slipped inside, navigating by the narrow but powerful blue-white beams of their torches.

Gabriel had been in mortuaries before, both in the army and as a Department agent. This one followed the pattern. Stainless steel, white enamel. Bright-yellow plastic bins for hazardous waste and others for sharps. In the centre of the room, a stainless-steel dissection table stood empty, waiting for its next inhabitant.

"He must be in one of those," Gabriel said, pointing at a row of six square steel doors.

He took a step towards them, then stopped. *Oh, God. And so is Britta.*

From beside him, Eli spoke quietly.

"Let me."

He stepped back and watched Eli open the first door. As she pulled the sliding steel tray out a foot or so, he turned away. He listened to the repetitive pattern of sounds, heartrate speeding up with each set:

clunk – handle down

huff as seal gives way – door open

rumble of roller bearings – tray out

another rumble – tray in

huff – door close

clunk – handle up

Four times Eli repeated the procedure and on the fifth time, she whispered to him.

"Found him."

Gabriel turned and walked over to the wall of body fridges. Protruding from the upper row, resting on its steel bed, was the body of the man who had murdered Britta. Gabriel was standing on the body's right side.

He looked down dispassionately at the ruined face. Everything from the centre of the forehead to the lower jaw was missing, revealing a sticky red mess of torn flesh, punctuated by sharp bone fragments and shiny white teeth. The upper right portion of the pectoral muscle had been burst open by Eli's high-powered pistol round.

"Serves you right, you bastard," Gabriel muttered.

"The phone, Gabriel," Eli hissed. "Come on."

Gabriel reached into his trouser pocket and extracted Kristersson's phone. He picked up the man's right hand and pressed the thumb against the circular button. The phone vibrated in his hand and flashed up a message.

Touch ID or Enter Passcode

○ ○ ○ ○ ○ ○

"That's what I'm trying to do," he muttered. "Shit! How many goes do you get on one of these?" he asked.

"Not sure. Three, maybe. Four, max."

"OK. We need to think it through. If it's three we have two more shots and then we're locked out."

"Can't you turn it off and on again?"

He shook his head.

"No. You have to enter the passcode to enable Touch ID."

"Right, what do we know about him? He was OCD. He liked the initials ABC. And he was a pro. So totally security-minded."

Gabriel closed his eyes. Thinking himself into Kristersson's head. Before it had been blown apart by Eli's pistol round.

I'm a Norwegian hitman. I like ABC.

He pictured two hands, spread out in front of him. Held them up so the backs were towards him. Superimposed letters on the fingernails, starting with A on the left little finger. *Would I go for the start, the middle or the end of the sequence? Which is the most unlikely?*

He opened his eyes.

"Did you notice whether he was right-handed?" he asked Eli.

She paused for a moment, closing her own eyes.

She opened them.

"Right."

"Sure?"

"Yup. After I hit him in the shoulder he switched his gun to his left hand."

"OK, good. I'm thinking, left little finger. It's the furthest from the right thumb, where I started. The least obvious."

"And awkward even for him," she added. "I'm thinking maybe he used his trigger finger. Right index."

Gabriel pursed his lips inside the ski mask.

"OK. Two chances. You happy with left little and right index?"

"Yes. You?"

"Yes."

Holding his breath, he took hold of the dead man's left little finger and pressed firmly against the button. The phone vibrated.

Touch ID or Enter Passcode
○ ○ ○ ○ ○ ○

Willing his pulse to settle before the final attempt, Gabriel dropped the left hand and picked up the right. He grasped the index finger and placed the pad dead-centre on the circle of plastic.

Touch ID or Enter Passcode
○ ○ ○ ○ ○ ○

"We're shut out," Eli said.

Gabriel dropped the dead man's hand but clenched his own tighter around the phone.

"No. We can't be. We need this. Shit! I need to think. What about the passcode. Can we figure that out?"

"I don't know. The screen was clean so we're starting with ten digits in any six-position combination or permutation. That's tens of thousands."

"It is. But that's only a problem if we try and use brute force. I've done this sort of thing before. I was on a farm in Michigan once, just before I got badged in to The Department. This South African arms dealer had combination locks on the barns where he kept all his merchandise. He hated the British because his grandfather had died in one of our prison camps during the Boer War. He used the end date of the Boer war as the combination: one-nine-oh-two."

"Which was super-clever, but how is it helping us now?"

"When we were at Bev Watchett's place, she mentioned that he'd used a fictitious alias. Not an ABC-one, which is odd in itself."

"Yeah, what was it again, Anderson and somebody?"

"Asbjørnsen and Moe. She said they were the authors of a book of Norwegian folktales. Maybe he loved the book as a kid."

Gabriel pulled out his own phone, pulled off his right glove and tapped the web browser icon. He tapped in "Asbjørnsen and Moe". The Wikipedia page gave him the dates he wanted.

"The first collection came out in 1842 to 43. The second in 1844," he said.

"If he was that much of a traditionalist or a book-lover, my guess is he liked the earlier editions best. So, try the digits in that order."

Gabriel nodded and puffed his cheeks out.

He pushed the home button to access the virtual keypad and began tapping in the dates of the first collection.

1 – 8 – 4 – 2 – 4 –

Sweat stung his eyes as he tapped in the separate digits and watched the empty black circles change to solid white. He inhaled again and let it out with a hiss. Then he entered the final digit.

3

9

The phone vibrated once more.

"Fuck it, I really thought that was going to be it," Gabriel said.

Suddenly, Eli grabbed the phone from his hand.

"No, no, no! I've got it! It's a double-bluff."

"What? What do you mean?"

"He went so simple, nobody would ever think of it."

She took off her own right glove and tapped feverishly.

2 – 2 – 2 – 2 – 2 – 2

The keypad disappeared and a grid of icons appeared over a background of a snow-capped mountain.

Gabriel huffed out a sigh as he disabled the phone's security.

"How the fuck did you figure that out?"

Pull up the keypad," she said.

He did as she asked.

"Look at the letters on the keypad.

The middle key on the top row provided the answer. Kristersson's obsession with order and patterns had become his undoing.

2
ABC

Gabriel nodded his appreciation.

"God, you're smart," he said. He nodded at the body.

"Let's put the bastard back in his box."

He slid the tray home and closed the steel door. The door behind them opened. The neon tubes flicked into life, throwing a cold blue-white light over the mortuary.

Gabriel whirled round, conscious that Eli was doing the same. This was not going to be a fair fight. Two experienced, and ruthless, former Special Forces agents against a single security guard from a private firm probably earning just a shade above minimum wage.

Standing in the doorway, hand still extended and covering the light switch, was a woman. Her white coat gave her away as a medic, not security. Maybe she was a pathologist. She looked tired, greyish bags beneath her eyes and a pallor to her skin that couldn't all be accounted for by the fluorescent lights, one of which was plinking above her head.

Seeing these two black-clad intruders, she backed towards the door, eyes wide, mouth open. Gabriel darted towards her before she could run and seized her left wrist. He pulled her into the room and Eli ran behind her to close the door.

"Who are you?" she asked, her voice a mixture of fear and outrage. "What are you doing here?"

"Tishe! My zdes' nikogda ne byli," Gabriel said. *Shut up! We were never here.*

It was a masterstroke, though he felt bad for pulling it. After the exposure of GRU agents using Novichok in his old home city of Salisbury, speaking Russian was a huge red herring that the local police would easily swallow.

Blinking, the woman shook her arm, but Gabriel's grip was ironclad, and she merely succeeded in wrenching her wrist. She cried out. Gabriel clamped his hand over her mouth, stifling further screams, though he could feel her lips working against his palm.

As if reading his mind, Eli took the woman's other hand and

bound both wrists behind her back with a cable tie. She marched her to the steel dissecting table, pushed her down onto her bottom, then looped another tie around her ankles and the sturdy leg, which was bolted to the floor.

Gabriel's heart was racing, but there was nothing else they could do. The worst case was that the medic would have to wet herself. But somebody would be along in the morning to discover and free her. They'd call the police, tell them the intruders spoke Russian, and that would be that.

"Do svidaniya doktor," Gabriel, laying the accent on with a trowel just to make sure there was no ambiguity. *Goodbye, doctor.*

"Wait!" she called as they turned to go. "You can't leave me here like this. Please!"

Gabriel stopped. The medic was right. And since when did their rules of engagement include brutalising British doctors? He put a restraining hand on Eli's shoulder.

He went back to the doctor and drew his Böker. Her eyes widened as the blade appeared and she shuffled away from him. He caught her by the wrists and slit the cable tie. Standing, he looked around, and saw what he was looking for on a steel workbench. He filled the glass beaker from the deep metal sink's cold tap and placed it within reach. He fetched a steel basin from a second bench and, again, placed it where she could get to it. She looked up at him with he wanted to believe was gratitude.

He'd shown he understood English, but it was a small price to pay for giving her some measure of dignity back. And it was a short phrase. Nothing to suggest they weren't Russian agents.

Outside, they marched to the car, climbed in and drove away, only removing their face masks once they had reached the brightly lit front of the hospital.

Once they were safely out of Ipswich and driving back along the country roads towards Aldeburgh, Gabriel spoke.

"Did you see her?"

Eli paused, then answered.

"Yes."

"OK. Good."

They didn't speak again for the rest of the journey.

Gabriel and Eli finally got to bed at 3.30 a.m. They'd agreed to leave all thoughts of working through Kristersson's phone until the morning. Once again, she amazed him with her ability to fall asleep seemingly within seconds of her head hitting the pillow. He counted her breaths. The third exhalation was longer, and deeper than the first two, and he sensed her muscles give up the last of the day's tension as she slipped away from him. He lay motionless beside her, staring at the ceiling. Thoughts chased each other round his head the way Seamus, his old greyhound, would race around with other dogs in the fields.

He slid out of bed and went next door to his office. Pulled a sheet of paper out of the printer tray, uncapped his pen and began writing.

* * *

The hitman killed Britta but carried on shooting. That means I was the real target. Who would send a hitman to kill me? Does it matter? It would help if I understood who, because then I might understand why. Why does the why matter? What matters is finding them and killing them. I've been here before with Lizzie Maitland.

What was it Smudge said to me when I was cruising on morphine at the British Embassy in Tehran? "*Ubey ikh vsekh*, boss. It means 'Kill 'em all.'" The mercs in the Merc were Russian, or at least one of them was. They could have been working for the same people as Kristersson.

What about Tim Frye? Did he betray us to the Russians as well as the Iranians? Don said it was a personal thing with him, not ideological. So was he just searching for anyone with the men and the resources to take us out? Wait. The Iranians had a reason for wanting us dead. We were going to destroy their missile factory. But what was in it for the Russians? Is it personal for them, too?

They, whoever *they* are, will pay. Each and every one of them. Official or unofficial business. I don't care which. There will be a day of reckoning. And a very great deal of blood.

10

SAKHA REPUBLIC, RUSSIA

Vitaly Kovalenko had been born and raised in the Russian capital. At fifty-five, the Muscovite was old enough to remember Soviet communism, and he didn't care for it. Not then. Not now. Sometimes, after the working day was done, he would take a bottle of vodka and a chunk of bread and the strong local garlic sausage out to the western edge of the mine and look towards the city he still thought of as home, over nine thousand kilometres away. And where had he ended up? In a self-contained settlement, a diamond mine at its centre, slap-bang in the middle of the Nakyn kimberlite field, about two hundred kilometres northwest of a shithole town called Nyurba in the Yakutia region of Mother Russia. If you wanted a whore, or a drink in a bar, you faced a six-hour round trip on roads that would shake your fillings loose. Mother of God, they didn't even speak the same language!

As manager of the Almaznaya Shakhta Novoj Galaktiki – the New Galaxy Diamond Mine – his job ran the gamut from hiring and firing to reporting the financial numbers back to the owners. And what owners!

He liked to refer to the partners, after he'd taken enough vodka onboard to lose his inhibitions, as "The Who's Who of People Not to Piss Off." The majority stockholder in the joint venture was Garin Group, the multinational commodities trading company owned by Tatyana Garin in its entirety since the death of her husband.

Next in the pecking order came Alrosa, the state-owned diamond-mining concern. And finally, the people he thanked God lived so far away that their presence on the papers of incorporation was the most tangible aspect of their existence: Compañeros Blancos LLP.

"White Partners" sounded so pure. And considering the ultimate source of their wealth, he could see the joke. The company was, solid-gold intelligence had it, owned lock, stock and pistol barrel by a Colombian drug cartel. El Nuevo Medellín.

Tongue clamped between his teeth, Kovalenko was writing his weekly report. Hearing shouts, he heaved his bull-like frame out of his chair and went to the door of his cabin. The noise was coming from the edge of the staff compound. This was the area, packed with rudimentary accommodation constructed from shipping containers, where the miners and ancillary staff lived. Men were yelling in that bastard local dialect that sounded like goats being slaughtered. And in Russian. Moscow Russian.

"What the fuck is going on?" he roared as he stepped into the sunlight.

They were the last six words Kovalenko would ever utter.

A shot rang out and he toppled backwards, blood fountaining from a hole in the centre of his forehead. In the centre of the compound in front of the office, a man lowered his arm, a sleek black pistol dangling in his fist.

Emerging from their huts, or climbing out of trucks driven by more black-clad men, were all of the mine's manual workers not currently labouring in the gigantic, three-kilometre-long, two-hundred-metre-deep pit.

Yet more men, this time armed with Kalashnikovs, stood around, indicating with raised rifle barrels that the miners should assemble in front of the manager's cabin. Once the mine workers were formed into a loose, roughly circular crowd surrounded by fifty heavily armed men, the pistol-wielding man took a bullhorn from a subordinate, clicked the mic switch and spoke.

"My name is Volodya Ignatyev. Volodya means ruler of the world. As of right now, I am the ruler of *your* world. I am the new general manager here. Your work will go on as normal. Your lives, if you work hard and behave yourselves, will go on as normal. For you, nothing will change. My investors and I wish only to share in the profits of this glorious enterprise. How we effect this redistribution of wealth does not concern you."

He turned and gestured at Kovalenko, now lying in a widening lake of his own blood.

"My predecessor rejected a sound business proposition that would have guaranteed New Galaxy protection from the rapacious local criminal gangs who would rob you of your livelihoods." He paused for effect. "And, come to that, your lives. Now he has resigned his position, you need not fear. My men and I are your guarantors of a peaceful life. Just do your work, put in the hours, and all will be well. Oh, and one last thing. Yegor!"

A burly, black-clad gunman prodded one of the workers in the back with the muzzle of his Kalashnikov. The man stumbled forwards, his fellow workers clearing a path for him that led all the way up to the platform on which Ignatyev stood waiting.

"What is your name," Ignatyev said, still speaking into the bullhorn.

"Chayevich," the man muttered, though the electronics meant even those at the back of the crowd could hear him.

"Well, Chayevich," Ignatyev said with a smile, "I hear you have been smuggling diamonds out of the mine and selling them locally, on the black market.

The man's eyes widened and he shook his head vigorously.

"No! Nothing like that. I am a good worker. Loyal."

"The man you sold your last stone to works for me. You are not loyal. And you are a liar. Kneel."

The man remained standing, and then, perhaps finding some final shred of defiance, he looked straight into Ignatyev's eyes.

"I will not."

Ignatyev shrugged. Then he aimed low and shot the man through the left knee, sending him, screaming, to the ground. Two of the heavies rushed forward and grabbed the man by his armpits and hauled him over to a rock-crushing machine.

He strolled over to the vast machine and pushed the start button. With a roar, and a clank from the ascending conveyor belt, the machine juddered into life.

"No!" the man screamed as the two men lashed his hands and feet together and dumped him onto the conveyor.

As the frantically wriggling Chayevich inched closer to the parapet above the hopper, Ignatyev spoke into the bullhorn again.

"Kuznitsa treats its people fairly. As long as they treat us the same way. Anything else is punishable by sanctions up to, and including, death."

The man screamed one final time as his body upended at the top of the conveyor and tumbled between the spiked steel wheels in the guts of the machine. The whine of the gears didn't change in pitch: compared to their usual fodder, a human body was soft stuff. A bloody, semi-liquid mess dripped and spurted from the underside of the machine, spattering the ground.

"Back to work," Ignatyev shouted.

The stunned crowd of men drifted away, back to their earth movers, trucks, drills, graders, backhoes and spades. Ignatyev signalled to his lieutenants. Now for the white-collar staff. He didn't imagine he'd have much trouble from them.

Later that evening, relaxing with a large tumbler of brandy as he pored over the accounts, Ignatyev consulted the dead mine manager's address book and made a call using the clunky, black, Soviet-style desk phone.

A woman answered.

"Hello, Vitaly."

Smiling, Ignatyev corrected her.

"I'm afraid Vitaly has resigned. Permanently."

Her voice sharpened.

"Who is this?"

"I am Volodya Ignatyev. I represent your new joint venture partners."

"What are you talking about? I have no new partners."

"Yes, you do. As of now, you are in business with Kuznitsa. We are taking a twenty percent profit share. We are also assuming day-to-day control of New Galaxy. I thought, as a courtesy, Mrs Garin, I should let you know. I would be happy to answer any questions you may have about our new working relationship."

He enjoyed listening to the ghostly echoes and unearthly harmonics on the line as the billionairess fell silent. He took a sip of his brandy, then a larger mouthful and swallowed it down, enjoying the burn at the back of his throat.

"Where is Vitaly? Let me speak to him."

"That's going to be difficult. Unless you have a hotline to the afterlife."

"He's dead?"

"I'm afraid so."

"No! I don't believe you. Your crude threats don't frighten me. You said you are my new partner. Do you know who our other partners are?"

"Those coke-head dagos in Colombia, you mean? They hold no fear for me. We fought the Taliban. Have *they*? And as for Alrosa, let's just say we have at least as many contacts inside the Kremlin as you do."

"You will not get away with this. I have powerful friends."

"Mrs Garin, when other *biznes* types talk about having powerful friends, guess what? They mean us! We *are* the powerful friends. No, we *will* get away with this. And if you want to continue to live out your," he paused, searching for just the right word, "widowhood, in the style to which I am sure you have become accustomed, I suggest you fall into line. The consequences of doing otherwise, as poor

Vitaly discovered – and as your late husband discovered – are far from pleasant."

Not giving her the chance to formulate a comeback, he ended the call. He refilled his glass and looked around what had just become his workplace. Yes, this would work very nicely. And his bosses back in Moscow would be pleased. Their deal with the Colombians to launder Kuznitsa cash through the diamonds-to-drugs pipeline just became a reality.

11

Though they'd never fought together in active service, Gabriel felt that he, Smudge and Britta made a great team. The mission was simple. Get inside the Kremlin and kill 'em all. Admittedly the injuries the other two were carrying would slow them down, but on the whole he felt unusually confident. As they ran across Red Square, Britta kept her right hand on the top of her head to keep her skull from falling apart. Smudge didn't seem so bothered. He'd stuck his lower jaw in a pocket and ran on, tongue flopping left and right.

Gabriel checked his weapon and felt a cold wave of panic envelop him. He was carrying a bright-green, plastic dummy rifle.

"Smudge, Britta, wait!" he called out.

But they couldn't hear him. Or maybe chose not to. They sprinted on, laughing wildly, losing parts of their bodies as they closed on the vast edifice of the Kremlin, its blood-red, five-pointed stars spinning on their towers like fairground lights.

He tried to follow, but his feet were leaden, dragging with each step until he was shuffling along like an old man. Now even the dummy rifle had gone. He carried a rugby ball in both hands.

"Kick it, Gable!" a young man called from the edge of the

crowd that had gathered to watch his ridiculously slow progress across the square.

Suddenly free, his legs started working again and he ran a few paces further before launching a mighty kick that sent the human head spiralling upwards and over the high walls of the Kremlin.

The crowd cheered at his try and he turned to take a bow, before realising he was naked. They were laughing now, shrieking hysterically, and pointing at him.

Then the crowd melted away and Gabriel found he was standing alone in the vast, windswept square, apart from one other person. A thickset man dressed in jeans and a vest, his torso protected by a bloodstained leather apron, stood behind an iron anvil. His arms and shoulders were massively muscled, and matted with thick curling black hair. He fixed Gabriel with a gaze so intense Gabriel felt his will draining from him like blood from an open wound. The man beckoned with a crooked finger, and Gabriel walked towards him.

As he walked, the man swung a huge hammer and brought it down on the anvil with a deafening bang. A flock of black crows clattered from the red-pointed stars. Again and again the hammer swung, so that its rhythm chimed with Gabriel's steps.

Finally he arrived in front of the man. The blacksmith.

"You're dead," Gabriel said. "You killed yourself."

The great man laughed, throwing his head back and roaring so that Gabriel could see to the back of his throat.

"No, fool! I am not dead. The one calling himself Blacksmith is dead, but he was small fry. I am the real blacksmith and you are in my forge. Look around."

Gabriel turned and discovered he was standing in a dark shed, dominated by a gas-fired furnace, glowing redly in the twilight. The blacksmith walked over to the evil-looking black construction and stretched out a hand to a dial on its greasy side. He twisted the knurled black knob from MIN to MAX, and, through a grimy inspection window, Gabriel saw the flames dance higher. All around, swords, spears, daggers and machetes were stacked in piles or propped together in tepees. The blacksmith resumed talking.

"We want you dead. We will *have* you dead. You killed our men. But we have plenty more."

"Please, Gabriel," Britta said. She stood to the blacksmith's left, unable to move thanks to the grip he had on her copper-red hair, glowing even brighter in the firelight. "Help me."

The blacksmith laughed once more.

"It's too late for her. Can't you see that? This was your doing."

Then he slammed Britta's head down onto the unforgiving surface of the anvil, raised the monstrous hammer over his head and brought it down with a clang so loud it made Gabriel scream.

"No! Britta!" he shouted, rearing backwards ...

... and upwards, finding himself sitting up in bed, panting and drenched in sweat.

Beside him, Eli was struggling to sit up. She drew him into an embrace, or tried to, but he struggled free.

"No!" he said. "I have to think. This was them. Kuznitsa. Of course it was! We killed their operatives, but they were sent for me in the first place. Then they sent Kristersson. Don't you remember what Don told us at his place? Kuznitsa. It's some sort of organised crime gang. Russian in origin. Before he killed himself, Frye told Don his contact was a man named Max. Max runs Kuznitsa."

"Slow down! You're rambling. Come on, you're not really awake yet. Hey," she said, softly, stroking his cheek, "Come on, Gabriel, come back to me. Come on." Then she kissed him, and at once the memory of the dream receded and he was back in the real world.

"Oh, God, I'm sorry. That was such a bad dream. Smudge was there, and I thought I'd laid him to rest – literally. And Michael. And Britta. We have to go to Russia. Moscow. That's where they'll be based."

Eli shuffled closer and embraced him, leaning back until he either had to go back with her or wrestle himself free. He chose the easier course.

"If they're in Moscow, that's where we'll go," she said. "But one step at a time, OK?"

· · ·

73

The following morning, as they ate breakfast, Gabriel's phone pinged. Terri-Ann Calder had emailed him to say she was leaving for Cambodia soon and did he want to sort out shipment of the Camaro? He recognised the question for what it was, a request that he get a move on so she didn't have any loose ends in the US.

He found a shipping company with a collection depot in Houston. As he'd half expected, the delivery port in the UK was Felixstowe, just thirty miles away. While Eli got dressed, he emailed the company to kick off the process of bringing Lucille to her new home.

Twenty minutes later, he and Eli were sitting in the garden, sipping from mugs of coffee and examining Kristersson's iPhone.

"Try Contacts first," Eli said.

Kristersson had taken care to ensure his contacts list was of little use to anyone but him. All the spaces for photos were blank, and instead of names, each contact was identified by a codeword.

"Recent calls?" Gabriel asked her, as he tapped the phone icon.

"Find his last client?"

"That's what I'm thinking."

The last five calls all came from numbers with a 47 country code. Gabriel looked it up. Norway. The sixth was prefixed by a 7. Russia. And the contact's codeword was *Hestesko*. Gabriel looked it up. Horseshoe.

He showed Eli.

"I think this is Max," he said.

She nodded.

"You make horseshoes in a forge, and we know that's what Kuznitsa means. Plus it's a Russian number."

"Should I text him? Say target down?"

Eli nodded, then frowned.

"Wait. Let's just play this one out."

"OK. Kristersson texts Max and says Wolfe is dead. Max sends congratulations or whatever and sends the balance of the fee."

"Unless he paid up front."

"Unless that, yes. What if there's an agreed code phrase?"

"Hang on, I'll check his messages."

Gabriel began scrolling back through all of Kristersson's outgoing messages. Finally, on March third, he found what he was looking for. The message, to a US number, was brief. Its content, to a professional killer, was unambiguous.

I scrapped the car. It won't be driving anymore.

He showed Eli.

"Send that to Max?"

She nodded.

"What's the worst that can happen? He thinks you're dead. You're confirming it. If the code's wrong he'll know Kristersson's dead instead. If he thinks you're the one who killed him, he'll be running scared."

At the last moment, Gabriel deleted the message and tapped in a shorter version.

Car scrapped. No more driving.

They sat side by side, sipping their coffee, and waited. A few seconds elapsed and then the phone pinged.

Good. It was becoming a chore to look after. Balance on its way.

Gabriel smiled, grimly.

"I'm coming for you, Max," he said in a low tone.

His own phone rang a few moments later.

"Yes, boss."

"Ah, yes, hello Old Sport. Just been on the blower with friend Ekström. Apparently Britta's funeral is all organised. It's next Tuesday. Uppsala. I can send you the details."

"Yes, please."

"OK, hold on, just click this here and press that and, yes," he paused. "All done."

"Are you going?"

"I can't. I want to, but I'm in an all-day planning session with some of my global counterparts in Paris. I tell you, if there's a more closely guarded secret than the location of our little pow-wow, I'd be very surprised."

"Eli and I can represent you, then."

"Excellent. I'll have a wreath sent."

The call ended, Gabriel looked at Eli.

"Her funeral's next Tuesday."

She nodded, looking him straight in the eye. He noticed the way the green hue in her eyes intensified in the sun.

Later that day he added a few more lines to his testament.

* * *

I don't know how this mission will work out. I might be successful and live. I might be successful and die. Or I might fail altogether. But of one thing, I am sure.

It is time to rebalance the scales.

Max Novgorodsky and everyone connected to him must die.

12

THE FOLLOWING TUESDAY | UPPSALA, SWEDEN

Britta's family were standing stiffly outside Gamla Uppsala Kyrka in a short, soberly dressed line. Behind them, the brick-and-stone church, with its stepped roofline, looked almost quaint compared to the grandeur of Uppsala's cathedral.

The drive from Stockholm in a rented Volvo had taken half an hour, through countryside that began as forest and ended in the wide, flat plain of Uppsala County, the land stretching away to the horizon without interruption.

Birds were singing in the blossom trees surrounding the small, grassy churchyard and, as if to lighten the sombre mood, the sun shone from a beautiful, clear blue sky. *The colour of your eyes*, Gabriel thought, as he and Eli approached the family.

Britta's mother and father occupied the leftmost places in the line. Both in their early seventies and trim, they wore the expressions he had had cause to witness at other funerals, in other countries, most recently for Damon Cheaney. Though that day had been cold and marred by a biting, sleety wind.

Britta's mother, Ebba, looked poleaxed, her red-rimmed eyes, paler than her daughter's, unreadable. Her hair had been blonde the last time Gabriel had met her, on a flying visit with Britta between missions. Now it was white, almost silver. A loose strand kept flicking against her cheek, though she made no effort to brush it away.

Her father, Sixten, stood a head taller than his wife. An old-school industrialist, managing director of a machine tool company, he appeared to be unmoved. His blond hair was cut short and neatly brushed in a side-parting. His blue eyes stared intently at each guest who came to shake his hand. His mouth was set firm, but curved upwards into a half-smile.

And beside their mother, Britta's older brother and sister, Karl and Freja, in their early forties. Karl maintained the same set expression as his father, but Freja's face looked ravaged by grief, eyes red and lower lip quivering each time she had to speak. Her hair was the exact shade of Britta's, and Gabriel's heart jumped as she glanced at him.

Gabriel and Eli waited their turn and then approached the quartet. Seeing him, Sixten smiled, properly this time, and shook hands, before drawing Gabriel into a hug. Gabriel winced as the older man patted him on the left shoulder. Sixten released him.

"Thank you for coming, Gabriel. I know things didn't work out between you two, but I know she still cared for you. Very much."

"How could I not? She was my partner and a dear friend, even afterwards. I am so sorry."

"Yes," Sixten sighed. "It is the hardest thing. Against God's order for a parent to bury a child."

Feeling a crushing sense of guilt for having been the cause of Britta's death, Gabriel moved along a step to where Ebba was just embracing a young woman, who, from her copper-coloured hair, might have been one of Britta's cousins.

"Hello, Ebba," he said, unsure how she would react.

"Oh, Gabriel. I am so glad you are here. Come."

She held her arms wide, as her husband had done, and hugged him before kissing him on both cheeks. Tears had sprung to her eyes again, and while she fished out a paper tissue to wipe them away,

Gabriel turned to Eli, who was speaking to Sixten, her right hand held in his as he mechanically pumped it up and down while speaking.

"Ebba, I'd like you to meet my friend, Eli Schochat. Eli, this is Ebba, Britta's mum."

Eli, dressed more soberly than he'd ever seen her, in a knee-length black dress and black high heels, stepped forward.

"I am so sorry for your loss Mrs Falskog," she said, shaking her hand. "*Ha'makom yenahem etkhem.* I am Jewish. That is what we say at funerals. It means, 'May God console you.'"

Ebba managed a small smile.

"Thank you, my dear. I hope you have not been to many funerals. You look too young."

Eli smiled.

"I have been to some. At home."

"Israel?"

"Yes."

"Thank you for coming all this way."

"Oh," Eli smiled, shaking her head. "I live in England, now."

"Still, though. Thank you."

Gabriel and Eli moved on to shake hands with Karl, who seemed even more reserved than his father, and Freja, and then it was time to go inside.

They took their seats in the middle row on the right-hand side of the church. The back of the wooden pew was at the perfect height to dig into the small of the back, perhaps, Gabriel reflected, to ensure congregants stayed awake, or at least upright during services. Around them, mourners were filing in, holding whispered or muttered conversations as they found seats. Eli sat to his left and reached out to take his hand in hers. She placed their intertwined hands on Gabriel's left thigh. He looked up.

The stone arches supporting the ceiling were joined in eight-pointed stars at the centre of each of the three roof sections. Where the English cathedrals he had visited displayed their devotion through ornate carving, these were plainly made, though not plain. Twining away from each square-section beam, and from the round columns that supported them, as if growing there, deep-red fronds of foliage were painted onto the greyish-white stone.

Sunlight blazed whitely through the windows on one side of the church, illuminating the dust motes in the crisp, cool air.

Is that all we are? he wondered, as he tried to follow the progress of a single, twinkling speck. *Dust? Did the old prayer have it right? One minute she was here, a living, breathing, flesh-and-blood woman, and soon she'll be just atoms, swirling away?*

The deep, sonorous voice of the priest, a middle-aged man in the traditional black shirt of Church of Sweden, filled the space. He spoke in Swedish, and although Gabriel had a passing knowledge of the language, much of what he said passed him by.

So he sat, head bowed, and thought of Britta, as the priest intoned prayers and, presumably, a eulogy. He stood when the congregation stood, sat when they sat and, when they sang a beautiful Swedish hymn, closed his eyes and let the swell of melodious voices wash over and through him.

Suddenly, he jerked into fully alert mode. Someone had begun speaking in English. He looked towards the front of the church to see Karl standing at the lectern. He was a tall, thick-set man, with a shock of reddish-blonde hair above a wide, open face. Like his sisters, he had those amazing, cornflower-blue eyes.

"To thank Britta's former colleagues, who have come from England, I want to speak a little about Britta in words they can understand."

Gabriel smiled at Karl but he was looking at a row of people across the aisle. Gabriel followed his gaze and saw a small group of young men and women, all sitting together along a single pew. They had the look he associated with law enforcement or military service. Something in their physical appearance and a familiar watchfulness in their gazes. Britta's former colleagues from MI5, he assumed.

Karl took a deep breath. "Britta loved her family. She loved Uppsala, where she grew up. And she loved Sweden, for all its faults," he added after a pause. A few knowing chuckles echoed around the church.

"She was a patriot, at a time when patriotism has become something of a dirty word in parts of Sweden, in parts of the world. But my sister," he looked towards Freja, "*our* sister, was not a narrow-minded, flag-waving patriot. She welcomed people who wanted to live in Sweden, and adopt our way of life, our values. But she was just as ready to defend her against those who came here to do the opposite. Britta, as some of you know, loved action." Gabriel saw a few people nodding. Karl continued.

"As you know, she served in the military and then worked in England for their security service." He nodded briefly at the row of people Gabriel had seen him look at a few moments earlier. "Only recently, she accepted a new, high-profile role based in Stockholm, working in counter-terrorism. It is a great shame for Sweden, as well as for our family, that her life was cut short. Especially since at the time she was not even engaged in any professional capacity, but was simply taking some time off from her work to visit friends."

At this point, Karl's voice cracked and he paused, looking straight at Gabriel. There was a hardness to his gaze, and all at once, Gabriel realised what was coming.

13

Karl cleared his throat and resumed speaking. He kept his gaze fixed on Gabriel, and the effect on the congregation was magnetic. First one, then another mourner, then whole pews, turned to see whom, precisely, Karl was addressing.

"I say friends, because the man she was staying with had once been her fiancé, though in the end, she rejected him. But I ask him now, in front of witnesses. How could a *friend* allow this to happen? Why was my little sister gunned down on an English beach? Was the bullet even meant for her?" He raised an arm and held it out, finger pointing at Gabriel. "Or did Britta die instead of you?" he cried, before leaving the lectern and resuming his seat.

Cries of "*Nej!*" and "Karl!" rang out in the church, bouncing off its hard stone walls.

Gabriel felt the earth's gravity pulling him down onto the unforgiving wooden seat and wondered if he'd ever have the strength to get up again. Eli squeezed his hand and leaned over to whisper to him.

"He's just upset. Don't take it to heart."

Freja didn't speak at all, and the priest concluded the service by inviting friends and family to bring up any flowers they had brought with them and lay them on the simple pine coffin placed on a bier at the front of the church.

Outside the church, the sun was beating down, and in his charcoal-grey suit, Gabriel felt both overdressed and overheated. The mourners were milling about before proceeding to the graveside. A pale-faced man in his midthirties wearing a navy jacket over black trousers materialised in front of Gabriel. Gold-rimmed spectacles magnified yet another pair of blue eyes, these ones free of tears but narrowed in implacable hostility. The narrow-lipped mouth was set in a hard line.

"Do you know who I am?" the man asked, in unaccented English.

"No, I'm sorry. Are you part of the family?"

The man shook his head violently as if he were trying to free it altogether from its moorings on the top of his spine.

"No! And nor will I ever be."

At a stroke, Gabriel realised the identity of the man facing him. Fearing the worst, he braced himself, physically and mentally.

"I'm Gabriel. This is Eli," he said, trying to deflect the man's evident wrath.

"Yes, I know who you are. Karl pointed you out to me before the service. Well, I am Jarryd. Jarryd Pålsson. Britta and I were engaged to be married. And you," he stuck out a trembling finger and poked Gabriel hard in the sternum, "you ruined everything for me. Everything!"

He had raised his voice and people were, once more, turning towards Gabriel to ascertain the source of the commotion. Sixten hurried over, his face creased with concern. Arriving at Jarryd's side, he took hold of the younger man's arm above the elbow and attempted to draw him away, back towards the main group of mourners. But Pålsson shook his arm free.

"No, Sixten! Leave me be. He needs to hear this." Then he

turned back to Gabriel. "You did this. You! She went to visit you, and now she's dead."

With his eyes, Sixten signalled an apology to Gabriel, as he tried a second time to stem the flow of anger that now seemed an uncontrollable flow.

"Come, Jarryd. You do not know that. Let's go and say farewell. Please don't cause more upset here."

"Jarryd, you're right," Gabriel said. "Britta is dead because of me. The man who shot her was aiming at me. If she'd stayed in Sweden, she'd still be alive. If I could give my life for hers, I would, to send her back to you, and to you, Sixten, and the family. But I can't. So I'm going to do the next best thing. I'm going to find the people who murdered her and bring them to justice."

"Ha!" Jarryd spat out. "A fine speech ... for a coward to make. You let her take a bullet meant for you."

Then he lashed out his right fist and caught Gabriel a glancing blow on his left eyebrow, opening a cut. Gabriel stepped back, flinching.

"Jarryd!" Sixten shouted. "That's enough. Come away with me, now."

He dragged the now-weeping Jarryd away, saying sorry over his shoulder. Eli pulled the display handkerchief from Gabriel's top pocket and held it firmly against the cut eyebrow.

"Are you OK?" she asked.

"Yeah, I'm fine. Poor sod. He's really suffering."

"Not a bad punch for a schoolteacher."

Gabriel laughed mirthlessly.

"I guess I'm lucky he wasn't carrying a gun."

"I wouldn't have let him shoot you. Come on, I think maybe we should watch from a distance."

After the priest had concluded his words at the graveside, and the gravediggers were approaching to begin their work, Gabriel took Eli's arm and turned away.

"There's coffee and cake and probably whisky at the family

home. We were invited but I don't think I'd be welcome. Can we get going instead?"

She smiled and squeezed his bicep with her free hand.

"Sure. Let's get back to Stockholm while it's still light. Your cut's stopped bleeding but a plaster wouldn't be a bad idea."

14

Gabriel drove the hire car away from Uppsala. The late afternoon sun was slanting across the E4 motorway from right to left, casting a golden glow over the road surface. He was thinking about the two encounters at Britta's funeral. The verbal one with Karl, and the physical one with Jarryd. At no point had he felt like offering even a whisper of defiance. And when Jarryd had thrown that clumsy, amateurish punch, which must have hurt his unprotected knuckles like hell, he had simply let him. *Because they were both right, Wolfe. She's dead because of you.*

He looked right, at Eli. She was checking her phone but caught the movement and looked up.

"You OK?" she asked.

"Not really, no."

"Want to talk about it?"

He wrinkled his nose and shook his head.

"No. No thank you, I mean."

She smiled.

"It's OK. I'm here if you change your mind, you know that."

"Thanks, Eli."

She resumed her scrolling, though she stopped long enough to squeeze and pat his right thigh.

He checked his mirror. The road had been quiet since they left Uppsala apart from the occasional truck and a few dozen cars. Compared to England, Sweden – or this part of it anyway – felt deserted.

Eyes front again, he thought back to Karl's speech and the coded references to immigrants. He and Britta had never talked in detail about her counter-terror role, but he imagined it would have been similar to many in the UK. Trying to identify and prevent hundreds if not thousands of terrorist plots to disrupt normal life, to maim and kill Swedish civilians. Radicalised Muslims, mainly young men, were being ordered to attack at random. Yes, bombs were impressive, but all you really needed to spread terror was a family car or even a kitchen knife. Were there other threats? Of course. Wherever Islamist terror reared its ugly head, neo-Nazi groups were close behind, or sometimes out in front.

Ahead, he saw a slip road joining the motorway and pulled over into the outside lane in preparation. Unlike drivers in southern Europe, who, in his experience, tended to regard a flashing indicator as a perfectly adequate safety measure before joining a flow of eighty-mile-an-hour, nose-to-tail traffic, Scandinavian drivers were more cautious. But even so, it did no harm to prepare the way for them.

As he passed the junction, he heard a distinctive roar. An exhaust note made by only one brand of motorbike. Harley-Davidson. First one, then two, then a handful of the big, vee-twin-powered bikes surged onto the carriageway. Eight altogether, mostly black or matte grey, though a couple sported flamboyant paint jobs, demonic skulls and twisting flames catching the sun and reflecting it in twinkling flashes of light.

Once all eight riders had joined the motorway, he pulled in behind them, expecting them to open their throttles and peel away. Instead they paced him, maybe a few bike lengths ahead. He felt his pulse tick up a notch. Then two of the riders moved out and slowed so that as he drove on, they appeared to be drifting backwards.

They took up position behind him. Two more formed up beside him in the outside lane, threatening, leather-clad outriders in a convoy.

Gabriel pushed down on the accelerator, closing the gap between his front bumper and the rear wheels of the men in front. The rider to his right drifted closer and the light dimmed fractionally in the cabin, Eli looked up.

"What the fuck!" she exclaimed, as she took in the closed ranks of the eight bikers.

"We have company," Gabriel said, grimly.

He eased the steering wheel a fraction to the right and enjoyed the way the two Swedish bikers had to hurriedly adjust their own road position. They wore open-face helmets and bandannas. Most had dramatic beard-and-moustache combos, a few with tattoos visible on their cheekbones.

Come on. Just try it. Please. We could have some fun.

"Gabriel," Eli said, her voice rising. "What are you doing?"

"Did I tell you I hate bikers?" he asked her in a flat tone. "Actually, no, did I tell you that I *really* hate bikers?"

"No, you didn't. Can you pull back a bit, please?"

"I don't think I can. Look behind."

Eli did as he instructed then turned to face front again.

"They're just idiots trying to frighten a couple of tourists."

"You're right. But we're not tourists, are we? We could have some fun with them. Eight against two? The police would have to take our side."

"Police! What are you talking about?"

"This," he said.

Then he jammed his foot down, closing the distance between him and the bikers in front to just a couple of feet. He saw wide eyes in their mirrors before they grabbed a handful of throttle each and roared away. Gabriel looked right and winked at the nearest rider. He pointed, first at his steering wheel, then at the biker. His meaning, he felt, was clear. But just in case, he began closing the gap between them, tweaking the steering wheel just a little to send the Volvo's right flank over the lane markers.

The Harley swerved away from him, its rider taking his left hand off the grip to give him the finger.

"Gabriel, you need to calm down," Eli said, her voice tight, anxious. "Let it go, whatever it is."

Gabriel hadn't told Eli what "it" was, and at that moment, he realised how much they didn't know about each other. He thought back to the time he'd watched a deranged English knight shoot dead a group of Hells Angels using a .50 calibre Browning heavy machinegun. And another, in Brazil, when he'd been forced to deal with another bunch of bikers intent on killing him.

The bikers surrounding the car now had the same dead-eyed look he'd seen on the faces of their North, and South, American cousins. The man on Gabriel's right pointed to the hard shoulder. His meaning was clear. Pull over.

Gabriel shook his head. *Not going to happen.*

"Shit!" Eli said. "Now what?"

Easing the car up to ninety, forcing the bikers ahead to pull away or risk getting flung from their mounts, Gabriel spoke, in a voice that surprised even him with its calm, detached tone.

"Well, I suppose we could do what he wants. But then we'd have to beat them all senseless or get kicked to death, and a couple of them would probably die. Or we could keep going, see how fast those bikes'll go. We might hit Stockholm doing a hundred and fifty, which could get interesting. Although if the cops took an interest we'd probably lose the bikers."

He edged his speed up towards three figures. The flat land to their left stretched away to the horizon: a hundred-mile-long billiard table of low-lying agricultural land. No trees flashing past to give a sense of their increasing speed.

"OK, look, I know being at Britta's funeral shook you up, but you need to get a grip, right now!" Eli was shouting, but he seemed able to screen her out.

He shook his head. *No. I've had enough of getting a grip. Of being in control. You're not my shrink. And I'm not sure she's got much I'd want to hear right now anyway. Because after all, what can they do, seriously, if I decide to deal with them? They might be armed. But shooting while riding a bike doing a ton-plus is a mug's game.*

He glanced at the speedo. One-twenty-five. The engine was on song. The Volvo's engineers had designed it to go fast. The turbocharger blasting exhaust gases back into the cylinders saw to that. He could feel a faint vibration through the leather seat but other than that, it was a pretty sweet ride.

So, what to do, what to do?

He decided.

15

Keeping his eyes forward, he felt around for the electric window button and gave it a push. As the drop-glass slid down, the cabin filled with the rush of wind and the heady smell of the bikes' exhaust fumes.

He turned to his right, stuck his hand out and beckoned the biker. Gabriel could see the frown lines in the man's forehead beneath the edge of his helmet.

When their heads were no more than a foot away from each other, Gabriel leaned out of the window, not taking too much care with the steering wheel, so that the biker had to weave to stay away from the Volvo's incoming steel flank.

"Speak English?" he yelled. The howling wind snatching the words from his mouth.

"Yes, you mad fucker! Pull over!" the man yelled.

Gabriel shook his head, ignoring Eli's yells from the passenger seat. He pointed at a sign indicating the turnoff for Norrtälje and Knivsta.

"Take it."

"What?" the man shouted.

Gabriel edged even closer then reached over, stuck the heel of his hand against the left handlebar grip and gave it a shove. The bike wobbled violently and the Gabriel watched as the man fought not to be thrown off.

Gabriel pointed at the upcoming turnoff markers.

"Leave! Now! Or die!" he bellowed.

Then – and afterwards, Gabriel came to believe this was what had prevented his killing the entire gang using the Volvo as the murder weapon – he grinned. A crazy, happy-go-lucky, why-don't-we-just-do-it-and-see-what-happens? expression.

Maybe it took as along as half a second. Maybe it was instantaneous. But something about Gabriel's expression must have flicked a switch somewhere in the reptilian part of the biker's brain that calculated life-or-death decisions. It was probably there to avoid sabretooth tigers, but it did a decent job now.

Shaking his head, the biker dropped back, gesturing to his associates with his left hand, pointing first at Gabriel and then tapping his left temple.

Gabriel surged forward, enjoying the way the whistle from the turbocharger sang over the roaring of the engine. The bikes in front pulled left and right to let him through and he watched in his mirror as they joined their leader, peeling off the motorway and heading round the long, sweeping curve that would take them to Norrtälje, or possibly Knivsta.

With the combined roar of eight high-capacity motorbikes fading, Gabriel eased back on the gas, letting the car slow to a more manageable eighty-five.

He turned to Eli.

She was rigid, staring out of the windscreen. Her lips, normally full and sensuous, were compressed into a thin, bloodless line.

"You OK?" he asked.

She didn't answer. Not at first. He looked ahead again, listening to her breathing through her nose, the nostrils pinched with tension so that each inhalation and exhalation was audible.

"Am I OK?" she asked, after a pause he counted through, reaching twenty. "Am. I. OK? Well, yes. I'm alive. I haven't just been involved in a nine-vehicle smashup on a Swedish motorway. But in case you hadn't noticed, we were attracting quite a few curious stares during that little dick-swinging contest of yours. If we don't get pulled over by a traffic cop it'll be a gold-plated, fucking miracle!"

Gabriel blinked in surprise. He hadn't noticed whether there'd been any other vehicles on the road during the – *dick-swinging contest? That's a bit harsh!* – confrontation with the bikers.

"They started it," he said, defensively.

Eli twisted round in her seat.

"How old are you? Five? Look, there's a service area coming up. Please let's pull in and get a coffee. Or a drink in your case. I'll do the rest of the driving."

Suddenly, Gabriel's whole sense of his awareness of his surroundings seemed to snap into a different mode, duller somehow. But more engaged with the everyday. His hearing softened. His vision seemed less acute, so that number plates that had been pin-sharp a few minutes earlier were now fuzzy. He realised he could no longer feel the grain of the leather steering wheel under his fingers. Hyper-vigilance, they called it. That state of combat-readiness that was every soldier's friend until you carried it away from the battlefield with you and couldn't let go. Sleep became impossible. You were anxious all the time. Hopped up on adrenaline. Short tempered and even shorter fused.

He signalled right, slowed, and took the service road, pulling into the first available parking space and killing the engine before the car had even stopped rolling. His heart felt fluttery in his chest, as if a small bird had been sewn inside him. He pushed two fingers into the soft place under his jawbone and counted how many beats throbbed against his skin while his watch ticked ten seconds away.

… eighteen … nineteen … twenty … twenty-one … twenty …

Six times twenty-one is a hundred and twenty six. Fuck! I really lost it.

He felt Eli's hand on the back of his neck and leaned back into it, closing his eyes so he didn't have to watch the bright, white sparks fizzing around the edge of his vision.

"Gabriel? What just happened?" she asked, in a softer voice than before. "Tell me."

He kept his eyes closed and began to speak.

"Honestly? I'm not sure. I was ready to kill those guys. I didn't care, Eli. Really. Not at all. I wanted to. I was actually looking forward to seeing them flying off their bikes. I've done it before. I thought it would be fun."

He heard the latch click as she undid her seatbelt. Then he felt her warm breath on his face. She kissed him softly and cradled his face in her palms.

"This is shock. Delayed shock. And I'm not a shrink but I'd say your PTSD was kicking off big time back there. Come on, let's go inside. Hey!" she said excitedly. "Look over there."

Gabriel opened his eyes. Eli was pointing across the carpark.

"What? That fat guy in the football shirt?"

"No, numbskull! There's a hotel. Right, give me the car keys, we're going to get our bags and check in for the night. No arguments, you hear?"

Gabriel smiled and it felt like a natural expression from the inside, not the manic fuck-off-or-I'll-kill-you grin he'd used on the biker.

"You're the boss," he said.

Then he unclipped his own belt and returned her kiss, harder this time, before burying his head in the crook of her neck.

"Thank you," he murmured into the soft skin above the neckline of her dress.

Gabriel woke early. Beside him, Eli was sleeping. He slid out of bed, not wanting to wake her, but there seemed little chance of that. Her breathing was slow, deep and steady. He dressed quietly and went for a walk in the landscaped grounds beyond the hotel.

Walking steadily away from the E4, he felt rather than heard the hiss of its morning freight of commuters and truckers diminishing beyond a row of trees. To his left, a covey of birds burst free of a fir tree's shelter. The noise made him look round, and wonder what had disrupted them. Then he stopped dead, his heart pounding.

Beneath the trees, a woman was running at right angles to his path. Long, slender limbs, tanned to the colour of caramel, the flash of scarlet trainers. And a bobbing, copper-coloured plait. She turned her head as though she sensed him there, though they were over seventy-five metres apart. And she waved.

He started to call out to her.

"Br—"

Then he stopped himself.

Fool. It's just another early riser like you. What, you think she was the only woman in Sweden with red hair?

He shook his head, aware, even as he did so, of the cartoonish nature of the gesture. When he looked back, the woman had gone. *Gone, gone?* he wondered. *Or just disappeared between a couple of trees?*

He decided not to investigate. He wasn't sure he wanted to know one way or the other. He strode on until he reached a fence line dividing the open heathland from a farm. Leaning on a five-barred gate he looked at the farmhouse, situated a few hundred metres further on, a large pond housing a flotilla of ducks and wildfowl to one side. Painted in the dark shade of wine-red the Swedes called *falun*, the farmhouse seemed undersized in the vast, flat landscape. A sudden wind tugged at his shirt sleeves as if urging him to turn back. He ignored it, watching the surface of the pond ruffle under its caressing fingers.

Checking it wasn't too early – *eight thirty, you'll probably be at your desk, boss* – Gabriel pulled his phone out and called Don.

"Morning Old Sport. What can I do for you?"

The older man's voice sounded muffled, or maybe he was eating.

"Sorry, boss, did I catch you with your mouth full?"

"Mm-hmm. Bit of bacon and eggs. Christine likes to see me off to work with a full belly."

"Oh, God, sorry, I forgot about the time difference."

"It doesn't matter. So, how did the funeral go?"

"Well, fine. I mean, Britta's brother more or less blamed her death on me from the lectern, and then her fiancé punched me in the face, but other than that, a rip-roaring success, I'd say."

"Ah. Grief takes people in different ways. Don't let their reaction get to you, if you can help it. And how about you. Coping all right?"

"Yeah, I'm fine. I'll mourn her in my own way. I've never been a massive fan of funerals. So, look, I wondered whether you'd dug up anything on the hitman who killed Britta. Clients, that sort of thing."

Don made his characteristic *hmm, mm-hmm* noise as he breathed in and out through his nose. Over the years, Gabriel had learned to interpret its many meanings. It could mean anything from "That's an interesting question?" to "That's the biggest load of bullshit I've ever heard and I think you'd better start telling me the truth before I truly lose my temper." This one seemed as if it might be closer to the former than the latter.

"It would help if we had his phone, although the police drew a blank. Funny thing," Don paused, and Gabriel had a guilty flash of intuition. *Rumbled.* "They finally tracked him back to an Airbnb room rented out by a local artist. She said you'd already been there. They searched his room thoroughly. According to the detective I spoke to, their methods made fine-tooth combs look like rakes. And the place was clean. No passports, no cash, no nothing. Isn't that funny? Nothing on the body, either. The lady of the house was certain you hadn't been in his room. So tell me. Do we have his phone? Or not?"

Gabriel decided. In for a penny …

"We do, boss. Plus a handful of passports including the real one. And before you have to hear it from anyone else, I broke into the mortuary at Ipswich Hospital. I thought he might have used Touch ID. He hadn't, but in the process I was discovered by a doctor, or a pathologist. I had to immobilise her for a bit. No violence, just cable ties. I made out I was Russian. If it comes across your desk, I thought you'd want to know, that's all."

Don said nothing. Gabriel could hear him breathing and counted to ten before he got a reply. Don's tone was harsh.

"Jesus Christ, Gabriel! What the hell are you playing at? And don't think for a moment all this first-person singular stuff is even remotely convincing. *I* did this, *I* did that. No doubt Ms Schochat was involved in your little expedition to the mortuary. Did you honestly not hear a word Ekström said?"

"But, boss. I thought you were just agreeing with him to give me cover. I thought you'd *want* me to get involved. I'm a Department asset, and someone – well, I know who, it's a guy called Max – is out to kill me. Doesn't that make it our business? *My* business?"

Don heaved a sigh.

"This conversation is giving me indigestion. And now Christine is giving me the evil eye from the other end of the table, so here's what I suggest. Get yourself back to England and get yourself down here to talk to me. We need to figure out what we're going to do about this Max character. Or, given the way your mind works, *how* we're going to do it. Yes?"

"Yes, boss. Sorry."

Don snorted as he ended the call, leaving Gabriel with the distinct impression of a very angry senior commander. He checked his watch then turned and made his way back to the hotel, all thoughts of the red-haired jogger erased from his mind.

After breakfast, Gabriel was finishing repacking his bag, and had just zipped it closed when his phone rang. He checked the screen and smiled. *Now there's a name I haven't seen in a while.*

16

ST PETERSBURG, RUSSIA

Tatyana Garin sat behind the vast mahogany desk that had once belonged to Peter the Great, the man some called the father of modern Russia. She had bought it for $130,000, plus the auction house's commission. The ranks of Russia's super-rich had swollen since then, and she knew their rediscovered interest in Russian history meant she could probably sell it for eight or ten times what she'd paid for it. Though sell it she never would. Her poor dead husband Genady had loved to sit at it and review contracts or sign cheques.

But now Genady was gone, blown up and burnt to death in his Rolls-Royce outside a casino by those murdering sons of bitches, Kuznitsa. He was gone, and his killers had called her the previous day to announce they had executed her mine manager in Nyurba and seized control.

She'd spent the rest of the day considering her options, sipping ice-cold vodka from a heavy-bottomed cut glass, pausing only once to go to the front door and sign for a package delivered by courier – a small box.

She could talk to her business partners, but what good would that do? Everybody knew the government was walking along hand in hand with the gangsters like Hansel and bloody Gretel. It's how they did business. She knew they would simply look the other way as long as they got their dividends. No! She and Genady hadn't built Garin Group by bowing before every swaggering gangster demanding protection money. They'd confessed to killing Genady. And now she knew where to find them.

Having slept on her decision, she came in to work ready to do battle. She picked her phone up from the richly figured wood and, with one perfectly manicured fingertip, called up a number.

The answering voice, when the call went through, was warm, and friendly. He sounded tired, though. And she detected a note of sadness beneath that.

"Gabriushka," she said, speaking English. "You were once my knight in shining armour. I need you again."

"How can I help you, Tanya? You know I am in your debt."

"Don't be silly boy. I introduced you to Ayesha, that is all. Was nothing."

"She helped me find the person who'd murdered my friends. And have you forgotten flying me out of Mozambique?"

Tatyana smiled. Of course she hadn't forgotten. But when someone owed you a favour, you didn't need to rub their nose in it.

"I enjoyed your company. But yes, I would like to enjoy it again. I have some," she paused, "trouble. At diamond mine I control. Some people are making life very difficult. Could you come and see me? I would prefer to explain in person."

Gabriel didn't answer at once. *That's not like you,* she thought. *You're a man of action. Why so hesitant?*

Before she could formulate a theory, he responded.

"Of course. I suppose I should ask which of your properties you're living in at the moment."

She laughed.

"Oh, Gabriushka, you are such funny boy. My *dacha* outside Saint Petersburg. I will send address. Come soon."

"I will. Do svidaniya."

"Do svidaniya."

Tatyana refilled her glass, slopping a little of the ice-cold spirit onto the pristine polished surface of the desk and tutting. She mopped it up with a paper tissue before it could mark the wood. As she cleaned the desk, swiping angrily from side to side, she knocked the small cardboard box that she'd signed for earlier. Now, it slid a few centimetres across the polished surface then tipped over when it reached the leather blotter.

The finger wearing Vitaly's Spetsnaz ring spilled out and rolled to a stop on the pale-blue blotting paper.

Tatyana thumped her fist onto the desk.

"*Nyet!*" she shouted to the empty office.

* * *

"Who was that?" Eli asked, coming up behind Gabriel and encircling him in her arms.

He swivelled, enjoying the way she loosened her grip only just enough to let him twist round to face her.

"That was a friend. Of which I have an increasingly small number. She's a Russian billionairess. I owe her a favour, and she's just called it in."

Eli frowned.

"Does that work with going after Britta's killers?"

"She's in Saint Petersburg, so it's the right general direction. And Tanya's incredibly well connected. It wouldn't surprise me if she knows people who know people who know Max."

"Good. Russia it is, then."

"You're coming?"

Eli widened her eyes and let her mouth drop open in mock outrage.

"What? Let my *boyfriend*," she poked him in the chest, "fly off to meet some glamorous Russian oligarch without a chaperone? I don't think so!"

"I didn't say she was glamorous."

"So she's ugly then?"

"No. She's very beautiful. And extremely stylish."

"See, I told you."

"We need to go and see Don. Clear the air. I think I've blotted my copybook."

"Sorry, you whatted your what?"

Gabriel smiled. Then he remembered the way he'd tease Britta whenever she tripped up on a piece of British idiom. The smile vanished as quickly as it had arrived.

"Blotted my copybook. It means I spoiled a clean sheet. Literally. Like kids getting ink splodges on their exercise books."

Eli nodded.

"Noted. Thank you. *Host du bie mir an avleh.*"

"What's that, Yiddish?"

"Mm-hmm. It means, So you made a mistake, so what?"

"Let it go and let's get on with it, you mean?"

"That's exactly what I mean."

They headed out and were checking in at the airport an hour later. With another hour to spare before they had to board, they strolled along the brightly lit concourse in the departure area. Eli pulled Gabriel over to a window displaying a glittering array of classy and very expensive watches.

"Look at those. They're nice, aren't they?"

Gabriel peered in at the Cartiers, Chopards and Patek Philippes on display.

"Very. Look at that one."

He pointed to a diamond-encrusted Rolex, twinkling beneath a carefully positioned halogen spotlight.

Eli sighed. Then she held her hand out in front of her, pulling her jacket sleeve up to reveal a black-rubber-cased Casio G-Shock watch.

"I think it would look perfect on my wrist, don't you?"

"You don't think it's a bit, I don't know, blingy?"

"No! How could you say that? It's so pretty."

At that moment, Gabriel realised something about the woman beside him. The woman whom, with every passing day, he realised he loved. Eli wasn't just a fantastic fighter. Not just a fierce patriot for her adopted country and, always, her beloved Israel. Not just fun, in bed and out of it. She also had a traditionally feminine side. She revealed it in her delight in fresh-cut flowers from the garden. In strikingly designed and brightly coloured clothes that showed off her figure. And jewellery. Just because she didn't always go full-on girly didn't mean it wasn't there. He smiled. Took her hand. And dragged her into the shop, ignoring her protests.

"Gabriel! What are you doing? Stop it!"

But she was laughing, and her tone was playful.

Gabriel marched Eli, both of them laughing now, to a glass-topped display table in front of a large, wall-mounted Rolex logo, gold lettering and crown on a metallic-green backplate. A salesman, immaculate in a sharply tailored navy suit and electric-blue tie, smiled as they approached, perhaps catching their mood.

"Sir, madam, good morning. How may I help?"

"My friend would like to try on a Rolex, please," Gabriel said, only now releasing Eli's hand. "Like the one in the window, with the light-blue face."

The young man smiled again, first at Gabriel then, for longer, at Eli. He wore his hair in a forties style, sharply razored sides and a slick parting. This close, Gabriel could see the faint depression of a vacant piercing in his left earlobe.

"Of course. Please wait. I will fetch one from our stockroom."

While they waited, Eli looked at Gabriel. She was still smiling, which he took to be a good sign.

"What the fuck are you doing, Wolfe?" she whispered, eyes wide.

"I want to buy you a present. Since we first met, I don't think I've ever given you anything."

"But I was only joking. I have a perfectly good watch already." She flashed the Casio again.

"So leave. I'll tell him you changed your mind."

Eli pouted.

"That would be rude after he's gone to the trouble of finding one for me to try on."

Gabriel nodded.

"Oh, of course. And we can't make an act of bad manners be our last act before leaving Sweden. It would be …"

"Disrespectful."

"Yes! Disrespectful. Plus, you couldn't wear a Rolex on an op, could you? So you'll still need the G-Shock."

Their bantering was interrupted by the salesman returning. In both hands, as if bearing a royal proclamation on a velvet pillow, he carried a green, leather-covered box.

Eli nudged Gabriel and whispered.

"Bloody hell! You could fit a pair of shoes in that!"

"Here you are, madam," the salesman said with a smile as he laid the box reverently on the glass-topped display case. He swivelled it round and opened it towards Eli. "Rolex Lady-Datejust 28 in 950 platinum on a platinum President bracelet. Ice-blue face surrounded by forty-four brilliant-cut diamonds. Shall I?"

He picked the watch up and unclipped the clasp, waiting while Eli removed her chunky G-Shock and laid it on the glass with a soft *clunk*.

Gabriel watched, delighted, as the young man slid the watch over Eli's wrist and closed the clasp for her. He stood back, hands behind his back, relaxed, seemingly enjoying himself. *Stand easy*, Gabriel thought.

Eli held her wrist out, turning the watch this way and that under more of the bright halogen downlighters. She held it out towards Gabriel.

"Well?"

"It looks fantastic on you."

She looked happy. That's what Gabriel thought. Happy in an uncomplicated way. Just here, with him, in this moment. No baggage beyond the case she'd checked in and the leather messenger bag over her right shoulder. He felt himself falling, about to sigh, then mentally straightened, chasing away the grey cloud that threatened to cloud his enjoyment of the moment.

"What do you think?" Eli asked the still-smiling salesman, offering her wrist at eye level.

He peered at the watch, then stood back and looked along the length of her arm before returning to look at the watch.

"It is a good look for you, madam. The face is in proportion to your wrist. It suits you very well, I think."

Eli grinned and turned to Gabriel.

"You really mean it? You'll buy it for me?"

He smiled and nodded.

"Yes, I really mean it. Please let me. I'd love to."

She laughed.

"OK, then. Yes, please."

"We'll take it," Gabriel said.

"Very good, sir. The Lady-Datejust 28 with diamond bezel is forty-five thousand euros. How would you like to pay?"

"Credit card, please."

The salesman smiled and nodded, clearly used to dealing with customers who had that sort of headroom on their credit cards. He reached for the watch but Eli pulled her wrist back.

"Oh, no! I want to wear it. Put my *work* watch in the box, please."

Smiling, the young man complied, closing the lid on the G-Shock.

Outside the shop, Eli took Gabriel by his shoulders and kissed him, long and hard, drawing appreciative calls of encouragement and whistles from a group of young men in matching white T-shirts, emblazoned with "Danny's Stag Weekend."

"Thank you," she said, when she finally freed him. "It's beautiful."

"So are you," he replied.

Later, waiting for their bags at Heathrow, Eli left Gabriel at the luggage carousel.

"I need to pee," she said

With Eli gone, he glanced around the baggage reclaim area, running through the different types and styles of traveller, assigning each a name he'd made up years earlier. The Weary Executive. The Wide-eyed Backpacker. The International Glamourpuss. Then his pulse raced upwards. There she was again. The woman with the red hair. She was half-turned away from him and her face was obscured, but he caught the line of her jaw and the glint of copper in the plait at the back of her head. He felt sweat break out under his shirt. He looked down, holding a hand out, and steadying himself on a nearby luggage cart. When he looked up again, the woman was gone.

Eli arrived.

"Bags here yet?"

"Nope."

She looked at him again.

"What's wrong, you look like you've seen a ghost."

Gabriel Wolfe said nothing. He looked away, over to the conveyor belt from which bags, holdalls and cases were falling onto the scratched black slats of the carousel like bodies being dumped into a mass grave.

17

MOSCOW

Inside the pine-panelled sauna, the temperature had climbed to almost fifty Celsius. The three men relaxing on the top level of its tiered benches ran Kuznitsa, a criminal organisation founded by returning Afgantsy, Russian soldiers who'd fought in its decade-long war with the Taliban. Each had entered the sauna carrying a knife.

They'd left their clothes, wallets, phones and pistols outside, in the lockers the health club provided. Despite the flimsy hardware, they had no concerns. They'd brought rather more substantial security. Three men who supplied personal, round-the-clock protection, men of few words but pronounced appetites for violence.

Their leader, Max Novgorodsky – the name acquired during a stint in prison – leant forward while his deputy scraped sweat and dirt from the pliant flesh of his back with an ivory strigil. Max enjoyed the feeling of the curved, blunt-edged blade sliding over his skin, gathering up the fine black worms of grime. He spoke over his left shoulder.

ANDY MASLEN

"Use some muscle, Krasivyj! I'm not some girl you have to pussyfoot around with."

The man behind him, as tall as his six-foot boss but almost twice his girth, shook his head and snorted.

"Fine. But you better be ready."

His nickname meant "handsome." Although he'd chosen it himself, in prison, it was ironic. His face was a mess, a swirl of pink shiny skin on the left side that dragged the eyelid down, the result of a mujahideen rocket-propelled grenade exploding against the side of his truck. His right cheek was disfigured by a jagged scar, a white trench carved into the sunburnt skin of his face.

He looked over at the third man, who sat on Max's other side, and winked. Nozh – "knife" – winked back.

Krasivyj applied more pressure, grinning as he brought forth a groan from his boss.

"That any better?" he asked.

"Just about. If it's the best you can do, I suppose I'd better be grateful."

"Careful, Max," Nozh said. "If he uses any more force on that thing, he'll do to you what he did to that Afghan we caught. Remember?"

Max nodded, closing his eyes and letting his mind drift back to a bitterly cold January day in 1988 towards the end of the war. He, Krasivyj and Nozh were part of a patrol clearing out an Afghan village. They called all Afghans *vragi* – enemy – and didn't trouble themselves distinguishing between combatants and civilians. They discovered a young man cowering inside a sheep pen, his turban soaked in blood. Beside him lay a Kalashnikov, its magazine missing.

"Where'd you get that from, eh?" Krasivyj had shouted, kicking the young man hard in the ribs. "Steal it from one of our boys, did you?"

The young man held his hands out in supplication, palms towards his captor, shaking his head. His beard was scrubby, like desert thorn bushes, and his teeth were brown and decayed as he grinned in fear.

"*Nyet! Droog!*"

Krasivyj sneered.

"'Friend'? Fuck your mother! You're all the same. Bloody sheep-shagging savages."

He bent to retrieve the rifle and at that point the young man sprang at him, slashing him across the face with a curved knife and spitting out a stream of that bastard language none of them could understand. Max could only make out a single word: Allah. He was a fucking muja like all the rest.

Reeling back, and clutching his bleeding face with his right hand, Krasivyj drew his Makarov and shot the man in the stomach. Over his screams, Krasivyj yelled at him, a fluent stream of obscenities involving his parentage, his sexual tastes and his diet, as he dragged him from the sheep pen and into the road.

"Hold him there!" he shouted at Nozh and Max. Then he rushed back to the sheep pen and retrieved the man's knife.

Marching back to the screaming Afghan and the two bemused Russian soldiers, he waved the knife back and forth in the cold winter sunlight so that its edge glinted like glass.

"Motherfucker! You ruined my face. What girl's going to want to kiss this, eh?" he shouted, wiping a huge paw across the freely bleeding wound and flicking blood over the Afghan.

He bent and grinned evilly.

"I tell you what. Compared to you, I'll look like a fucking movie star!"

And then he drew the blade right across the man's forehead and down the sides of his face in three crudely joined-up lines. The man's struggles and screams seemed only to excite Krasivyj. He looked up at his two comrades.

"Watch this," he said.

Then he turned back to the screaming Afghan.

"Good luck getting a date now, *friend*," he said.

Then he dug his fingers under the flap of skin on the man's forehead and pulled down.

He let him writhe there in the dust for a full minute before drawing his pistol again and shooting him dead.

. . .

For a few days, they'd tried out the nickname *Kozha* – Skin – but it hadn't taken and they'd reverted to *Loshadik* – Horsie – for his prodigious ability to drink.

It wouldn't be until prison that he chose his own name, the one that finally stuck.

* * *

Max leant forward and ladled a little water onto the hot coals. It boiled instantly with a hiss. He watched the brief whiteness spiral into the superheated air before disappearing altogether. As he took his place on the bench again, he moved the three knives along a little.

Someone rapped sharply on other side of the pine-panelled door. Max nodded grimly to himself, then made eye contact with his two most trusted lieutenants.

"Yes," he barked.

The door swung inwards and a hunched figure stumbled forward, his progress aided by a sturdy push in the small of his back from a thickly muscled forearm. He straightened. His eyes, a pale blue, flicked between the three naked men in front of him. Somehow, in his chain store suit, scuffed brown shoes, beige shirt and narrow, custard-yellow tie, it was he who appeared embarrassed by his state of dress. He pushed a hand through wiry black hair then stuck it in a trouser pocket. He took it out again and folded his arms, then uncrossed them. He cleared his throat and ran a finger round the inside of his shirt collar.

Max stared. The man trembling before him, sweat gathering on his forehead, cheeks and top lip, looked after mining contracts for Kuznitsa. His job involved bribing officials in the Federal Agency for Mineral Resources. Word had come to Max from an impeccable source – the Deputy Head of the Ministry himself – that his man had begun informing for Sledkom, the Investigative Committee of the Russian Federation.

Dark stains had blossomed under the arms of the man's suit, changing the colour from brown to black. His face had reddened. It glistened with sweat that evaporated and reformed, evaporated and reformed. Max leaned back, resting his elbows on the bench behind him. He spread his legs apart.

"Daniil," he said softly. "Why?"

The man's lower lip trembled.

"Why what, boss?"

"Why did you betray us to the Feds?"

"I … I didn't. I don't know where you got that from, but you're mistaken."

Max laughed. He turned, first to Nozh, then to Krasivyj. They laughed too, three baritone voices raised in enjoyment of the joke. Then he leaned forwards and addressed his betrayer again.

"Are you calling me a liar, Daniil?"

The man's eyes widened and he gulped down some air as he realised his error.

"N-no! Of course not! I just meant someone is trying to discredit me with you. I live to serve you, Max, you know that. You gave me my chance, and I have always repaid your generosity with my loyalty."

Max smiled and shook his head. The man was a good actor, he'd give him that, at least. More than one man had pissed himself faced with a similar encounter. But enough was enough. Max kept his ears open, he heard the whispers in the air, the rumours spreading amongst the other gangs. Ever since that monumental fuckup with the four guys he'd sent after the English agent and his Jewish partner, the whispers were being repeated, louder this time.

"Daniil, you are," he paused, "a goat."

The man's face drained of blood. It amused Max the way the flush from the heat whitened in just a few seconds. But then, he reflected, calling a man a goat – an informer, a faggot, a jerk, a bastard – well, that was the worst insult in the criminal lexicon. If it hadn't produced some sort of reaction, he'd have wondered if Daniil was actually there in the sauna with him, or just a hologram.

"Max, please," Daniil said, moving to take a step closer and then staggering as his knees buckled at the enormity of the insult.

Max stood. Beside him, Nozh and Krasivyj rose to their feet.

"No!" he roared. "Here is your choice. Die on your feet, like a man, or on your knees like a bitch. Are you a bitch, Daniil? Or a man?"

The man who had informed against Kuznitsa rubbed his right fist against his eyes, then shook his head. He took a few steps backwards until his shoulder blades bumped against the pine. Then he unbuttoned his suit jacket, grasped the translucent cotton of his shirt — wet enough that his nipples and black chest hair were visible through the thin fabric — and ripped it open, baring his chest.

He inhaled for the last time and screamed out, "Take my soul!"

The three men closed the gap between them and the goat and plunged their knives into his chest over and over again, getting covered in spurting blood and not minding — no, not at all, for was this not the Kuznitsa way?

Max withdrew his blade for the last time and let the lifeless body slide down the wall until it sat, legs splayed, in a spreading puddle of blood.

"Come on," he said, breathing heavily. "A shower and then a swim."

Later, as Max was knotting his bronze-and-sea-green Gucci tie, his phone buzzed. He looked down and read the text.

Car scrapped. No more driving.

He smacked his right fist into his left palm.

"Yes! Kristersson came through. That English bastard is dead."

"Wolfe?" Nozh asked.

"Who else? Yes, Wolfe. Counting Daniil, I make that two for two. Not a bad day's work, eh lads? Let's go and eat. I'm starving."

· · ·

Strolling down Tverskaya Street, Max looked around him. This Moscow – *his* Moscow – had changed beyond all recognition from the drab Soviet city of history.

Yes, GUM, the vast flagship department store on Red Square, still plied its wares. And the state had managed to preserve its own landmarks: the infamous Lubyanka prison, Saint Basil's Cathedral, the vast expanse of Red Square, and the Kremlin itself. But here, on Tverskaya Street, this was the new Russia.

Ferrari dealerships rubbing shoulders with those for Bentley and Aston Martin. Ten-a-penny BMWs, Audis and Mercedes with blacked-out windows, sweeping down newly resurfaced streets, their whisper-quiet engines only raising their voices when their owners wanted them to. *Not like those shitty old heaps we used to churn out like tractors. No, that's unfair to tractors. At least they had charm.*

And look in the shop windows! Turnbull & Asser. Valentino. Gucci. Prada. Rolex. Burberry. J.Crew. Sweet Jesus, you could be in Milan or Manhattan or Paris or London.

Russians had changed, too. Or those with the wits, or the balls, to seize the opportunities that sprang up all around their feet like spring crocuses. He eyed up a trio of young women walking ahead of him. Their long, beautifully slender legs ending in towering high heels, their blood-red soles semaphoring wealth, self-confidence, sexiness.

Each woman clutched an iPhone, rose-gold models they all surely must have bought together. Their hair was sleek, fastened with tortoiseshell clasps or gathered into shining ropes at the napes of their necks. Hairdos like those would cost more than their grannies made in a month. In three months!

And nobody cared anymore. That was the beauty of it. Nobody cared. What mattered was getting on. Getting ahead. Getting one over on your competition.

Max didn't really see what he and his fellow board members did as crime. Not in the sense it used to carry. Of course, there were times when rules needed to be enforced, examples made, but most of what he did relied on conversations, the discreet digital transfer of funds from one offshore account to another. When the recipient of those glorious ones and zeroes was a minister or a party secretary, a general or a foreign CEO, how could that be considered a crime? If Max ran a criminal enterprise, then the whole world was a criminal enterprise.

Max walked on. Master of the New Moscow. Master of the New Russia. Smiling broadly, he pushed a handful of 5,000-ruble notes into the cup of a beggar wearing scraps of an old Russian army uniform, the jacket mismatched with the trousers, one boot sole flapping loose like a lolling, black tongue.

"There you go, Grandad. Get yourself a meal and a bed for the night."

Yes, it had been an extremely satisfying day so far. With steaks at Café Pushkin to look forward to, along with a bottle of Château Pédesclaux claret – Max's favourite and, at 12,650 rubles a bottle, quite honestly a steal – an afternoon with his new mistress, the wife of an oil and gas tycoon, and then the opera that evening, a new production of *Otello* at the Bolshoi. All this, and the new diamond mine way over in Yakutia, which would soon be bringing in a solid new income stream and making Kuznitsa's balance sheet look even healthier.

But better, much better than all of these ticks on the credit side of Max's personal balance sheet, was the news that his torpedo had struck the target and blown it to shit. Even UK security agents were not beyond his reach. No more Wolfe. Max's reputation as a hard man restored. The challengers to his authority slinking back into their holes.

Max smiled and strode on.

18

SHOREDITCH

I am writing this for myself. I have no intention of showing it to anyone. Not Eli. Not Don. Definitely not Fariyah, although God knows she'd have a field day reading it. No, this is for me. I have come to think of it as my testament. Something has happened inside me. Not a bad thing, not really. But I've changed. If people I get close to are in danger, then it stands to reason I have to raise my game. I have to kill my enemies first, before they kill me, or those I love. Because I won't be beaten. I won't give up on life. But it has to be life on my terms.

That business outside Stockholm with the bikers was the clearest signal yet of the way I have to go. Not Yinshen fangshi. The Way of Stealth has its place. But this is a new path. I feel sure Master Zhao would approve. I could have pushed that handlebar grip with just a few more pounds' pressure, and that fat thug would have been rolling down the E4 on his arse at a hundred miles an hour. I gave him a choice. I won't do it again.

I saw pure rage on the faces of Karl and Jarryd at the funeral. Now I can feel that same emotion heating up in my brain, like a pressure cooker. It's starting to hurt, starting to hamper my thinking. It's two in the morning and I'm wide awake. Eli's upstairs, sleeping the sleep of the just. I'm going out. To put my theory to the test. The world is full of bad people. They choose their path, just as I have chosen mine.

First, I need to borrow Eli's Rolex.

I was out for two hours and twenty minutes. It's now 4.23 a.m., and I have just shown some people the consequences of their chosen paths.

It's a warm night, which made my little experiment easier. I went out in my running gear. The T-shirt meant the Rolex was visible, those twinklers flashing under the streetlights like an advertising sign saying, "Rob this stupid rich guy."

Maybe by day, Shoreditch is London's new hipster paradise. The German cars on Eli's road and the artisanal coffee shops say it is. But at night – proper night, I mean, not late evening when the execs and artists are still rolling from restaurants to bars, bars to clubs – all the herbivores go home to sleep and they leave the neighbourhood to the meat-eaters. The jackals, the hyenas, the leopards and the lions.

I jogged down Shoreditch High Street, but it was too bright, so I took a random turn and ended up on a much less salubrious road. But still. My feeling is, a citizen, even a rich one – even a rich, stupid one – should be able to go for a run at two in the morning and not get mugged. It's like those old fart judges on the bench who used to dismiss rape cases on the grounds that a girl in a mini-skirt was "asking for it." Running while wearing a Rolex isn't a crime, nor is being stupid, for that matter.

I'd gone about fifty yards when out popped these three likely lads. Two black, one white. They all had the same expression. A kind of dead-eyed stare, slack mouths. Maybe they think it's intimidating. It might be on a member of the public. But I've seen worse. Far worse. Black men in Africa with gold teeth, tribal scars incised all over their faces and vicious glints in their eyes that say they're going to enjoy inflicting pain on you before killing you. Militiamen in Bosnia, so pale their skin is translucent, and you can see the veins in their temples like blue-green rivers, with children's ears threaded onto leather thongs round their necks. Masked Middle-Eastern terrorists who enjoy raping women and castrating men before dunking them in containers of concentrated caustic soda, all in the name of religion.

The leader, a big lad, maybe eighteen or nineteen, six-five and at least fifteen stone, pointed at the watch.

"I'll 'ave that, bruv," he said. He was the white one, but he affected the accent they all seem to use nowadays.

I stood still, and looked at the watch, then back at him.

"No," I said. "You won't."

He looked left and right at his two lieutenants and grinned, then he dropped the smile and looked back at me. He pulled a knife, and the others followed suit. Big ones, too. Complete overkill for urban muggers. Serrated top edges, the works. Rambo knives, they call them. That or Zombies.

He took a step closer and pointed the knife at my face.

"I said, I'll—" is as far as he got.

His intention was clear. He was carrying a deadly weapon and had just threatened me with it. Reasonable force was justified. *Pre-emptive* reasonable force.

I stepped in, fast, slid inside his reach and head-butted him in the face. I heard the crack as his nose broke. I caught him with a knee on the way down. I may have broken his jaw. I relieved him of his blade as he crumpled.

And then I turned to the others.

They didn't hang back. Maybe they'd trained themselves not to run. Together, they came at me, slashing wildly with the knives, yelling insults. Fucking this, cunting that.

I almost felt sorry for them.

Dodging their wild thrusts was child's play. One guy took a foot to the balls. He went down screaming in that high-pitched tone men do when you kick them there. I had time to register the clink of his knife as it hit the pavement.

The second I took out with an elbow to the right cheekbone. It broke, I think.

When they were all on the ground, and I was sure they weren't going to get up, I collected the other two knives. I knelt close to the first guy's face and leaned down, just touching the tip of his knife to his cheek.

"If I see you again, I'll kill you," I said, in a conversational tone. "Do you understand?"

"Yeah, yeah, bruv, whatever!" he said, still sticking to the streetwise accent.

"Tell your friends," I said.

Then I ran on, back towards the High Street.

It took another thirty minutes before I got contacted again.

It was round the back of a pub.

I heard raised voices. Male voices, mostly, maybe a couple of females. I thought it was worth a spin of the wheel.

I jogged left and found myself running into the middle of some sort of, I don't know, gang palaver, I suppose I'd call it.

Anyway, five guys and a couple of girls, smoking dope and arguing about some mobile phones they'd lifted. I went to jog round them, but they saw me coming and stopped what they were doing. They spread out across the road, each one of them looking straight at me. Under the pinkish-orange glow of the streetlight I could see the way their eyes kept flicking down to the watch.

As they started coming towards me, the question going round and round in my brain was, *When did everyone in Britain start carrying knives?* They weren't much older than the three thugs I had dealt with earlier. A couple of the men might have been touching thirty, but the rest were anywhere between eighteen and twenty five.

Street gangs are predictable. The leader, who usually elects himself, is basically the one with the height and the muscle. He probably went through school beating up smaller kids and came to believe that bulk equals bravery.

This guy was turned out in a quilted gold bomber jacket. It made him easy to spot, for sure. More for form's sake than anything else, I gave them a chance to escape unharmed.

"Please, I don't want any trouble," I called out as they closed the distance between us to ten feet.

"Well, then," he answered with a cocky smile, "you should have stayed out of our fuckin' enz, shouldn't you?"

I'd heard this word once before and looked it up. "Enz" equals "ends" equals the ends, i.e., the perimeter of a gang's territory.

"I was just out running. I have insomnia," I said.

"Yeah? Tell you what. I've got some pills that'll help you sleep. I'll give you two for that Roly on your wrist."

The others all sniggered at his shaft of wit.

After that, the laughing stopped.

I ran at him and chopped him to the ground with a move Master Zhao taught me. It's not too dangerous if you aim properly. I caught him pretty much dead-on: a spot below the jawline rich in nerves and blood vessels.

While he was still upright, eyes rolling up in their sockets, showing white, I took out two more with Krav Maga combinations I've been practising with Eli. I had to scale the power back. I didn't want to kill them. Although I may have broken one guy's elbow. The clinking of metal on concrete as knives fell from unresponsive hands was almost musical. The rest fled.

Then I came home.

I feel calmer now. My head is clear again. I suppose apart from anything else, I got a couple of hours' good hard exercise.

I'm going back to bed. I could probably jump in beside Eli from the top of the wardrobe without waking her. Joke. I'd never do that. She says she loves me. I know she means it. I can see it in her eyes. And I love her, too. But she's in danger. I need to keep her safe, protect her. Ah, Fariyah, what would you make of me at the moment? Perhaps I'll let you find out.

19

YAKUTIA

Ignatyev liked to think of himself as a hands-on manager. Not for him, the abstract world of spreadsheets and forecasting reports. That was what the *apparatchiks* in the air-conditioned offices were for, after all. No. He believed in, what had that Western management book he'd read called it? Ah, yes. "Managing by Walking Around." Although, to be fair, he'd probably have retitled it, "Managing by Walking Around and Kicking People's Teeth In If You Don't Think They're Working Hard Enough, and What About That Short Little Fucker Who Gave Me a Funny Look So I Pulled Him Out of Line and Shot Him in the Leg to Teach Him a Lesson?"

In any case, it was too far to walk all the way from the compound to the mine, so he took a 4x4. A very nice BMW SUV in sparkling, deep-blue paint. The white leather interior was perhaps not the most practical colour, but it sent a strong signal to passengers. We can engage in the dirtiest of activities, but we always come out cleaner than a virgin's conscience, as the saying had it.

As he drove, he sang. An old folk song from his part of Russia, a small, agriculture-dependent province to the south of the Urals near Yekaterinburg, characterised by rolling pastureland, endless summers and short, sharp winters that would freeze your cock off if you took a piss out of doors.

The weather here reminded him of his childhood summers. Dazzling sunshine that bounced hard light off every flat surface, from drilling equipment to the broad, flat hood of the BMW. Low humidity, so you could actually enjoy the heat. And a soft, sweet-fragranced breeze blowing all the way down from the distant, snow-capped purple mountains of the Verkhoyansk Range. If it weren't for the mosquitoes, who God, in His infinite wisdom, had equipped with bites like miniature Kalashnikovs, the place would be pretty close to perfect.

The mine was to his left as he powered round the long, looping bend in the road that ended at the heavily guarded perimeter. With a flamboyant skid, anti-lock brakes juddering at all four corners, he brought the SUV to a halt outside the gates. He hit the centre of the steering wheel hard, three times, sending demanding blares from the horns echoing out across the open-cast pit.

A uniformed man shambled out from a small guardhouse built of white-painted cinder blocks, scratching his stubbled cheek. When he saw who was demanding access, he snapped to attention and saluted clumsily, before rushing to whack the circular rubber button that would open the steel gates.

Ignatyev drew level with the man and then stopped, buzzing the window down. He looked left.

"Get yourself a proper shave. And where's your weapon?"

"In-inside, sir."

"It's not much fucking good in there, is it? Go and get it. Now!" he barked.

The man turned and rushed inside, appearing moments later clutching an ageing AK-47.

"You keep it clean," Ignatyev asked.

"Y-yes, sir," the guard answered, his eyes locked onto Ignatyev's.

Ignatyev climbed out of the BMW. He held his hand out.

"Give it to me."

The guard handed his rifle over, and Ignatyev was gratified to see the hand that held the gun was trembling.

Good. We need to get you guys sharpened up. A bit of fear never hurts. And compared to what I have planned, this little interaction is nothing.

Ignatyev dropped out the magazine. Then he pulled back the charging lever and let it go with a loud clack in the still summer air. Satisfied that there was no round in the action, he turned the AK-47 round and peered into the barrel. He caught the gleam of smooth, oiled steel. Surprised, he reversed his grip on the rifle and pushed the magazine home. He handed it back to the guard, who visibly relaxed once his own hands were curled around the pistol grip and wooden fore-end.

"What's your name?" he demanded.

"Elley Aysenovich, sir."

"Very good, Aysenovich. A good soldier knows his rifle is his best friend, yes?"

"Yes, sir. I served in the Second Chechen War, sir."

"Did you, now? Which regiment?"

"Border Guard Service of the Federal Security Service, sir."

"And were you a courageous fighter for Mother Russia, Aysenovich?"

The man nodded. He looked relieved now he was on more familiar territory.

"Yes, sir. In fact, I was awarded the Medal of Ushakov for my part in a raid on a Chechen stronghold outside of Grozny in oh-eight."

Ignatyev raised his eyebrows. *So not everyone working here is on the take or a coward.*

"OK, Aysenovich. Good work. Listen, come see me in my office at eight tomorrow morning. I think I can use a man like you."

Aysenovich smiled broadly, revealing greyish teeth. He straightened still further and slammed off a salute that nearly took his head from his shoulders.

"Yes, sir!"

Smiling to himself, Ignatyev climbed back into the BMW's padded driver's seat and drove through the gates, watching Aysenovich in the rearview mirror. The man spun on his heel as the SUV entered the mine, shot out his right hand to the close the gates, then marched with exaggerated military bearing back into his office.

Ignatyev drove on for five minutes, skirting the western edge of the vast pit scraped, blasted and dug out of the earth and rock. Two hundred metres down, the trucks, earth-movers, crushers and wash plants resembled the toy vehicles he liked to buy for his sons back in Moscow. How fast they were growing up. Alexei nearly seven and Eduard already five and almost as tall as his older brother.

He piloted the BMW along the access road that spiralled down into the pit, descending in a series of graceful curves cut into the dark-grey shale. With the window down, the sound of the heavy machinery reached his ears: the wail and whine of high-powered gears, the deep-throated roar of vast diesel engines, the hard, double-bangs of piledrivers, and the distant crack-thump of demolition charges exploding. Together they created a most unmusical sound, which nevertheless made him smile.

Arriving at last at the bottom, he killed the engine and stepped out onto the graded floor of the pit. All around him, men and machines were biting, grinding and tearing at the soft substrate; buckets, grabs, drills and conveyors raking out millions of tons of dross to find the few precious kilos of diamonds that made all this effort worthwhile.

He pulled out his phone and called the shift manager. They'd spoken earlier and planned this moment carefully.

"Yes, boss," Gerasimov said, answering on the first ring.

"Is he here?"

"Yes. He's operating the number four line. Huge fucker, built like an ox. Blond hair, orange-and-yellow striped hi-vis over a bare chest. You can't miss him."

"I don't need to miss him," Ignatyev snapped. "You're the one who's going to get him. I want him in front of me in ten minutes. And the entire shift gathered to watch."

"Of course, boss. Sorry. It's just, you said, you wanted to make an example of him."

"Don't worry about that," Ignatyev said with a smile. "After today, nobody's going to forget Boris Yegorevich in a hurry."

While he waited for Gerasimov to bring him Yegorevich, Ignatyev lit a cigarette, flicking the spent match away. Inhaling deeply, he turned slowly through a full circle, taking in the vastness of the pit and trying to visualise how many tonnes of diamonds might still lie interred in its black depths. The keening cry of a bird of prey drew his eyes skywards.

High above him, though still readily identifiable by its forked tail, a black kite wheeled and stooped, trying to escape the attentions of a trio of crows mobbing the interloper and seeking to drive it from their territory. The larger bird performed a sharp turn and seized one of its tormentors in its talons. Together, kite and crow fell vertically, locked in a whirling death-spiral. Ignatyev watched, entranced, as the spectacle played out before him.

The two birds fell below ground level, right into the embrace of the cathedral-like interior of the pit. Just as he imagined they would smash into the ground, killing themselves from pride, fury or just a dumb animal's unwillingness to change course, the kite unhooked its claws and wheeled away, banking to starboard and flapping its broad wings lazily as it climbed, cresting the rim of the pit and disappearing. Cawing angrily, the crow followed in an untidy, effortful attempt to avoid hitting the ground.

The stressed engine note of a truck being driven in too low a gear snapped Ignatyev out of his reverie. He looked over at the Toyota Hilux pickup, painted in the black-and-silver livery used on all of New Galaxy's official vehicles.

Gerasimov climbed out, followed by a giant in a multicoloured hi-vis vest, his face half-hidden by swags of thick blond hair. The giant wore a surly expression. Gerasimov prodded him in the back with a pistol. Dragging his boat-like boots, the man edged closer to Ignatyev.

Ignatyev was six-three. When the giant arrived in front of him, he still had to look up into his eyes.

"You are an animal," he said in a low voice.

"What?" the giant replied, staring down at Ignatyev, and looking as though he wanted to eat him. Or break his spine at the very least. He flexed his arms and balled his massive hands into fists, but Gerasimov's Makarov was proving a sufficient deterrent.

"You heard me! You steal diamonds. That is bad enough. But you have been misbehaving, haven't you, Yegorevich?"

The man glowered at Ignatyev, his wiry blond eyebrows knitting together so that the grey eyes beneath them almost disappeared.

"I don't know what you mean."

"No? Then I'll have to remind you. Last month, on your day off, you took a company truck, drove to Nyurba, got drunk, then visited a brothel, where you had your way with three whores, leaving one of them with a broken jaw and internal injuries."

Yegorevich shrugged.

"Is that it? The bitch got what she deserved. She tried to cheat me."

Enjoying the fact that he knew how the game would end, while the dumb ox in front of him was just playing the piece in his hand, Ignatyev, a keen chess player in his admittedly limited spare time, made his final move.

"No, that's not it. I agree with you. A whore knows what she's getting into the first time she spreads her legs for a few rubles. But after you smashed that woman's jaw like kindling and sent her to the hospital, you roamed the streets didn't you?"

The big man's brow furrowed again, but from doubt this time, not aggression. Ignatyev saw the change on his man's face. Smiled as he waited for an answer.

"Maybe I did. So what? I had to clear my head, you know? I drank a lot of vodka."

"A lot? More like a fucking bathful! Then you broke into a house on Kusakova Street. You beat up the owner, a Mr Rodion Variseyevich, rendering him unconscious. And you raped his wife and teenaged daughter at knifepoint."

"No! I swear to God, I didn't—"

"Don't swear!" Ignatyev roared. "You finish that sentence, and I'll have Gerasimov here gutshoot you and leave you out for the wolves."

"What are you going to do?" Yegorevich mumbled.

"Wait and see," Ignatyev replied.

20

Over the next fifteen minutes, 178 men assembled in front of Ignatyev's BMW, just as the whole staff had gathered when he took control of the mine. While he waited, he retreated to the BMW's cabin and listened to an Eagles CD, smoking a second cigarette. Judging the time to be right, he descended again and walked to the rear of the SUV. He blipped the fob to open the tailgate. He pointed to a couple of men and beckoned them over. He pointed inside.

"Lean that up against the side facing your colleagues."

The men's eyes widened as they took in the apparatus Ignatyev had brought with him – he'd had the head carpenter construct it for him the previous day – and what lay coiled beside it. They were staring at a tapered wooden plank that stretched the length of the cabin, from the rear door over the folded-forward passenger seat to the windscreen. Seven feet in total, a foot wide at one end, three at the other.

They hauled it out of the BMW's cavernous interior and did as Ignatyev had instructed them. He appreciated the care they took to lower its top edge against the roofline to avoid scratching the pristine paintwork. A swell of murmurs from the assembled workers let him know that at least a few recognised the gravity of the situation facing their shift-mate.

Cut along the top edge of the plank were three semicircles – a larger central cut and two smaller. Ignatyev beckoned Gerasimov, who jabbed his pistol into Yegorevich's back.

"Move!" he commanded.

Yegorevich shambled forwards and, when he was facing the plank, Gerasimov shoved him hard and held him flat against the sloping wood.

Ignatyev stepped closer and, taking a hank of the giant's thick, blond hair in his fist, shoved his jaw over the lip of the larger semicircle.

"Put your wrists on the other two," he whispered.

Perhaps realising he was backed into a corner, Yegorevich complied.

He turned his head towards Ignatyev.

"What are you going to do to me?"

"I'm going to make an example of you." He turned to the two men he'd co-opted. "You and you, get the rope from my car and tie him down."

They rushed to comply, and Ignatyev supervised them as they lashed Yegorevich to iron rings bolted through the plank at head and ankle-level.

Once Yegorevich was secured, Ignatyev leaned closer and muttered a couple of sentences before turning away to face the workers gathered before him. Over Yegorevich's pleading, he repeated the words he'd just whispered, this time at a volume that even the men at the back of the crowd could hear.

"Kuznitsa does not tolerate animal behaviour from its employees. And, in case you had forgotten, that's what you are now. This man, this Boris Yegorevich Berezin, is a thief, which is bad enough. But he is also a rapist. Of children. Yes, my friends. Good, honest, Russian whores weren't enough for him. Last month, he got himself drunk enough that he could rape a fourteen-year-old girl and her mother. Maybe some of you already know this. Maybe some of you have done the same. So, workers of

New Galaxy Diamond Mine, know this. My name is Volodya. Ruler of the World, as I told you before. As Kuznitsa's representative here, I am the law. You are all witnesses to Kuznitsa's justice. I do not take pleasure from what I am about to do, but it is necessary."

Ignatyev strode to the back of the BMW and grabbed the wooden-handled coil of leather that had so clearly horrified the two men he'd ordered to help him.

He stood beside Yegorevich and shook out the whip to its full length, eight feet of sun-dried leather, traditionally cured in milk until all its pliability had been replaced by a metallic hardness.

A few men gasped, others shouted, "Nyet!" They all knew what he held in his hand.

The knout.

The fearsome whip had been used to punish criminals for centuries, and had even replaced the death penalty once that had been abolished for crimes except those against the state. Ten lashes would render a person unconscious. Fifty could kill.

"Silence!" he roared. "Innocent Russian women and their daughters, asleep in their beds, should be free to dream without the fear that men like this are roaming the streets, drunk out of their skulls, intent on violation."

He ripped the hi-vis vest from Yegorevich's back and cast it aside. Then he marched back four paces, turned, shook out the knout and, in a smooth back-and-forth motion like a fly fisherman casting onto the surface of a trout stream, laid the one-inch wide strip of leather across the rapist's sunburnt skin.

Yegorevich screamed, and a violent shudder shook his body as the skin of his back split under the impact of the knout, and blood spurted from the wound.

Ignatyev flicked the wooden handle to bring the thong behind him, then laid it on again, harder this time, eliciting an even louder scream from Yegorevich, who bucked under his restraints.

With each repeated flick and lash – Ignatyev quickly lost count – droplets of blood flew from the thong until his face, hands and the clothes on his back were spattered with scarlet. He turned and leered at the crowd of men, most now wearing horrified expressions on their faces.

"Behave yourselves! Or else!" he roared at them, before turning towards the lolling Yegorevich and snapping the knout forwards, ripping another gobbet of flesh from his bleeding back, exposing a rib deep inside the shredded musculature.

He intended to continue, but a hand on his free arm stilled him mid-strike.

"Sir." It was Gerasimov.

"What is it? Can't you see I'm busy here?"

"He's dead, sir, Look."

It was true. Under the onslaught, Yegorevich's heart must have given out. He hung from his bindings, head twisted all the way to one side, eyes rolled upwards in their sockets.

Just to be sure, Ignatyev walked over and stuck two fingers under the man's jaw. Feeling nothing, he placed his ear against the left shoulder blade and listened. No pulse.

He coiled the knout and dropped it at Gerasmiov's feet.

"Find a bag for that. And point me to the nearest shower. I need to freshen up."

Later that day, Ignatyev's phone rang. He glanced at the screen and immediately straightened in his chair.

"Yes, boss. Ignatyev here."

"Well, of course it's you, idiot! Who else would be answering your phone?"

"Sorry."

"Never mind that. Did you deal with Yegorevich?"

"Yes, boss. Just like you asked."

"Did it work?"

"He's dead, so—"

"Yes, obviously, he's dead. I meant, did it have the desired effect on the others?"

"Oh, yes. I mean, one hundred percent yes. We won't have any more trouble."

"Good. I have to call the police chief in Nyurba. Smooth things over. And Volodya?"

"Yes, boss?"

"See that it doesn't happen again, won't you? Or I'll come down there myself and it'll be you under the knout. Understand?"

Ignatyev swallowed.

"Yes, boss," he managed to choke out before the call was cut off.

He poured himself a tumblerful of brandy and glugged half of it down in one. Compared to Max, he was a pussycat.

21

LONDON

Don had summoned Gabriel and Eli to Whitehall for their briefing. Sometimes it suited him to use a Central London location, and there were always people willing to lend him their accommodations. He was owed plenty of favours.

He watched as his two agents settled into the leather club chairs facing him across the uncluttered desk. He'd arranged coffee a few minutes before they arrived and waited now while the PA brought in a tray laden with a cafetière, jug brimming with hot, frothy milk, mugs and a plate of biscuits.

"Thanks, Diana," he said with a smile as she straightened the tray before leaving.

The door closed, he waited a moment, knowing that he needed to play the meeting carefully. There was a look in Gabriel's eye he hadn't seen for a long time. A dangerous look.

Start softly, he thought.

He smiled at each of them in turn.

"How are you doing, Old Sport? I'm sorry things kicked off at the funeral."

"I'm OK, boss. I think they just needed someone to blame. I made a pretty decent scapegoat."

Don scrutinised the younger man's face, looking for telltale signs that he might be dissembling. But Gabriel appeared relaxed. No tension drawing the skin tight around his eyes or mouth. Reasonable colour in his cheeks. He turned to Eli.

"And you?"

"Me?"

She seemed surprised. As if to say, *Why would you even be asking?* Since he'd hired her out from under the nose of his old friend Uri Ziff, he'd never been anything other than hugely impressed. She seemed completely unflappable. "Competent" didn't even get close to her levels of technical and tradecraft skills, and she was far more willing to follow orders than her partner. More, in fact, than half of the awkward buggers who comprised his team.

"Yes. I know you and Gabriel are an item these days. If he's under stress, that has to affect you, too. So, how are you?"

He noticed a blush stealing across her cheeks. Then it faded as quickly as it had arrived. *Either you have superhuman control of your autonomic nervous system, my lady, or there's actually very little that truly bothers you.*

"Honestly, boss, I'm fine. I only met Britta once, and I thought she was lovely. But in my life, sad to say, I have lost many friends. I try to keep moving forward. I have an eye out for Gabriel, but for me, no. I'm good."

Don rubbed his hands together. *No point pushing any harder. We'll take it on trust.* He poured three mugs of coffee.

"I spoke to Ekström again. He was adamant that you shouldn't play any part in the investigation, Old Sport. I had to let him know, as gently as possible, of course, that while I'd be taking his comments under advisement, as our American friends say, I would retain the final authority on when and where my people are deployed and to what ends."

"So you're saying I'm official?"

"Mm-hmm. Half-official. The Swedes are mounting an investigation and Six is helping them. Sort of a joint taskforce.

They're very keen to get to the perpetrators first. But as Kristersson was sent after you, and there was that whole business on the way down to Marlborough Lines, I think we also have standing. So I'm running my own operation. Call it housekeeping, if you like. Purely a Department matter."

Eli grinned.

"Boss, you're not going off-books yourself, are you?"

He smiled back.

"No idea what you're talking about, young lady. I may have inadvertently forgotten to brief the Privy Council or the PM, but as I said, this is Department business. I'll handle any flack if it comes our way. Now, to business. What do we know? And what do we need?"

He stood and crossed the expanse of soft, thick-pile carpet to an ornate marble fireplace above which hung an oil painting of the Duke of Wellington. Beside the fireplace stood a whiteboard. The flimsy construction of shiny white plastic and spindly metal legs looked almost embarrassed, as if a cadet had taken a wrong turn and ended up in the officers' mess. Selecting a black pen and uncapping it, he waited.

"Put Kuznitsa at the centre, boss," Eli said, breaking the silence. "They're the spider at the centre of the web, after all."

The squeak of the pen on the shiny surface was the only sound in the room. Don inhaled, enjoying the pear-drop tang of the volatile ink. He added "Kristersson" and "4 x Mercs in the Merc," connecting them to Kuznitsa with solid lines.

"Max Novgorodsky. He's the boss," Gabriel said. "Ex-Russian army. Veteran of their Afghan war. Ex-con, too."

The pen squeaked again.

"One of the mercs had a tattoo in Russian," Eli said. "'Kill 'em all,' wasn't it?" she asked Gabriel.

"Yes. It's a Spetsnaz slogan."

Don nodded, adding more text to the whiteboard.

"Hmm, mm-hmm. So we're up against tough opposition. Special Forces training. And the Afgantsy are no pushovers."

"Nor are we," Eli said, folding her arms across her chest.

"Indeed not," Don said, smiling.

"What's our objective, boss?" Gabriel asked him.

Don frowned. Gabriel seemed unsure. Not like him at all.

"Well, what do you *think* our objective should be?"

Gabriel shrugged.

"We could cut off the head?"

He paused and Don wondered, *What are you waiting for, Old Sport?*

"We could do that, of course," he replied. "But it might be like the hydra and just grow two more." *There, that should give you the opening you're clearly looking for.*

"If it were up to me, I'd do what we did to the warlord in Cambodia. Total wipeout. Search and destroy. Apart from anything else, it would send a fairly big signal to other organised crime gangs not to tangle with us. If we can destroy an Iranian nuclear facility, I'm sure we can deal with Kuznitsa. Even if it is stuffed with former Spetsnaz."

Don frowned. Gabriel had never told him all the details of his trip with Eli to Cambodia. He'd brought back photos of the dead warlord, an ex-Khmer Rouge commander named Win Yah. But Don knew that the man had under his command several dozen fighters, maybe more. Discreet enquiries with the security service in Cambodia hadn't yielded much in the way of reliable intel, but they'd been adamant that the northern province that Win Yah had controlled was now free of his reign of terror. There had been muttered references to a "killing field." He wrote two more words on the whiteboard.

Russian Govt?

Then he connected them with dotted lines to Kuznitsa.

"You'll need to tread carefully. We can't go crashing in there and upsetting the Ivans. I know we have relatively powerful patrons down the road," he said, pointing in the vague direction of the Houses of Parliament. "But there are some places where discretion isn't just advisable, it's mandatory."

"Understood," Gabriel and Eli chorused, before looking at each other and smiling.

Don looked on, amused, wondering whether they'd shout "Jinx!" next. They didn't.

"Good. Thoughts on cover?"

"*Biznes!*" Gabriel said. "It's the new religion over there, isn't it? We'll head for Moscow posing as hedge fund managers. Hide in plain sight. I'll hire a flashy car, we'll dress the part, nobody will bat an eyelid."

Don smiled.

"It's a fine idea, Old Sport. But the Department's budget doesn't stretch to rented Ferraris. I'm afraid even we aren't immune to budget cuts."

Gabriel shook his head.

"This is personal. They murdered Britta, and they were aiming for me. I'll pay for the cover myself."

Don didn't bother arguing or saying, "Oh, no, you can't, that's far too generous." This wasn't a vicarage tea party.

"Fine. We'll furnish the materiel. We can get it to you in the diplomatic bag once you're there. Compared to Tehran, Moscow is an easy place to move stuff into and out of. Our Embassy is ready to help."

Gabriel frowned. The expression lasted less than a second, but it was enough for Don to notice.

"What is it?" he asked.

"Uh, we may need to make a detour."

"A detour? Where to?"

"Saint Petersburg."

"Why?"

"I have a contact there. I owe her a favour. She called it in. But she could be helpful. She's extremely well connected. And extremely rich. She could be an asset."

Don smiled as he recrossed the room and took his seat again.

"Listen," he said, taking in both Gabriel and Eli in his gaze. "This isn't Six. You know that. We do things our way. What did their last boss but one call us?"

"'A bunch of bloody mavericks running around shooting anything that moves,'" Eli said.

"Yes. So once you're on the ground, you run it the way you need – or want – to. Just get the job done."

22

Gabriel and Eli were sitting in her kitchen, waiting for a Department driver to arrive and take them to Heathrow. Gabriel had booked two first-class tickets on the 9.25 a.m. flight to Pulkovo International Airport in Saint Petersburg. Pushing back the French cuff of his shirt, Gabriel checked his watch – 6.55 a.m. – and frowned.

"He should be here by now."

Eli leaned across the table and laid a hand on his forearm.

"Relax. He's probably hit a little traffic. All those ad agency hipsters striving to get to work early and impress the boss."

Gabriel had travelled all over the world, first as a soldier, and then as a Department operative, and until now, he'd never felt nervous. Excited, yes. Revved up before action, certainly. But not this insistent yet vague anxiety. His stomach was churning, and for a moment he thought he was about to bring up his breakfast. He swallowed hard and took a deep breath.

"Are you OK?" Eli asked, her forehead furrowing. "You look pale."

He looked at her and shook his head, aiming for a reassuring smile. Even to him, it felt forced.

"I'm fine." He rubbed his left shoulder beneath the lightweight wool and cashmere fabric of his suit jacket. "This still hurts like hell, even with those industrial-strength painkillers they gave me."

Eli blew out her lips. She looked relieved. Gabriel was pleased.

"I'm not surprised. You heard what that A&E consultant said at the hospital. Six weeks minimum to recover from a gunshot wound. Even a through-and-through flesh wound like yours. You didn't even give it a week."

"I know! I'm not stupid," Gabriel snapped, then instantly regretted it, watching with alarm at the way Eli's eyes popped wide open at the sharpness of his retort. "Sorry. I'm sorry," he said, running an open hand across his face.

What he wanted to tell her was that the red-haired woman had been appearing more and more frequently. Always with her face turned away or hidden by a hood or a passerby. With every fibre of his being, he knew it wasn't Britta. He'd watched her coffin being lowered into the warm Swedish earth hadn't he? But what then? A hallucination? Please, God, not that. He'd had enough of that with his dead friend and comrade Smudge Smith to last him a lifetime. Then again, at least the redhead was keeping her head intact. He didn't think he'd be able to cope if she appeared before him with the top of her skull blown away like a boiled egg.

"Listen," Eli was saying. "Let's just get on the plane and then relax, have a few drinks. It's what, a three-hour flight to Saint Petersburg?"

"And twenty minutes."

"OK, so a three-hour-and-twenty-minute flight. You can relax, maybe get a little extra sleep. I think you just need to be back in action. I know what a strain it's been, seeing Britta killed in front of you, then getting all that grief, literally, from her brother and Jarryd at the funeral."

"You're right. I'll try," he said. *I wish I believed that. I wish I could feel that things were going to be OK.*

The doorbell rang, interrupting this negative train of thought.

Eli stood up and smiled down at Gabriel.

"Well? How do I look?"

Gabriel took his time, willing himself to enjoy checking out his girlfriend and ignoring the flare of fear as he thought of what might happen to her. And of what effect that might have on him. She'd put her auburn hair up in a bun and was wearing more makeup than usual, though she'd toned down the kohl she usually rimmed her eyes with. In her role as a successful hedge fund manager, she'd selected a navy pinstriped Hugo Boss trouser suit, paired with a crisp white shirt and a pair of black Prada high heels.

"You look fine," he said. "Let's go. We can't keep the man waiting."

"The man" turned out to be "the woman," midthirties, short, efficient haircut, athletic physique visible despite the less expensive version of the suit Eli was wearing. Her erect stance and watchful gaze told Gabriel she was ex-military.

"Morning, sir, ma'am," she said briskly. "Heathrow, yes? Terminal Five?"

"Yes, please," Gabriel said.

She blipped the fob in the general direction of the Jaguar's boot and took Eli's case from her, swinging it over the boot lip and carefully laying it inside. Gabriel laid his own case beside Eli's and closed the boot with a muffled *clunk*.

She drove with the minimum of fuss but the maximum amount of speed, purring to a stop at the Terminal Five drop-off zone at 8.10 a.m. Although it was early, Gabriel took Eli's advice and had a glass of champagne in the first class lounge. The hit of alcohol eased the tension in his stomach. He leaned back in the chair, rolling his shoulders and closing his eyes. He let his thoughts wander wherever they wanted to.

Which turned out to be his missing sibling.

I'm going to find you. Even if you're dead, like Michael, I'm going to find you. But I hope you're alive. I don't know how Mum and Dad could have kept you a secret, but maybe the whole business with Michael just screwed them up more even than I thought. I have a lawyer in Hong Kong. I have money. I will find you. Maybe we could get to know each other. I'd like some family again after all this time. I'd like it a lot.

* * *

"Ladies and gentlemen, this is Captain Rennie. Welcome to Saint Petersburg. The local time is 3.40 p.m. So we made our stand a few minutes earlier than scheduled, which is good news. It's a very pleasant twenty-five Celsius outside, no clouds and low humidity. Thank you for flying with British Airways and have a good stay."

Gabriel and Eli looked at each other. They could read each other's thoughts. It wasn't difficult. *It starts now.*

Once they'd cleared Immigration, Gabriel called Tatyana Garin. He spoke Russian.

"Tanya, it's Gabriel. We just landed. We're at Pulkovo."

"Gabriushka! My darling man! It's so good to hear your voice and know you're here. You have the GPS for my dacha?"

"Yes. Already plugged into my phone. We're going to head into Saint Petersburg and hire a car, then we'll drive straight out to see you."

"Good. I have so much to tell you. I'll cook for you. You like steak. Pah! What am I saying? All men like steak. I have two big ones marinating already."

"Better make it three if you can manage it."

"Three? Oh! You brought someone?"

"Yes. She's my partner. We're going to work this together."

He detected a tiny pause.

"And when you say, 'partner' …"

"For work."

"Not pleasure?" A teasing tone had crept into Tanya's voice.

"OK, yes, for pleasure as well. She and I, we're a, you know …"

"Oh, Gabriushka! You don't need to sound quite so embarrassed about it. A handsome young man like you should have a girlfriend. Is she pretty?"

Gabriel looked at Eli and smiled. She returned the expression.

146

Her Russian was OK, and although he was speaking fast, he sensed she could tell she was the subject of the conversation.

"Yes, very. Listen, I should go. I'll see you later."

"Were you talking about me?" Eli asked as soon as he ended the call.

"Was it that obvious?"

"So you *were* talking about me?"

"Tanya asked me whether you were pretty."

Eli raised her eyebrows.

"And?"

"I said you looked like the back end of a bus."

Eli's mouth dropped open. And her fist collided with Gabriel's right bicep. Not for the first time. She had unerring aim.

"You bastard!" she said, smiling nonetheless. "You're lucky I don't dump you on your arse right in front of all these people."

"That would hardly fit the cover story, would it? Two hedge fund managers arrested by the Russian cops for brawling in the arrivals lounge. Unless you want to spend your first night here in jail."

"No thank you," Eli said, primly. "I'd rather spend it with some civilised female company. I hope *Tanya*," she laid heavy emphasis on the familiar diminutive of Tatyana, "is a good cook. Or is she too important and has a personal chef?"

"She's doing steaks. Herself," Gabriel said, rubbing the injured muscle through his sleeve. "Now, come on. Let's get a cab into town. I made the arrangements while we were in England. There should be a very nice set of wheels gassed up and ready to go, just waiting for us."

Installed in the back of the taxi, Gabriel watched out of the window as they covered the twenty or so kilometres into the centre of Saint Petersburg. Not much to see. Manicured trees lining much of the route and the usual big-box stores that were gradually turning every suburban landscape around the world into carbon-copies of each other. Even when they hit the centre, the traffic was light, or light compared to London.

The wide boulevards that reminded him of Paris seemed designed for many times more vehicles than were currently sweeping along, around and past them. Soviet delusions of grandeur, he supposed, before realising that the city had been built by Peter the Great centuries before the Russian Revolution. The cab driver twisted his head round and told Gabriel there were roadworks ahead and did he mind leaving Nevsky Avenue and taking the river route? Not at all, Gabriel replied, and the driver, satisfied, executed a nifty left turn that took them down towards the great Neva river.

Beside him, Eli gasped.

"It's beautiful!" she said.

He followed her pointing finger and had to agree.

Low, plaster-rendered buildings with classical porticoes and pediments, painted in pastel shades of blue, yellow, pink and green lined the wide waterway on both banks. None of them were more than three or maybe four storeys high, emphasising the width of the Neva.

"Pretty, isn't it?" the driver asked in Russian. Then, for Eli's benefit, in English. "Pretty? Like Venice?"

When they arrived, Gabriel paid the driver then climbed out of the car onto Inzhenernaya Street. A warm breeze brought with it the smell of the river. A not unpleasant mixture of old, wet wood, the water itself and a faint tang of diesel that reminded him of boat engines.

He gestured up at the array of logos above the plate glass frontage of the car dealership – a winged *B*, a three-pointed star, a prancing horse, a snorting bull – and turned to Eli.

"Shall we?"

Inside, the owners of the luxury car rental business had opted for what Gabriel always thought of as "New-Money High Style." Glittering white marble flooring. Black leather and mahogany armchairs. A vast, free-standing glass vase filled with a couple of dozen bird of paradise flowers, their orange and blue blossoms indeed resembling the creatures they were named for. Black-framed posters of Grands Prix and Le Mans 24-hour races from the twenties and thirties. And chrome light fittings sending shafts of rainbow-tinged halogen light down onto the polished paintwork beneath.

And what paintwork! Clearly, the post-Soviet years had found their ultimate expression in the several million pounds' worth of luxury cars on display. Compared to the exotic engineering, the bird of paradise flowers made rather dull companions, governesses at a debutantes' ball.

Gabriel navigated his way between a low-slung, scarlet Ferrari and a lime-green Lamborghini, the pair resembling aggressive insects more than cars, towards the reception desk. On the way, he turned to Eli and murmured, "Pull your shirt cuff up a little. Let the dog see the rabbit."

The woman behind the pale wood counter looked up and regarded the pair of customers with an icy smile. Her long blonde hair was cut immaculately, ending in a dead straight line at her shoulders. High, Slavic cheekbones emphasised the planes of her face, which, Gabriel reflected, could just as easily have been gracing the cover of Russian *Vogue* as the reception desk of a Saint Petersburg car-hire joint, albeit an outrageously expensive one.

"Good afternoon, sir, madam," she said, in flawless, lightly accented English.

"Good afternoon," Gabriel replied, noticing the way her grey eyes flicked from his wrist to Eli's then over their tailored jackets. And how, clearly reassured by what she saw, she relaxed, just a little, allowing her shoulders to drop as she moved.

Always the same routine in these places, he thought. *Check the watches, then the clothes*. He'd had a similar experience in a Ferrari showroom in England during a rare break in their routine on their last mission. That time, the salesman hadn't survived the encounter unscathed, being released from a hypnotic trance halfway round a full-tilt "test drive" that had left him in need of a dry cleaner.

"My name's Wilkie. I booked a Bentley Bentayga for a few days."

He placed his credit card on the satin-finished countertop. The simple black and white design centred on a logo: a Gothic H&Z. It told the knowledgeable observer that its issuer was a discreet Swiss bank called Händler und Ziegelhaus. Gabriel had met the managing director on a trip to Zurich, only to discover that "Walti Krieger" was in fact Amos Peled, a sleeper agent for Mossad, gathering information on former Nazis and their contemporary fans.

The receptionist picked up the card and glanced at the name before tapping her glossy purple nails on a hidden keyboard.

"Ah, yes. I have you," she said, raising her eyes to Gabriel and widening her smile to reveal small, even, and blindingly white teeth.

"All the paperwork was completed online. I just need you to sign and then, she is yours."

She held his gaze for a fraction longer than was necessary as she said these final three words. With Eli watching him – amused, he could tell from the tiny, bracket-shaped dimple that had appeared at the right corner of her mouth – Gabriel signed for the car. He had time to notice the swingeing penalties in the small print for anyone returning one of the thoroughbreds in less-than-mint condition.

Then it was done. He capped his pen and slid it back into his inside pocket.

Paperwork completed, and with a smartly overalled technician offering a salute, they were soon driving away in the vast, bronze-coloured SUV emblazoned with winged *B* logos. With the satnav lady guiding him, Gabriel piloted the Bentley away from the rental place, back the way they'd come, avoiding the roadworks and giving them another chance to enjoy the magnificent view along the Neva. As he turned the big vehicle left into Sadovaya Street ready to rejoin Nevsky Avenue, he saw an old man shuffling along, wrapped, despite the summer heat, in a stained and tattered army greatcoat.

On an impulse, he stopped the SUV, pushed the transmission selector into Park and got out.

"Won't be a minute," he said.

He approached the old man, who, he now saw, was clutching a mostly empty vodka bottle in one filthy hand.

"Hey, grandpa," he said, in Russian.

The old man turned, slowly and peered up at Gabriel from inside a bird's nest of greasy matted hair.

"What the fuck do you want with me?" the man said.

With a jolt, Gabriel saw that behind the grime and the unkempt appearance the "old man" was probably only in his fifties.

"I wanted to help. Could you use a little cash?"

"Cash? Of course I could use a little extra cash. This is the New Russia, or hadn't you heard? No cash, no future. At least in the old days, we got looked after. We kept our noses clean, and the Party looked after us. Now, those fucking kids in their flashy cars look at people like me and laugh! They'd have had Chechens and Arabs raping their arses if we hadn't fought to keep them safe."

Not wanting to discuss Russian military campaigns with the clearly embittered veteran, Gabriel pulled a couple of twenty-dollar bills from the nest of rubles in his wallet.

"I'm a veteran, too," he said, quietly. "Maybe these will help you. At least for a while."

The man looked astonished as he took in the two insignificant-looking banknotes. His hand darted out and snatched them from Gabriel's fingers. Behind them, the Bentley's horn parped twice. Gabriel turned and saw Eli frowning through the open passenger window. He signalled to her with an upraised index finger. She folded her arms and faced front.

"Thanks, comrade," the veteran said. "Not many like you around anymore."

Then he shuffled off, head down, without saying another word. Gabriel climbed back into the Bentley, slid the selector into Drive and pulled away.

23

Perhaps it was the literary associations of the word *dacha* that had led Gabriel to jump to conclusions about Tatyana Garin's summer house. He realised he had been imagining some rural Russian fantasy house straight out of a novel by Pushkin or Tolstoy. A simple, clapboard construction, gaily painted in primary colours, with window boxes full of geraniums or pansies, and a small vegetable garden and maybe some fruit trees groaning with apples, pears or cherries.

But then he recalibrated his expectations. Tanya was a billionaire, and however generous, however friendly, still very much a member of Russia's elite. Her dacha sat in the centre of a huge landscaped garden that stretched down to a slow-moving river. The lawn was easily big enough to host a football match, though the owners clearly preferred tennis. A couple of grass courts and two more with royal-blue artificial surfaces occupied one corner.

The house itself was a mishmash of architectural styles. Here a cast-iron balcony that could have come straight from New Orleans, there a covered porch with rocking chairs and a glass-topped table. Bay windows sitting in carved white frames that resembled those on the houses edging the Neva. Dutch gables beneath which tiny windows peeped out like shy children. The whole edifice was resplendent in a deep-red and forest-green paint job that glistened in the early evening sun.

Gabriel trundled the Bentley up the tarmac drive to the front of the house, where several cars and SUVs were haphazardly parked in a gravel half-circle. Stepping out, he immediately broke into a sweat as the heat and increased humidity of the countryside hit him. The next sensory impression that registered was the scent of honeysuckle. He looked around, searching for the source. Growing over and through a pergola was an old plant with a main stem as thick as a man's wrist, its pink and gold flowers so abundant they obscured all but a few of the leaves.

"Nice little place in the country, eh? How the other half lives."

Gabriel smiled at the irony in Eli's voice.

"Other half? More like the other one percent. Come on, let's go and meet our hostess. I think you'll like Tanya."

Eli rolled her eyes.

"Oh, I'm sure I'll *lurve* Tanya. After all, she's clearly smitten with you!"

"It's not like that. As I think I mentioned before," Gabriel replied as he led Eli up to the ornately carved front door. Its surface had been decorated with a bas relief of the Church of the Saviour on Blood in Saint Petersburg, right down to its myriad onion domes, and then varnished so thickly, the wood resembled toffee.

Seeing no bell push, he pulled down on an old-looking, stirrup-shaped iron handle. From somewhere inside the house, a bell jangled. He turned to Eli and smiled, before straightening his jacket.

"You look fine," she whispered. "In fact—"

The door swung inwards, and there stood the lady of the house.

The last time they had met, Tatyana had flown Gabriel out of Mozambique when he needed to leave the country in a hurry. In the intervening years, she seemed not to have changed. Her hair was still a lustrous golden-blond, now cut into a sleek style that just kissed her shoulders. She was attractive rather than beautiful, her smiling face dominated by large, wide-set eyes of pale blue.

"Gabriushka!" she exclaimed in English, holding her arms wide. "You are here!"

Just as she had done in their previous encounters, she enveloped him in a hug, kissing him three times, left, right, left, before releasing him from her perfumed embrace and turning to Eli, who smiled and held out her hand.

"Hello, Mrs Garin. I'm Eli Schochat."

Tatyana pouted and waved away Eli's hand, hugging her just as she had Gabriel.

"Call me Tanya," she said. "And I shall call you Eliya."

Eli smiled.

"That's my nickname at home, too."

Tanya nodded and smiled before addressing Gabriel.

"You are very naughty boy. You did not tell me that Eliya was so pretty."

"Yes I did! You asked me."

"Pah! You said 'Yes,' like 'Oh my girlfriend is OK looking.'"

She turned back to Eli.

"She is very, very beautiful woman. You are lucky man. Now, come inside. I will have Mishka take your bags upstairs to the guest suite."

Assuming Mishka would be a member of Tatyana's staff, Gabriel merely nodded and followed his hostess, who had threaded her arm through Eli's, into the dacha, whereupon he gasped. The exterior of the house might have been created by a builder awarded a trolley-dash through the past hundred years of Western architecture, but the interior was dazzlingly modern.

The entire ground floor appeared to be a single, unbroken space stretching from the front door at least a hundred feet to a set of folding sliding doors, which were currently concertinaed back on themselves to reveal yet more landscaping. Walls, rugs and woodwork were off-white. Sofas, chairs and cushions were purple. And everywhere, gold glittered, from light fittings, door handles, sculptures, light switches. The rule the interior designer – or their client – had specified clearly read, in its entirety, "Gild it."

"Wow!" he said, feeling no need to lay on any kind of false flattery. "This is amazing."

"Is not too vulgar?" Tatyana asked.

"It's beautiful," Eli replied. "Your favourite colours?"

"Since I was little girl. When I married Genady, and we set up Garin Group together, he asked me for colour scheme for brand identity. It was no-brainer. Now, come. You must be thirsty. Hungry maybe?"

"Just thirsty," Eli said.

"Champagne is best for thirst."

Gabriel, Eli and Tatyana sat in wicker armchairs by an ornamental pond the size of Gabriel's entire back garden in Aldeburgh. A fountain set off to one side was sending a scurry of silver bubbles across the otherwise mirror-like surface. Sprays of soft-blue water irises dotted the bank. And waterlilies, their pink and yellow lotus-like flowers so perfect they looked unreal, speckled the water like confetti.

Tatyana had just topped up their glasses – "Krug, my darlings, not that Georgian rubbish." – and was asking about their journey from England to Saint Petersburg.

Gabriel told her about the alcoholic veteran he'd helped out in Saint Petersburg. Tatyana's face fell.

"Is very sad. Many soldiers who fought for Motherland returned to find Motherland had forgotten about them. They were," she paused and looked up for a second, "embarrassment. The New Russians want nothing but to make money. Old soldiers who killed Afghan children or Chechens are not *kul'turnyj*. You know this word, Eliya?"

"I can guess. Cultured?"

"Yes. In Soviet times, which sadly I am old enough to remember, it meant also how rulers thought of themselves compared to proletariat. New Russians want only BMW, Louis Vuitton, Chanel, or," she winked at Gabriel, an expression he noticed Eli noticing, "Birkin."

"Something you're not telling me?" Eli asked Gabriel, raising one eyebrow and then taking another sip of her champagne.

"Is how we met," Tatyana said. "In Islington. Two *grabiteli* – what is English word, Gabriushka?"

"Muggers."

She smiled.

"Aha! Such good word. Two *muggers* – very ugly boys – knock me down, take my Birkin bag. Very expensive. Made from saltwater crocodile. Gabriushka chases muggers, beats them up and brings back Birkin. Since then, we are friends."

"I didn't beat them up. I just gave them a scare, that's all."

"Oh, scare. Then you should have beaten them. Or killed them."

Eli leaned forwards and held Tatyana's gaze. She looked serious. Gabriel wondered what she was going to say.

"Tanya. That is the biggest diamond ring I have ever seen. It's beautiful."

Tatyana looked down at her extended left hand. The ring on her fourth finger, snug behind a twisted rope of white, rose and yellow gold, threw off splinters of pink, pale-blue and yellow light. Gabriel found himself staring at the hazelnut-sized gemstone, unable to tear his eyes away from its lustre.

"Is engagement ring. Genady found diamond himself in Mozambique. He dug it from earth. Had it cut for me."

Then her eyes welled up. Gabriel watched, astonished, as tears overflowed her lower lids and splashed down onto her trousers, turning the pale-grey linen to the colour of lead.

"Tanya? What's the matter? Why are you crying?"

She looked at him, her eyes reddening as he watched.

"They killed Genady. Just two weeks ago. Now they threaten me."

Eli jumped up from her armchair and crossed the small space between her and the older woman to crouch at her feet. She took her hands in her own and squeezed them.

She offered the same Hebrew prayer she had spoken to Ebba Falskog.

"*Ha'makom yenahem etkhem*. May God console you. But tell us, who killed your husband, Tanya? Who did it?"

Rather than answer, Tatyana looked towards the dacha.

24

The man striding across the grass towards them was well over six feet tall, dressed in a grey two-piece suit. The jacket flapped in the breeze that had sprung up, revealing a shoulder holster beneath his left armpit. His head was shaved, revealing white scars among the black stubble. At some point, his nose had been broken and reset, badly.

He stopped when he arrived at the trio of chairs and stood perfectly still. Waiting. Tatyana broke the silence.

"Gabriushka, Eliya. This is Oleg Stakhansky. Oleg is Garin Group head of security." She turned to the man. "These are my friends from England. You remember, I mentioned Gabriushka in particular."

Gabriel and Eli got to their feet and shook hands with the heavily built newcomer. Gabriel felt his balance go, just for a second, then it returned. *Something's not right*, he thought. For a moment he wondered whether Tatyana had added a Mickey Finn to his drink. Then he dismissed the thought as unworthy. *What would she have to gain, anyway? We're here willingly to help her.*

"How do you do?" Stakhansky said in a low, almost melodic

voice. "Forgive me for intruding, Tatyana. We have received news from Nyurba. It isn't good."

Gabriel recognised the expression on the man's face, and the subtle movements of his hands and head. He wanted to take his boss away from the social gathering so he could impart bad news out of earshot of the unknown-quantity guests.

Tatyana waved her hand. Then pointed to a fourth wicker armchair.

"Pull up chair, Oleg," she said. "They have come to help. Anything you can tell me, you can tell them."

Looking as though the invitation to sit had been made by a dentist, Stakhansky pulled over one of the large outdoor chairs as if it were made of balsa wood. When he sat down, it creaked, loudly. Gabriel wondered whether the big man would go right through the woven seat and onto the floor. The wicker held.

Stakhansky drew a meaty hand down over his mouth and chin. He sighed.

"They've killed another one. Ignatyev used a knout on him. It's like martial law over there. My guy had to get out in the middle of the night and find an internet cafe in town. He said something's not right with Ignatyev."

Unlike Tatyana, Stakhansky spoke English without a trace of an accent, and he used it like a native, too. No Russian syntax bolted on to the foreign language to make it easier in the mouth.

Tatyana's face had paled at Stakhansky's mention of the word *knout*. She turned to Gabriel and Eli now.

"You know what is *knout?*" she asked them.

"Some sort of weapon?" Gabriel replied. It wasn't exactly a Holmesian piece of deduction.

"Is whip. From time of Ivan the Great. I forget which century."

"Sixteen," Stakhansky said.

Sixteen. Sixten. Gabriel's mind flew back to the funeral in Uppsala. *He didn't blame me. Nor did Ebba. Or Freya. Maybe I'm innocent. Yeah, right. Because Kristersson was just in England on a walking holiday.*

"Gabriushka? Are you all right?"

"What? Sorry."

Tatyana was looking at him, her eyebrows drawn together, her lips downturned.

"Did you hear me?"

"I'm sorry, Tanya. Could you repeat it?"

"I said, Peter the Great knouted his son, Alexis, to death. Is fearful thing, to lose a son. But to have him tortured before your eyes with whip, at your own orders, is worse. Much, much worse."

Gabriel thought back to his first encounter with Tatyana. She'd told him over coffee that her son had been killed in Mayfair. Burnt to a crisp in his Ferrari in a collision with another rich kid in a Lamborghini.

"Who is Ignatyev? And what is in Nyurba. *Where* is Nyurba?"

The man nodded, evidently happier now he was on solid ground, discussing facts. He leaned forward and clasped his hands together between his knees. As he was about to speak, a whistling sound made all three of them look up. Above their heads, a flight of swans cruised over the garden in a loose V-formation, their broad wings creating overlapping layers of sound. Once the flypast had finished, Stakhansky tried again.

"Nyurba is a city – no, more of a town, really – in the Sakha Republic. The far east of the Russian Federation. They are closer to Beijing than Saint Petersburg. We operate a diamond mine there. And apparently, Volodya Ignatyev is the new manager." He practically spat out this final phrase.

"So fire him," Eli said. "You're the head of security. Can't you just fly over there and kick him out?"

Stakhansky shook his head.

"It's not that simple. Ignatyev represents our new business partners. I can't just terminate him. Though believe me, that is what I would like to do."

Stakhansky balled his right hand into a fist and smacked it onto his open left palm for emphasis.

Eli frowned.

"What kind of business partner puts in a manager who kills employees with a whip?"

Gabriel had a flash of insight. He knew exactly what kind of organisation Stakhansky was talking about. The kind who would go to any lengths to pursue its goals. From suborning British prime ministers to paying Mozambican warlords to track down and murder British security agents. He and Tatyana had talked about diamonds a few years earlier in her private jet. How they made an excellent untraceable currency, but that, without a Kimberley Process Certificate asserting that they weren't the so-called "blood diamonds," they were harder to trade than a stolen Picasso.

"You're talking about organised crime, aren't you?" he asked Stakhansky. *And I think you and I are going to be making common cause.*

Stakhansky nodded.

"They call themselves—"

"Kuznitsa."

Stakhansky's eyes widened and he leaned back in his chair, slapping his hands palms-down onto his knees.

"Yes! How did you know?"

"They sent a team of people to kill us. That failed. Then they sent a hitman. He missed me but killed my friend."

Stakhansky pursed his thick lips.

"I am sorry about your friend. But at least you know the kind of people we are fighting. They are ruthless. They are rich. And they are powerful. Political connections. Military. Probably in the intelligence service, too. Either FSB or GRU. I can't be sure."

Gabriel scratched at his scalp, ruffling his hair into spikes.

"You want them gone."

"Of course."

"I want them dead."

"Ignatyev and his men?"

Gabriel shook his head.

"All of them."

"You are crazy, then. There are hundreds of them. Ex-Spetsnaz, Russian Armed Forces, police, and your, what do you call them, common-or-garden gangsters."

"We're going to kill the leaders. The ground troops will disperse or join other gangs. I don't care. It's the bosses I'm after. And one in particular. His name is Max. Max Novgorodsky."

"If you know about him, you know maybe of his record. He is a hard man to find, let alone to kill."

"Did any of your sources tell you about an explosion in an Iranian nuclear plant last month, Oleg?" Eli asked.

He frowned.

"Yes. We have people in Tehran. They launched saffron futures contracts on the Iran Mercantile Exchange last May. Perhaps Tatyana told you: we are the world's number one trader."

Gabriel smiled. He couldn't help himself. Amidst an earnest discussion about whether they could wipe out the top tier of management of a powerful global criminal gang, Stakhansky couldn't resist the chance to boast of his company's market dominance.

"Gabriel and I blew up the plant," Eli continued. "And four Russian-built tactical nuclear missiles. Pioneers. On our own."

She was twisting the truth. But only slightly. They'd had tactical support from the Israelis, but the on-the-ground work had been all their own.

Stakhansky said nothing. Gabriel counted. Five seconds passed. Finally he offered a small smile.

"Perhaps I have misjudged you."

"You should not do that, Oleg," Tatyana said topping up the glasses and offering hers to him, an oddly intimate gesture, Gabriel thought. "Gabriushka is very brave, very resourceful. I have made enquiries of my own. Eliya is no doubt just as talented. Is that right, Eliya?"

Eli nodded. She placed a hand flat against her chest.

"IDF. Kidon. Mossad. Many of Israel's enemies are dead. I am alive."

Stakhansky nodded his appreciation of this stripped-down, but eloquent résumé.

"Then perhaps we shall triumph over Kuznitsa after all. I have men, vehicles, money, weapons, whatever you need."

"It is getting too hot out here," Tatyana said. "And you have finished your drink, Oleg. Come. We will continue our talk inside."

With that she led the other three members of what appeared to be Garin Group's counter-terror squad towards the rear of the dacha.

25

MOSCOW | LONDON

Max reclined against the pillows, filled with the finest goose down money could buy and sheathed in maroon silk edged in gold thread. Absent-mindedly tousling the blond hair splayed across his stomach while the girl he had hired for the evening attended to him, he made a call.

"Yes, Max? What can I do for you?"

"I want you to do a little digging for me."

"Go on."

"A British Government agent. Gabriel Wolfe. He died last week. In his home town of Aldeburgh. He was shot. Find out all you can."

"And when you say shot …"

"It wasn't a hunting accident, if that's what you mean."

He ended the call, allowed himself to come, then sent the girl packing with a hundred-dollar bill and a well-aimed slap on her ample behind.

* * *

Robert Finnie, or to give him his full title, Lord Finnie of Marston Ash, stared down at the phone in his hand. As a Labour peer sent to the upper chamber by Tony Blair, he'd discovered he had even better access to the levers of power than he'd previously had as a mere MP.

Consultancies and non-executive directorships with a handful of London-based but global companies kept him, his wife and their teenaged children in the style to which they'd become accustomed. Loyal to the last seriously effective Labour prime minister to the point of fanaticism, Finnie was now out of favour with the current hard-left leadership. But freed from the five-yearly trudge round the constituency to get out the vote, he could relax on the patinated red leather benches of the House of Lords and enjoy watching his former colleagues struggle.

Russia. That was his first love. As a lawyer, his profession before, during and since his stint as a member of parliament, he had come into contact with a great many Russian businessmen, and occasionally businesswomen. His firm specialised in smoothing the way in their commercial and personal lives. Whether it was speeding them through the process to get permanent residency – "just put ten million into Government bonds and you're in after two years, Sergei" – or helping them navigate UK customs and tax regulations, Finnie was the go-to partner at the firm.

So when he'd been approached in the late nineties at his London club by a superbly dressed Russian calling himself Max, and offered a two-hundred-thousand-a-year retainer, he hadn't even blinked.

"*Da*," he'd said.

Over the years, his relationship with Max had deepened, and the retainer had increased, as had the volume and magnificence of the gifts Max bestowed both on Finnie, and his wife and children. Free use of a two-thousand-square-foot ski chalet in Klosters. Diamond jewellery from Boodles for Angela Finnie. Brand-new Mercedes SLK convertibles for each of the children on their seventeenth birthdays. Max's generosity knew no bounds. And from time to time, as a favour to Max, Finnie would ask questions in the

House, or steer amendments to bills through their committee stages.

Finnie's conscience was untroubled. Max, as he had explained to Finnie over Chateau Lafitte in the club on that first, fateful evening, was an old soldier. Loyal to the socialist principles that had created the Soviet Union and brought so many millions into the twentieth century from the virtual serfdom of the nineteenth. He knew that Finnie believed, broadly, in the same things he did. And Finnie had been only too eager to agree.

And then Max had appeared at Finnie's club for a second time, having transacted their business in the interim exclusively by phone and email, bar the occasional face-to-face in Paris, Hamburg or Singapore, when Finnie was on a fact-finding mission or government business.

"I have a problem, Robert," he said, lighting a preposterously large cigar and puffing gently on its end. "The UK tax authorities are clamping down. One of my businesses is under scrutiny. I need legal," he paused, puffed, continued, "assistance."

"Of course. I can assign our best tax barrister to you. The woman's a genius. She——"

Max shook his head.

"No, my friend. Not that kind of assistance. A tax official was killed. Well, murdered, actually. By one of my people. It was a mistake, but there you are. We all make mistakes, don't we?"

Max winked at Finnie and blew a stream of richly-scented smoke towards the ceiling. And for the first time in their decades-long partnership, as he watched that silver-grey coil drift upwards, Finnie wondered whether he had made the right decision, saying "Da" all those years ago.

Once Max had presented Finnie with a few home truths about the exact nature of his business, and, by the by, some hidden-camera footage of Finnie enjoying the company of a high-class prostitute in a Mayfair hotel, the lawyer-politician had been only too ready to comply with Max's wishes. He had arranged through an intermediary to bribe the senior investigating officer in the murder case. The Russian returned home untroubled by the grip of a

British detective on his shoulder, and Finnie's life continued much as before. Except in one important respect. He was now, as Max had explained in none-too-subtle language, Max's *suka*. His bitch. The money, the gifts, the holidays: all were his for the asking. But now, whenever Max needed a favour, of any kind and on either side of the line between legal and illegal, Finnie would do it.

He replaced the receiver and looked to his right. From his lofty perch on the nineteenth floor of the architect-designed building on St Thomas Street in which Langham, Finnie, Hall and Robinson LLP had its offices, he had a panoramic view. All the way from Tower Bridge just a few hundred metres to the east to St Paul's Cathedral to the northwest. He stood up and went over to the floor-to-ceiling glass wall. The boats on the Thames left white wakes on the greenish-brown water. He followed a pleasure cruiser from the London Eye until it disappeared round a bend in the river. Then, heaving a deep sigh, he returned to his desk, sat down and started work.

His first call was to a private investigator he knew in Essex. A former Metropolitan Police detective sergeant who'd taken early retirement before a case of sexual abuse of a vulnerable witness could be brought. Scott Randolph had even fewer scruples than did Finnie. Just as well.

26

TATYANA'S DACHA

Over more drinks, then the promised steaks, the quartet discussed the problem posed by Kuznitsa. Gabriel asked why, given his obvious access to men and weapons, Stakhansky hadn't simply gone in all guns blazing and cleared New Galaxy of the interlopers.

"You want to know why? OK, I'll tell you. And this should come as no surprise to a man with your background. Kuznitsa, they rose quickly. In Russian underground circles, the one currency people respect more than the dollar is violence. Hmm, maybe honour, too. But mainly violence. Kuznitsa have always been ready – happy, actually – to use violence against their enemies. Worse violence, and more violence. When other groups stop, that is when Kuznitsa starts. You know they killed Genady?"

"Yes."

"So, families are no longer sacred. There was a time when Russian *Mafiya* played by a certain set of rules. That time is past. They are completely, utterly ruthless."

Gabriel shrugged and swallowed another mouthful of the succulent beef.

"So are we. And we have the element of surprise on our side. Max thinks I'm dead."

"Then you should make the most of it. You clear the chief blacksmith from the forge, then we will eradicate whoever is left and doesn't run. With no one to protect them and pay their wages, they won't stick around in that godforsaken place for long. As you will soon discover for yourselves," Stakhansky included Eli in his look, "Nyurba does not offer much beyond mining, drinking and whoring."

"Can you fly us in?" Eli asked.

"Of course!" Tatyana answered. "You fly from Pulkovo on a Garin Group plane direct to Yakutsk. Is nearest big airport to New Galaxy. From there, we fly you in light plane."

The group disbanded just before midnight. Tatyana showed Gabriel and Eli to what she described as "my little guest room." This turned out to be a suite of rooms including a vast bedroom complete with four-poster bed, a wooden-floored bathroom centred on a claw footed bath easily big enough for two, and a sitting room furnished in more of Tatyana's off-white, purple and gold.

Lying next to Eli in cool, luxuriously smooth sheets – "Organic Egyptian cotton, single-ply, three hundred thread count," Tatyana had said, proudly – Gabriel stared at the ceiling. After Rioja and then chilled vodka, his brain was mercifully still, and he found himself able to think, if not clearly, then at least freely.

I'm Max. I sent a hitman to take out Wolfe. I received coded confirmation that he was dead. What would I do next? Celebrate? No. Why not? No proof. When I kill people, I see their dead bodies. I smell the blood. I watch the spark of life dim and then vanish from their eyes. When I can't do it myself I want the next best thing. I want to see them, dead. Kristersson didn't send me a photo. So I can't be one hundred percent sure. But I need that certainty. That's how I built my business. On solid, unshakeable foundations of certainty. Doubts come back and try to kill me. I want to know Wolfe is dead.

Beside him, Eli whispered.

"You OK?"

"Yeah, you?"

"Yeah, I'm fine. Bit drunk."

"Me too."

"What are you thinking about?"

"Max. He doesn't know I'm dead."

Eli propped herself up on her elbow and swept her hair clear of her eyes.

"What? What do you mean? You *aren't* dead."

"That's what I mean. He isn't sure I'm dead. He'll want proof. The text we sent him wasn't enough."

"Are you sure? He replied almost straight away."

"I'm not completely sure, no. But if I were Max, I'd need proof before I could totally relax."

"Shit! A photo, you mean."

"A photo. Or maybe I'd settle for an eyewitness. I'd be thinking there was a slim chance my torpedo double-crossed me. But somebody else, somebody unconnected with me, them I could trust."

"We need to get onto Don. Ask him to run interference in Aldeburgh. If Max sent someone to sniff around, we don't have much time."

Gabriel reached for his phone. This was an encrypted device that all Department operatives used on active duty. Sending a secure message involved two steps. First, entering an innocent text to "Mum", then the operational message, using the exact same number of characters. The phone scrambled the two together then sent the combined message to "Mum," adding false metadata, from time sent to location, in the process.

Hi Mum. LA is amazing. Universal Studios tomorrow. Food amazing. Huge portions! Everyone looks like a movie star – maybe they are! Dave x /
Think Max will be looking for proof I'm dead. Keep watch in A. Can you get me a photo? No need for materiel – have that in hand.

He sent the message, then placed the phone, screen down, on the night stand.

. . .

After three days of air travel, Gabriel and Eli stepped down from a Cessna Citation X business jet onto the apron outside the quaint, wooden terminal building at Nyurba Airport. From the row of seats behind them, they collected their luggage. To an observer, the silver hard-shell cases would simply convey a sense of their owners' wealth. To anyone connected to them by the handles they'd convey a sense of being packed with something far more substantial than just fine tailoring and expensive toiletries. Glock 17 semi-automatic pistols, for example. Heckler & Koch MP5K submachine-guns. Shoulder holsters. Slings. Quantities of ammunition for both weapons. Russian-made Kizlyar Delta D2 titanium daggers. Military-grade binoculars equipped with night vision.

27

Although Nyurba was hardly a thriving centre of cosmopolitanism, there were enough suited-and-booted mining engineers, management consultants, investment banking types and lawyers thronging its hotel bars and restaurants that Gabriel and Eli could fit in without trying. On their first morning, they hired a car and drove out of the small town into the surrounding countryside along a single-track road on which goats outnumbered vehicles by three to one.

Gabriel pulled off the road by a stand of birch trees and killed the engine. They got out and stood by the bonnet. Gabriel pointed off to their right.

"Flat, isn't it?"

"Mm-hmm. I reckon we can see all the way to China."

"How do you think we should do this?"

"Find the boss-man—"

"Or woman," Gabriel interrupted, keeping a straight face.

"Or woman," Eli echoed, her own face not betraying whether she found his avowal of a woman's right to be a gangster amusing or not. "Capture him," she said, pausing. Gabriel didn't take the bait. Mainly because he didn't want one of her signature punches to the right bicep. "Or her. Exfiltrate somewhere safe and interrogate him. Or her. Until he. Or she—"

Gabriel laughed.

"OK, OK, I get the point. We'll go for a guy. It'll halve the time it takes you to talk."

"Thank you," Eli said, with a sweet smile. "Interrogate him until he gives up Max. Then kill him."

"He'll have muscle."

"We kill the muscle."

"Agreed. Then get our Garin Group travelcard out and head back to Moscow or wherever Max is at the moment. Kill Max. And anyone else we can find who's at the top."

Eli frowned.

"What is it?" Gabriel asked.

"You've changed. You used to be a bit less ready to start spraying lead around."

"I used to have more living friends."

With her back to the car, Eli placed her hands on the bonnet behind her, one heel on the top of the tyre, and pushed herself up until she was sitting a couple of feet higher than Gabriel. She held out her hands and he stepped inside the circle of her arms. He let her pull him close and turned his head to the left so his right ear was over her heart. He listened to it beating while she stroked the back of his neck. Inhaling, he caught her familiar scent and smiled despite the black clouds that sat, unmoving, at the back of his mind these days.

After a few minutes, when he listened to the soft thumps of her pulse and concentrated on slowing his own heartrate, he spoke.

"Let's get a little closer."

"If you get any closer I might have to suggest we take our clothes off," she replied.

Gabriel pulled back. He'd meant closer to the mine. He looked around, at the thousands of square miles of empty landscape. An unbroken, flat plain stretching to the horizon, where the snow-covered peaks of a distant mountain range broke through low-lying cloud.

"Come on, then," he said. "Lots of soft, dry grass around here and we're hardly likely to be interrupted.

Her lips parted and she blinked with surprise. Then she nodded, quickly and without a word began to undress. Gabriel followed her and then he was above her, looking into eyes that seemed to change from hazel to emerald, depending on the way the light hit them.

They settled easily into a rhythm that suited them both.

"I thought you were never to going to make love to me again," she panted as his thrusts became more urgent.

Then talk became impossible. Together they slid away from reality and into that private space only lovers know.

Crying out, Eli clutched Gabriel, her fingertips digging into his back. As he reached his own climax, he forced himself to keep his eyes open and held her gaze.

And then it was over. Gabriel rolled over, next to Eli, and laid his head on her breast, listening to her heart again, its rapid-fire thumps matching his own.

A keening high above them made him twist his head away to search out the bird of prey. Many hundreds of feet above them, a tiny black doodle in the sapphire sky, an eagle, or perhaps a large buzzard, described lazy circles, drifting on a thermal to which he felt they had just added their own heat.

"Can it see us, d'you think?" Eli asked.

"Probably. They can see for miles."

"What's it thinking?"

"It's thinking, 'I wonder whether those two are good to eat. She looks tasty enough but he looks a bit rough round the edges.'"

"I like you a bit rough round the edges. But I thought I was losing you."

Gabriel frowned.

"When?"

"Since, you know, Britta. You've been different. I thought you had feelings for her after all. Your midnight ramblings, that diary of whatever you've been keeping. I love you, Gabriel, and I don't want to lose you to your grief."

He propped himself up on one elbow, feeling the sun warming

the whole side of his body. He stroked her cheek with his free hand, and brushed the back of his finger across her lips.

"You aren't losing me. I know I've been difficult to live with these last few days. But you're what's keeping me anchored, Eli. I love you back, believe me. But I struggle with this … I don't know, this feeling that there's something out to get me. Something evil, that waits for me to prize someone's friendship, or love, and then picks the perfect moment to snatch them away from me. I'm just frightened it's going to do it to you as well. I don't think I could bear that. I couldn't live with myself. God knows, sometimes it's hard enough to live with myself now."

"Listen, OK? Just listen to me. Plenty of people have tried to kill me and, like I said before, they're dead, not me. We none of us know what's around the corner, waiting for us. But we can't live our lives expecting it, either. When God calls me I'll go, but not before, and while I'm here, I'm assuming he wants me alive, doing good. You should try to live the same way."

"You believe in God, then? Even after all you've seen? After the people you – we – have gone up against? You still believe?"

She smiled. And once again, he was struck by her unaffected beauty.

"Yes, I believe. Not in some old guy in a white robe up there, somewhere," she pointed at the bird, which was still circling high overhead, "hurling thunderbolts, though I wouldn't blame him. But in God as, you know, just this power that wants us to be better people and love each other and find beauty in the world, and kindness, and look after the weak and protect them against the strong, yes."

The mine complex appeared on the horizon, seeming to float a few feet above the hard-packed ground. As they drove north, the shimmering heat lifted the mirage higher until it appeared to be a small city, floating in mid-air. Gabriel could see individual buildings, cooling towers and spoil heaps wavering in glassily clear focus that was as disorientating as it was beautiful. Ten minutes' more driving, and the apparition sank, first to the ground, and then in on itself, until all that was left was a collection of low, greyish-brown shapes some two miles distant.

The terrain between them and the mine was more of the flat, scrubby prairie, uninterrupted by even a stand of trees, much less any human habitation. Low shrubs and tussocky grass offered the only cover.

Gabriel spun the wheel and drove the car off the road, heading due east, on a course parallel to the boundary of the complex. Finding a slight depression that might have been a dry lake bed, he drove into its centre and turned off the engine

"I think this is as good as we're going to get," he said.

Eli nodded.

"Let's get changed, then."

From the Jeep's load bay, they pulled out the rucksacks containing their camouflage gear. The Mossy Oak camo was a decent match for the colour and type of ground that lay between them and the New Galaxy Diamond Mine. With sand-coloured boots, bandannas, net vests and baseball caps rounding off their outfits, they'd have a good chance of blending in, especially as Kuznitsa's mine security people would hardly be expecting surveillance.

Walking twenty feet apart so they didn't present a single, large silhouette, Gabriel and Eli walked in a zig-zag line towards New Galaxy. Whenever they came to a shrub or a frond of foliage or dried twigs, they'd stoop to collect it and thread it into the netting that covered their torsos, creating improvised ghillie suits that further disrupted their outlines and allowed them to merge seamlessly with the background.

The heat was fierce, and mosquitos plagued them, but by pulling up their bandannas, they managed to prevent themselves inhaling the whining little insects. Once they were close enough to use the binoculars, they simultaneously dropped to their bellies.

Gabriel raised his binos to his eyes and adjusted the focus. New Galaxy popped into bright, pin-sharp detail. He could see trucks laden with black-brown spoil, so big that their vast knobbly tyres stood higher than the men gathered round them. The mine itself, he knew, would be invisible, consisting as it did more of an absence than a presence. A monumentally big hole in the ground that Tatyana had shown them on a satellite image, its sides descending in ridges that appeared to be tiny steps but which, in reality, were some thirty or forty metres across.

No physical security. That's good. Is it odd? Why would it be? Look around you. There's literally nothing and nobody for two hundred miles in any direction. It's like those old Siberian labour camps the Soviets built. They had no need of fences. If you left, you froze to death or starved. The only question was which got you first, the cold or the hunger.

Then Gabriel realised something. If you were a diamond miner, out here in this godforsaken place, earning enough to support yourself or your family, it wouldn't really make much difference to you who was running the show. Kuznitsa would keep paying the men their wages. In fact, if they had any sense, they'd probably give them a pay rise. The man they'd whipped to death would have served as a potent symbol of the sanctions the new bosses would impose on anyone who broke the rules, but why break them anyway? New Galaxy was pretty much the only game in town. It was probably one of the better-paying gigs. So why run?

As far as he knew, miners had always tried to smuggle out stones, whether they were diamonds in South Africa or emeralds in Venezuela. Some even had their back teeth hollowed out by dentists to create hiding spaces. You'd want to stay close to the source to give yourself a chance, however remote, of making that big score. Who cared if an organised crime group had just taken over the running of the mine?

It would be the same with Alrosa. They'd just demand, and receive, their share of the profits. They were probably in league with Kuznitsa anyway. That just left the mysterious Compañeros Blancos LLP. "White Partners." Tatyana had said they were a legitimate Colombian business group. Private equity. But she was lying; he was sure of it. Put Russian diamond mining together with Colombian private equity, and if you didn't come up with a drug cartel, you were a fool. Gabriel was not a fool. It certainly made things interesting. God knew how many new enemies he'd be making by snatching the boss man. But if he was the kind of God that Eli had described – that Eli believed in – maybe he wouldn't look too unkindly on a pair of his servants trying to right a few wrongs in his world.

Shaking his head and smiling at himself for indulging in theology when he should be mission-planning, Gabriel lowered the binoculars and looked across at Eli.

"Seen enough?" he called.

"Yup."

"Shall we go, then?"

She flashed him a toothy grin.

"Steaks and beers for lunch back in Nyurba?"

"Be more like teatime when we get back."

"Excellent! Big steaks and lots of beers!"

28

HONG KONG

Beneath the restaurant's thick, turquoise glass deck, fish swam, their silver scales flashing as they rolled and flipped, chasing prey or evading bigger fish. The late afternoon sun slanted down into the water, spearing the schooling fish.

Mei glanced down, then pointed.

"Look, Master. An octopus."

The leader of the White Koi triad placed his chopsticks on the bone-china rest and leaned sideways, so that he could look through the glass floor at Mei's side.

She watched, rapt, as the octopus undulated along a submerged pipe. A slender dogfish, silvery-grey with reddish spots, feinted then attacked, darting towards the softly undulating sac. The octopus threw out half its limbs and enveloped the attacking fish, clutching round its midsection and foiling the attack. The dogfish flailed, thrashing left and right before the octopus released its suckered grip and the chastened predator fled for deeper waters.

Fang Jian laughed loudly, drawing a few curious glances from other diners, who, on seeing from whom the sound emanated, looked hastily away again.

"Are you suggesting I draw a lesson from the octopus, Mei?" he asked, smiling as he picked up his chopsticks again. "You think El Nuevo Medellín have many arms? That they will reach out and snare us?"

She touched the groove on her top lip then smiled delicately and shook her head.

"No, Master. Look."

She pointed downwards with her own chopsticks, then took a mouthful of the succulent spider crab, ginger and spring onion dish on the tiny plate before her.

Five dogfish were zeroing in on the octopus, which was flicking out tentacles and flushing a deep, angry red. Working seemingly as a team, they circled it. Then, all at once, they struck. With so many antagonists, the octopus had little chance, Although it managed to fasten a couple of tentacles onto the attacking dogfish, the fish darted in and severed the remaining limbs, which floated away, still twisting and coiling as if alive. Before long, the battle was over. Spewing black ink into the otherwise crystal-clear water, the now-limbless octopus slid off the pipe and, as it sank, was consumed by the voracious mini-sharks.

"El Nuevo Medellín may have many tentacles. But cut off, they are useless. Then the octopus is easy to kill."

"I thought we already took the head away?"

"We did. But it will grow a new one. The only way to defeat it is to destroy the whole creature, all at once."

Jian finished his glass of champagne and signalled a waiter for another bottle. He belched, almost as loudly as he had laughed earlier. This time, nobody looked round.

"They have many soldiers."

"So do we."

"They will be planning their revenge for Ruíz."

"Exactly. They will be focused on their own plans. They will be thinking it is their turn to strike. But this is not mah-jong. We don't need to wait for our turn."

"How many people do they have in total?"

"In Medellín, the people we need to worry about, twenty-seven only. The rest are just muscle, runners, intelligence staff. They'll disappear once we kill the main group."

"And how do you propose to kill twenty-seven Colombian gangsters?"

Other employees of Jian might have backed off at this point, sensing their boss's question as an implied instruction. Not Mei. She knew the question for what it was. A genuine inquiry into logistics, strategy and tactics. And she'd come prepared. Once the arriving waiter had uncorked and poured the new bottle of champagne, she spoke.

"They are holding a council of war two days from now. At the home of the deputy leader. Well, he's the leader now. A man called Domingo Fabricas. He has a waterfront house a few kilometres outside Guatapé, on a reservoir. It's a town about eighty-two kilometres east of Medellín. It's protected, but badly. Low-level security. Nothing we can't deal with. Wūshī could probably disable it remotely from that skanky apartment of his. We go in at 3.00 a.m., set charges. Retreat to an island to wait for the fireworks."

Jian frowned.

"As simple as that?"

Mei smiled.

"As simple as that. Master," she added, dipping her head and offering a demure smile, her eyes looking up at him from beneath lowered lashes.

"How many people would you need?"

"Me and two others."

"Who?"

"Xi Peng and Doi Mah."

"Explosives? Timers?"

"I arranged matters before I flew back to see you. A contact in the Colombian National Intelligence Directorate. We have worked together on occasion"

"He is trustworthy?"

"I would trust him with my life, Master."

Jian smiled, showing a new gold tooth, then nodded, lowering his heavy eyelids as if to blank out the world while he pondered his subordinate's suggestion.

Mei was content to wait. She sipped her champagne and popped a king prawn wrapped in *pak choi* into her mouth. She looked around. Checking the exits. Noting who had arrived at a table, and who had left. It was an old habit, and given her dining companion, probably unnecessary. *Better safe than sorry*, she thought.

Jian opened his eyes.

"Make the arrangements."

Mei nodded, and dabbed her lips with the thick, white napkin. She looked down. Beneath her feet, the dogfish were still there, picking among the scraps of octopus tentacles half-buried in the silt.

29

GUATAPÉ, ANTIOQUIA DEPARTMENT, COLOMBIA

Dressed in a black outfit of skintight yoga pants, a tight, long-sleeved T-shirt, facemask and plimsolls, Mei lay on her back in the crawlspace beneath the house belonging to Domingo Fabricas that backed onto the Peñol-Guatapé Reservoir. She threaded two long, black cable ties through holes she had just made with a hand drill in a joist. Then she looped them around a 1.25 pound M112 Demolition Block of C4 plastic explosive, pushed the tapes into the pawl and cinched them tight with a faint *zzzp*.

Beside her, dressed in an identical black outfit, Peng was fixing his own charge to a gas pipe linking a series of squat, metallic-blue propane bottles to the kitchen. He had an economical way of moving that she admired. No wasted energy. Inside the house, Mah was setting three further charges: one rolled flat and then duct-taped to the underside of the heavy oak dining table, a second shoved up hard at the back of the stainless steel sink in the kitchen, a third at the back of an airing cupboard in the master bedroom suite.

· · ·

The three White Koi assassins gathered in the garden that sloped gently down to the water.

"Charges all set?" Mei asked.

She knew the answer, but this was one of her rules. You checked and double-checked. Everything. Every time.

"Yes," her two subordinates chorused.

"Detonators?"

A second "Yes."

"Timers?"

A final affirmative. She'd elected to use electronic detonators triggered by signals from cheap, disposable mobile phones. Nothing fancy, but reliable and free of trailing wires that would give the game away on the charges set inside the house.

"OK, then. Let's go."

They scurried down to the water's edge and pushed off in a black rubber dinghy, heading for a small, tree-covered island five hundred metres offshore.

The next morning, Mei woke at dawn. She kicked off the camouflage blanket covering her and strode over to the other two. Prodding them gently with the toe of her plimsoll, she waited until they were properly awake before speaking.

"We eat. Then we wait. When they're all inside, we wait for five minutes, then blow it. The muscle will either die in the blast or rush inside. Once they do, we go ashore and clean up."

Peng and Mah nodded. Neither was given to talkativeness, which suited Mei fine. If there was something to say, she knew they'd pipe up. Silence was preferable. It allowed her to think more clearly. After a breakfast of vacuum-packed fish and rice, and bottled water, the trio settled in to wait. Peng took the first two-hour watch, monitoring the road beyond the shoreline for traffic heading towards the house.

Mah sat cross-legged on the ground, a square of grey ripstop nylon in front of her, and began field-stripping the IWI Micro-Tavor assault rifle provided by Mei's contact in the Colombian NID.

Mei listened to the series of clicks, snaps and scrapes as Mah methodically took the stubby, all-black weapon to pieces before reassembling it. Mei didn't think they'd need it, having calculated that the six and a quarter pounds of C4 they'd attached to the house would reduce it, and its occupants, to a fine, wet dust in about a tenth of a second.

At the end of Peng's watch, he shuffled back to join the others. Mei checked her watch.

"I'll take the next shift," she said, reaching for the binoculars.

At 9.55 a.m., as her shift was coming to an uneventful end, Mei heard a noise from beyond a low ridge to the east of the house. A low, asynchronous growl that spoke of multiple high-capacity engines.

"They're coming," she said. "Get ready."

Continuing to watch the road through the binoculars, she listened as Peng and Mah collected their weapons. They'd each brought an FN 509 semi-automatic pistol, chambered for 9x19mm Parabellum rounds. Peng also carried the Micro-Tavor. All three carried knives in black sheaths on their belts.

Mei observed closely as the convoy of black SUVs appeared over the ridge and made its slow progress along the last remaining hundred metres or so of road before pulling off the road and down onto the grassy parking area in front of the lake house. She counted seven vehicles altogether. Gratifyingly, they had all parked close to the house, presumably to save their occupants from having to walk far. *The blast should take out the SUVs too*, she thought. *Good*.

The doors began opening, and in the silence once the engines were switched off, Mei could hear their conversation floating across the water. They were too far away to make out individual words, but the men were clearly in good humour. The odd guffaw signalled they were relaxed.

She counted. Thirty men. Dressed in a variety of clothes, from light-coloured suits, pale chinos and Hawaiian shirts, to jeans and bomber jackets. Most of the men made their way inside. Six toting submachine guns split into pairs and began patrolling the exterior, wandering in circuits of the house before heading for the water's edge. One pissed off a jetty into the water to mocking laughter. Then they all walked back up to the house and stationed themselves, four at the front, two at the back.

She frowned. *That's not right. If there are thirty of them, it should be twenty-seven gangsters and three bodyguards. Three cartel bosses are missing.*

There was no time to ponder the whereabouts of the missing men. Mei looked left and right and nodded. Peng and Mah nodded back. Mei pulled out the burner phone that would trigger her charge. The other two did the same. Mah's three charges were linked by a radio relay that would send the detonation signal to all of them simultaneously.

Mei set the timer on her watch for five minutes. As the minutes counted down, she focused on her pulse rate. It had jumped higher than she found comfortable, and she preferred it to stay at a nice, steady sixty beats per minute. Allowing her breath to slow, she willed her heart to follow suit.

You will be pleased with this one, Master. A definitive blow against El Nuevo Medellín and a warning to anybody else who thinks they can muscle in on White Koi business.

She had time to notice a little egret picking among the weeds at the island's sloping shoreline, before her watch beeped, startling the white, heron-like bird into taking flight.

Three thumbs pressed down on three hard little plastic buttons, each printed with an apple-green icon. *Funny they still show old-timey phones*, Mei thought.

With a shattering bang that morphed into a deep-bellied boom, the C4 charges exploded. The mostly wooden building transformed in a split-second from a house-shaped cuboid into a cloud of shrapnel, exploding propane and wet, pink mist as its twenty-four occupants were blown apart and vaporised in the heat. A blindingly bright white flash dulled to a yellow-orange fireball that rolled up and out from the ground, trailing black smoke like a tail behind a kite.

"Get ready!" Mei shouted. Then the three assassins pushed the rubber dinghy into the water before jumping in. Peng yanked the outboard's cord, and it roared into life, though they could barely hear the little engine above the secondary explosions onshore as more propane tanks exploded. As they motored towards the house, fragments of wood and metal began spattering the water's surface.

Mei kept her eyes on the blast site. She detected no movement. The three SUVs closest to the epicentre of the explosion had been reduced to blackened hulks, little more than twisted bodywork loosely attached to chassis twisted by the force of the explosion. The other four, shielded to a degree, were burning merrily. As they beached the small craft, one of the petrol tanks blew with a dull *crump*, enveloping the SUV in a fresh tangerine-coloured fireball.

Moving along pre-agreed paths, Mei, Mah and Peng made their way as close to the house as they could manage before the intense heat stopped them. There, they circled the blazing remains, looking for survivors. There were none. Several of the trees and shrubs in the garden were on fire, their fruits crackling and spitting as the heat burst them.

Here and there, Mei came across a blackened body part. But of life, there were no signs. Using her phone, she documented the devastation in stills and video, taking over a hundred pictures from every angle she could find. Something caught her eye about fifty metres from the side of the house. A black cube sticking into the soft earth on one of its points. She trotted over to get a better look.

Up close, the cube resolved into a safe, its steel casing dented and crushed as if by a monstrous fist. The blast had destroyed the combination lock and the door was hanging from one hinge, prevented from opening fully by the earth wedged against it.

Mei bent down and placed her right shoulder against the safe and pushed using all her strength, concentrating on her breathing and channelling every thread of her mental energy into the force she was exerting on the steel. Slowly at first, then with a quick *thump*, the safe righted itself.

Mei pulled open the door, wrapping her hand in a piece of cloth first. Inside, she found thick, half-burnt chunks of currency. Dollars mainly, but also sterling and euros, the notes in the centres of the bundles less damaged than those on the outside, but all reduced now to worthless hunks of ink on dead trees. Behind the charred currency, which she hooked out with her swaddled fingers, a steel box, of the type used in offices to hold petty cash, rested on its side. She could see that at one time it had been bright red, but the heat had burnt most of the paint away and blackened the cheap metal beneath.

She pried the lid open with her knife. What she saw inside made her frown. Colour photographs, their pigments altered by the heat to an alien palette of purple and green, showed a young woman with blond hair engaged in sexual intercourse with a large, broad-shouldered man. At the edge of the shot a pair of clearly male legs could be seen. She flipped through the pictures, noticing that although the girl was always the same, the man she was with varied between photographs. Underneath the photos lay a rectangular plastic case, also blackened, and melted into a solid block.

"Mei!" Peng called. "Come on! We have to go!"

She gathered the photos and the plastic case, stuffed them into her backpack and moved away to finish her circuit of the house. Having satisfied herself that nobody had escaped the blast, she extracted a deep-red plum from her backpack. It wasn't ripe, but the skin was flawless. She tossed the hard fruit into the centre of a pile of smouldering ashes and turned away. She met the others at the back of the house again.

"It's done," she said. "Let's go."

They pushed off from the little beach and were heading west long before the sirens began to wail.

30

NYURBA

Gabriel and Eli were zeroed in on the single, mission-critical goal they needed to achieve: Identifying Volodya Ignatyev. They'd discussed the options the night before.

Option one: surveillance. Or, in Gabriel's old SAS parlance, a "lurk." They dismissed it. Too time-consuming. And unnecessary.

According to Stakhansky, who'd sent an update the day they arrived in Nyurba, out of an initial force of fifty armed men, all but six had left the mine, presumably needed for other duties. Kuznitsa had secured the miners' loyalty in the simplest way known to man: by increasing their wages. When a twenty-percent stake in a hugely profitable diamond mine had come their way at the cost of a few bullets and some airfares, they could afford to be generous to their new workers. Ignatyev's performance with the knout had also played its part in ensuring compliance among any of the more militant-minded employees.

Option two. A full-frontal assault. Charge in behind the wheel of a 4x4, all guns blazing, shoot anyone carrying a gun, get the last man standing to point out Ignatyev. Seize and exfil before interrogating him. Pros: fast, element of surprise, brutally effective. Cons: risk of wounding in firefight, may not find Ignatyev.

Option three. Infiltration. Make a direct, non-threatening approach posing as Alrosa lawyers there on a basic site inspection. Or maybe from El Nuevo Medellín. A visit from legal counsel for a minority shareholder would be less likely to raise suspicions than from Garin Group itself. Meet Ignatyev face-to-face. Either snatch him right then or return later. Pros: less risk of full-on shootout with Kuznitsa soldiers. Might get Ignatyev away without discovery. Cons: ploy could fail, no opportunity to use anything bigger than a pistol.

In the end, they'd agreed on the third stratagem. From the briefing Stahkansky had given them at Tatyana's dacha, Ignatyev sounded like a psychopath. Among the various characteristics he would likely display would be a towering ego and a belief in his all-encompassing power. That, and his lack of empathy, would make him less likely to be suspicious of newcomers, especially if they were to heap flattery on him for his genius for management and commercial insight.

Before leaving the hotel, they had assembled what they'd need for the trip in the identical black leather briefcases they'd brought from Saint Petersburg. Into the lower compartment of each went a Glock 17 pistol, a spare 17-round magazine and a Delta D2. With tight-fitting dividers closed over the hardware, the upper compartments held sheaves of densely typed but in fact utterly content-free documents, prepared by Stahkansky and stapled, tagged and clipped into official Garin Group file folders. Eli also had a slim, zipped grey leather case, the size of a paperback book. Gabriel had some packets of duty free cigarettes, Marlboros he'd bought in Saint Petersburg.

They weren't expecting to be searched. But they had a Plan B: a very simple Plan B.

PLAN B
1 Revert to Option 2.
2 Attack.
3 Disable.

4 Kill all armed men.

5 Shoot way out taking Ignatyev with us.

After the comfort of the Bentley Bentayga they'd driven in Saint Petersburg, the well-used Toyota Landcruiser they'd hired felt more like a Willy's Jeep. But it was the best the hire-car place could offer them at short notice, the manager explained apologetically.

"We have Chevrolet Suburban," he'd said the previous afternoon, looking from Gabriel to Eli and back again and smiling ingratiatingly. "But visiting trade delegation from China, they take it for whole week. Toyota is good vehicle. Never let you down."

Gabriel didn't doubt the man. He'd fought against people driving Landcruisers and their pickup cousin, the Hilux, on four continents. The most popular modification was a heavy machinegun mounted in the truck bed. Though he'd seen others, up to and including ground-to-air missiles.

Now, they were ready. Dressed impeccably in their suits, though with practical boots for Eli where a lawyer would probably be sporting low-heeled shoes.

As Eli's Russian was perfunctory, they'd decided to make use of the fact, rather than go for more complex deceptions. They were Americans. She had no Russian, he was fluent. Joe Boyd and Ellen Hicks. Representing the US law firm GTR Partners LLP and the interests of Compañeros Blancos.

Gabriel turned Eli to face him, holding her by the shoulders.

"Let me look at you, Ms Hicks. Yes, very smart. I like you with your hair up. Very … lawyerly."

He flicked a piece of lint off her left shoulder.

"How do I look?" he asked.

She frowned and took her time looking him up and down.

"Very Ivy League, Mr Boyd. I could put my makeup on using your toecaps. And the tailoring just screams ambition. You'll make senior partner this year, I'm sure of it!"

Gabriel grinned.

"Let's go then."

. . .

After a four-hour journey, they drove through the main gate of the New Galaxy Diamond Mine. The sign directing visitors was printed in English and Cyrillic, English first. No guard post. Just a youngish guy in a generic, deep-blue rent-a-cop uniform with a peaked cap, though he was toting a highly polished AK-47.

Gabriel rolled to a stop and buzzed the window down. Beaming, and employing his best American accent, he spoke to the guard, who, up close, he realised couldn't have been more than midtwenties.

First, echoing the site's own stated preference, in English.

"Hi! Joe Boyd and Ellen Hicks to see Mr Ignatyev."

Then again, in Russian.

"*Privet! Joe Boyd i Ellen Hicks, chtoby videt' Gospodina Ignatyeva.*"

The guard raised his eyebrows so that they disappeared beneath the pulled-down plastic visor of his cap. In heavily accented English, he replied.

"You have appointment?"

Gabriel increased the wattage of his smile.

"No! Kind of a mystery-shopper thing. Where's his office, please?"

The guard stared at Gabriel for a few moments, then looked past him at Eli. She smiled back, exposing far more of her teeth than she normally did. Gabriel was impressed.

"Hi there! Ellen Hicks, pleased to meet you."

She leaned across Gabriel and stuck her hand out of the window. Uncertainly, the young man shook it and then let go. He pointed to a cluster of buildings about three hundred metres away, across a broad swathe of tarmac, on which huge yellow trucks and pieces of mining equipment were haphazardly parked.

"Is white block. New Galaxy logo. Is his office. Also house."

"Thanks," Gabriel said, feeling that his face might split apart if he smiled any wider. "You're a star. Hey! You smoke?"

"Sure, I smoke." The young man said, straightening up.

"Cool, cool. Here, take a couple packs. I picked 'em up in Saint Petersburg. American, yes?"

He fished a couple of packets of Marlboros from the glove box where he'd stashed them and handed them over. The guard snatched the proffered cigarettes, perhaps afraid this generous American might take them away if he hesitated. He smiled, revealing a row of greyish, stained teeth missing an incisor.

"*Spasibo*. Er, thank you."

"*Pozhalujsta*. You're welcome. OK, gotta run. Take care now!"

Gabriel pulled away, keeping things nice and relaxed, and drove across the expanse of tarmac towards Volodya Ignatyev's headquarters.

Eli pointed over to the far edge of the compound.

"Look. Couple of guys who don't look like miners."

Gabriel followed her pointing finger. Yes. Two beefy men leaning against a wall, smoking, dressed, despite the heat, in black bomber jackets and jeans. They had that ex-military look, instantly recognisable the world over. Maybe the stance was just a little too balanced to be that of someone who was truly relaxed. Maybe the way the heads kept turning, every few moments, to check out their immediate surroundings.

They looked in the direction of the Landcruiser, then turned away again. Clearly a single, reasonably well-presented SUV was not considered a threat in their playbook. So much the better. Gabriel felt alert but relaxed. Heart ticking over nicely, maybe a few beats above resting, but still capable of pumping a lot more blood round his system should he need it. Headroom, a military doctor had called it once. Though Gabriel supposed "heartroom" would have been more accurate.

He pulled up directly outside the door to the white building, which he now saw was little more than a blockhouse, and killed the engine. The positioning, which some more courtesy-orientated visitor might have concluded was impolite, was perfect. It shielded the front door from all but the most persistent observers. Perfect for bundling their captive into the back of the Landcruiser.

He and Eli climbed out and retrieved their briefcases from the back seat. He marched up to the front door and, seeing no bell push or intercom, simply knocked, loudly, on the painted plywood. He listened intently, but no clatter of footsteps or even angry shouts met his inquiry.

Then, from behind him, a shout broke the silence. He and Eli turned round, smiles plastered onto their faces. The man rounding the front of the Landcruiser was clearly in a bad mood. His face was flushed and his lips were drawn back from his teeth.

"Hey!" he shouted in Russian. "Who the fucking fuck are you and what the fuck do you fuckwits think you're fucking doing parking that fucking shitheap in front of my fucking front door?"

Impressive, Gabriel thought, *I've met infantry sergeants who couldn't swear as fluently as that.*

Answering the man he was sure was Ignatyev in fluent Russian, though minus the foul language, Gabriel kicked the plan off. He held his hands up in mock surrender.

"Whoa! Sorry friend. We meant no offence. We're looking for the big man, you know? The head honcho. The guy running New Galaxy these days."

Ignatyev slowed to a stop in front of Gabriel, hands held out at his side. He was panting. Perhaps he'd been exercising. He was thickly muscled and stood a head taller than Gabriel. He ignored Gabriel's outstretched hand. After a few more seconds, Gabriel let it fall – the disappointed social caller – rubbing his thumb and fingertips together as if perhaps his interlocutor had spotted grime on his hand that he had missed. Ignatyev jutted his chin forwards.

"I'm in charge here. Like I said, who the fuck are you?"

"We're lawyers. My name is Joe Boyd. We represent your minority shareholders, Compañeros Blancos. We've come to take a look around. Our clients heard there had been some management changes here and wanted to reassure themselves their investment was secure under the new boss."

Ignatyev's narrowed eyes widened a touch and his arms dropped to a more natural position at his sides, reducing his simian appearance. Less gorilla, more man.

"Huh. OK, well, nobody informed me of any site visit."

"And we're very sorry about that oversight, Mr—?"

"Ignatyev. Volodya Ignatyev. I'm the site boss here like I said. What's the matter with the woman? She doesn't speak Russian?"

Gabriel turned to Eli and smiled and murmured a translation in English. Eli faced Ignatyev and smiled. She held out her own hand.

"Ellen Hicks. I'm afraid the only Russian I know is *spasibo* and *pozhalujsta*."

Under the searchlight power of Eli's smile, accentuated with scarlet lipstick, and her coquettish pronunciation of the two Russian words, Ignatyev cooled down a few more degrees.

"Volodya," he said, again, smiling wolfishly, and laying a hairy hand flat against his chest. And, in English, "Pleased to meet you, Ellen. Maybe we should speak English then, for your sake?"

She lowered her eyelids and then returned her gaze upwards into his fierce blue eyes.

"That's very sweet of you, Volodya. I'm sorry if my colleague upset you. Joe can be a little too, " she paused for effect, "*American*, at times. Tell me, what does *Volodya* mean?"

Ignatyev stood tall and held his hands out wide.

"Ruler of the world. I like to tell my men, around here, I am ruler of *their* world. My little joke. Are you thirsty? It is a long drive from Nyurba. I have tea or coffee or vodka. I am Russian, after all."

"Coffee, please, Volodya."

"Then come inside. Let's find out what your *clients* are so worried about. I am sure I can help you put their minds at rest."

The interior of the building was starkly designed, as if someone had been keen not to waste any money on creature comforts. A rudimentary reception area housing a battered plywood desk and a grey filing cabinet plus a couple of tatty cloth-covered armchairs. Ignatyev led them past the desk to an internal door. Opening it, he stood aside and waved them through.

Gabriel let Eli lead, so that he formed a human barrier between her and Ignatyev. Beyond the door, a narrow hallway led to a third door.

"Open it, it's not locked," Ignatyev called.

Gabriel pushed through and found himself in altogether more sumptuous accommodation. A thick fur rug covered most of the floorspace not occupied by tobacco-brown leather sofas, coffee tables in varnished timber and a gigantic flat-screen TV, bolted to the wall above an expensive-looking hi-fi. Venetian blinds screened the view through a sizeable window, though they let plenty of light into the living quarters.

"Take a seat, Ellen" Ignatyev said. "I will fetch coffee." He turned back. "You also, Joe. But as they say, *laydeez furst*." He uttered the last two words in an American accent so comically over-the-top Gabriel had to bite the inside of his cheek to stop a smirk.

Once Ignatyev had disappeared, Gabriel turned to Eli.

"So far, so good," he whispered.

"I think he likes me," she whispered back, winking.

"Poor sod."

"He won't know what's hit him."

They shut up as the door opened again.

Ignatyev stood there. In his left hand he held a tray on which were balanced a pot of coffee and three mugs, milk and a bowl of sugar with a silver teaspoon sticking out.

In his right, he held a pistol.

31

Gabriel reared back in his chair, hands held out in front of him.

"What the hell? What the fuck is that?"

Ignatyev set the tray down on a low coffee table, not taking his eye off Gabriel and not letting the muzzle of the pistol – a Makarov, Gabriel noted – waver. He straightened.

"Lawyers, eh?" he asked in Russian.

"Yes, like I said. We represent—"

"Yes, I heard you the first time. Those Colombian cocksuckers, Compan-whatever."

"We really mean you no harm, Mr Ignatyev," he said, affecting a hurt tone and keeping his gaze on the Makarov's muzzle. "Like *I* said, we are here merely on a fact-finding visit. Due diligence, that's all. An hour or two of your time and we'll be out of your hair."

Open the cases," Ignatyev ordered in a low growl. "Let me see what you've got in there."

Gabriel shook his head, hoping he was judging his opponent's strategy accurately.

"I'm afraid I can't do that. They contain legal documents. *Privileged* legal documents. Of the confidential variety."

Ignatyev grinned, and pointed the Makarov at Gabriel's groin.

"You know what this baby contains? Bullets. *Privileged* bullets. Of the hollow-point variety. Now, either you open the cases and show me what you and little miss sexy American lawyer have got in there, or I'm going to do some due diligence of my own."

Gabriel held his hands out wide.

"OK, OK, fine. But this is highly irregular."

He turned to Eli and said, in English, "Ellen, *Mister* Ignatyev wants us to open our cases. Would you mind?"

She shook her head and tightened her lips, doing a fair impression of a chicken in a fox's den. In concert they flipped the catches so that they opened with four closely-spaced clacks, lifted the lids, and swivelled the briefcases round to face Ignatyev.

Now we'll see how this plays, Gabriel thought, calculating that Eli would be following the same train of thought. *If you're happy with what you see, fine. If you go to lift the inner lid, you're a dead man. You'll be within range and you'll be distracted. Not a good position for someone within a foot of Ms Schochat's right hand.*

Ignatyev leant forward. Gabriel tensed. Ready to move. To strike. Out of the corner of his eye, he saw Eli shift her weight in the chair, moving forwards so that her centre of gravity shifted ahead of her hips. Using the Makarov's muzzle, Ignatyev poked at the folders in Gabriel's case, then repeated the perfunctory search on Eli's.

He looked at Gabriel.

"Why've they got Garin Group logos on them? You said you were with the Colombians."

"Garin Group's Finance Department prepared the files for us and couriered them to us in Saint Petersburg."

"Huh. Usual admin bullshit. I hate it. It's bloodsucking lawyers like you who stop honest working men like me from getting on with things. Running things."

Gabriel relaxed his posture, though it was for show.

"I know. And I'm sorry. But if you can just let us do what we have to do here, we'll be on our way, out of your hair, and you can go back to being the ruler of the world."

He was considering using hypnosis on Ignatyev but worrying whether the techniques would work on the mind of a psychopath.

The skills Master Zhao had taught him weren't one hundred percent effective, and the last thing he wanted was an enraged Ignatyev, tooled up and ready to shoot a pair of "bloodsucking lawyers." No, for now, the straightforward approach seemed to be working. *Carry on.*

Suddenly, Ignatyev's mood seemed to flick over from hostile to friendly. Almost as if a switch had tripped in his brain.

"What the hell! Why not? It's not as if anything much happens around here. Come on, let's have a coffee and maybe a shot of vodka in it. Then we can go look at a fucking big hole in the ground, and you two can report back to the Colombians that everything is fine, yes?"

"Yes," Gabriel said. "Thank you. That would be perfect."

Ignatyev became talkative after his second, three-finger shot of vodka. He slopped even more into his empty coffee mug, and Gabriel began to think Ignatyev was going to do their job for them.

"You ever been to a diamon' mine before, Joe?" he slurred, switching back to Russian.

"No. Our first time," Gabriel said.

"'S not all it's cracked up t'be, I tell you. Fuckin' big pit, little guys at the bottom look like bugs all scurryin' roun' down there. Digging those little chips out of the ground. 'Casion'lly we get to do a bit of blastin' but tha's rare. Hey, you wan' more vodka?"

He waggled the half-empty bottle at Gabriel. Pleasingly, his gaze was unfocused, the eyes doing their best to look in two directions at once.

"I'm good, thanks. Plus, we have to drive back."

"Oh, you don' wanna bother 'bout that. I'm as good as the law roun' here. Fuckin' peasants all of 'em. Hardly even real Russians, know what I mean? More like Chinks, if you ask me."

Ignatyev finished another monster shot of vodka and clunked his mug down on the table. He missed the edge and the mug spun onto the carpet, spraying the last few drops of vodka onto the rug.

"Balls!" Ignatyev said, sliding off his armchair onto his knees to retrieve the mug.

While his head was down, Gabriel signalled to Eli with a nod. *Now would be a good time.*

In a slow, clear voice, speaking in English, Eli addressed the kneeling Ignatyev.

"Er, excuse me? Volodya? I'm a diabetic. I have to inject my insulin, OK?"

Without waiting for him to answer, she retrieved the leather pouch from her briefcase, leaving the lid up, and unzipped it. It contained a diabetic's blood glucose testing kit complete with a pair of syringes and a packet of disposable needles.

"Wha' she say?" Ignatyev asked Gabriel, placing the mug with exaggerated care dead-centre on the table.

"Diabetic," Gabriel said.

"Ah! OK. Yeah. My sister is the same. Fuckin' pain in the arse, you ask me. Min' you, they're about the only pricks she gets inside her, know what I mean?"

Ignatyev roared with laughter at his own joke, sending a gust of high-octane breath sailing across the few feet separating the two men.

Gabriel could feel his pulse starting to pick up speed as he watched Eli select a syringe, and fit a needle to the barrel. Ironically, had it been filled with insulin it would have been fatal to a non-diabetic like Ignatyev. As it was, the clear liquid inside the narrow-bore plastic cylinder was ketamine, which they'd bought quite legally from a vet's in Nyurba the day before, regulations concerning the supply of horse tranquilisers in the Sakha Republic being lax to the point of non-existence. The fact that they'd paid in dollars may have had something to do with it as well.

Eli looked up at Ignatyev, who was watching her with a drunk's intensity, the whites of his eyes now flushed pink, the eyelids starting to droop.

"Hurt much?" he asked her in English.

She smiled.

"A little. I need to ask a favour, Volodya. Could you hold my shirt up, please? I'd do it myself, but I hurt my left hand yesterday."

To a sober man, it might have been a transparent ploy. Although Gabriel had seen the way Ignatyev's gaze kept flicking to Eli's chest whenever he thought she wasn't looking. It was one of the things he admired about the Israeli. Despite her Special Forces training, which had equipped her to kill with everything from her bare hands to the most sophisticated modern weapons systems, she was quite happy to use the oldest trick in the book to disarm – sometimes literally – male opponents.

"Sure!" Ignatyev said, sliding to his knees for the second time and shuffling round the coffee table until he was next to Eli.

He leaned closer and then plucked the front of her shirt out from the waistband of her trousers and lifted it until four inches of tanned skin were visible.

"Like this?"

"Perfect," she said. "Now, I just need to get this ready."

She rotated the syringe in her hand until she was holding it in a stabbing grip, thumb over the plunger. Gabriel visualised black crosshairs on the exposed side of Ignatyev's neck where she'd drive the needle home. She moved her hand closer to her exposed belly.

Gabriel readied himself, every muscle primed to go, his hands already pushing down on the arms of his chair, feet brought underneath the seat to give him a fast exit from its comfortable embrace.

"Could you lift it a little higher, please, Volodya?" Eli asked.

As the drunk Russian complied, clearly enjoying every second of his proximity to so much bare American female flesh, Eli drew her hand back.

32

A mobile phone rang. Ignatyev swung his head round, away from Eli. Her incoming hand stopped in midair.

"What the fuck?" Ignatyev said, sharply.

As Ignatyev got to his feet and went to retrieve his phone from a side table, Eli glanced at Gabriel. Her meaning was clear.

Now, what?

He gave a fractional shake of the head. *Stay calm. Try again in a minute.*

Ignatyev was standing, unsteadily, one hand stretched out and laid, palm-out against the wall.

"What did you say?" he asked, after listening for a dozen seconds, his voice suddenly clear and authoritative.

He shook his head.

"Impossible. They're already here."

He frowned.

"The lawyers! Two of them. They're right here with me. I'm looking at them now."

He turned and pointed, irrelevantly, at "Joe" and "Ellen." He listened again, staring at Eli.

"OK. Do that."

He ended the call. He didn't return to his position as diabetic's carer on the floor beside Eli.

Gabriel checked out the position of the Makarov. It lay on the end of the coffee table furthest away from Ignatyev. The pistol was the wrong way round for the Russian, and he'd have to lean right across the table to reach it.

He saw Ignatyev follow his gaze.

Ignatyev backed up until he hit the wall. He looked left and right, as if summoning help, but for now, at least, it was just the three of them.

Eli and Gabriel stood.

"You're not with the Colombians," Ignatyev rasped out. "That was my man in Moscow. Three of them just left Medellín. They're coming here. Who the fuck are you?"

Gabriel leapt towards Ignatyev, aiming a blade-hand at the man's throat. Simultaneously, Eli dived for him, syringe out in front, aiming for his neck. But the big Russian wasn't ready to give in without a fight.

He ducked under Gabriel's incoming blow, grabbed the narrow metal pole of a standard lamp and swung it like a bat at Eli's torso.

Eli doubled over with a gasp as the aluminium rod caught her in the chest. The syringe shot from her fingers and skittered under a chair.

"Bastards!" Ignatyev yelled, aiming a huge fist at the side of Gabriel's head.

His punch was wide of its target but connected with Gabriel's left shoulder. Gabriel screamed with pain as the flesh compressed under the massive weight of the Russian's fist.

Eli was on her belly, stretching out her right hand to get to the syringe. Ignatyev kicked her hard in the side. Gabriel saw her roll away from the blow. How was this drunk Russian besting them? It didn't make sense. He let himself stagger backwards, fast, and deliberately hit the coffee table with his calves. Rolling over its polished surface, he grabbed for the Makarov, and snagged the grip just as he rolled off onto his knees.

He brought the pistol up and yelled at Ignatyev.

"Dvigajsya i ty pokojnik!" *Move and you're a dead man!*

Ignatyev froze, his right leg lifted ready to stamp down on Eli's stomach. The blow, had it landed, would have crushed internal organs, started massive haemorrhaging, and probably killed her.

She scrambled to her feet, gripping the syringe and plunged the needle into Ignatyev's neck, just below the angle of his jaw.

His eyes rolled up in their sockets until only the whites were visible. He fell sideways with a crash, smacking his skull on the wall as he went down. Gabriel dropped the magazine out of the Makarov and pocketed it, racked the slide twice to eject any round in the chamber, then flung the empty pistol into a corner.

"Come on!" Eli shouted, grabbing the diabetic kit and sticking it into an inside pocket.

Grabbing their Glocks from the open cases and sticking them into their waistbands, they grabbed Ignatyev under the armpits and by the ankles and carried him out of the room, Gabriel going backwards, with the Russian's head pressed into his midriff.

At the front door, he stopped.

"Wait!" he said. "Drop him."

Ignatyev's relaxed form practically bounced off the cheap, nylon carpet. Gabriel lifted a slat of the Venetian blind.

"Shit! Four incoming. Pistols only."

"They'll have to come in," Eli said, breathless. "Wait! I've got it. Help me get him out of sight."

They dragged Ignatyev's inert form to the hinge-side of the door so the arriving muscle wouldn't see him as they entered the reception area.

Eli dashed for the reception desk and sat behind it, concealing her Glock in her lap and picking up the desk phone with her left hand. She pasted a wide smile on her face.

Gabriel stood, Glock raised, behind the door, straddling Ignatyev.

He heard the clumping of four pairs of boots. The door swung open and he caught the handle and held it so he, and the better part of the slumbering Ignatyev, were hidden.

Four beefy men rushed over to Eli, pistols out but not raised.

"Where's Ignatyev?" one shouted.

Eyes wide, she put the phone down with a shaking hand and pointed at the door leading to his private quarters.

They headed for the door.

Eli shot the first two before they'd even reached it. One in the back of the head, the other between the shoulder blades.

Gabriel aimed for the leading figure, blowing the side of his skull away in a spray of blood and brain matter that spattered the white-painted wall.

The fourth man, alive only because he'd been shielded by the other three, whirled round, gun arm coming up. But he was too slow, and too late. Gabriel and Eli hit him with two shots apiece. He fell backwards, stumbling over the bodies of his dead friends, one eye socket pierced dead-centre.

With the sharp stink of gunsmoke and burnt propellant stinging his nostrils, Gabriel stuck his pistol into his waistband. Eli was doing the same.

They lifted Ignatyev, who was now snoring loudly, and carried him out through the open door. A few figures were making their way, cautiously, across the tarmac towards them. Gabriel took one hand away from Ignatyev's armpit, grabbed his pistol and fired a few shots over their heads. They ran for cover, but he knew it wouldn't be long before the rest of the Kuznitsa enforcers arrived.

They slung Ignatyev in through the open rear door and slammed it shut before racing round to the front and climbing in. The Toyota's engine, more bulletproof than the dead Russians, started with a roar. And they were away, slewing round in a wide, rubber-burning circle, before powering out of the compound towards the main gate. From behind them, Gabriel heard the rattle of small arms fire. He flicked his eyes up at the rear-view mirror. Several more men had arrived and were letting loose with submachine guns. The lack of accuracy of the weapons themselves, coupled with the men's feverish rush to defend their master, meant that not a single round hit the retreating Landcruiser.

Engine roaring, the Landcruiser shot out of the main gate,

speed nearing seventy. Gabriel had his right foot jammed down against the threadbare carpet under the throttle pedal.

"Come on, come on!" he yelled.

The SUV might have been high-mileage, but it also had a 4.5L V8 diesel engine under the bonnet. A few seconds after leaving the perimeter of New Galaxy, they were travelling at 125 mph. The road was just about able to accommodate vehicles travelling at half that speed, and at times it felt as though the Toyota might part company with Earth for good, leaping over bumps in the rutted surface, all four wheels spinning freely in the air with an alarming whine.

Gabriel glanced at the mirror again. *Nobody in pursuit. Odd.*

"There's no one behind us," he said.

"Maybe their orders are to protect the mine, not the man," Eli answered.

"Maybe he gave them a taste of the knout, too."

"Mutiny?"

"Don't know. Can you call Stakhansky? Let him know he's clear to go in?"

"Wait, what about the Colombians? Ignatyev said three of them were on their way out here."

"What about them?"

"They find out we've snatched Ignatyev, then we've brought a drug cartel down on Stakhansky's head as well as Kuznitsa."

"Kuznitsa are a short-term problem," Gabriel said grimly. "As for the Colombians, I just, just don't know. I need to stop. My shoulder feels like it's on fire."

Gabriel swung off the road and slowed to a stop. He climbed out and swapped places with Eli. Back inside the Landcruiser, Eli looked across at him, frown lines furrowing her forehead.

"You OK?"

"I think so. Ignatyev got in a good punch right on the wound."

Eli leaned over and lifted Gabriel's jacket away from his shoulder. He winced as the healing bullet wound protested. She bent her head over still further and sniffed, then wrinkled her nose.

"It smells pretty bad. I think it's infected."

"I'm maxed out on painkillers and antibiotics. So, unless you want to shoot me up with some of that ketamine, I guess I'm just going to have to gut it out."

Eli's eyes popped wide.

"Of course! That's exactly what we'll do. I did a course in battlefield medicine. Combat medics use ketamine all the time. Shit, what was the dose for analgesia?"

"Google it?"

Eli nodded. She fished her phone out and called up a browser.

"Bugger it! No service. OK, let me think."

"Not being funny, but we don't have time to think. How much did you give Ignatyev?"

"A thousand and eighty milligrams."

"OK, so he's what sixteen stones?"

"Yeah, that's what I used to calculate the dose."

"Right. I'm eleven. We want analgesia not anaesthesia."

Eli looked upwards. Then she closed her eyes and began to recite.

"Battlefield medicine course, module five, combat trauma pain relief. Ketamine dose for acute pain relief is … is … " Her eyes snapped open and she looked at Gabriel, smiling. "Is a half to one milligrams per kilo. You're eleven stones. That's roughly seventy kilos. If we go for the maximum dose that's seventy mills. Way less than a tenth of what I gave our friend back there."

"OK, let's do it, then."

Eli fetched the zipped leather case and took out one of the spare syringes. Gingerly she inserted the needle into Gabriel's left deltoid and depressed the plunger a fraction.

"There," she said. "That's my best guess at seventy mills. It should kick in almost immediately."

Gabriel rolled his head on his shoulders. Miraculously, the drug that had knocked out the sixteen-stone Russian — still sprawled, and snoring on the back seat — was already working, numbing the pain from his inflamed shoulder until he could feel nothing at all.

"Thank you, Dr Schochat," he said, grinning. "That feels

absolutely marvellous! Now, why don't we find somewhere nice and quiet to interrogate our captive?"

Having driven at ninety degrees to the road for a mile or so, Eli pulled into the centre of the one of the rare clumps of vegetation in this expanse of low-lying land.

"Are we there yet?" Gabriel asked with a smile.

"What?"

"Are we there yet?"

"Yes. If by *there* you mean *here*. Come on, help me get Sleeping Beauty out of the back. I think I could cheerfully shoot him just for that racket he's been making."

"OK, boss. Whatever you say. By the way, and please don't think I'm being forward, but you really are an extraordinarily pretty girl, did anyone ever tell you that?"

Gabriel felt so happy to be out here in the countryside with Eli. As they manhandled – *man-and-woman-handled*, he mentally corrected himself with a grin —Ignatyev out of the rear seat, he considered proposing to her. *Right here and now. It's the perfect setting. OK, maybe not perfect. No bower of roses. No gypsy violins playing, but you know, not bad. The pink kestrels are a nice touch. And once we're married, I can protect her from harm. Like I should have done with Britta.*

With Ignatyev lying on the ground between them, Gabriel straightened and eased a kink out of his back. He took a few steps backward, then ran at Ignatyev and kicked him as hard as he could in the ribs.

"Hey, shit-for-brains! Wake up! I wanna talk to you!" Gabriel shouted, leaning over the now grunting Russian and spraying him with a fine mist of spittle.

"Gabriel! That's too much!" Eli shouted, grabbing him by the right arm and pulling him away.

He shook himself free and pushed her hard in the sternum.

"No, it isn't, *dorogoya moya*! He killed Britta. And I promised Tanya I'd torture him to death."

"No, you didn't! Shit! I must have overcooked the ketamine. You have to back off Gabriel. Let me handle this."

Gabriel held his hands wide. What was she wittering on about? He had no intention of backing off. He was only getting started. He stepped across Ignatyev's chest then sat heavily, driving the air from the waking man's lungs with an *oof*.

He dug his thumbs into Ignatyev's eye sockets and pushed. Ignatyev came fully awake, writhing under Gabriel.

"Get the fuck off me, you crazy fucker!" he screamed in Russian.

Gabriel pushed harder. *Funny things, eyes. Squishy.* Something seemed to slide past his right thumb. *Oh, no, my bad. That was my thumb sliding in.* He hooked it and pulled, leaning back as the attaching muscles strained to hold on. With a jerk, the eye came free and Gabriel rocked back, laughing.

"Oh, Jesus, I bet that hurts!"

Over Ignatyev's screams, he flung the eye away, flicking the blood and clear fluids off his fingers.

"Gabriel!" Eli shouted, wrapping her arms around his chest and trying to drag him off the yowling Ignatyev. "Stop! You'll kill him."

"I thought that was the IDEA!" he roared, resisting her tugging. He lashed out with his right hand and caught her a glancing blow across the cheek. She staggered back.

He returned to Ignatyev who was bucking beneath him and attempting to wriggle free, though the anaesthetic remaining in his system was weakening his muscles.

"You've still got one peeper left, Volodya," he said. "But now I'm the master of your world."

He dragged the Glock from his waistband and poked the muzzle into Ignatyev's empty eye socket.

"Where is Max?"

"Who?" Ignatyev groaned.

"Where is Max? Where is Max?" Gabriel chanted. "Where is Max? Maxy-Max?"

Gabriel took the pistol out of Ignatyev's eye socket, turned round and shot him through the left thigh.

"Last chance saloon, pardner. You no-tellee, me go-shootee. Savvy?"

The fight went out of Ignatyev. Alternatively moaning and howling with pain, he nodded, causing a rivulet of blood to overspill his empty eye socket and track down over his cheekbone into the dust beneath his head.

"Moscow. Krivoarbatsky Lane. Thirteen."

Gabriel climbed off Ignatyev.

"Thanks, matey!"

Then he stood back and shot Ignatyev in the face, and kept pulling the trigger until the last round left the magazine and the gun dry-fired.

He turned to Eli, who was standing some way off, arms folded across her chest, defensively, he thought. He dropped the Glock to the ground and held his hands out wide.

"What?"

"Have you finished?" she asked him.

He looked behind him at what had once been the Russian's head. Then back at Eli.

"Looks like it. So," he clapped his hands. "Moscow, then. Krivoarbatsky Lane. Number thirteen. Unlucky for some, eh?"

Eli just shook her head.

"Get in, Gabriel. We need to head back to Nyurba and then get the fuck out of here. Things are going to get very messy, very quickly."

While Eli drove, Gabriel closed his eyes. He felt deliciously, supremely, relaxed. Wonderful, in fact. Life should feel this way all the time. The thrum of the Landcruiser's engine was a lullaby. No pain from his shoulder. No pain anywhere. Not even in his soul. The dead were asleep. Even Britta. The Super-Swede was in some cinnamon-scented heaven, skiing or ice-rallying or sniping at distant targets.

"Is that what you think, *hej*?"

Gabriel's eyes snapped open.

Britta took her right hand off the steering wheel and poked him in the ribs.

"I asked you a question, Gabriel."

"Aren't you, then? In Heaven, I mean?"

"Do I look like I'm in Heaven?"

She turned to him and smiled. The gappy grin went on widening until her teeth were showing all the way round to the back of her head. She reached up and took a handful of that amazing coppery hair and yanked. The top of her head came away. Gabriel's lips stretched wide in a silent scream.

Britta toppled sideways, her brains spilling from her open skull. The Landcruiser carried on in an arrow-straight line back towards Nyurba.

33

COUNTRYSIDE NORTH OF MOSCOW

Tatyana Garin wasn't the only Russian in Gabriel's life who kept a dacha. Max Novgorodsky also maintained a summer residence, though his was north of Moscow, a few hundred kilometres from his multi-million-dollar apartment on Krivoarbatsky Lane.

Despite his wealth, which, though not on the same scale as Tatyana's, was enough to land him firmly in the ranks of the world's super-rich, he did not care to flash it around in the countryside. His dacha was a comparatively modest affair. Two storeys, six bedrooms, all with en suite bathrooms, but no swimming pool, no tennis court, no rifle range, recording studio or bowling alley. Just a traditional wooden structure with prettily carved green balconies, a veranda on all sides apart from the front, and matching fretwork trim around the doors and windows.

What was distinctive about Max Novgorodsky's dacha was the beast he shared it with. It had a large, heated kennel outside, and free access to the interior of the dacha. A 500- by 250-metre garden to range in. And, when Max was in residence, the opportunity to hunt in the vast expanse of thick forest and lakes beyond the high fence that served as his property boundary.

Pyotr, he called it. After not one but two heroes of his. Peter the Great and the boy, Peter, from Prokofiev's symphony. Pyotr measured one metre seventy from his cold, black nose to the blackish hairy tip of his tail. A big specimen even for *Canis lupus lupus*, Pyotr weighed in at seventy-one kilos. People had initially complained after spotting Max out and about with Pyotr.

"If a man wants a pet, he should buy a dog," one neighbour had written in a formal complaint to the local authority.

The official who received the complaint had acknowledged it courteously. But there was no way he was going to go head to head with their newest resident over his preference for keeping a Middle Russian forest wolf rather than a Siberian Husky or a Borzoi.

While Max was away in Moscow, Pyotr's needs were met by a local man who dumped three kilos of fresh butcher's meat over the fence every day. Water he could get from a stream that ran through the property from east to west. And, if so minded, he could always top up his diet with rabbit, hare, pheasant or any other specimen of the small game that lived, if not happily then at least in a state of natural coexistence, on Max's land.

Sometimes, Max would engage Pyotr's services in a semi-professional capacity, when, for example, he felt a business situation had reached the point that it required a show of strength. Then, the recalcitrant businessman, or perhaps a mid-level drug dealer or local crime boss, would be taken out to the dacha and introduced to Pyotr. Personally.

Depending on the severity of their transgression, the introduction might take place each side of a chain-link fence. For the most serious offences against the Kuznitsa code, no fence was provided. Video would be posted on the Dark Web and a discreet "press release" would be issued, alerting members of the wider global community that Kuznitsa had, once again, flexed its muscles. Pyotr usually slept for most of the following few days, and tended not to need any meat from the butcher.

. . .

While Gabriel and Eli were disrupting his operations in Nyurba, Max was out in the forest with Pyotr on a long, strong, rope leash. Crouching at the foot of a fat-trunked oak tree he brushed some dead leaves away from the stem of a beige-capped mushroom.

"Look, Pyotr," he murmured, although the wolf was ten feet away, relieving himself against a bush. "A puffball. We used to call these 'grandpa's tobacco' when I was a kid."

He picked the bulbous mushroom and placed it reverently in the wooden basket at his side. Nestling in the folds of a red-and-white gingham cloth were a dozen or so assorted wild fungi, their caps mostly brown or white, although a couple blazed a vivid shade of yellow in the sunlight slanting through the forest canopy.

He straightened, wincing as his knees cracked, and moved on through his hunting ground.

34

NYURBA

Gabriel opened his eyes. He was looking up at a white-painted ceiling into which was set a bright, white lamp on some sort of cantilevered metal arm. He turned his head to the left. A man wearing a white coat stood with his back to Gabriel, consulting a computer screen. He looked right. Eli sat in a hard chair, reading a magazine. He went to check the time but found his left arm wouldn't move. Feeling a wave of panic, he fought to control his breathing before trying to move his other arm. No response. The white-coated man turned away from the screen and crossed the room to look down at Gabriel.

"Miss Hicks. Your colleague is back with us," he said in Russian-accented English.

As Eli dropped the magazine and hurried to his side, Gabriel lifted his head and looked down at his wrists. With a flood of relief, he saw leather straps buckled tightly across his skin. *Not paralysed, then.* Eli looked down into his eyes.

"Hi, Joe. Back with us?"

"Uh, yeah," Gabriel said, essaying an American accent, which, even to his ears, sounded about as real as a three-dollar note.

"You were pretty far gone back there. Dr Usbayev here said I must have overdosed you on the painkiller. He's given you something to counter the ketamine."

The doctor, midthirties, balding, adjusted the thick, tortoiseshell-framed glasses that magnified his brown eyes.

"You may feel a lingering sense of unreality, Mr Boyd, but this should fade in a day or so. Miss Hicks tells me you are on other medication."

"Yeah. Uh, paracetamol, ibuprofen, Tramadol, some antibiotics. I have a shoulder injury."

Usbayev pursed his lips, an oddly prim expression for a young man.

"Yes, well, combined with ketamine, that is a fairly," he paused, clearly searching for the right word, "*potent* combination. I'm surprised you didn't have some sort of psychotic break."

Gabriel glanced up at Eli and widened his eyes a little. *Did I? I can't remember much after we left the mine.* She dropped her eyelids for a beat. A tiny left-to-right movement of her head.

"Just really sleepy, doc. Maybe some funny dreams, you know?"

Usbayev unbuckled the wrist straps. Gabriel rubbed his wrists in turn, massaging some feeling back into them.

"I think it would be best if you stuck to *retail* painkillers," Usbayev said.

"Gotcha, doc," Gabriel said, pushing himself into a sitting position on the bed and swinging his legs down. "Advil and Tylenol only from now on."

"How much do we owe you, Dr Usbayev?" Eli asked, reaching for her purse.

"Five hundred, please. Dollars." A beat. "Cash."

Eli smiled.

"Naturally. And thank you."

She counted out the requisite number of bills.

. . .

Back at their hotel, behind the locked door of their room, Gabriel sat heavily on the edge of the bed.

"What the fuck happened?"

Eli shrugged as she uncapped a bottle of beer and took a long pull.

"You went on a pretty wild trip out there. Do you remember what you did? What you said? Anything?"

Gabriel closed his eyes and tried to visualise the interior of the Landcruiser. Him and Eli in the front, the snoring Ignatyev in the back. He opened them again.

"Nothing. I think I can remember feeling my shoulder flaring up and you gave me the ketamine. After that, it's just blank."

"God, I'm sorry. I must have miscalculated the dose. Or maybe I just remembered wrong. Maybe it was 0.1 mils per kilo, not one."

Gabriel burst out laughing.

"Jesus! I hope not. Ten times the dosage of horse tranquiliser? I'd have been out like Ignatyev."

Eli wasn't laughing.

A flicker of memory ignited in Gabriel's brain. A wispy image. A man, supine, one bloody eye socket filled with purplish-red mush.

"What did I do to Ignatyev?" he asked. Knowing the answer. Dreading it.

"You did what you said you'd do. More or less. Pulled one of his eyes out, shot him in the leg then emptied your Glock into his face."

Gabriel rubbed his palms across his face, squeezing his eyes shut.

"Did he give up Max before I killed him?"

"Yes. He gave us an address in Moscow: Thirteen Krivoarbatsky Lane."

Gabriel shook his head, wanting to unsee the image now floating in front of his eyes. He reached for the beer bottle. Eli shook her head and held it out of his way.

"Uh-uh. No alcohol for forty-eight hours. That's what Dr Usbayev said. Unless you want to play Russian roulette with your consciousness. No pun intended," she added, winking.

"I suppose a shag's out of the question, then?"

Her eyes popped wide open.

"You're joking, right? You do know you slapped me back there? Even if you were tripping."

"Oh, God. I'm sorry, Eli. My bad. I was just trying to lighten the mood."

"OK, well you may have misjudged that one."

"Moving on, what about Stakhansky?"

"I called him while you were flying high. Told him three Colombians, probably cartel members, would be arriving in Nyurba in a couple of days. He's already assembled a squad to retake New Galaxy. I don't think they'll encounter much resistance. Now that Ignatyev's dead, the others have probably already buggered off. He said he'd pose as Ignatyev. Give the Colombians the guided tour, get them drunk, have them driven back to Nyurba. If all goes to plan, they'll jump back on a plane. If not, he said he'd have them disappeared."

Gabriel lay back on the bed and closed his eyes.

"God, I'm knackered."

"I'm not surprised," Eli said, coming to lie next to him.

She stroked his cheek.

"Get some sleep," she said. "I'll call Tatyana. Arrange our transport out of this one-horse town."

"Stay with me. There, I mean."

Eli opened out her arm and Gabriel lifted his head and lay it on her chest. Her heart beating softly against his ear, he drifted away.

* * *

By the time they arrived back in Saint Petersburg, the infection in Gabriel's wound had almost completely cleared up. The flesh was pink, rather than red, matte rather than shiny, and no more pus was leaking from between the stitches.

Picking up the Bentayga at the airport, they drove out to Tatyana's dacha, arriving just after eleven in the morning.

They found the lady of the dacha in the garden, snipping roses with a pair of red-handled secateurs. Each long-stemmed scarlet bloom went into a wooden trug she carried in the crook of her left elbow. Her gardening attire was remarkable. A loose cobalt-blue top made of some silky material that shimmered in the sun. A pair of tight, white jeans cut off at mid-calf. Wedge-heeled espadrilles, their natural rope soles a contrast to the tangerine ostrich skin from which the rest of the shoes were made. As they approached, she straightened and turned, placed the secateurs in the trug beside the roses, and waved.

"My two darlings are back in civilisation!" she called, smiling broadly. "Oleg was pleased. So am I. Now I have two knights in shining armour!"

She placed the trug at her feet and held her arms wide. When they were within hugging distance, she embraced them, first Eli, then Gabriel, kissing each three times and leaving multiple lip-prints on their cheeks.

Eli laughed at the Russian woman's extravagant display of affection.

"You are one of a kind, Tatyana!"

"No, Eliya! I insist you call me Tanya, like Gabriushka, here," she said, reaching out and pinching Gabriel's cheek. "Now, come inside and let's get you some coffee. Or would you like tea? Or champagne? Yes! Champagne. To celebrate liberation of New Galaxy from those Kuznitsa thugs."

Inside the dacha's kitchen, which, thanks to the air conditioning, felt deliciously cool after the heat of the Saint Petersburg summer, Tatyana pulled a bottle of Krug from her fridge. She held it out to Eli.

"Here you are, my darling. You open it. Is feminist, yes? To ask woman to open wine?"

Eli grinned at Tatyana, who seemed to have adopted Eli as a daughter.

"Very feminist. We'll serve Gabriushka first. And the women last."

Tatyana clapped her hands together and laughed, clearly

enjoying herself now that the threat posed by Kuznitsa had been removed.

"Oh, yes. Gentlemen first!"

The champagne poured, and a tray of blinis, sour cream and caviar laid out on the table, the three unlikely friends – Russian billionaire, English and Israeli assassins – toasted the success of the operation.

"*Za tvoe zdorov'e!*"

Gabriel took a long pull on the bone-dry champagne.

"Has Oleg cleared Kuznitsa out of New Galaxy then?"

Tatyana placed her flute on the table.

"One hundred percent. All vermin gone. Pah!" She clapped her hands. "Oleg and his men shoot all Kuznitsa men dead. Bury in worked-out part of mine. Is fitting, yes? What you call poetic justice. They wanted share of mine. Now they are there for all of eternity."

"Did he say anything about a visit from any Colombians?"

Tatyana frowned.

"No. Why?"

"Just before we snatched Ignatyev, he took a call. Someone evidently told him that three guys from Compañeros Blancos were coming," he paused briefly, "from Medellín. We said we were their lawyers, so things got kinetic for a while."

Tatyana frowned.

"What is *kinetic*?"

"Sorry. Army jargon. Ignatyev attacked us. We had to fight him to a standstill."

Tatyana turned to Eli.

"You are good fighter? Israelis very tough people."

Eli nodded.

"I'm an excellent fighter, Tanya," answered, earning herself a smile for her use of the nickname.

Gabriel could see how Tatyana was attempting to lead the conversation away from the Colombians. He wanted more information. He wasn't sure why. She was entitled to do business with whoever she wanted, up to and including members of a drugs cartel, he supposed. But why had she been so eager to present them as honest businessmen? He decided to try again.

"Are there a lot of private equity firms in Colombia?"

She shook her head, wary again; he could see it in the way the muscles at the corners of her eyes tightened a fraction.

"Not many."

"But Compañeros Blancos fitted the bill as investors?"

"Yes. Like I said before."

Was that a flash of irritation in her voice? Her eyes had widened and he'd caught the briefest expression of, what – hostility, anger, fear? – flitting across those normally unblemished features.

"And none of the firms in London, or New York, or even Moscow met the necessary criteria?"

Tatyana clanked her drink down on the table.

"Why so many questions, Gabriushka? You cleared out rats from New Galaxy. We celebrate, yes? Not conduct due diligence into my business partners."

Her face was pale. She glanced at Eli, clearly looking for support, but Eli remained silent.

"They're a drugs cartel, aren't they? Medellín? I mean it's not exactly overburdened with exportable commodities, is it? And as far as I'm aware, the only people making enough money out there to invest in a diamond mine are the ones in the drugs trade."

Tatyana glared at Gabriel. He looked away for a second, to lower the threat level he knew he was posing. A basic animal instinct, to break eye contact. The difference here was that he was no subservient creature in the pecking order, however large the disparity in their assets. Not a predator, either, but someone who, as a friend, wanted a straight answer to a straight question.

She took another long pull on her drink, emptying the glass. Then she refilled it.

35

Fixing Gabriel with an icy stare he had not so far witnessed, Tatyana began to speak.

"In 1976, I was very young girl. Sixteen. Our town was allocated to manufacture of machine tools. My mother was cleaner in nearby lathe plant. No money. No husband. No," she frowned, "anything. Just working all time to put little more food on table, keep children warm. Nobody got fat under Communism. Except Party bosses.

"I did not want to be burden. My mother, she had three more kids apart from me. All younger. So, I left home. Travelled to Moscow. When I arrive, I get job as cleaner in Ministry of Labour and Social Problems. Just like my Mother. One day this *apparatchik* – you know this word, Gabriushka?"

Gabriel nodded.

"A Party functionary. A minor official."

She nodded and took a sip of her champagne, then gestured for Eli to refill her glass.

"Yes. So, this man, he sees me at work. He is working late. He asks my name. Soon afterwards, he is working late again and again. In end, he asks me to come for a drink with him in special club for men like him. Party men.

"Of course, I say yes. Maybe he likes me, I think. Maybe he will buy me gifts. Maybe he will marry me." She sighed. "Instead, he rapes me. Then his friends, they rape me also. They have Party photographic artist there. He takes pictures and also eight millimetre films."

Gabriel heard Eli inhale sharply.

"After this moment, my life is changed. I become Party whore. But, in process, I get to know very powerful, important men. One of these men, I do marry. In 1989. Two years later, Soviet Union," she puffed out a breath and spread her hands in a slow, unfolding gesture. "Poof! Gone. Exploded. Now, money men take over. Deals are done everywhere. Factory bosses sell their factories to themselves, or their friends, in secret auctions. 'Yours for one thousand rubles, Comrade.' Generals, they sell off weapons. Pride of Soviet Union sold for couple of cents on the dollar. Does not matter who is customer, as long as they have cash. Good old greenbacks, yes?

"My husband, he is in charge of three power stations and gas pipeline also. One day he is manager, on salary of two hundred rubles per month, next day he is managing director. Now he pays himself one million US *per annum*, and has also eighty-five percent stake in newly named ElectroGaz.

"Trouble is, for my husband, he has double-crossed business partners. I do not know who this outfit are, but he says they are Latin Americans. He boasts that they are stupid. Calls them *suka-pidorasy*, all worst insults. One day, he flies to Colombia to have meeting with these stupid bitch-faggots. Guess what? They shoot him in face, then cut his throat and pull out tongue through hole in throat. They send pictures. Not just of dead husband. Also of me. From time at Party club. My stupid husband, he takes porn photos of his wife to Colombia to show off.

"Now, I am widow. But also rich widow. One year later, I meet Genady Garin. We fall in love. He proposes to me in Saint Petersburg, on steps of Saviour on the Spilled Blood. So Tatyana Levtoshenko who became Tatyana Talikashvili became Tatyana

Garin. Genady was already successful businessman. But with my money, Garin Group expands. Moves from gemstones into precious metals and then saffron and other extremely rare commodities. All is going so well. Grigori is born in 1995. Then all changes.

"Those Colombian *suka-pidorasy*, they arrive in Saint Petersburg, in HQ building of Garin Group. They bring simple proposal. Cut them in or world gets to see porno of Tatyana Garin, CEO of Garin Group. We had no choice. Stock price would go into freefall. So they become minority partners in New Galaxy. Rest, you know."

She shrugged, and drained her champagne, then gestured again to Eli for a refill.

In the silence immediately following Tatyana's story, Gabriel could hear a clock ticking, and his own pulse rushing in his ears. He could think of no words. Nothing that might offer some comfort to Tanya.

"If the Colombians from Compañeros Blancos were the same guys who've been blackmailing you, there's a good chance they're already dead," Eli said. "Is it possible? That they're the same, I mean?"

Tatyana nodded.

"Yes. Is possible. Is highly possible. I would say, one hundred percent possible. CB is front company. Money laundering operation. Behind is small outfit called El Nuevo Medellín. But suppose Oleg did not kill them. Maybe they arrive and leave before he gets there with his team?"

Gabriel worked through the timings in his head.

"No," he said. "When we were there, Ignatyev said they were on their way. We called Oleg the same day. He went into action the next day. There's no way the Colombians could have got to New Galaxy before he did."

Tatyana nodded. Then her brow furrowed.

"I must make call. Immediately. To Oleg."

She stood up and left the room.

Gabriel looked at Eli.

"Wow! Some story. Talk about from rags to riches."

"Aren't you forgetting something?" Eli said in a flat voice. "There was another 'R' in her journey. Rags to *rape* to riches, Gabriel." Her lips tightened and she shook her head, eyes closed, as if trying to dislodge the image of a young Tatyana being gang-raped by Communist Party officials. "I hope he was alive when they gave him the necktie," she said, finally. "Sometimes they make you watch in a mirror. I hope they did that to him."

Tatyana arrived back a few moments later. She was still frowning.

"Not good news?" Gabriel asked.

"No. Oleg showed Colombians round mine, then they left. He said they told him they were visiting all global assets."

"What does that mean for you?"

"Oh, for me? It means I am still being blackmailed. For Garin Group, it means we still do business with *suka-pidorasy.*"

Tatyana insisted that Gabriel and Eli stay with her while they waited for Oleg Stakhansky to return from Nyurba. When he did, a week later, it was with a mixture of news.

Over coffee and delicious ginger biscuits Tatyana had had flown up from Saint Petersburg – "the best baker in whole of Russia, I swear," she said, presenting the delicate spiced biscuits on a Sèvres porcelain plate – Stakhansky presented his report.

When he and his men – fifty hand-picked ex-Russian Army fighters, seasoned in the mother country's wars in Afghanistan and Chechnya – arrived at New Galaxy, they discovered that all of the Kuznitsa enforcers had either fled or were lying dead from gunshot wounds in the mine's central administrative compound.

He'd interviewed as many staff as he could find who'd seen or heard anything and pieced together what he felt was a reasonably accurate story.

One miner returning from a shift had seen Gabriel and Eli arriving. He'd described them as, "Finance-types. You know, westerners. You could tell by their clothes." After the shootout with the guards and the kidnapping of Ignatyev, the remaining Kuznitsa men had fallen to arguing. One, named Varyonovich, a "sadistic bastard," according to a second miner, had called the staff together and announced that he was now in charge as Ignatyev's second in command. He had been immediately shot by another guard, at which point a full-blown firefight erupted between the remaining Kuznitsa men. The staff scattered, diving for cover or running for their lives if they were far enough away from the boiling centre of the fighting.

The site foreman had ordered the bodies to be collected and slung into the scoop of a massive earthmover and driven to a remote area of the mine, as far from the road as it was possible to get without straying beyond the perimeter. There, the bodies were dumped in a pile, to be disposed of by scavengers. By the time Stakhansky arrived to see the dead for himself, airborne and ground-dwelling creatures had begun the task of reducing the bodies to bones, and sometimes not even that.

"What happened with the Colombians?" Gabriel asked.

Stakhansky shrugged.

"They arrived a couple of days later. Three of them. Dressed the way gangsters do when they hit the big time. Armani suits, Gucci shoes. They stank of cologne. One had alligators tattooed on his cheeks. Odd look for private equity," he said, flicking a look at Tatyana, a glance Gabriel registered, even though it disappeared almost as soon as it arrived on Stakhansky's weather-worn features.

"What did they want?" Eli asked.

"To look around the place. I drove them down into the mine in an SUV, gave them each a few rough chips as souvenirs, which they loved, by the way," he said with a crooked grin. "Showed them over the books, gave them a decent dinner, got them drunk on the directors' stock of wine, put them up in the guest quarters, then I drove them personally back to Nyurba."

"Did they say anything out of the ordinary, Oleg?" Tatyana asked, breaking her silence for the first time since he had begun his narrative.

He shook his head and then took a swig of coffee before speaking.

"Nope. Told me they were on a global tour of their investments. Big talk, you know? *Khvastalis'*," he added, switching to Russian. Then he looked at Eli and smiled. "Sorry, where are my manners? It means *bragging*. They were full of it. How much money they had in mining, forestry, foreign companies, the works. Real arrogant types, especially Mr Alligatorface."

As Stakhansky finished the story, Gabriel was putting the finishing touches to his own particular version of events. The three men were clearly at the top of the cartel known as El Nuevo Medellín. Maybe at the very top. The private equity cover was a reasonable one, since virtually nobody outside that elite club of players really knew what it meant. *A bit like hedge funds*, he thought. But the equity stakes they took in legitimate businesses were funded by drug money, of that he had no doubt. He'd come up against a Colombian drug boss once before, a particularly nasty specimen named Diego Toron, but unofficially as "El Bautista" – The Baptist. Toron's speciality had been to "baptise" his enemies, drowning them in a few inches of bathwater. Like many of the evil men, and occasionally women, who had crossed Gabriel's path down the years, Toron was now dead, rotting away in a Brazilian jungle.

So, Mr Alligatorface and his two cronies were the men blackmailing Tanya. Maybe after he'd tracked down Max, he could offer her a measure of peace of mind by going after the Colombians, too. He added it to his mental watchlist. A virtual "most wanted" board with blown-up images of people he'd either killed or intended to, the faces of the dead obscured with black crosses, those of the living unadorned. For now.

Later that day, Tatyana reconvened what she'd dubbed her "Council of War" in the dacha's dining room, a large, rectangular space painted deep red, and decorated with gilt-framed mirrors and paintings by Russian masters. One in particular caught Gabriel's eye. In contrasting halves of grey and gold it depicted a pair of Christlike figures in simple robes and headdresses, astride donkeys, beneath a series of complex mathematical equations.

"You like it?" Tatyana asked, as she took her seat at the head of the table.

"Yes. Who is it by?"

"He is Russian artist. Anatoly Belkin. A genius. During time of Communists, Anatoly risked prison, and worse, for painting without Soviet approval. Brave, like you and Oleg here." She turned to Eli. "And you, Eliya. This painting is called Principles of Equilibrium."

"I like the title," Eli said. "It's what Gabriel and I do. Restore equilibrium. When we can."

She smiled at Tatyana, who nodded her head, returning the smile with one of her own.

"So, Gabriushka. You restored equilibrium in Nyurba for me. Now, I and Oleg," she turned to Stakhansky, who nodded, "will help you restore it for yourself, and for your poor, dead friend. Question. How will you get to Max Novgorodsky?"

"I'm assuming that at some point, he'll learn about what happened in Nyurba. He'll be told that two westerners – 'finance types' according to Oleg's source at New Galaxy – were responsible. I don't know how many westerners he's pissed off enough to want to take out an entire operation, but it must run into the hundreds. Since he's been told I'm dead, I think we still have the element of surprise with us. We know his street address in Moscow, but going in all guns blazing isn't high on my list of strategies."

"A full-frontal assault would be a very bad idea," Stakhansky said. "Kuznitsa is still too strong. Even if you know his address, he will have plenty of protection. You are just two people. He will have dozens of men at his disposal."

Gabriel shook his head.

"Actually, I do want to go in through the front door. Just not as an opponent."

Eli's head jerked round. She stared at him, open mouthed before she shut her jaws with a clack of teeth.

"What?" she exclaimed, outrage visible on her face as clear as the mathematical symbols on the painting behind her.

"It's the only way I can think of that guarantees a shot at Max. I need to be on the inside. I need him to trust me. Then, when he lowers his guard," Gabriel paused and aimed an imaginary pistol. He pulled the trigger.

"Are you literally out of your fucking mind?!" Eli said, raising her voice. "Don't you think there might be oh, I don't know, one or two heavily armed ex-Spetsnaz around him who'll blow your head off the moment you pull out a gun?"

"I'll have to get rid of the muscle first, obviously," he said, calmly. "Then, when it's just me and Max, I'll have plenty of time to explain the way things were, the way things are, and the way things have to be."

Eli opened her mouth to answer, then her phone rang. She clamped her lips together in irritation and pulled her phone out. She glanced at the screen and then frowned.

"It's my dad," she said, sounding genuinely surprised. "I'd better take it. He never calls me."

Gabriel watched her closely, fearing the worst. When people who never called, called, it was rarely to announce a new job or a house move.

As she listened, a single tear rolled from the corner of Eli's left eye. She nodded a couple of times, tremulous, jerky movements as if animated by electric shocks.

"How is she?"

She nodded again and brushed the tear away from the angle of her jaw.

"OK. Yes. Yes. It'll take me day or so."

She placed the phone on the polished tabletop and turned to Gabriel.

"There was an attack outside the Knesset. A gunman. My mum was hit. She's in intensive care. I have to go. I'm sorry. I have to."

Gabriel jumped to his feet and rounded the table before crouching at her left side and hugging her.

"Of course you do. It's OK. Oleg can provide backup. You need to be with her. And your dad."

Tatyana leaned forwards and took Eli's hand.

"Eliya. If you will permit me, I will fly you home on Garin Group plane. It will be less stressful for you, and we can get you there sooner than scheduled flight."

Eli sighed, then nodded.

"Thanks, Tanya. Yes, please. That's very kind of you. Excuse me. I need to pack."

Then she stood, Gabriel at her side, and embraced him, squeezing hard, before running from the room.

* * *

Gabriel drove Eli to Saint Petersburg, Oleg riding shotgun to sort out the details once they arrived at Pulkovo. Gabriel tried to stay off the topic consuming his girlfriend, but she seemed to want to discuss it.

"Dad called again while I was packing. He had more details of the attack. The shooter was an Arab-Israeli guy. Young. Twenty-one, Dad said. He loosed off with an AK-47 on Eliezer Kaplan Street. My mum was about to take a group of schoolchildren round the Knesset. Two of them were killed outright. Another three are in the hospital with Mum. God, those bleeding-heart leftists in the UK, like that idiot I decked at the party. 'You're on the wrong side,' he said to me. Can you believe it? 'The only side in the Middle East that promotes liberal western democratic values,' I asked him. 'You think sharia law would be better?' Fuck! She might die, Gabriel."

"She won't. They have some of the best trauma surgeons in the world. She'll be OK," he said, feeling less confident than he sounded. He'd seen plenty of dead people in his life, and more than a few had gone to their graves with 7.62mm rounds from Kalashnikovs inside them.

. . .

At Pulkovo, Gabriel and Stakhansky escorted Eli into the departure lounge. Stakhansky pointed to a door marked "VIP Security."

"That's us," he said. "I arranged a take-off slot. We have excellent relations with air traffic control at Pulkovo. It helps that we're a majority shareholder in their parent company, but we still have to hurry. I'll need to escort Eli through to the plane door."

Gabriel and Eli exchanged hurried goodbyes.

Gabriel kissed her hard and hugged her.

"Get a message to me when you can, OK?"

"OK."

Gabriel watched Eli's receding form as she left with Stakhansky for the departure lounge. He puffed out his cheeks, feeling a weight in his heart as if someone had encased it in lead. He turned to go and almost collided with a paunchy, middle-aged man wearing a sharp suit and carrying a burgundy briefcase. Behind him walked two hulks in dark suits, cut more to accommodate their muscles than to flatter their physique. They bristled at this stranger's unwanted proximity to their boss, but he waved them away.

Apologising, Gabriel disentangled himself from the trio and wandered back towards the parking lot where he'd left the Bentley. He found a small shade tree and sat with his back to the trunk. *Let her be OK, please. But if she has to die, let Eli get there in time to say a proper goodbye. Let her hold her Mum's hand and kiss her and not find her already dead.* He closed his eyes and let the sun warm his face.

It's down to you, now, Britta whispered from somewhere far away. *Eli won't be coming back. Her mum's going to die. She'll be grieving. Like my parents. Like Theo and Freja. Like Jarryd.*

You don't know she's dead. Eli said she was in the ICU. If anybody can treat a gunshot wound, it's an Israeli trauma surgeon.

You know that's not the way it works. Death follows you around. You wrote it. Don't you remember?

Maybe it does. But what happened to Eli's mum had nothing to do with me. Nothing! Some crazy gunman thousands of miles away doing what he no doubt thought was justified. How can that be on me?

I dunno, Wolfie. So listen, how are you going to avenge me, hej*? Tell me that. You going to go charging in there like a horse in a china shop?*

It's 'bull.' As I'm sure you know. I haven't decided yet. But I need to get close enough to Max to be sure of a kill. He's too well protected for anything long range. Plus I want to see it in his eyes. The moment when he realises that I'm the one taking his life, and understands why.

Up close and personal. I like it. You should join Kuznitsa.

Join? I was thinking more of going in posing as some kind of tradesman or delivery driver.

Nah. Too many problems. He won't talk to people like that directly. He'll have a minion. That's the right word isn't it?

Yeah. Spot on.

So, he'll have this guy who takes care of all the daily shit the rest of us have to deal with ourselves.

What then?

You remember that guy in the departure lounge? The little guy in a suit?

Oligarch plus bodyguards.

Exactly.

You think I should get a job as Max Novgorodsky's bodyguard?

Why not?

Why not? Well, for a start, because that's pretty well impossible. I mean, what do you suggest I do? Stroll up and ring the front doorbell and say, "Oh, hi, I'm looking for work protecting a crime boss. Gizza job?"

Don't be a fool! Of course not!

What, then?"

I don't know. But you're a smart guy. You can work something out. You always do. Talk to Oleg. I bet he's got some good contacts in helpful places. Head of security for Garin Group? If he hasn't got some dodgy people in his little black book, then I'm not dead.

Gabriel opened his eyes. He'd remembered something. A time when he'd pulled off a cute move. Tracking down the kidnapped wife and daughter of a British pharmaceuticals executive, he'd got a job as a nightclub bouncer by the simple expedient of nobbling the existing muscle, leaving him unconscious on the pavement then waltzing in and demanding his job from the bar manager.

Oleg appeared on the pavement outside the terminal building, checking the traffic before jogging across the road and back to the Bentley. Gabriel joined him, and they climbed in together.

"Did she get away OK?" Gabriel asked.

"Everything's fine. She'll be airborne in about ten minutes."

Contacts. Strings you could pull. It all came down to that in the end. Well now Gabriel felt he needed to start tugging a few strings of his own.

On the motorway heading back to the dacha, Gabriel spoke. Now that Eli was gone, he used Russian.

"I've got an idea for how to get Max. I need to be close to him. Really close."

Stakhansky turned in his seat to look at Gabriel.

"What do you mean 'close'? He always has plenty of female company, so ..."

Gabriel shook his head impatiently.

"Not that kind of close. Close like personal protection."

"Okaay," Stakhansky said, drawing out the two syllables in the universal sound of doubt mixed with curiosity. "How?"

"How about we stage an attack? Knock out a couple of his minders. Then I put myself in the right place at the right time to get hired?"

"Why not just kill Max if we're in position to knock out the minders?"

"Because I want to look him in the eye. This is personal. Otherwise, I could just plant a bomb under his car."

"I'm not sure you could, but in any case – no wait!"

Gabriel detected the sudden increase in interest from Stakhansky. It was the sound of a man seeing, in a flash of insight, a way to make things happen.

"What?"

"It's actually not a bad idea. Plenty of Russian crime bosses have been killed by insiders. It's either them or rival soldiers conducting an ambush." He spread his hands, "Or their health fails. But you don't want to wait on the off chance Max goes down with cancer, do you?"

Gabriel shook his head.

"No. No I don't. Even if he only had a day to live I'd still put a bullet in his brain. The question is, how do I get to him?"

Stakhansky looked up at the ceiling. Then back at Gabriel.

"I have an idea. But it's risky. Very risky."

"How risky?"

"It depends."

"On what?"

"On whether you could cope with a spell in a Russian prison."

"I coped with being tortured in the Iranian security ministry. And I escaped."

"Fair enough. So, I've been researching Kuznitsa. I have a few contacts in that world."

Told you so, a disembodied Swedish voice said from somewhere between Gabriel's ears.

"And?"

"And they recruit their muscle from one specific state correction institute. Maximum security. Its official name is Penal Colony Seventy-Three."

"And its *unofficial* name?"

"Red Dog."

"How did it get the name?"

"The guards there used to feed the bodies of prisoners they'd shot while escaping to the guard dogs."

"Charming. So where is Red Dog?"

"It's about one hundred and twenty kilometres west of Nizhny Novgorod, which is—"

"Max's hometown, yes. I read his file, brief as it is. So he's loyal to his alma mater, is that it?"

Stakhansky shrugged.

"I don't think loyalty has much to do with it. Red Dog houses some of the worst criminals in the Russian penal system. Murderers, rapists, arsonists. Not the really crazy ones, though. They're all down in Black Dolphin. Even you wouldn't want to spend time there, no matter who you wanted to kill."

"That bad, eh?"

"Depends what you mean by 'that bad.' How about cannibals, serial killers, terrorists, paedos and maniacs? That's an actual Russian legal category, by the way."

"All right, so Black Dolphin, no, but Red Dog, yes. What shall I do, kill someone?"

"You'd do that to get to Max?"

"At this point I'd be quite happy to kill lots of people to get to Max."

"No need. The quickest and safest route would be to assault a cop. Our current president takes a very dim view of that kind of thing."

"But how could I guarantee I'd get sent to Red Dog?"

"You couldn't. But Lavrenty Boykov could."

"Who's Lavrenty Boykov?"

"He's the Moscow Deputy Attorney General, and he's married to the sister of Garin Group's chief legal officer. Boykov has expensive tastes, but not the salary to go with them. We help him square the circle with a retainer as a legal consultant."

Gabriel smiled.

"So your contacts go from the lowlifes to the high, is that it?"

"Something like that. You get yourself arrested. I'll see to it that Boykov has you sentenced to Red Dog. What will you do when you're inside?"

"Prisons operate by rules, set by the governor and by the prisoners. But I'm not going to play by any rules. I'm going to make a holy terror of myself. And if that's where the killing starts, so be it. While you monitor me, I'll find the biggest, ugliest, toughest inmate and beat the shit out of him. Then the next biggest. Then the next. Then maybe a couple of guards. Then I need you to pull me out. I reckon that will be enough to bring me to Max's attention."

"That simple, eh?"

"Have you got a better plan?"

"Hey, you're the one on a mission, not me. You want to go and cause trouble inside Red Dog, be my guest. I can get you in, and I can get you out. But if some twenty-stone fucker decides he wants you to call him Daddy, don't come crying to me."

"Fine. I won't."

36

ALDEBURGH

To his irritation, Scott Randolph discovered that every single hotel, pub, Airbnb and plain, old-fashioned B&B in Aldeburgh was full when he began calling round to book his accommodation. Finally settling for a room in a chain hotel just off the A12, twenty-five miles from his destination, he threw some clothes and the essentials of his trade into a battered leather holdall and set off.

The following day, a Tuesday, he changed into what he imagined would allow him to blend in with the holidaymakers and left the hotel for Aldeburgh. The brown leather boat shoes, faded pink cargo shorts and pale-blue-and-white hooped polo shirt were like a cloak of invisibility. Almost every single man strolling along the High Street wore a version of this middle-class mufti. One guy a few years older than Randolph had done a double take as they passed outside a fish and chip shop. So closely did their outfits match, he must have thought he had a doppelgänger in town.

Over his right shoulder, Randolph had slung an army surplus

messenger bag in faded khaki canvas. Another bullseye. But whereas his fellow men might have filled their bags with sun cream, well-thumbed thrillers and the keys to their Audis or BMWs, his contained an altogether more practical assemblage of items: a ruggedised laptop capable of functioning after being dropped from up to six feet; a compact digital SLR with telephoto lens; a burner phone; a pair of wigs, one blond, one a striking shade of red; two pairs of sunglasses; a set of lockpicks; a small bottle of Rohypnol – the "date rape" drug; and, because above all else, Scott Randolph was a cautious man, an eight-inch leather tube filled with lead shot, with a looped handle stitched securely into one end.

He caught sight of his reflection in a plate glass shop window, and smiled. He fitted right in. OK, so he was a little on the heavy side, and the calves beneath the hems of his shorts were whiter than the tanned legs on display elsewhere in the town. But in all other respects he was, he felt, Mr Average. Even the receding hairline disguised by a super-short buzzcut put him slap-bang in the middle of the bell curve.

So, Scotty, he said to the man who looked out of the shop window at him, *let's get to work, shall we?*

Yes, but where? These days most of Randolph's work was computer-based. Despite the popular image of the private eye snooping through bedroom windows or following straying spouses to out-of-the-way hotels, he could get ninety-nine percent of what he needed from databases these days. However, he hadn't completely forgotten how to be a proper investigator.

He sauntered through the town, heading for the beach south of the Brudenell Hotel. The local plod had done a reasonable job of shutting down press coverage beyond the basics, but the basics were enough to start with. He decided to ask the first uniformed copper he saw.

He passed the last house on the right, beside a busy boatyard, and turned left, crossing a full car park, and walking onto the stony beach. He fished a large white handkerchief from a pocket and mopped his forehead, which was dripping with sweat. Out on the water, small sailing boats heeled over, making swooping turns into the wind. Yachts? Dinghies? Randolph wasn't a sailor and could no more have distinguished a catamaran from a cutter than he could a barge from a banana boat. They looked pretty, though and added to what he thought of as the timeless charm of the English seaside.

Crunching over the stones, he scanned the beach and spotted his target. A uniform was talking to a guy dressed in a waiter's outfit of black trousers and a white shirt outside the Brudenell Hotel. He wandered over and waited for them to finish their conversation.

"Still talking to people about the murder?" he asked in a conversational tone.

The PC shrugged. He towered over Randolph and looked cool despite the heat, no sweat dripping from beneath the black baseball cap.

"Someone has to, sir," he said, none too warmly. "And you are…?"

"I used to be job. Did my fair share of door-to-doors while my mates were off chasing villains. I'm a PI now. You know anything about what happened here?"

"Yes."

That's all? Yes? You're a tough one to crack, aren't you?

Randolph essayed his best we're-all-mates-together smile.

"Hey, I'm not looking for inside info or anything. Just, the guy who was killed. He was a local, right?"

PC Man-mountain glared down at Randolph.

"I'm afraid I can't say anything about that."

"All right, I get it. I'm not ex-Suffolk Constabulary. Just some nosy bugger from Essex."

He made a show of looking both ways and behind him. A comic-book move, but one he had found seemed to work. *He lowered his voice.*

"There's a ton for you if you tell me where I can find out a little more. If not from you, then someone with lower morals."

The uniform stared into Randolph's eyes.

"I'm going to count to three. If you're still here, I'm going to arrest you for attempting to bribe a police officer."

Randolph turned on his heel and left. *Uptight twat.*

. . .

Having found a friendly-looking pub, he perched on a bar stool, sipping a pint of lager, idly attempting to chat up the barmaid, who was half his age and probably half his weight, too.

"I heard you had a bit of excitement up here a week or so ago," he said.

"Oh, yeah! It was like something off the telly. This guy, right, he was just walking on the beach and he got shot. Like, actually shot! And this woman, too, which is really sad."

"Local boy, wasn't he?" Randolph asked, keeping his voice casual despite the feeling he had hit pay dirt.

"I think so. I'm just here for the summer. Down from uni. My parents live here. In Church Farm Road."

Randolph finished his pint and ordered a second.

"And one for yourself," he added.

"Thanks," she said with a smile. "We put the money in the tips jar, if that's OK. I don't actually drink, so, you know …"

"It's fine," he said. "Smart girl. Spend it on something more useful than alcohol."

He accepted the brimming glass with a nod of thanks, but then a rowdy group of young men came into the pub and demanded her attention. Randolph didn't mind. He'd made a start. He wandered over to a table by the window looking out onto the High Street. An old man sat there absent-mindedly scratching the head of a black lab while he read a local paper.

"Mind if I join you?" Randolph asked.

The old guy looked up from his paper and smiled.

"Be my guest."

Randolph sat, placed his glass in the centre of the table and sighed.

"Such a shame something like that had to happen here, of all places."

"You from round here, then? Don't think I've seen you before."

Randolph shook his head.

"Not any more. My parents have a place over on Leiston Road, but I moved down to Essex years ago. For work."

"Probably for the best, for a young guy. Not much here except bar work and the boat yard. What line of work you in, then?"

"Police. Was, I mean. I'm an investigator now. I still work with the force now and then, as a civilian consultant." A lie, but a plausible one.

"You investigatin' the shootin', then? Place was crawlin' with coppers a week ago but it's died down now."

"Me? No. Just a holiday." Randolph made a show of looking at the man's pint glass, which was a quarter full. "Can I get you another?"

The man smiled.

"Never say no to a pint, that's my motto. Yes, please. Pint of Adnams Southwold Bitter. And some cheese and onion crisps if you've a mind to be generous. For Bess."

He nodded at the dog, who, hearing her name, raised her head and seemed to Randolph to smile at him.

He laughed.

"Does she want something to drink, too?"

"Ha! That's good. No, just the crisps, thanks."

Randolph returned with two pints and a packet of crisps for the lab. He opened the packet.

"What d'you do? Feed them to her one at a time?"

The old man shook his head.

"Too slow. Just put it on the floor."

Randolph did as he was told and watched, amused, as the dog delicately placed one forepaw on the sealed end of the bag and proceeded to scoop the crisps out with the other, before gobbling them down.

He raised his glass.

"Cheers!"

"Cheers! Didn't catch your name."

"Bob."

"Cheers, Bob! Good health."

Randolph waited while the old man took a long pull on his pint.

"He was a local boy, the guy who got shot. That's what I heard," Randolph said.

"Oh, yeah? Well, you've been listening to the wrong people, Bob. He weren't no local. It was a newcomer what got shot by him but not the one who got shot dead, if you see what I mean."

Randolph frowned, trying to untangle the man's grammar as well as his strong Suffolk accent.

"Sorry, so the newcomer?"

"Lad called Wolfe. Took one in the shoulder. I expect they had him over down to Ipswich to patch him up."

"But he's not local?"

"Well," the old man drawled, "he bought a place here a year or so back, but he's hardly what you'd call local, is he?"

The penny dropped. Randolph realised he was speaking to a member of that special breed of Englishman who reckons you a stranger unless your grandparents are buried in the churchyard.

"No. I suppose not. But if he wasn't the victim, who was?"

The old man furrowed his brow.

"You ask a lot of questions for someone who reckons he's not investigatin' the case."

Randolph spread his arms wide and aimed for a contrite smile.

"What can I say? Old habit? Once a copper, always a copper."

This seemed to satisfy the old man.

"Eh, well, you're probably right. Merchant Navy, me," he said, placing a gnarled hand on his chest, fingers spread. "Thirty years, man and boy. Still get a thrill when I see the old girls out on the water."

Randolph smiled.

"Here, finish that and I'll get you another," he said, calculating that the third pint would be the tongue loosener, whereas the fourth might send his informant into the land of Nod.

Over their newly purchased drinks, Randolph asked the old man another question.

"Must be hard seeing a stranger turning life here upside down. Coming in, firing a gun. Even at a newcomer."

The man's watery eyes opened wide.

"Oh, complete chaos for a day or two. Holidaymakers practically abandoned the beach. Then, you know, one goes back, then another, and pretty soon it's back to normal. But it were a funny two days, I can tell you."

"Was he staying here, then? This stranger?"

The old man nodded.

"Over at Bev Watchett's place. Right at the end of Thorpe Road."

Randolph nodded, as if familiar with the address.

"Oh, yeah. Thorpe Road."

Having got what he needed Randolph finished his drink, thanked the man for his company, scratched the dog under the chin. And weaved towards the toilets. *Next stop, Thorpe Road.*

An hour later, sitting in the shade cast by a huge steel sculpture of a scallop shell, Randolph pulled out his phone and called Robert Finnie.

"Yes, Scott. What do you have for me?"

"Wolfe was shot but not killed. The dead man wasn't from round here. I spoke to a neighbour of the woman who rented a room to him. She said he was tall and blond."

"Name?"

"Didn't know or couldn't tell me if she did."

"And you're sure Wolfe's alive?"

"I spoke to some old boy in the pub. The type who knows everyone's business, you know? He said he was wounded. That's all."

"OK, good. Thanks, Scott."

* * *

Finnie walked to the end of his garden. He'd been sitting under an apple tree, enjoying a gin and tonic, when his man had called, but felt he needed the security of another thirty metres between him and the house for his next call.

The gravel-voiced Russian sounded amused to hear his voice.

"Robert! How is my favourite milord?"

"Fine, thanks, Max."

"And the delightful Lady Angela? In good health?"

"Perfectly well, thank you."

"And your children. Doing well at university?"

Champing down on the bit of his impatience, Finnie maintained the fiction Max seemed to find amusing that this was merely a social call.

"Yes. Tom is enjoying himself at Liverpool and Emily is about to graduate from Queens in Belfast."

"Well, that is good to hear. And you, Robert. What news do you have to share with me?"

Finnie dropped his voice, even though his garden backed onto the Thames and the next pair of human ears on this bank were at least sixty yards distant.

"Wolfe's not dead. He was wounded and taken to hospital. A man *was* killed, though. Tall and blond."

Finnie listened to the ethereal hiss of the silence between Richmond upon Thames and Moscow. Wondering whether he had angered Max in some way. Fearing, not for the first time, that he had got himself irrevocably entwined with absolutely the wrong man. Finally Max broke the silence.

"Thank you, Robert. Give my regards to Lady Angela and your two darling children. In Liverpool. And Belfast."

Then the line went dead, leaving Finnie with the uneasy feeling that he shouldn't have told Max the cities giving temporary shelter to his children.

* * *

In his office at MOD Rothford, Don Webster was in the middle of a phone call, just as Finnie's was ending. His caller headed the intelligence branch of Suffolk Police. The woman was speaking now.

"I don't know if it means anything, Don, but a man identifying himself as a private investigator has been asking questions in Aldeburgh about your boy, Wolfe."

"Hmm. Mm-hmm. Give a name, did he, this gumshoe?"

"Bob. That's all we got. Probably not his real name."

"Did you—"

"Get him on CCTV? Yes. Aldeburgh's not London, but I had one of my DCs go through what public and private footage there was, and we picked him up. I'm emailing you a couple of pictures and a few additional notes."

"Thanks, Polly. I owe you one."

"Careful, Don. I might hold you to that. Our police commissioner's making a complete pain in the arse of himself."

Don chuckled.

"Want me to send in a kill team?"

She groaned with theatrical despair.

"If only …"

His call with the intelligence commander ended, Don immediately dialled an internal number. It belonged to a man everyone called Mr Fixit, an intensely private individual with virtually no social skills and a fiercely guarded workspace containing, it was rumoured, over four hundred hand-painted Star Wars action figures, arranged in order of their first appearance in the series of movies. Mr Fixit – real name Keith Took – lived a monkish existence away from the rest of the operators and agents, but roamed freely over the internet like a migrating swallow.

"Yes, Colonel Webster, sir?"

"I'm sending you a couple of pictures of a private investigator. Ex-Essex Police. Can you see if you can track him down for me, please, Keith?"

"Yes, sir."

37

MOSCOW

At 10.45 a.m., a week after getting back from Pulkovo Airport with Stakhansky, Gabriel swaggered into a barber's shop on Merzlyakovskiy Lane in central Moscow. He'd bought a bottle of vodka from a minimarket on the way and had worked his way through a quarter of it already. He was now Tikhon Lisanovich, a taxi driver, and had fake Russian identity documents provided by Stakhansky to prove it.

For his debut and, he hoped, only performance within the Russian penal system, he'd selected an outfit he felt sure would send the right signals to its functionaries. A knock-off Louis Vuitton-branded T-shirt, the LV logo almost comically badly rendered in fluorescent orange ink; acid-washed jeans, their normally tough fabric bleached, denatured and partially disintegrated by the action of the chemical; and a pair of cheap, caramel-coloured cowboy boots.

One of the white-jacketed men cutting, combing and clippering behind the polished chrome-and-black-leather chairs glanced up as the bell above the door pinged, then back at the cropped head of his customer.

"Nothing for thirty minutes, chief," he said without looking round.

"Tha's OK, I'll wait," Gabriel slurred in Moscow-accented Russian, before slumping on the padded bench that ran along the back wall of the shop.

Eighties-era, American heavy metal belted out from ceiling-mounted speakers. Gabriel contented himself with frequent pulls on the bottle and borderline-aggressive stares at the three other men waiting their turn for a haircut.

The barber who'd originally spoken to him beckoned him to the now-vacant chair.

"What're you looking for, chief?" he asked, looking at Gabriel in the mirror above the varnished pine shelf on which the tools of his trade were arrayed.

"I wan' it very very short and very very blond. Like him," he said, not having to act drunk anymore, as he pointed at a punky-looking model in a poster

The barber nodded.

"No problem. We take cash here. That OK with you, chief?"

Gabriel laughed and fished out a wad of notes Stakhansky had provided.

"This all right?"

The barber smiled and began work.

After a final tweak and a rub with hair gel, Gabriel, now thoroughly oiled, staggered from the dimly lit shop into the bright Moscow sunshine and immediately collided with a pair of glamorous young women striding along on towering heels, their wrists crooked to accommodate half a dozen glossy shopping bags each, slathered with brand names known from Los Angeles to Beijing.

"Hey! Watch where you're going, idiot!" one of them said,

before they disentangled themselves from "Tikhon Lisanovich" and carried on their way.

"Sorry, ladies!" he shouted after their retreating backs.

He turned away and headed for Red Square, the venue he'd agreed on with Stakhansky for his command performance.

Outside a branch of McDonald's on Mokhovaya Street, he stripped off the T-shirt and chucked it into a bin overflowing with greasy food wrappers and crushed Coke cans. Vodka bottle swinging from his left hand, he marched into the centre of the square, singing "Sex Bomb" by Tom Jones at the top of his voice. Not a good singer when sober, Gabriel was woefully off-key drunk and began attracting stares from passers-by that ranged from anxious to amused, irritated to hysterical. A couple of younger men snapped him on their phones and he mugged for their pictures, striking heroic poses and using the opportunity to scan the milling tourists for his target. He spotted him almost at once.

Aha! There you are! Come on, then, do your civic duty.

He continued singing, switching to a medley of rock songs he'd listened to while waiting for his haircut. A small crowd had gathered around him and he worked it hard, sashaying up to a couple of teenaged girls, who were shrieking with laughter as they videoed him, and going down on one knee as he wailed up at them.

"I wanna make luurve to ya, all niiight long, baaaybee!"

Then, like a dropped ice cream on hot summer tarmac, the crowd melted away. *Showtime!*

He got to his feet and turned round to find himself face to face with one of Moscow's finest, a city cop, eyes narrowed, hands on hips, which meant the right lay on the butt of his pistol. *Makarov,* Gabriel thought, unable to resist categorising the handgun, even in his inebriated state.

"Oh! Morning, ociffer!" he said cheerily, making sure to blow a gust of vodka-infused breath towards the cop's face. "Sorry, I don' do requests."

"Get your shirt on, lose the bottle, and get the fuck out of my square," the cop deadpanned, jerking his not inconsiderable chin in the direction of Varvarka Street.

"Ah. Now, y'see, tha's the problem. 'Cause, one," he held up his left thumb and bent it back with his other index finger, "I los' me shirt somewhere. Two, I just bought the vodka. An' three, it's not your fuckin' square, it's mine!"

He shouted the last word and pivoted through 360 degrees, arms outstretched, playing to the gallery. The crowd, now forming a rough circle around the pair, applauded wildly.

He felt the cop's hand enclose his left bicep in a vicelike grip and let himself be spun round to find himself staring into the Makarov's muzzle.

"I'm being nice because it's nearly the end of my shift," the cop said in a low voice, too quiet for the smartphones to pick up. "But if you don't fuck off right now, I'm taking you in."

Gabriel squinted at the cop along the pistol barrel. He made a show of thinking, scrunching up his face and looking upwards into the beautiful, clear, summer sky above the city. Then back at the cop.

He nodded.

Then he grabbed the pistol by the barrel, twisted it out of the cop's grip and tossed it away.

"Oops! Too slow, Starsky!" he said.

Even with the alcohol interfering with his judgment, Gabriel was able to anticipate the right hook. He leaned back so that the cop's swinging fist passed harmlessly in front of his face, then butted him on the bridge of his nose.

The cop screamed with pain as the delicate mesh of nerves and blood vessels absorbed the impact of Gabriel's forehead.

Gabriel turned away, arms wide again and bowed to the crowd, waiting for the inevitable.

As they cheered, he noticed a few people's eyes widening, hands flying to cover mouths opened in wide O's, and braced.

A flash of white.

A burst of stars.

An explosion of pain.

Darkness.

* * *

Nose still sheeting blood, the cop handcuffed the prostrate figure in front of him, sheathed his rubber baton, then stood, clutching a handkerchief to his face.

"OK, fogues," he shouted, nasally. "Show's ober."

The crowd dispersed, leaving Police Private Ulanov to radio for a paddy wagon to bring him and the troublemaker in to Police Headquarters at Petrovka 38.

"Say again, Officer Three Eight Six. You're not coming through clearly, over."

Gritting his teeth in pain and frustration, Ulanov tried again, enunciating each word as if to a class of foreign language students.

"I'b id Red Sgware. I deed a prisder dradbord to HQ. Charge: assaultig a bolice obicer. Ober."

"OK, got it that time," the dispatcher said with what Ulanov felt sure was barely concealed laughter. "Stand by. Out."

Ulanov hooked his radio back onto his belt, replaced his blood-soaked handkerchief over his nose and looked down disgustedly at the drunk sprawled unconscious in front of him.

He drew back his right foot and kicked him hard in the ribs.

"Whode square iddit dow, eh?"

* * *

Someone was slapping Gabriel's face. Rhythmically. And none too gently. Left. Right. Left. Right. He opened his eyes to find himself staring up into grey eyes of depthless hostility.

"Ah, so you're awake, now, are you, scumbag?" the police officer asked, giving Gabriel's left cheek a final blow. "Well that's good news for us and shit news for you. You're up before the city magistrates in a couple of days."

The man left, slamming the door behind him.

Gabriel hauled himself to a sitting position and took stock of his situation, trying to think clearly through the throbbing from the back of his skull. He touched a spot near the epicentre of the pain and found a goose egg so tender he had to clench his teeth together to avoid yelling. His living space had been reduced from the guest suite in a billionaire's dacha to a grey-painted cell, maybe seven feet by five, that stank of urine and stale sweat. A stainless-steel toilet and a concrete bench with a thin mattress constituted the entire furnishings of the cell.

His vodka hangover played a dull counterpoint to the sharp jolts of pain from the place the cop had whacked him. Fair play to the guy, though. He had just had his nose broken. Gabriel looked down. During the time he was out, someone had removed his acid-washed jeans and cowboy boots and redressed him in loose, grey pyjamas and a pair of dirty white flip flops.

He heard a scrape of key in lock and looked up.

The cop he'd assaulted was standing there, smiling. Beside him stood a man twice his size, also dressed in the uniform of a Moscow city cop. Not smiling. Both cops entered the cell, and Broken-Nose closed the door behind him.

* * *

After a sleepless night – the pain from his testicles and kidneys kept him awake far more effectively than any amount of caffeine – Gabriel started as the door was flung open.

This time his gaoler was a woman. Sturdily built, with a severe haircut, reducing her brown hair to little more than a spiky cap.

She barked an order at him.

"On your feet!"

He struggled to get up. She crossed the tiny cell in two strides and hauled him to his feet, causing him to emit an involuntary yelp as his bruised groin protested.

Prodding him in the small of the back with a long baton, she marched him down a corridor into a larger cell, though this one contained a handful of other prisoners, all with the same red-rimmed eyes and deathly pallor. She shoved him between the shoulder blades, propelling him into the centre of the cell, and slammed the door shut.

Gabriel looked around at his new cellmates. *Time to do some reputation-building.* He leered at one who seemed to be taking the closest interest in him.

"Hey, pussy. If anyone round here's going to get fucked, it's not going to be me, understand?"

The man looked away hurriedly. Gabriel sensed movement to his right and whirled round.

Two hulks with red, drinkers' noses and thick brow ridges were glaring at him. The man to Gabriel's left slapped his huge hands down onto his thighs. Both little fingers were missing. Someone had inexpertly tattooed a Russian word – убийца – across the remaining six fingers.

"Killer, eh?" Gabriel said. He sauntered over and planted himself in front of the inked giant. "Fuck your mother!"

The giant and his matching companion jumped to their feet, only to stagger backwards and collapse against the wall, gasping for breath and holding their wounded throats where Gabriel's blade-like hands had just lanced in against their larynxes.

Gabriel spun round and eyed the other men in the cell. All avoided eye contact.

"Anyone else?" he asked in a playful tone, not easy as his pulse was hammering in his ears and the pain from the hangover and internal injuries were making him dizzy. "No? Good! Now, I fancy a kip. Hey, fatso!" he said to an overweight, balding guy who'd snagged a corner seat on the bench. "Give me your space and keep this bunch away from me or I'll eat your fucking eyeballs right out of your thick skull."

The fat man complied at once, and Gabriel folded himself into the space he'd vacated, closing his eyes and focusing on slowing his heartrate and smoothing out his ragged breathing. To his relief nobody attacked. Eventually he slept.

* * *

"You!" a man's voice woke him from a dreamless sleep.

Gabriel opened his eyes slowly, but not so slowly he'd get a kick for his trouble. He needed to rebuild his strength.

"Yes, boss?"

"Lisanovich, right?"

"Yes, boss."

"Come with me. Don't know why but somebody's fast-tracked your case. You're up before the magistrate in fifteen minutes."

"What about a lawyer?"

"One's been assigned to you. From the public defender's office," he added with a smirk. "So good luck with that."

Gabriel got to his feet and preceded the cop out of the overcrowded cell. He looked over his shoulder as he went through the door.

"Laters, losers!"

The cop shoved him hard, and Gabriel heard the cell door clang shut behind him.

38

EXAMINING MAGISTRATE'S REPORT

Case number: MOPD31/547768/B544
    Identity of Accused: Tikhon Lisanovich
    Internal Passport No.: 65 92 745509
    Occupation: taxi driver

Charge: Assaulting Police Officer
    Arresting Officer: Police Private P. Ulanov, Badge Number 386.
    Arrest Location: Red Square
    Arrest date: 22.06.18
    Magistrate: Ippolit Matarovsky

Accused was observed by Police Private Ulanov creating a disturbance in Red Square while under the influence of alcohol. Accused was advised to dress himself and move on, at which point, accused assaulted PP Ulanov, breaking his nose. Accused subsequently arrested and charged at Moscow Police Headquarters.

Accused questioned in Moscow Central Magistrates' Court. No evidence in mitigation was offered by accused or his lawyer. Accused appeared hostile, belligerent and several times had to be cautioned for abusive language.

Verdict of the court: GUILTY.
Sentence: two years and four months. No parole.

Accused to serve sentence at Penal Colony Seventy-Three on personal recommendation of Moscow Deputy Attorney General, A. Boykov.

PRISONER TRANSIT REPORT

Prisoner T. Lisanovich collected from Cell 6883, Lefortovo Remand Block D, 07.45, 24.06.18.
Delivered to Prisoner Reception Block, Penal Colony 73, Vyazniki Vladimirskaya Oblast', 13.13, 24.06.18.
Nothing to report. Prisoner docile throughout journey.

PRISON INTAKE REPORT

Prisoner: Tikhon Lisanovich
Internal Passport No.: 65 92 745509
Received from Federal Prisoner Transit Authority 13.13, 24.06.18.
Penal Colony 73, Vyazniki
Vladimirskaya Oblast'.

Interview and assessment conducted by Governor I. Kratovsk.
Prisoner :-
- assigned prison number: 35976264
- made aware of prison rules and procedures
- had rights explained
- scheduled for medical examination
- property recorded and confiscated:
one disposable plastic toothbrush, one western paperback book:
Killing Floor

Prisoner 35976264 indicated he understood rules, procedures and rights,
including property confiscation. Signed acceptance form GN/100487.

* * *

The doctor looked at Gabriel, who was standing naked before him
in the examination room.

"You're a taxi driver, eh?"

"Yes. When I can get the fares."

"Is that how you picked up all those?" the doctor asked, pointing
at the biroed crosses on a human outline drawing on the form on his
desk.

Gabriel grinned.

"What can I say, doc? Sometimes passengers cut up rough."

The doctor smiled. His face had an unhealthy grey tinge. He
looked exhausted, Gabriel thought.

"Ever serve your country, Lisanovich?"

Gabriel shook his head.

"What, and get my balls cut off by Afghans or Chechens? Do I
look stupid?"

The doctor shrugged.

"Well, you just got a couple of years for breaking a cop's nose in
front of witnesses and now you're about to enter the hell they call
Red Dog, so on balance, I'd say, yes, stupid is exactly what you look
like."

Now it was Gabriel's turn to shrug.

"Fair enough. Are we done here?"

"Get dressed, prisoner 35976264."

The doctor signed the medical report with a flourish of a gold fountain pen, then pressed a button mounted on the grey-painted wall to the left of the desk.

"You want me to sign, too?" Gabriel asked as the door opened and a burly guard entered, hand resting on the butt of his Makarov.

"Are you a doctor?"

"No, I'm a taxi driver."

"Then, no, I don't want you to sign. Take him away, guard."

PRISON MEDICAL REPORT

Prisoner: Tikhon Lisanovich

Internal Passport No.: 65 92 745509

Date/time of medical examination: 24.06.18, 16.10.

Doctor: V. Velanovich

Prisoner in good general health.

No obvious signs of persistent or extreme alcohol abuse.

Identifying marks: scars: left cheekbone, left thigh, right thigh (bullet wound), left hand, left trapezius (bullet wound – recent). No tattoos.

Bruising to testicles and kidneys. Probable result from fall.

* * *

Gabriel marched across a sunlit exercise yard in his black prisoner uniform of baggy shirt, trousers and black work boots, which scratched and scuffed in the dry, gritty surface. Every few steps the guard prodded Gabriel in the small of his back with the muzzle of his rifle, a Kalashnikov AK-74. He'd been instructed to keep his hands on the top of his head. The black baseball cap he'd been given felt rough under his fingertips.

"Prisoner, halt!" the guard shouted as they reached the first of a set of three iron gates leading between two steel fences topped with rolls of razor wire.

Gabriel waited while the guard unlocked the first of the gates and ushered him through. The gate banged shut behind them, and, after locking it, the guard pushed and prodded Gabriel along the ten-metre path leading to the middle gate. Twice more the guard repeated the procedure, giving Gabriel time to look around and take stock of his new home until he caused enough trouble and Stakhansky extracted him. He could see no other prisoners, so he guessed they were all being kept inside in communal areas or, probably, given what he'd managed to find out on the internet, in lockdown in their cells.

"Hey! No daydreaming!" the guard shouted. "Get moving."

Gabriel shuffled on as they approached a three-storey block, constructed from brick the colour of thunderclouds. Then he was being shoved into a cell already occupied by three other men, none of them much taller than Gabriel, one a little shorter, and all of them bearing the unmistakeable signs of malnutrition: sunken cheeks, a hollow look about the eyes and a yellowish-grey pallor.

The door slammed shut behind him.

Gabriel sized up the three men looking at him from their bunks. One of the two steel constructions had a free bed on the bottom. His, presumably. He swaggered over to it, then sprang up, using the upper bed rail as a gym bar and bounced to a stop right next to the man occupying the top bunk.

"You're in my bed, shit-for-brains," he said, then seized the man by the shoulders, twisted him round and flung him bodily off the bunk. The man landed awkwardly. Gabriel heard a bone snap.

"You cunt!" the man roared, half in rage, half in agony as he writhed on the hard cell floor. "I'll cut your balls off for that! Get him boys!"

Gabriel jumped down before either of the other prisoners could move. He kicked the prostrate man hard in the left hip, in a spot where the femoral nerve rose to just a couple of centimetres from the surface and which, if injured, would cause immense pain. Over the man's shrieks, he spoke to the other two, who were now regarding him with looks of frank terror.

"Don't know what you're in for," he said, grinning. "And I don't care. I tried to kill a cop, but the little fucker escaped. But while I'm in here, I'm the boss, you understand?"

Neither man said a word.

"You understand?" Gabriel roared.

"Yeah, yeah, we understand, OK? Just calm down," the smaller of the two men said, holding his hands out. "You'll have the guards in here, and you really don't want that."

Gabriel lunged at the man, then squatted and leaned forwards, still grinning manically, into the other guy's face.

"You have no idea what I want. As from now, you work for me. You tell me what you hear. You tell me what you know."

He sensed movement behind him. The wounded man had hauled himself into a sitting position and was pulling something from his trouser pocket.

Gabriel whirled round and stamped on the man's wrist, not hard enough to break it, but enough to force his hand to open. He picked up a dropped toothbrush, the handle sharpened to a needle point. He held it between thumb and forefinger and turned it in the pale light entering the cell through a high-set, grimy window.

"Nice," he said. "You weren't thinking of using this on me, were you?"

The man grimaced, teeth clenched to prevent any more cries of pain. Through clamped jaws he muttered something.

"What was that, comrade? Couldn't quite catch it."

"I'll fucking kill you."

"Ah. Well that's a problem. See, I don't want to be killed by a little billy-goat like you."

The use of the worst imaginable insult was deliberate. The man's eyes bulged and he tried to push himself upright, but the broken bone in his left arm wouldn't allow it, and he slipped sideways, howling with pain.

Gabriel knelt on his thighs, letting his weight dig down onto the quadriceps, a painful move at the best of times, but for a man with an injured femoral nerve, excruciating. Gabriel cocked his head to one side, then flipped the sharpened toothbrush round and held it in a knife-fighter's grip, brush head in his palm. He angled it like a fencer's rapier and advanced it towards the man's left eye.

The man flinched, and turned away. Gabriel grabbed an earlobe in the pincer-like finger and thumb of his other hand and brought the man's head back round to face him.

"Shall I pop your eyeball out on your own toothbrush, my friend? Shall I eat it? Shall I? I could, you know. I mean, if the mood took me. You see, the cop wasn't my first. Just the first I got caught for. There are ten more buried on my grandma's farm out east. Rural plods, couldn't find their arses with both hands, if you know what I mean. I made a mess of them before I killed them. Dunno why. I just don't like cops, I guess. So, am I gonna pull your peepers out for you or not?"

The man managed an infinitesimal shake of the head.

"Not. Please." He swallowed noisily. "OK. You're the boss," he said.

Gabriel jumped to his feet and pocketed the improvised stiletto. He addressed the three men as a group, still with his maniac's grin plastered to his face.

"Good! That's settled, then. And just in case any of you are thinking of staging a night attack, you should know three things about Tikhon Lisanovich." He counted the points off on his fingers. "One, he's a very light sleeper. Two, he doesn't take kindly to people creeping about his cell at night. And three, if one of you tries anything, I'll kill him. Then I'll kill the other two of you for not stopping him. You!" he pointed at one of the uninjured men. "Get a guard in here. Your cellie just fell off his bunk and broke his arm. He needs to see the prison doctor. Get to it!" he barked.

While the big man was being treated in the hospital wing, Gabriel looked down from his bunk. The other two men were reading cheap paperbacks that looked as though they had served longer sentences than the prisoners themselves, so battered were their covers.

"Hey!" he called down. "I need some information."

"What do you want to know?" one of the men asked. He wore glasses and for this reason alone Gabriel had mentally nicknamed him the Prof.

"Ever hear of Kuznitsa?"

"Of course! Everybody in here's heard of them."

"I heard they recruit their enforcers from here. Torpedoes, too."

The man shrugged. "I don't know. I've only been here a month."

"I do," the other man said. His eyebrows met in the middle, creating a dark streak across his otherwise pale forehead. "You're right. It's 'cause their boss came from round here. He takes his pick of the hard cases. When they get out, he has them collected from the gate in a fucking Mercedes, if you can believe it. New suit, washbag full of toiletries, fat envelope of cash, and bam!" he snapped his fingers. "They're set for life. Good job with Kuznitsa. Money, booze, girls, everything, all laid on."

"What if they don't want to work for him?"

The man snorted.

"What? Don't be stupid. It's the dream."

"OK, the dream. Who's his talent scout?"

"What do you mean?"

"Oh, come on! If the boss man is picking out enforcers he must have an inside man who's feeding back to him. I want to know who it is."

"What're you going to do?"

Gabriel grinned and tapped the side of his nose.

"Believe me, comrade, you don't want to know. Now, who is it?"

The man shifted on his bunk and glanced at the door. Then back at Gabriel.

"You didn't get this from me, OK?"

Gabriel shrugged.

"Whatever."

"His name's Ratimir Vladinovsky. But everyone in Red Dog calls him Vlad the Impaler."

"Cool nickname. Why?"

"It was what got him in here in the first place. A rival gang went up against Kuznitsa in southwestern Moscow. Tried to take over the heroin trade. Triads, or something. Maybe Yakuza. Some fucking bunch of slant-eyes, anyway. Their plan failed. Kuznitsa had a man on the inside feeding back intelligence the whole time. Vlad took a team to deal with them. He put the whole leadership on oiled stakes in Gorky Park at two in the morning. You know, naked, with the stakes up their arses. Apparently they took all night to die."

"Sounds like my kind of guy. What does he look like?"

"You can't miss him. He must be at least one metre ninety and a hundred and ten kilos. All muscle. Big fucking knife scar right down the left side of his face. Plus look out for his tattoo. Eyes just below the collar bones. That means 'I'm watching over you.'"

"Thanks, comrade," Gabriel said.

Looks like I just found my route to Max.

39

Gabriel's third cellmate returned to their shared accommodation with his right arm in a cast. He glared at Gabriel but said nothing. During the night, as he tried to sleep, Gabriel thought of Eli. Hoping she was OK. Hoping her mum was alive.

The following morning, as they queued to slop out their toilet bucket, Prof murmured a few words to Gabriel.

"He's been telling the others how he's going to kill you, so you'd better be ready."

"Oh, really? You think he's serious or just bluffing to cover up the fact I beat him like a bitch?"

Prof shrugged and compressed his lips into a thin line as if to stop any words physically from leaving them.

Gabriel wasn't too worried about the big man. For a start, he'd noticed he was right-handed, so his good arm was out of action. And having the top bunk meant a surprise attack at night was even less of a problem: the metal springs stretched between the bed rails were old, rusty and tired, and they squawked in protest however gently the occupant might try to shift his weight in the night.

As for a daytime attack, Gabriel dismissed it. The guy was big, but out of condition. Whereas, for now, and despite his gunshot wound and the monotony of the prison diet, which consisted of dark-brown bread, a watery vegetable soup and the odd scrap of fatty meat, Gabriel was well-nourished and in great shape.

Each day, Gabriel maintained a strict routine over and above that imposed by the prison authorities. As Red Dog was not a maximum security prison, discipline, while harsh, was not punitive. Prisoners were allowed to mingle with each other for one hour a day out in the prison yard and there was a further hour of "free time" after the evening meal, served with depressing regularity at 5.00 p.m. every day except Sundays when it was shifted back by half an hour.

Gabriel spent each of these periods of communal activity watching Vlad the Impaler. His cellmate had done the man only partial justice in his description. Physically, he'd been spot on, although he hadn't mentioned the dead-eyed stare that never left Vlad's huge, flat-planed face. Or the way eyes, nose and mouth each seemed to occupy its own discrete area in that impassive area of pale, Slavic flesh, as if unwilling to acknowledge each other's presence.

According to Prof, who had adopted readily the role of Gabriel's informant within the prison, word had spread that Tikhon Lisanovich was not a man to be trifled with. He'd been instantly classified by the other inmates as a *chasovaya bomba*. A time bomb. A man with a ticking clock in his head and a readiness to explode at short notice. The cop killer story Gabriel had invented on the spur of the moment had solidified into fact and even gained a few extra details, like unexploded RPGs sticking out of the protective corrugated armour of a tank.

The other men mostly ignored or avoided him, which was fine. Although it gave him too much time to mull over the event that had brought him here, to the heart of the Russian penal system, where he was surrounded by rapists, paedophiles and murderers. Each night, while his cellmates slept, sometimes snoring, at others calling out for lost lovers or their mothers, he lay awake until two or three, trying to keep Britta alive in his mind, struggling not to lose his memories of her, her salty laugh, her random way with the idioms of the English language and the times they'd spent together as a fighting unit.

And from the depths of sleep, she'd call to him. Or arise from the grave, smiling and talking to him. Sometimes whole, sometimes with her head burst open. Then they'd have long conversations – whether as part of a dream or a hallucination, he wasn't sure – in which she'd plead with him to exact revenge on her killer.

"Not that Norwegian *torpedo*," she'd scolded him on his first night. "He was just the trigger man. I mean Max. I mean all of them. You'll do that for me, won't you, darling?"

And he'd agreed. Readily. On waking, whether in the pre-dawn gloom or at the harsh grating of the prison buzzer that shattered everyone's sleep at 6.00 a.m., he'd find his face powdery with dried salt that had collected in the corners of his eyes or maybe tracked down across his cheeks.

His PTSD, which he'd striven so hard to overcome since resigning his commission, he now let have its head. Being in a state of constant hypervigilance helped, if that was the right word. From the moment he woke to the moment he fell, finally, into sleep, he felt the adrenaline coursing through his arteries and veins, was alive to its every minute variation in blood-concentration. It decreased his appetite, and by the third morning he noticed he'd already lost a little weight. Given the quality of the prison food, maybe that wasn't such a bad thing, he mused, grimly. And he felt ready to fight. On a hair trigger.

Back in the UK, he had to work to resist the occasional rages that flickered into life at the slightest provocation. Slow-witted drivers, officious civil servants, overloud businessmen yelling into their phones on trains. All were enough to have him reaching for an imaginary pistol or knife. But here, in Red Dog, he simply surfed the emotions as they arose in his breast. By the fourth day, he'd solidified his reputation for unpredictability, a quick temper and a willingness to lash out with fists or boots.

The guards seemed not to care. As long as prisoners stuck to the rules and avoided eye contact with them, did what they told them the moment they issued their orders, they seemed content. Maybe it was all just too much trouble to police every single instance of prisoner-on-prisoner violence. They'd never get anything else done, Gabriel mused, after he'd seen two scrawny prisoners beat the shit out of a third and then steal his cigarettes.

However, what Gabriel had planned would, he felt certain, attract the guards' interest, if not their fists and boots.

He chose as his moment the free association period on his fifth day. The sun was blazing down from a cloudless sky, and most of the men had stripped off their shirts. The pallid skin thus revealed was like an art gallery. Virtually every man had at least a couple of tattoos, and some were clothed in them. Religious icons, dollar bills, devils' heads, wild beasts, weapons. A vast array of designs, all executed in a blackish-blue ink he'd heard was usually made from melted shoe soles, urine and soot.

He was sitting with Prof on a metal table to which benches were welded, watching a football match: murderers versus an all-comers eleven. Prof nudged him and pointed as a muscular guy with a shaved head ran past.

"See that one? On his shoulder? The girl catching her dress on a fishing line?"

"Yeah."

"That means he's in for rape."

Gabriel pointed at the murderers' goalkeeper, a short, fat man with a dagger tattooed on his neck as if stuck right through the thick column of muscle.

"And that one?"

"He murdered in prison, and he's available for hire to do it again."

They spent a companionable fifteen minutes with Prof schooling Gabriel in the meaning and significance of the prisoners' inky code. A double-headed imperial Russian eagle meant a hatred for the USSR. A Madonna and child, that the bearer had been a thief since an early age. A rose on the chest, that the man had turned eighteen in prison.

Vlad the Impaler, who was playing for the murderers as a striker, had the most impressive set of tattoos of them all. As well as the watchful eyes beneath his collar bones, he wore epaulettes on both shoulders, with skulls replacing the usual pips. "High-ranking criminal," Prof translated. The Impaler's back was covered with a single design, a man in a loin-cloth chained to a rock, with an eagle tearing at his torso. Gabriel recognised the myth of Prometheus, the Titan who gave the secret of fire to man. In revenge, Zeus tortured him by having his liver pecked out every night, only to regrow the following morning. Other, smaller designs included revolvers, medals, fans of playing cards, poetry and a coffin overflowing with skulls.

The match ended with a cheer from the murderers, as Vlad booted the "ball," a heavy-looking, lumpy leather sphere, over the head of the all-comers' goalkeeper. He strutted in a circle, arms aloft, revealing yet more ink on the undersides of his massive triceps: coiled snakes with wide-open, fanged mouths.

The cheering subsided and the two teams dispersed into ones, twos, or small groups, watched over with stony faces by the Kalashnikov-toting guards.

His heart racing, palms slick with sweat, Gabriel pushed himself forward, off the metal table.

"Where're you going, boss?" Prof asked.

"Solitary."

As Prof's face crumpled in puzzlement, Gabriel strode across the exercise yard, arms swinging and legs kicking out in an exaggeratedly military gait. A few of the players still hanging around on the rectangle of tramped-flat earth that served as the pitch noticed him coming and shuffled aside. Out of the corner of his eye, he saw that two of the guards were watching him, too, hands resting along the tops of their rifles.

Perfect, just the right kind of audience. Now then, boys. Watch Tikhon Lisanovich earn his place on the Red Dog Honour Roll of Solid-Gold Nut Jobs.

Gabriel came to within four metres of the big Kuznitsa recruiting sergeant.

Combat appreciation, Captain Wolfe. Yes, sir! Target acquired. Target description? Immense Russian fucker covered in prison tats. Arms like hams, legs like tree trunks. Tactics? Gain target's attention through strategic use of prison insult, deploy maximum devastating violence until target is down. No mercy, no quarter. Wait for guard's gun butt. Sit out solitary until Stakhansky pulls me out. Very good. Carry on.

40

Gabriel drew in a breath, filling his lungs, then bellowed loud enough for everyone in the yard to hear.

"Hey! Vladinovsky! I've seen paedos play better football than you!"

Vladinovsky turned round to see who was addressing him in such disrespectful tones. His face darkened, and he bunched his massive hands. He opened his mouth to speak.

"Oh, yeah? Listen you little fucker. I—"

Gabriel sprinted to close the gap between them and launched a flying kick that connected with Vladinovsky's mouth, shattering teeth and breaking his jaw. As the big man stumbled backwards, roaring with pain, Gabriel sensed the drawing in of a crowd of onlookers, prison fights being high on everyone's list of preferred entertainment. A cheer went up, smoke-roughened voices echoing off the nearest cell block.

Vladinovsky must have bitten his tongue: blood was flowing freely from his broken mouth and sheeting down over his chest, obscuring one tattoo after another. His eyes were blazing. He rushed Gabriel, arms pumping, fingers curved into talons. But it was hopeless. Gabriel had spotted the red-haired woman in the centre of the crowd, in a small space of her own. She held up a hand and then chopped it down.

Gabriel ducked under an incoming haymaker and kicked Vladinovsky on the side of his right knee. Ligaments popping as they separated from bone, Vladinovsky collapsed sideways, screaming. Gabriel lunged, pushing his leading knee under the back of the falling gangster's neck. As Vladinovsky's head jerked backwards, Gabriel chopped down with a blade-hand, across the windpipe, wreaking irreparable damage to the soft tissues of the larynx and oesophagus. He heard the clump of running boots. Time to finish off Kuznitsa's top dog at Red Dog.

He thrust his right arm straight down past Vladinovsky's right ear, wrapped his left arm across his face and around his head and gave a single, convulsive jerk against his rigid right arm using every ounce of his strength. The neck broke with an audible snap. Gabriel stood and held his arms wide in triumph. The red-haired woman was applauding. Some of the prisoners were, too. Perhaps Vladinovsky was a hated figure after all. Then a few of the men's expressions changed. Eyes widened. Mouths opened in wide O's. Faces turned away.

Gabriel felt his guts churn as the guard reached him and drove the heavy wooden butt of his AK into the back of his skull. A metallic taste filled his mouth. A starburst obliterated the men's faces. A sound like the sky tearing itself in half. He fell, down, down, spiralling into the black …

Red Dog's governor, like many state officials – like the Deputy Attorney General of the city of Moscow – wanted a bigger slice of the capitalist cake than he could afford on his official salary. Fortunately, there were plenty of private enterprises around whose bosses would pay him handsomely for the occasional favour or morsel of intelligence. One such was Max Novgorodsky. And it was to this particular benefactor that he was speaking now.

"Your man Vladinovsky was killed today."

"Shit! Who did it?"

"That's the thing. A new guy. Not even been here a week. He kicked the crap out of one of his cellmates within minutes of being assigned, too. Broke the guy's arm and threatened to eat his eyeballs. A real nutcase."

"Who is he?"

"Name's Lisanovich. Tikhon Lisanovich."

"What's he in for?"

"That's the thing. All he did was to assault a Moscow cop. I mean, it's bad all right. But they don't normally send low-level thugs like that to us. But this was on the express orders of Lavrenty Boykov. You know who he is, right?"

"Of course I know who he is! So why's Boykov taking a personal interest in some guy who beat up a cop?"

"I don't know. Above my pay grade."

"OK. Look, send me a photo of this Lisanovich. And keep Ratimir on ice. I'll send some people to collect the body. He was married with five kids. We need to give him a proper send-off."

Max ended the call and the governor sat behind his cheap desk, staring at the buzzing handset. He shook his head. *Way above my pay grade.*

He pulled up the intake report file and searched for Lisanovich. When he found the record, he right-clicked on the photo, saved it to the desktop of his ageing PC, then attached it to an email and sent it to Max.

* * *

"This is a very dangerous time for you, Wolfe Cub."

Gabriel opened his eyes. His stone seat was surrounded by a pool of inky-black water that had no edge. He looked up: more blackness, no stars. Yet he could feel a cool breeze on his skin so he must be outdoors. The silver light forming curling crescents on the mirrored surface of the pool seemed not to have a source. Or none that he could detect.

"Is that you, Master?" he asked the darkness.

A figure wearing loose, white cotton trousers and a belted jacket walked across the water. Gabriel gasped, then realised stepping stones were submerged just below the surface. He could see white circles glimmering in that odd, silver light.

"Yes. It is I, Master Zhao. You have put yourself in grave danger, Wolfe Cub."

Gabriel looked up at the face of the man who had raised him after he'd proved too difficult for his embattled parents to deal with. He realised his breath was coming in short gasps.

"I had no choice, Master. And solitary confinement is a good idea. It will keep me out of harm's way until Stakhansky can get me out. Then I can approach Max with the right credentials to get a job."

Zhao Xi shook his head, his mouth downturned.

"No, that is not what I meant."

"Then what, Master?"

"Your brain is injured. A bleed. That's what the Russian doctor said when he examined you."

"How do you know? You don't speak Russian."

Zhao Xi smiled.

"Nor am I alive, in the strict sense of the word. But you heard him as you drifted, briefly, into consciousness. He said it's touch and go. You must focus on your recovery. Direct all your strength to that single goal. Focus on the candle, Wolfe Cub."

"What candle, Master?"

"There."

Zhao Xi extended an arm and pointed. Sitting atop a smooth black pyramid of stone, a single, white candle burned, its tulip-shaped flame the only colour in the otherwise monochrome world Gabriel inhabited.

Gabriel watched the unmoving flame and began to calm his breathing. He focused all his attention on the flame and was neither alarmed nor surprised to see it grow in size until it obscured Zhao Xi altogether. He remained like this, staring, breathing – for how long he wasn't sure. He felt no pain, so if a brain bleed was a bad thing, the prison doctor must be a good one.

. . .

He heard voices. Russian voices. Both male.

"He's coming round."

"Good. The drugs worked."

Gabriel opened his eyes. He was looking up into a pair of glasses with thick black rims. The eyes behind them were dark, and hugely magnified. He could see individual eyelashes and the tiny, meandering rivers of blood vessels on the whites.

"Welcome back, Prisoner 35976264. Do you know where you are?"

Gabriel moved his eyes away from the glasses-wearing man and let them traverse the ceiling and then the upper reaches of the walls. He saw a ceiling fan. Anatomical posters. Boxes of what appeared to be medical supplies.

"Hospital?"

"Correct. And which hospital? Do you know that, too?"

"Red Dog?"

The doctor nodded.

"Not that we acknowledge our unfortunate nickname, but yes, you are in the prison medical facility at Penal Colony 73, Vyazniki. And do you know why you are here?"

"A brain bleed?"

The doctor raised his eyebrows, which Gabriel noticed were speckled with flakes of dry skin.

"As it happens, yes. Not a large one, or you'd be in the common grave beyond the prison perimeter fence, but large enough to put you into a coma for three weeks."

"Three weeks!" Gabriel repeated, feeling as if he were speaking through a mouthful of dry oatmeal.

"Yes. But relax. We kept you hydrated, and our glucose drip is at least as nutritious as that swill they serve you from the kitchens. We couldn't operate. Too risky, plus, to be honest, too expensive. But we've a ..." he paused, "... a relationship with a large pharmaceuticals firm. They give us experimental drugs to try out on prisoners in return for access to their case notes. The trials aren't always a success, but there is no shortage of willing subjects. And, fortunately for you, it seems a new clot-dispersal therapy may have a promising future. If you notice any side effects, please let me know when you rejoin the general population."

"Side effect? Like what?"

"Oh, the usual," the doctor said, breezily. "Nausea, dizziness, mild feelings of unreality. The inmates call our pharmaceuticals 'prison brandy,' you know. You wouldn't believe the malingerers I get queuing at my door asking for pain relief, tranquilisers, antidepressants, what have you. Anything they can pop to escape reality for a few hours."

"When—"

"—can you leave us? A soon as I pronounce you fit. Which will be in a day or two. But I'm afraid the only thing that awaits you is a lengthy period in solitary confinement. Ratimir Vladinovsky was an influential man, both inside and outside our little community.

41

MAX'S DACHA

The evening was warm, and Max was sitting on the veranda. Pyotr had stretched out at his feet and fallen asleep, and Max watched as the beast's ribs rose and fell. With each inhalation, the tips of the coarse hairs of his coat caught a slanting beam of sunlight and glittered like silver. A soft breeze had sprung up, rustling through the slender birch trees at the far end of the garden and setting their delicate leaves fluttering like tethered butterflies. He sipped his whisky and reached forward to scratch behind Pytor's soft, hot ears. The wolf grunted softly in his sleep and a hind paw twitched, twice.

Max's phone pinged. He glanced at the screen. Incoming mail. He was looking into the brown eyes of Prisoner 35976264, AKA Tikhon Lisanovich. He frowned as he flipped through his mental card index of low-lifes in the Russian underworld, looking for a match. The punk haircut put him off for a moment, then his eyes widened. And then he grinned.

"Well, well, well. Not dead, indeed. And come all the way to Russia, only to mysteriously end up in Red Dog under a false name.

Mr Wolfe, have you come for some payback for the fact I tried to have you killed?"

Max threw his head back and laughed, waking Pyotr, who got to his feet and stretched before nuzzling his master's left thigh. Max grabbed a handful of the baggy skin at the scruff of Pyotr's neck and shook the head gently from side to side.

"Maybe we'll have two wolves at the dacha, Pyotr. What do you say?"

The wolf yawned, exposing two-inch long canine teeth and the black and pink interior of his mouth.

"I'll take that as a 'yes,'" Max continued. "But first I think we need to send a message to the Moscow judiciary. We can't have them sending foreign assassins into *my* prison and taking out my best men."

* * *

Aleksei Boykov returned home to his plush Central Moscow apartment after a long and challenging day dealing with a backlog of cases. Mostly gang-related, and complicated by the need to avoid upsetting his unofficial paymasters. Not Garin Group—they were easy enough to keep sweet. Their favours were usually bloodless, and triflingly easy for an experienced prosecutor to arrange. The other people keeping Boykov in German automobiles, French wines and Italian suits were the Mertvye Loshadi gang.

The "Dead Horses" had given themselves the gruesome name after a dramatic landgrab on another Moscow gang's turf. Literally. They'd taken over the gambling concessions one bloody night at the Central Moscow Hippodrome, Russia's largest horse racing track. In the process, as well as murdering ten members of the gang's security team, they'd slaughtered three Arab stallions belonging to their boss.

Boykov reflected that it would be a lot easier to keep Mertvye Loshadi sweet if the existing Attorney General could meet with an accident, and he could step behind his boss's desk. Maybe there was a win-win deal he could work out with them at their next meeting. He sat back in his thickly padded recliner, an Italian import in teal leather, with a glass of ice-cold vodka in one hand and the TV remote in the other.

"Right. Let's see what Netflix has to offer," he announced to the darkened sitting room.

He pressed the ON button.

The blast blew out the floor-to-ceiling windows in Boykov's sitting room, sending razor-sharp splinters flying forty or fifty metres outwards before they smashed to the tarmac and paving stones seven storeys below. Thanks to the above-average quality of the building materials the property developer had specified for the apartment block, the flats above and below Boykov's suffered only minor cosmetic damage. An automatic sprinkler system extinguished the flames before they had a chance to take hold, though not before a handful of expensive Western art prints had been scorched beyond recognition.

Very little of Boykov remained. The half-kilo of C-4 had been duct-taped to the underside of his Natuzzi recliner. The blast had reduced ninety-five percent of the former Assistant District Attorney to his constituent atoms. The five percent that remained undamaged, owing to some freakish concordance between the matching teal ottoman and the blast wave, was the feet. In scarlet velvet Gucci slippers, embroidered with golden tarantulas, they lay on their sides under a radiator, their blackened ankles ending in jagged smoking stumps.

Diagonally across Taganka Square from Boykov's block, sitting in a less well-appointed, but more intact apartment, Yerik Belov, a Kuznitsa torpedo, sent a short text.

Job done.

42

VYAZNIKI

The two burly guards threw Gabriel into the solitary cell. He had just enough presence of mind to roll to his right, avoiding mashing his still-painful left shoulder against the concrete floor. The thick steel door clanged shut behind him, leaving him in total darkness. The smell of the guards – body odour and cigarette smoke – lingered in his nostrils for a few seconds before leaving him.

He got to his knees, and, gingerly, stood, expecting at any moment to bang his head on an over-low ceiling. But no impact occurred, and he was able to stand erect. Eyes wide open, praying that once they adjusted, he'd be able to pick out a few details, he stretched his arms out wide, fingers spread.

His left hand met a wall before his elbow was half extended. His right, held out straight, was in free air. He took a step to his right and immediately crimped his fingertips against another wall. In humans, arm span roughly equals height, so his cell was about five feet ten inches wide. He rotated through a quarter turn clockwise and repeated the exercise.

This time he had to keep both elbows bent as his outstretched fingertips reached cold, sweating concrete. Five foot three, he estimated. He stretched his hands upwards and found the ceiling was barely much higher than the crown of his head. A six-footer would have to stoop if he wanted to stand erect. *Small mercies, Wolfe, small mercies.*

Having calculated the dimensions of the roughly cuboid box that was now his home, he began exploring the floor, crouching and running his fingertips across the rough surface. In one corner, which he mentally labelled north, he found a metal bucket. No lid. South, east and west were empty, as was the rest of the cell. No blanket. No bench. Nothing.

And it was cold.

He was somewhere beneath the prison compound, he guessed, judging from the number of steps he'd taken as the guards marched him away from the hospital block. Outside, it might be high summer, but here, where the warmth of the sun couldn't penetrate, let alone its light, it felt more like winter. He shivered. His thin prison uniform felt worse than useless, scratching at his skin and raising goosebumps.

He consulted memories from his time in the SAS. It was time to revisit his military training. The US military had created their SERE training program – Survival, Evasion, Resistance, and Escape – based on the experience of British pilots shot down in the Second World War. Special Forces around the world had all developed their own variants, and the SAS were no exception.

The first thing was to establish a routine. Time quickly becomes elastic in the absence of external markers like the transition from day to night. If captured and placed in solitary, troopers were to build a series of activities of known duration and use these to demarcate their time. For Gabriel, yoga, meditation and his martial arts training at the feet of Master Zhao were the natural place to start. Keeping his eyes open, even though the cell was devoid of the tiniest glimmer of light, he began a sequence of stretches, fighting stances, lunges and yoga moves that he knew took precisely one hour. After that he meditated for twenty minutes, using a numerical sequence of breaths that allowed him to track, more or less accurately, the passage of time.

After four rotations, he sat cross-legged in South Corner and closed his eyes. Sleep wouldn't come for a while yet, but he felt relaxed and able to think clearly.

Unless they wanted to kill him, and surely there were quicker and easier ways than this, the prison authorities were exacting punishment. Or possibly revenge. Their aim would be to break him, physically and psychologically, and turn him into a docile member of the prison "community." The bucket indicated that he wasn't to be reduced to the condition of a savage. Buckets had to be emptied. That meant a guard would visit. And as there was no hatchway in the door, it would have to be opened. Light. Fresh air. Human contact. He could hack it. At least nobody was nailing his hand to a table.

He slept. And when he woke, he realised he'd lost contact with the external calendar. That was the problem with the training. Yes, you could mark time while you were awake, but the ship of your sanity drifted as you slept, the anchor holding you secure in the flow of time dragged along the seabed.

He got to his feet and performed the hour-long physical routine again.

"Come on," he said in the darkness. "This is fine. You can do this."

He started again. Halfway through, he heard footsteps approaching on the far side of the door. He turned in their direction and waited, hands by his side, standing straight in the centre of the floor.

Key-scrape.

Handle-crunch.

Huff as door swings open.

Gabriel squeezed his eyes shut as the light from the corridor flooded the cell.

The punch landed in his guts, doubling him over. The shove sent him stumbling backwards until his back hit the wall and he slid to the ground.

He managed to open his eyes a crack, just long enough to see a uniformed guard drop a metal tray to the ground and stand a tin mug next to it before retreating and closing the door.

He crawled forwards, stomach cramping from the blow, and felt around with his fingers. They encountered something wet and soft, Some kind of porridge, maybe. He traced the rectangular outline, and although he found several other depressions pressed into the thin sheet of metal, they were all empty. No spoon. He worked his hand to the right, aiming for the last-known sighting of the tin mug and knocked it with the side of his hand. He heard it go over.

"No, no, no! Shit!"

He picked it up, but it was too late. Whatever liquid it had contained was now soaking into the floor. He bent forwards on all fours and placed his lips to the cool wet surface and licked what precious moisture remained, ignoring the foul taste, the gritty texture, and the rank stench of human excrement rising from the concrete.

The porridge was almost as gritty as the floor. It seemed to consist of roughly milled grains of some kind, mixed with water. It was cold, but he was hungry. He took solace from the fact that even food as bad as this was still, technically, food. So they didn't intend to starve him to death, just to weaken him.

The porridge eaten, he turned his attention to the two metal objects they'd left with him. Could they be fashioned into weapons? Yes. The mug would make a fine, if crude, knuckle duster and the tray might be foldable to create a striking or stabbing weapon. And then he realised. If they were happy to leave them, it meant they didn't consider the threat one worth bothering about. Even supposing he could take out a well-armed, well-fed, well-trained prison guard with two bits of bent alloy, he was at the end of a corridor with a guard post and security barriers at the far end and a single solitary confinement cell at the other.

He scratched a gate mark on the wall with a corner of the tray, then placed the mug on top and slid it over to the door.

43

Gabriel woke up from a dream in which he'd been flying above the prison. He felt along the wall and found his gate marks. Five. His stomach had long since given up growling and felt like a hard knot of scrunched-up sinews in the centre of his torso.

Footsteps sounded in the corridor. He stood, stumbled sideways and shot out a hand to steady himself against the wall. *Which wall, Wolfe? North-west? South-east? I don't know. I don't care. Too late. Attention!*

The door opened. Gabriel covered his eyes with the back of his left hand. Felt himself being seized by the biceps. Allowed himself to be dragged out of the cell.

With his eyes open, stinging in the electric light of the ceiling-mounted bulbs, he walked along in front of the guard, trying to maintain the pace that would avoid sharp jabs from the man's rifle into his kidneys. Could he take him? Back into the muzzle then duck and turn under it? Maybe. Could he shoot his way out of a high-security Russian prison? Probably not. Did he even want to? *Absolutely* not! This was the mission. To stay here until Oleg sprang him "legally," and he could make his way to Moscow. And Max.

"Where are you taking me?" he asked the guard.

"Shut the fuck up!" the guard shouted, before clouting Gabriel across the side of the head with his rifle barrel.

Gabriel shut the fuck up.

After passing through the guard post and two more sets of security gates, Gabriel and his escort emerged into daylight. Gabriel almost wept. He dragged lungfuls of warm, sweet air deep down and stared up at the sky, grinning as the sunlight heated his skin.

"Keep moving, shit-for-brains!" the guard shouted, shoving Gabriel so hard he stumbled.

On the other side of a high chain-link fence Gabriel saw prisoners standing around in small groups, smoking, chatting, tossing a football between them. Even laughing. One noticed him and yelled across the thirty metres that separated them.

"Hey, Lisanovich! We gave you a new nickname. Crazy Fox! Good, huh?"

Gabriel smiled but said nothing, guessing any response would earn him another blow from the guard's rifle.

But it *was* a good name, he reflected. *Lisa* meant "fox" in Russian. He'd chosen the name out of habit, Fox being an alias he'd used once or twice before.

Gabriel found himself sitting at a bare metal table in a long, narrow room divided into cubicles. The guard took up a position at the far end of the room, rifle at the port arms position, held diagonally across his body.

A door opened, and in walked Oleg Stakhansky. Stakhansky wore a grey suit, white shirt and dark-red tie. Every inch the corporate executive. To say he looked out of place in this grim institute of correction would be an understatement. He looked over at the guard and barked at him.

"Hey! I paid your boss a thousand dollars for a private meeting with my client. So unless you want to give up your post and go back to pig farming, I suggest you fuck off out of here!"

Shooting Stahkhansky a look of the purest venom, the guard about-turned and let himself out through a side door.

Glad I won't be going back to solitary, Gabriel thought. Stakhansky sat. A thick, scratched sheet of glass separated them. Stakhansky looked, not worried, exactly. But there was a tightness about the eyes and a set to his jaw that Gabriel didn't like. Stakhansky picked up the heavy black phone handset on the left of the partition, and Gabriel did the same.

"Hey! Ya come to spring me, boss?" Gabriel asked in a cod American gangster accent. Jimmy Cagney with everything turned up to ten.

Stakhansky didn't reply at once, and Gabriel's sense of foreboding ticked up a notch. He felt a worm of anxiety lazily uncoil in his stomach.

"Hey, come on, Oleg. Talk to me. You're the first human being I've seen in about a week. Not counting Lurch over there," Gabriel said, jerking his chin in the direction of the door through which the guard had exited.

Finally, Stakhansky spoke, his voice rendered as a rough squawk by the primitive electronics of the old, Soviet-era intercom.

"We have a problem. Someone blew Boykov's apartment to shit three days ago, with him in it. And that means our plan just hit a major fucking bump in the road."

Gabriel felt the sensation as a physical drop in the centre of his torso. Hope falling away from him.

"Fuck! What about his boss? Please tell me he's on your payroll, too."

Stakhansky shook his head.

"Nikita Zaytsev likes to be known as 'The Cleaner.' He came in on an anti-corruption platform. Needless to say, it isn't working, but as for the man himself, you'd be better off trying to bribe the President. Actually, come to think of it, that wouldn't be much of a stretch. The guy's practically a—"

"Hey!" Gabriel hissed into the intercom. "I get it, OK? But you must have a Plan B, yes? Some other way of getting me out of here? I've done my part, put down Kuznitsa's recruiting sergeant in here. But I'm in solitary now, and after you told Lurch out there to fuck off, well, I'm not seeing myself getting a job in the prison library any time soon."

Stakhansky frowned.

"Like I said. I'm working on it."

"How?"

"Option one, we buy the governor. He doesn't have the power to commute sentences, but obviously he could arrange your escape. Problem there is he's probably in Kuznitsa's pocket. Option two, we bring in a chopper and haul you out that way. But for that, we need you in the exercise yard, not buried in a hole in the ground."

"Yeah, well thanks for reminding me of that, Oleg."

"Look, I'm on it, OK? Tatyana pulled me off everything else until we have you out of here."

Gabriel was about to reply when the guard re-entered the visiting room.

"Time's up," he shouted down the length of the room, not bothering to conceal a smirk.

"I'll be back as soon as I can," Stakhansky said, then replaced the handset in its cradle.

Gabriel made the return journey to his cell lost in thought. Maybe disarming the guard and shooting his way out was an option after all. Then a dagger of pain shot through his guts, so fierce that he doubled over, gasping for breath. The guard kicked him, hard, in the rear end and he stumbled on, realising that his daily ration of gritty porridge and water was hardly the stuff to fuel a physical assault on an already wary guard.

294

44

In the dark, Gabriel pushed himself back into the south corner, jamming his spine against the concrete. So his stay was going to be prolonged a little. Fine. He'd just have to double down. What would Fariyah Crace, his psychiatrist, advise? He decided to consult her.

Fariyah had been helping him overcome his PTSD for six years. By and large he felt they had made excellent progress. But since Britta's death at the hands of the Kuznitsa torpedo, he'd let much of the good work they'd done together wither, preferring to revel in the mental instability and rage that his condition afflicted him with. Why bother trying to stop nightmares when your every waking moment is a living nightmare? Why strive to control sudden violent rages when violence is the only way you can see to get out of your current troubles? And why try to tamp down your ever-present anxiety when being hypervigilant is a condition of survival?

Eyes closed, Gabriel began to transform his cell into Fariyah's office at a private hospital in Mayfair. The walls lightened from bare concrete, stained with God knew what, to a shade of off-white she'd told him the decorator referred to as "bone." The raspy floor acquired a dove-grey woollen carpet. He hung a loud, splashy abstract painting in black and yellow on one wall, a less startling piece in muted shades of dark-brown and charcoal on the one facing it. Covered one wall with medical and psychiatric diplomas in silver frames, another with rows of textbooks on psychiatry, psychology and philosophy. Fariyah's desk came next: pale wood, aluminium legs, a black, tower PC in one corner, a sleek petrol-blue phone in the other.

No, not good enough, Wolfe! Which corners?

OK, PC to her left as she sits behind it. Phone to her right.

Really? So she picks up the phone with her right hand and writes notes with her left? Isn't she right-handed?

Wait! Wait. Please. No, you're right. The PC's on my left. Her right. The phone's on her left. So she can keep her right hand free.

Thank you. That feels much more accurate. How about family photos? Remember her children's names?

Of course, I do! Persia, Juno and … and …

Yes? I'm waiting.

Hold on, it's on the tip of my tongue. Persia, Juno and Alexis. Two girls and a boy. I bought them fountain pens and notebooks. And her husband's name is Simon, before you ask.

I wasn't going to. Carry on.

* * *

Gabriel sits in a low-slung armchair, upholstered in blue-and-grey digital camouflage fabric.

No. No I don't. That's what the guards wear.

He shakes his head and reupholsters the chair.

That's better.

It's covered in a nubbly cloth the colour of aubergines. It faces another across a pale, wooden, circular coffee table with a thick sheet of turquoise glass set into the top.

He wills Fariyah into existence. She is a plump, Muslim woman in her midforties with an olive complexion, round cheeks and large, almond-shaped brown eyes. He dresses her as for their previous hospital-based sessions: a black, tailored trouser suit and a hijab. Her headdresses are always brightly coloured. He gives her a cherry-red one today. She sits opposite him and smiles.

"Hello, Gabriel," she begins. "How are you feeling?"

It's her standard opening question.

He inhales deeply and sighs the air back out.

"Not so good, to be honest. I'm in the belly of the beast, only the beast doesn't want to cough me out. I'm worried I'll lose my shit before Oleg gets me out of here."

"You've been in worse situations than this before. What makes this so frightening?"

Gabriel steeples his fingertips underneath his nose. It's a good question.

"As far as my real people are concerned, I'm off the grid. As far as my replacement people are concerned, I'm on it but inaccessible. I'm getting weaker by the day. Nobody here knows who I really am, so they don't see me as an asset to be traded, or even tortured. I'm just human garbage to them. Human garbage who nutted a cop and then killed one of Kuznitsa's top people in here."

"Oleg said he has a backup plan, though, didn't he? Two, in fact."

"He did. But he also said each had a problem. A pretty fucking big one."

"So, Gabriel. What do you want from me? I'm afraid prison breaks are a little outside my field of expertise."

"I don't know. But you've always been good to me. Good *for* me."

Fariyah smiled and nodded at the compliment.

"We could talk about your family, if you like. As we're here."

"OK. Let's do that. It's not as if I've got anywhere else to be."

"I'm interested in the baby we talked about last time. Do you remember?"

"Of course! The baby I thought was Michael until you pointed out its age was all wrong."

"Yes. So although you lost your little brother at a very young age, it seems your parents had a third child. A middle child. I wonder where that child is now."

Gabriel snorted.

"Huh. Knowing the luck of the Wolfe family, probably dead."

"You don't know that."

"No, but why do I have no memory of the baby growing up? It must have died."

"I wish you wouldn't keep referring to your sibling as 'it,' Gabriel."

"What would you prefer? I don't know its name. And 'baby' sounds ridiculous."

"Your parents seemed to have a preference for naming their children after the archangels. Gabriel. Michael. How about Raphael?"

"*Raphael?* Really? A bit poncy, don't you think?"

"Shorten it, then. Like you did in the army."

Feeling like a sullen teenager, Gabriel assented.

"Fine. Rafi."

Fariyah smiled.

"Rafi it is, then. Who may be alive somewhere in the world, right now. If you lose your shit, as you put it, you may die in here and lose for ever your chance to reconnect with Rafi."

"So, you're saying I should hold it together because there's a vanishingly small chance I might have a living brother 'somewhere' in a world of seven billion people?"

Fariyah nodded.

"That's exactly what I'm saying."

Gabriel nodded back. It was good advice. If the worst came to the worst, he could behave himself for the rest of his time at Red Dog. Surely they'd let him out of solitary eventually. Then he could keep himself to himself, and his nose clean, and in a couple of years, he'd be free.

"Thanks, Fariyah," he said.

Then he opened his eyes.

.   .   .

The soft, reassuring atmosphere of the psychiatrist's office evaporated at once, leaving only a faint trace of Fariyah's perfume. Gabriel climbed to his feet and began his exercise sequence.

45

Gabriel opened his eyes. He'd been sleeping. His bladder was complaining and he groped his way over to the bucket and relieved himself. He felt along the wall for his gate marks. Eyes wide open, still searching for the chink of light under the cell door but finding none, he traced the scratches with his fingertips. Four verticals. A long, crooked diagonal. A fifth vertical. A sixth. A seventh. That made eight trays of food. Eight meals. Were they feeding him once a day? Twice? Four days or eight? He couldn't tell.

He stood and began exercising.

Then the cell door opened.

He hadn't heard footsteps and wondered, briefly, surreally, if the guard had removed his boots.

"Don't be stupid, Wolfe!" he said to himself as light flooded the cell, forcing him to squeeze his eyes shut against the glare.

"Hey, shit-for-brains, you got a visitor," the guard said. "Come on, let's go."

Despite the customary insult, there was something in his tone that put Gabriel on edge. Urgency coupled with, what? Fear? No. Respect, then? Maybe. He stumbled out of his cell and walked down the corridor, ahead of the guard, who this time refrained from trying to puncture Gabriel's kidneys with the muzzle of his rifle.

Once again, Gabriel found himself being marched past the exercise yard, empty this time, and towards the administration block. But when he turned towards the visitors' building, the guard was quick to correct him.

"Not that way. The governor's office."

Gabriel course-corrected without saying a word. But his heart leapt. Oleg had come through! He'd gone for option one and bribed the governor to let him out. It made sense. For Garin Group, money was like game counters. They could find a few thousand dollars down the back of the corporate sofa without even stretching.

The corridor leading to the governor's office felt like a world away from its sister beneath the prison. This one was carpeted, so that Gabriel's cheap prison boots – and the more expensive, military-issue items worn by the guard – made no sound as they marched towards the mahogany-effect door at the far end. Paintings on the wall replaced the unfinished rough-cast concrete. And daylight entered through windows that allowed the curious to look out onto the yard, the watch towers and the miles of razor-wire-topped fencing.

"Halt!" the guard said, as Gabriel reached knocking distance of the governor's office.

Gabriel executed a passable British Army drill move, bringing his right heel down beside his left with a thump, eyes front, arms tight against his sides, thumbs in line with his trouser seams.

The guard came up close, so close that Gabriel could smell a discomforting combination of garlic and cheap aftershave. Gabriel maintained a stiff, eyes-front stance. He stared at the painted aluminium nameplate screwed to the door, marginally off-centre and tilted so the right end was a shade lower than the left.

I.KRATOVSK, GOVERNOR

He thought the italics undercut the authority of the post somehow, and the metal plate looked cheap. Like something you might pick up at a DIY store's "While-U-Wait" counter. Arriving for his assessment interview a week or so earlier, he'd found it amusing. Now, knowing he'd be leaving Red Dog within the hour, he found it oddly touching. The guard spoke, hissing his speech into Gabriel's right ear.

"You behave in there, OK? Be a good boy. You speak when you're spoken to, do what you're told, and when he's done with you, it's 'Yes, sir, thank you, sir,' then you about-turn and knock. I'll be right here waiting."

Gabriel nodded, too focused on the conversation with the governor to worry about pleasing or displeasing the guard. His stomach was jumping, even in its impoverished state, and he could feel the excitement making his fingertips tingle. He struggled to keep a smile from breaking across his face.

The guard leant past him and knocked, twice, on the thin wood of the door. The voice beyond was muffled. But the single word was clear enough.

"Come!"

The guard, still leaning past Gabriel, twisted the doorknob and pushed the door open. Gabriel turned his head to the right to look at him, eyebrows arched in an unspoken question. The guard nodded. Gabriel leant forward, gripped the doorknob and stepped into the governor's office. Ready to meet him and hear the good news. Ready to leave.

Closing the door behind him, he turned to face the governor. And stopped dead in his tracks. Of Kratovsk there was no sign. In his place sat a much taller, stronger-looking man. Short, silver hair, a face seemingly constructed only from angles and planes, with not a soft edge of curve anywhere. Dark eyes beneath silver eyebrows, one bisected by a scar, the only sour note on his otherwise handsome features. And where Kratovsk's suit had been an off-the-peg number, this man's jacket sat like a second skin over his massive shoulders and barrel chest. A gleaming white shirt complemented by a lustrous gold silk tie with a discreet yet noticeable Gucci logo shrieked, "Money!"

The man sitting behind the governor's desk smiled.

"Hello, Tikhon. My name is Max."

46

Gabriel's heart stuttered in his chest. It took all his willpower not to spring at the man behind the desk. Then he thought, *Wait! Max is a common Russian name. It could be anyone. Hear him out.* Making sure to keep his Moscow accent in place, Gabriel replied.

"I am pleased to meet you. In fact, as you are sitting in the governor's chair, maybe I should say I'm *honoured* to meet you."

Max laughed. A deep baritone that seemed to emanate from his chest rather than his mouth.

"The governor and I are old friends. I asked if I could borrow his office, and he was only too glad to oblige."

"It is good to have friends, sir."

Max frowned, his tall forehead bunching and his brow deepening the shadows over his eyes.

"No need to call me, 'sir,' Tisha – may I call you that? Max is fine. It is what my mother called me, after all."

"Thank you, Max. Er, why did you want to see me?"

"Sit first. Then I'll explain. Are you thirsty? I bet they don't take much care of you in here."

Gabriel nodded. He realised at that point he had been thirsty the whole time he'd been incarcerated at Red Dog. A simple enough additional control method. Max smiled and swivelled round in the governor's leather chair. He opened a cabinet and pulled out a bottle of Stolichnaya and two glasses. He poured two generous measures and handed one to Gabriel.

"*Za tvoe zdorov'e!*" Max said, draining his glass.

"*Za tvoe zdorov'e!*" Gabriel drained his own vodka, noting its coldness. The cabinet was a fridge.

"Another?"

"Yes, please."

With their glasses refilled, Max clasped his large-knuckled hands on the desk blotter and leaned forwards.

"Tisha, you killed a man named Ratimir Vladinovsky."

"He was threatening me. It was self—"

Max held up a quietening hand.

"I don't want to hear it. Ratimir was a friend of mine. A good friend. Also an employee. Did you know who he worked for when you killed him?"

Gabriel thought fast. Would a new guy, a trigger-happy thug, get the inside scoop on a Kuznitsa enforcer on his first day? He could easily have asked. It would make sense. But that would mean telling Max, who he now knew was his nemesis, that he had deliberately killed his right-hand man at Red Dog. Saying no would remove that risk factor. But would it be credible? *Quick Wolfe! You're playing for the highest stakes here.*

He shook his head.

"He worked for Kuznitsa. I take it that name, at least, rings a bell." Gabriel nodded. "Well, my full name is Max Novgorodsky. I built Kuznitsa up from a shitty little street gang into a global organisation."

Inwardly, Gabriel rejoiced. *Target acquired.* But he also knew the next exchange would be crucial to his getting out of Red Dog and close enough to Max to exact his revenge. He aimed for just enough defiance in his answer.

"He was throwing his weight around. And I guess you know he

had a lot to throw. Called me a pussy. A faggot. You can't let that sort of thing go. Not in a place like this. I only meant to send a message. You know. Lay off or else. I guess he had a glass skull."

Max smiled.

"A glass skull. I like that. Must have taken a lot of guts, and skill, to put a man like Ratishka down. What are you, some sort of super-soldier? You ex-military Tisha, is that your guilty secret?"

Gabriel shrugged, wondering if he could tell most of the truth and get under Max's guard.

"I served for a while, yes. Booted out for insubordination. I decked this snotty-nosed lieutenant from the Moscow Higher Military Command School."

"Aha! So a quick temper even back then."

"My father was the same."

"Well, Tikhon Lisanovich, let's cut to the chase, as the Americans say. I am always on the lookout for men who can think quickly and use appropriate force when required. You killed one of my toughest men. How would you like to replace him?"

No! This was never part of the plan. You could have me locked up here for good if you wanted, I can sense it.

Gabriel tried to keep his voice level though it felt as though a belt was being tightened, notch by notch, around his ribcage.

"You mean in here, as your recruiting sergeant?"

Max laughed again and shook his head.

"No. Not in here. I'll need to find a new Ratishka for Red Dog. I meant, how about you come to work for me? I'll find you some much juicier skulls to knock heads with than some two-bit Moscow cop."

Feeling relief wash through him like summer rain cleansing the dusty prison yard, Gabriel nodded at once.

"Yes. Please. Thank you, Max. I won't let you down. I promise. Protection duty, hitman, enforcer, you name it, I'll do it. But—"

"—you're stuck in here at the thick end of a two-year-four-month sentence?"

"Yes. Exactly what I was going to say. And, you know, what with the business with Ratimir I haven't exactly wormed my way into the governor's good books."

Max waved his right hand over the surface of the desk then extended the gesture so his sweeping palm took in the contents of the meagrely appointed office.

"All this? This judicial power? It means very little when confronted with another kind of power. *My* kind. Sit tight, Tisha. We'll have you out of here in a day or two. Guard!"

And with that shouted order, the interview was at an end. The guard, who practically fell into the room in his eagerness to please Red Dog's visitor, saluted sharply, then, perhaps remembering who his nominal boss was, lowered the blade-like right hand and pointed at Gabriel.

"Come on, then, Lisanovich. I've got a nice, dark little box waiting for you."

Gabriel stood, then turned to Max.

"Perhaps—"

Max nodded, just once, and so slightly Gabriel felt sure the guard missed it. He addressed the guard in a friendly tone, though there was no mistaking the calm authority beneath.

"I think maybe your governor was a little ... overzealous ... in his punishment for this prisoner's misbehaviour. He was new to the penal colony when he attacked this Vladinovsky character, and perhaps had not absorbed the rules as fully as he might have done. I think a return to the general population would be in order now."

The guard opened his mouth to respond, then clamped it shut again. Clearly the man was torn between two loyalties. One to the job and the governor, the other to a system of favours and rewards that Gabriel felt sure was more financially appealing.

"Yes, sir. I'm sure Prisoner *35976264*," heavy emphasis on the dehumanising number, rather than his name, "has learnt his lesson. Come on, you!"

Gabriel marched out of the office without a backward glance and, arriving at his cell, reinstalled himself on the still-vacant top bunk. The other men were outside somewhere, he guessed, to judge from the good-natured shouts drifting in through the tiny slot window from the exercise yard. Gabriel looked at the ceiling, and the cobwebs hung with the miniature, black mummies of soon-to-be-consumed flies.

You think you're the powerful one, Max. Rocking up here and rewriting the rule book. Hiring a violent nutjob as an enforcer right from under the governor's nose. But I've got news for you. Power is like blood. You only have to push a knife in at the crucial point and it all leaks away. I am that knife. And I know exactly where to push.

Max was as good as his word. The following day, Gabriel was summoned to the governor's office for the third, and final time in his brief stay at Red Dog.

Kratovsk looked uncomfortable behind the desk, as if he knew he were only borrowing it from a more powerful man. His bald head shone in the light from the pendant lamp in the ceiling. He looked at Gabriel, peered at some papers, pushed his glasses higher up on his beaky nose, then glanced up again.

"Prisoner 35976264, it appears there was an …" he paused and swallowed, as if a lump of something indigestible had become stuck in his throat.

Gabriel watched the man's Adam's apple bob up and down. He almost felt sorry for him. Almost. Kratovsk made another start.

"The prosecuting authorities appear to have made an … error. There was an irregularity in the way your case was handled. The Moscow District Attorney has overturned your conviction. You are free to go. Report directly to the administration block to collect your possessions and sign your release paperwork. I believe transport has already been arranged."

Apparently, that was it. Blushing furiously, the governor bent his head and began sifting through the documents on his desk. Gabriel stood.

"Thank you, governor, sir."

· · ·

Gabriel had to sign eight different documents at a counter divided from the storeroom beyond by a metal grille. He pushed the sheaf of paperwork through a slot to a clearly bored prison official, who made brief eye contact then turned away and reached for a brown envelope in a wire pigeon hole. He pushed the envelope back through the slot beneath the grille. Having fulfilled this meagre duty, the official left his side of the counter and disappeared behind a tall row of shelves.

Gabriel couldn't help smiling. Jobsworths were the same the world over, from storemen in British army camps in Iraq to stockroom managers in Russian prisons. He upended the envelope, which wasn't sealed, and tipped the paperback and the toothbrush into the palm of his hand.

The sun was shining, as if on cue. Inhaling deeply, Gabriel walked ahead of the guard escorting him to the front gate. He met Prof coming the other way, carrying a large cardboard box. Gabriel slowed down, and for once, the guard behind him didn't reward this deviation from routine with a jab in the kidneys with his rifle.

Prof smiled.

"You off, then, Timebomb?"

Gabriel grinned.

"Free and clear. They fucked up my case. Here," he said, placing the paperback and toothbrush on top of the box. A leaving gift."

Prof smiled.

"Thanks! You're all right. See you on the outside."

"All right you two lovebirds," the guard broke in. "Get moving, Prisoner 35976264, we don't have all day."

Gabriel winked at Prof.

"Don't you mean, Mister Lisanovich? I'm a free man, now, aren't I?"

"While you're inside the fence, you're just a number to me, smartarse. Now move it, or my rifle might accidentally go off."

Gabriel sauntered down the gravel track leading to the main gate. Beyond the steelwork, the chain-link and the razor wire he could see a sleek, black Mercedes S-Class waiting. The rear and side windows were all darkened. *I suppose gangster chic's a legitimate look for actual gangsters*, he thought.

And then, with no further ceremony, he was outside. A free man. Even though getting sent to Red Dog had always been part of the plan, he felt a mighty sense of relief to be beyond its perimeter fence. As he walked towards the waiting Mercedes, he looked over its roofline at the landscape beyond. A wooded plain that stretched to the horizon, dotted here and there with settlements of brightly coloured wooden houses, some with thin columns of whitish smoke curling from their chimneys. A long, straggling V of geese moved slowly east to west, the same route he would now be taking.

As he reached its highly polished flank, the car's front passenger door opened. He grabbed the handle, pulled the door wide and slid into the softly cushioned seat. He glanced over the headrest, but the rear of the car was empty. Max was sitting behind the wheel, immaculately dressed, as before, though in a lighter-weight suit of pale-grey silk. No tie either, his white shirt open at the neck to reveal a few silver hairs in the notch of his throat.

"Tisha!" he said, smiling and leaning over to give Gabriel an awkward hug. "Welcome back to freedom and a new job with Kuznitsa. Let's go. I bet you're aching to see the back of that shithole?"

"You could say that. I'm going to trash it on Trip Advisor as soon as I get a phone."

"Ha! Trip Advisor. I like that! Tough and a joker. That's an unusual combination. Thirsty?"

"My stomach thinks my throat's been cut!"

"Open the glovebox. There's a bottle in there. Help yourself."

Gabriel leaned forward and popped the catch on the glovebox. The hatch fell open slowly to reveal a frosted bottle of Grey Goose vodka. It was cold to the touch. He pulled it clear. Then hesitated for a second before closing the hatch. The vodka had been resting on a pistol. He cracked the seal and unscrewed the cap, then took a hefty pull on the cold, clear spirit.

"Ah, fuck your mother, that tastes good. Thanks, Max."

"You're welcome. Keep it. Plenty more where that came from." Max coughed, then cleared his throat, a rough, growly sound that seemed to shift something liquid deep in his lungs. "Fucking cigarettes. The doctor says I should give them up for my health before they kill me. You know what I told him, Tisha?"

"No, what?"

"I said, 'Doc, the fucking Afghans couldn't kill me with RPGs. The fucking Chechens couldn't kill me with AKs. And the fucking government couldn't kill me with taxes. If God wants to have a crack with cigarettes, bring it on!' Eh? Bring it on! Ha! You should have seen his face."

Gabriel laughed. It was funny enough, and the vodka was making him feel happy and relaxed. Plus, of course, he was sitting within striking distance of the man who'd murdered Britta. He took another pull on the bottle and considered wrenching open the glove box and despatching Max here and now. But then stopped himself. Suppose the gun wasn't loaded. What if it was a test? *Hold your fire, Wolfe. You're thousands of miles from anywhere useful with no way out except through Tatyana Garin. Play it cool and wait for the right moment to strike. Plus, we're doing well over a ton. Bit risky to shoot the driver at that sort of speed.*

"It's a good story," he said, finally.

"I know. You ever do much killing, Tisha?"

"Me? No. Like I said. I got booted out of the army before I could do any proper fighting."

"Ah, yes. You decked that twit from the Academy, I remember." Max paused, and scratched his chin. "Your name, Tisha, it's unusual."

Startled by the change of tack, Gabriel turned to Max.

"Tikhon, you mean?"

"No. Lisanovich. It means 'Son of the fox,' as I'm sure you know."

"What about it?"

"Oh, nothing. Well, maybe not completely nothing. Foxes. Funny little animals, aren't they. They look like predators, sure enough, but they're really just scavengers, aren't they? I mean, we all know a fox'll go through a henhouse like a Spetsnaz in an enemy camp – Kill 'em all! – but they're opportunists. I mean, you see them in Moscow now, dragging away fucking McDonald's cartons for fuck's sake. Hardly a glorious way to live is it, Tisha Lisanovich?"

"I guess not. But even scavengers can be useful."

"Oh, of course, don't get me wrong. We're all God's creatures, after all. But when it comes to *real* predators, you know the animal I like the best? I'll give you three guesses."

"Lions?"

"No."

"Tigers?"

Max made a harsh guttural sound like a buzzer. "Ah-ahh! No, again. Your final chance."

"I give up."

"No! Tisha Lisanovich, you don't! You have a third chance to guess. Take it."

"OK. Great white shark?"

"Not bad. But no. You lose. You want to know the real answer?"

"Yes."

"The wolf. I have one as a pet, you know. Big fucking Middle Russian forest wolf. Name's Pyotr. After the little boy in Prokofiev's symphony, you know?"

"I guess so."

"Oh, come now, Tisha Li-sa-no-vich. What Russian doesn't know the story of Peter and the Wolf?"

"Oh, yeah, I remember now. All the characters are done with different instruments."

Max took his hands off the steering wheel and clapped, steering with his knee.

"That's it! You've got it! Ah, I tell you, nothing beats having a tame wolf around the place. Want to know where I got him?"

"Where?"

"Arkhangelsk. See, there's another interesting name. A wolf from Arkhangelsk. Maybe I should've named him after one of the archangels. You know, Uriel, Michael—"

Gabriel sensed what was coming. Tensed every muscle. Ready to strike Max in the right temple with his left elbow then grab the steering wheel. But the vodka was blurring his senses, slowing him down.

47

Max finished his sentence.

"Or Gabriel?"

At that precise moment, as Max's lips formed the name of his passenger, Gabriel began to move, pulling his left arm across his chest prior to accelerating it out sideways, aiming to smash Max's temporal bone.

And something silvery and very, very thin flashed in front of Gabriel's eyes.

Then his throat seemed to close of its own volition, and he felt a searing pain round the soft part of his neck and across his windpipe.

Gasping for breath, groaning in agony, tongue protruding, he scrabbled to get his fingers beneath the ligature slowly choking him.

"Ease off a bit, Fedya, we don't want to kill him," Max said.

Gabriel gasped as the pain eased a little and he could drag a lungful of air down.

A high-pitched voice close to his right ear: "Don't struggle, Foxy. This is piano wire. One bump in the road, and I swear it'll go through your neck like it was cheese."

Gabriel forced himself to sit still, panting and aware of warm wet blood running down the front of his neck and soaking into his shirt front.

"Maybe it's time we had our first honest chat, Gabriel," Max said. "I've been looking forward to meeting you for years. And by the way, the Glock in the glovebox isn't loaded, so you passed that test, at least."

Then Max slowed the car and pulled off at the side of the road. From the inside of his jacket, he pulled a slim semi-automatic pistol. Some kind of Walther, Gabriel judged, though most of it was enfolded in Max's fist.

"Out! Don't run. There's a Dragunov sniper rifle in the footwell, and Fedya back there is an excellent marksman."

Gabriel felt rather than saw the piano-wire garotte lifted over his head and clutched his injured throat. His palm came away sticky but it was dark, venous blood and already slowing to a trickle. He coughed, then winced as pain flared. He climbed out of the Mercedes, walked to the front of the car, then turned to get a look at his attacker.

At first he didn't understand. The rear door opened and he saw a pair of black shoes appear beneath its lower edge and step onto the ground. But no head or torso appeared. Then all became clear.

The man who rounded the sculpted edge of the car door was no more than four feet tall. He'd been scrunched up in the footwell all the time, with plenty of room to breathe despite the confined space. Perfectly proportioned, just scaled down to child-size, he had an athletic build and a lively, open face dominated by large brown eyes with absurdly long eyelashes.

Fedya had the same expensive taste in clothes as his boss. A navy-blue suit clearly made to fit his diminutive frame, a pale-blue shirt and a burgundy and navy striped tie. He was carrying a sniper rifle that was taller than he was. He sloped arms and stood silently, watching Gabriel. Max had got out too and was leaning against the door frame, resting the Walther on the roof, the pistol aimed at Gabriel's midriff.

"How did you know who I was?" Gabriel asked.

"I've known about you since you killed Strickland. In case you never learned his name, he was my man in Mozambique. Together with Britain's then Prime Minister, Barbara Sutherland, he had thrashed out an extremely lucrative deal to take over their diamond reserves and then, given time, the whole country."

Gabriel closed his eyes, trying to ignore the burning pain in his neck. He was remembering.

An early morning meeting with Sutherland in the Peak District. Pitch dark, well before dawn. A helicopter bringing a heavily armed assassin to finish him off after three others had failed. Just when all had seemed lost, Britta, camouflaged in a ghillie suit, had appeared right behind the man and driven the blade of a combat knife deep into his neck, killing him instantly.

So without realising it, Max's torpedo had killed the right person after all. No! Not the right person. It was he, Gabriel Wolfe, who should be lying dead, not Britta. It should *never* have been her. He opened his eyes.

"This was all about revenge?"

Max shook his head.

"No. Not revenge. You cost my organisation an amount of money that you cannot even begin to imagine. But when you killed Strickland, you stole something from me more precious than a mountain of diamonds. You stole my honour. And a man without honour loses other things quickly. His reputation. His subordinates' respect. And his power. Without power, a man is nothing."

"So why am I still alive?"

"That is the sixty-four-thousand-dollar question. And here is the answer. You killed one of mine. You stole respect from me. I tried to have you killed. Twice. Both times, you escaped. Then you came for me. Put yourself in Red Dog just to get a chance at *your* revenge. I respect that. And I've done a little digging. I want to offer you a deal. I still want you to come and work for me. But not as some low-level muscle. With your connections, your military skills, your special forces training, you could build yourself a kingdom!"

"What happened to your concerns about your lost honour?"

"It's true that there have been murmurings. You can imagine the sort of thing. Competitors get wind of a thing like that, they get ideas. One man in particular has been making noises in my world that have begun to be echoed elsewhere. I intend to make an example. I want you to help me. The meaning will be clear. Max Novgorodsky is more powerful than ever. Even those who would stand against him end up working with him. The forge burns brighter than ever, and anyone who thinks otherwise will be beaten on its anvil."

Gabriel frowned.

"Let me get this straight. You sent a squad of mercenaries after me. I killed them. Then you sent a hitman. He's dead, too. And even though I came to Russia to kill you, you're saying, no hard feelings. Let's go into business together?"

Max grinned, though the Walther's muzzle didn't waver.

"Do you have a better idea? At this point, all I can think of is letting Fedya here put a bullet in you and leaving your body for the crows."

As if to emphasise his boss's point, Fedya worked the rifle's bolt, the dry metallic clicks loud in the silence.

Gabriel looked from one to the other. His earlier supposition was correct. Max clearly had no idea about Britta. He thought this was some sort of brotherly misunderstanding that could be cleared up with a handshake and a bottle of vodka. He could bide his time a little longer. He spread his palms out. And smiled as best as he was able.

"You know what? The British Government pays me fuck all for what I do for them. And it's a zero-hours contract as well. No pension. No sick pay. And younger guys coming up behind me all eager for a slice of the pie. So, why not? I crossed the line between good and evil years ago."

He held out his bloody right hand.

Max advanced on him, transferring his grip on the Walther before shaking hands. He enveloped Gabriel in a bear hug and then, when Gabriel moved to pull away, held him tighter and placed his mouth against his ear.

"You won't regret this, Gabriel. Don't make *me* regret it."

Then he released him.

Gabriel looked the older man in the eye.

"I have a question."

Max smiled.

"Good. I like men who ask questions."

"How do you know I won't double-cross you and kill you?"

"Is that what you intend to do?"

"No. But I'd be wondering the same thing in your shoes."

"Number one, I'm not an idiot. Fedya here is the best bodyguard I've ever had. How many men have tried to kill me, Fedya, since you came to work for me?"

"Three," the little man answered in his high-pitched voice.

"And how many women?"

"One."

"And where are they now?"

"Pig farm."

"Working there?"

Fedya giggled.

"Fattening the pigs."

Max turned to Gabriel again.

"He's always there, in the shadows or in plain sight, whenever I'm out and about. If he isn't, it's because I'm with my two oldest friends. You'll meet them tomorrow. Nozh and Krasivyj. They're what you might call the loyalest of the loyal. Number two, you won't be armed unless I arm you. Number three, you're on probation for a year. I'm going to set you a series of, hmm, tasks, that will prove to me, beyond any doubt, that you, like Fedya, Nozh and Krasivyj, are loyal. I'll see the way you perform them for me. And I'll know. Number four, the money is better than you can imagine, Gabriel. And the perks aren't bad either. You like girls? You want to see football matches? Operas? You want to fly everywhere first class? Drink the finest champagne? Dine off Kobe beef and caviar every night? These are pipe dreams for most men, Gabriel. But for you, they can be the stuff of everyday life."

Gabriel smiled again. It was a good speech. Inspiring. He touched his throat again. The blood had already dried.

"I told you, I'm not planning to kill you anymore. You went for it. You failed. So did I. I failed as well. It's time I made a decent living in this business. And you can offer me something my former employers couldn't so I'm in. And I want to prove my loyalty to you, Max. In a way I hope you will find convincing. Do you have a knife?"

"Fedya!"

Fedya reached into a trouser pocket and tossed a little silver penknife to Gabriel.

Gabriel prised out the larger of the two blades: four centimetres of glittering, mirror-polished steel. He tested the edge against his thumb. He inhaled sharply, filling his lungs and ignoring the burning in his throat. Then he closed his eyes and visualised a cloud-filled sky. He opened them again, shot the breath in out in a noisy "whoof" and placed the edge of the blade against the skin on the inside of his left forearm.

The first cut was a short vertical.

48

The second cut began at the tip of the first and continued downwards in a diagonal.

Jaws clamped, Gabriel continued, repeating a short mantra in his head …

Pain passes like clouds on a windy day …

The blood from the cuts fanned out across the pale flesh of his arm and began dripping onto the ground, where it raised little puffs in the dust.

When he was finished, he held his arm up for Max to see.

MAX

Max nodded once. Then, saying nothing, he pulled the display handkerchief from the breast pocket of his suit jacket and held it out to Gabriel. Gabriel wrapped the square of cotton around his arm and climbed back inside the car, where he took another long pull on the vodka. He heard Fedya clip himself into the seatbelt. Beside him, Max leaned round and handed his pistol to the midget.

"Here," he said. "Take this."

He started the engine and pulled away.

. . .

Four hours later, they arrived at the dacha. Gabriel had drifted in and out of sleep during the three-hundred-kilometre journey. His arm was throbbing in time with the cut in his neck.

"Wake up, Gabriel," Max said, loudly but not unkindly. "We're here."

Gabriel opened his eyes. He climbed out stiffly, wincing as his newly incised arm caught on the seat belt.

A rapid-fire thumping coupled with a deep-throated growling alerted him to the imminent arrival of something four-legged, fast and ferocious. He looked left then right. Round the far corner of the dacha, a huge wolf galloped into sight, leaning into the bend to maintain traction between its vast paws and the sandy soil. Despite years of training with Master Zhao, Gabriel lost control of his heartbeat, which raced upwards into three figures – hundreds of thousands of years of human evolution wiped out in the face of one of its oldest enemies.

Every muscle tensed, Gabriel adopted a balanced stance, one foot behind the other, and turned sideways on to the attacker. His primal fear had released a flood of adrenaline, and his senses kicked up into a hyperalert state. He had time to see the long yellow canines, the pink interior of the wolf's mouth, its yellow eyes with dark pinprick pupils, the way its ears were flattened against its skull, the subtle gradations of colour in its pelt, from an ashy grey to a tawny brown and on to silver and black.

"Pyotr! Stojte!" *Halt!*

The wolf skidded to a stop less than a metre from Gabriel. Its chest was heaving and long strings of drool dripped from its red-rimmed mouth, from which a long, pink tongue flopped, quivering as it panted.

"Droog!" *Friend!*

The two words of command were enough. The wolf, magically transformed by Max's words into an oversized house pet, trotted up to Gabriel and sniffed his right thigh. It completed a slow circle, sniffing at his knees, his dangling hands and, finally, his groin. Its ears, which up close Gabriel realised were as big as the palms of his hands, were fluffy and pricked now, signalling alertness, but not fear or aggression. He stretched out a hand, knuckles bent under, and offered its back to the wolf. It sniffed and, under the sudden cold touch of its nose, Gabriel's mind flew back years to his beloved Seamus, the greyhound he'd acquired, and then lost, when he still lived in Salisbury.

The wolf turned a quarter-circle and leant against Gabriel's right leg, almost pushing him over.

Max laughed.

"He likes you!"

There was something so ridiculous about being adopted by a wolf that Gabriel laughed too. Only Fedya stayed silent, maintaining a distance and cradling the Dragunov under one arm, finger straight over the trigger guard.

"Come on," Max said. "You look like shit! You need a shower, a change of clothes and a decent meal inside you."

Gabriel found himself in a luxurious guest suite, complete with its own bathroom, dressing room and fridge stocked with alcohol. He uncorked a bottle of white wine – Svyashchennaya Bereza, the label said: *Sacred Birch* – and poured himself a glass. It was high in alcohol, off-dry and fruity. He drank half, then refilled it and went into the bathroom. Everything was a dazzling white, set off by gold details: taps, plugs, mirror surround, towel rail, shower head, even the radiator. He ran a bath.

Submerged in the steaming hot water, with his bandaged arm resting along the edge of the tub, he considered his options. Yes, he had to kill Max. But he realised he wanted to get away safely. This was no suicide mission. He had Eli. Jesus! How was she? He wished there was a way he could get in touch, but for now, that would have to remain a secondary priority. She knew the nature of the game. She wouldn't worry, and besides, she had more important things to worry about.

Max wouldn't trust him completely. Not yet. The demonstration of loyalty with the knife was a good start: inspired. He'd noticed the way Max's eyes had widened as the blade went in. But it wasn't enough. No. Max would have plenty of muscle besides Fedya. They would all have to go before Gabriel finally dealt with Max, taking his time to explain exactly why he was dying.

He drained his glass and set it carefully on the shelf behind his head with a clink. The water was easing the accumulated pain and stress of his time in Red Dog. He closed his eyes and sighed.

Oh, Britta! I'm so sorry. Just when you had everything you wanted. I'll kill him for you and I'll go and see your parents. And Jarryd. He hates me, and I don't blame him, but I'll explain what I did for you. Maybe it'll give him some peace.

Britta was sitting on the edge of the tub in a wedding dress in desert camouflage fabric.

"Hej! Stop beating yourself up. It was Kristersson who pulled the trigger, not you. I'm sure Fariyah would agree. Wouldn't you, doc?"

"Absolutely! You work in a dangerous world, Gabriel. So does Eli. So did Britta. Sadly, death in service is practically a condition of employment. You wouldn't get many insurance companies willing to write a policy on your life, that's for sure. And what on earth is that on your arm?"

Gabriel looked down at the inside of his forearm. The bleeding had stopped. In stark, red, ragged-edged letters, his knifework was revealed in all its glory.

Убей их всех

He looked up at the two women perched on the edge of the tub.

"It means, 'Kill 'em all,' and it's what I'm going to do before I leave here." Then he looked at Fariyah. "Er, should you be in here with me like this? Religion-wise, I mean?"

Fariyah smiled and shook her head.

"Not as such. But you need me right now. Don't worry, I'm not going to climb in with you."

Britta grinned her gap-toothed grin.

"But I might," she said.

Naked now, she climbed in and sat facing him between his legs, her knees drawn up to her chin, while Fariyah looked on indulgently.

"Careful of the head, my dear," she said. "I may not be a medical doctor but even I can see it's not looking too good."

Britta leaned forward to examine her reflection in the water and released a torrent of blood from her burst-open skull. As she swirled the blood into the bathwater, turning it a deep rose-pink, she smiled crookedly at Gabriel.

"Oops! My bad."

Then she slumped back, cracking what remained of her head against the gold taps with a sickening wet crunch. From the top down, her flesh began slipping and shifting, sliding down the smooth white surface of the tub and slopping into the water.

Gabriel screamed, thrashing to get away from the rapidly liquefying body of his dead ex-fiancée.

The bullets were flying.

Crack-thump.

Crack-thump.

Crack-thump.

Thump-thump-thump.

Gasping convulsively, and thrashing wildly, Gabriel heaved himself up from under the cold water and sat upright, staring down and seeing nothing but his own pale limbs.

Someone was hammering on the bedroom door.

Thump-thump-thump.

"Hey! Gabriel! Everything OK in there?"

It was Max.

"Yeah!" Gabriel shouted back. "I'm fine. I'm fine."

"OK, my friend. Come downstairs and let's get some food inside you. Don't take too long."

And then he was alone.

"Oh, shit!" he said to the empty bathroom.

. . .

Max's intelligence-gathering operation had clearly extended to Gabriel's measurements. In the dressing room he found a selection of suits, shirts, sports jackets and trousers. A chest of drawers revealed underwear, socks, T-shirts, thin cashmere sweaters, jeans and hoodies. A row of shoes and boots stood waiting in line. He dressed in jeans and a white T-shirt, then laced up the sturdiest pair of boots on offer.

Before going downstairs, he conducted a quick survey of his accommodation, looking for anything that might make an improvised weapon: a wire coat hanger, a doorknob with a long screw, a steel runner from one of the drawers. And found nothing. Either Max was more cautious than he'd anticipated or just had a fondness for all-wood furniture. No matter. A place like this would have a kitchen. Outbuildings. Concealed firearms. All Gabriel had to do was be patient. And find them.

49

Max was waiting for him at the foot of the stairs, beside a stuffed bear. The taxidermist, clearly of the old school, had positioned the bear reared up on its hind legs, snout wrinkled in a snarl, long claws extended in a ferocious ten-pointed welcome. Max held his arms out, unconsciously mirroring the bear's pose.

"Here he is! My newest recruit. Come, Gabrisha! Come and eat."

At the foot of the stairs, Gabriel felt himself grabbed and enfolded in Max's crushing grip. He had no other option than to return the embrace. Then Max held him a little distance away, examining his face and staring deep into his eyes, before pulling him roughly forward and kissing him three times on alternate cheeks.

"Everything OK? You sounded like you were facing the devil himself in there," he said, jerking his chin in the direction of the first floor.

"I'm fine. I just get bad dreams from time to time. It's nothing."

"OK. I understand. It's something all us old soldiers have to deal with, isn't it? Civilians, they don't understand. They want to know all about the glorious actions you took on their behalf, then you tell them how you fucked up a whole village with white phosphor grenades and suddenly they lose interest, eh?"

Max led Gabriel into a dining room dominated by a long, rectangular mahogany table. Two places were laid at one end. A platter of roast meat and vegetables sat between them, accompanied by a jug of delicious-smelling brown gravy. A loaf of what looked like home-baked bread had been roughly sliced on a wooden board, and a white plate held a chunk of pale, almost white, butter. A bottle of wine was open, and two glasses brimmed with the blood-red liquid.

"Come on," Max said. "Let's eat. I'm starving. God knows what you must be like. Your stomach thinks your throat's been cut, eh?"

The food was good. Gabriel munched his way through two platefuls of meat, potatoes and carrots, slathering them with gravy and then mopping up the remainder with thick slices of bread. He ignored the griping from his stomach, suddenly overburdened and struggling to cope, and took a swig of the wine.

Once he'd sated his hunger, he put his cutlery down, resting them against the rim of the plate.

"Oh, Jesus, Max, that was good. Thank you!"

"You liked the meat. Venison from the forest just beyond my property line. I shot it myself. We'll go hunting one day, you and I. I bet you're an excellent shot."

"Not bad. Others were better." *Like Britta.*

"You're too modest. Hey! Pyotr! Come!" Max shouted towards the open door.

Gabriel heard the rhythmic clicking of the wolf's claws on the polished wood floor then the great beast appeared in the doorway. It sat.

"How about that?" Max asked, looking at Gabriel. "Well trained or what?"

"Very impressive. What's the command for him to come in?"

"Here."

Gabriel twisted round in his chair and looked at the wolf, which was waiting patiently, long tongue lolling from its jaws.

"Pyotr! Here!" he said in a tone of command.

The wolf stood up fast and trotted in to wait at Gabriel's left side. He scratched the top of its head and it repeated its trick of earlier, leaning against him so that his chair shifted sideways under the additional load.

Max forked a mound of the venison onto his plate and set it down on the floor.

"Eat!" he said.

The wolf left Gabriel's side and bent its head over the plate, devouring the thick slices of meat and then licking the gravy and juices from the plate until it sparkled.

"You said you had enemies, Max," Gabriel said, once the wolf had finished eating and lain down beneath the table at its master's feet.

"Yes. A great many. And not just here in Russia, either. The trouble with running a global business, Gabrisha, is that you have to deal with global enemies, too. The irony of capitalism, eh?"

"Here in Russia, though. Who's causing you the most trouble right now?"

"Right now?" Max stared at the ceiling for a few seconds, then returned his gaze to Gabriel. "That would be Kasimir Byko."

"Who is he?"

Max's face darkened as he began speaking.

"Byko's from Gory, in Georgia, the same little shithole town that gave the world Stalin. Byko likes to be called Little Stalin. Thinks it makes him sound cool. Thinks he's a real man of the people. Giving to veterans' charities, all that, even though he's never done a day's military service. He moved to Moscow about ten years ago, started small, the way they all do, but just recently he's been throwing his weight around, letting it be known he's the real player in the city and people like me are just the 'old guard' – his words – like the greybeards Stalin got rid of in his Party purges. That's what I was talking about when I told you how honour is more important than money."

"What line of business is he in?"

"Oh, the worst. Sex trafficking. Prostitution. Kiddie porn. Drugs when it suits him to finance his other shit. He's got what he calls a 'supply chain' from Southeast Asia into Saudi Arabia, Pakistan, all those countries where they like their chicken as young as possible. Fucking paedophiles, the lot of them."

"Where's he based?"

"His business, you mean?"

"No. I mean where does he live?"

"Volkhonka Street. Number Seventeen. Why?"

"I'll kill him for you."

"What?"

"I'll take him out. To prove my loyalty. Again."

"He's heavily protected. You wouldn't get within a kilometre of him without being spotted. I only just recruited you, Gabrisha. I don't want to lose you to that cocksucker before you've even started work."

"This is my work. You said I was on probation. OK. Give the probationer something to do."

Max stared hard at Gabriel, who stared back. His breathing felt nice and easy. His pulse was ticking over nicely at just below sixty a minute. He smiled at Max.

"What would you need? *If* I said yes? How many men?"

Gabriel shook his head.

"No men. I'll tell you what I need."

Over the next ten minutes, Gabriel outlined his plan. Max listened attentively, nodding occasionally and grunting his approval. Asking the odd question but otherwise staying silent. At one point, the wolf got up from under the table, stalked into the middle of the room, shook itself violently from nose to tail then curled up in the centre of a Turkish carpet before the fireplace, filled, as it was summer, with a display of dried flowers.

One of Max's men drove Gabriel to Moscow a couple of days after the briefing. They arrived at 8.45 a.m., and the driver dropped Gabriel off in Lenivka Street, a narrow street lined mostly with apartment blocks, running at right angles to Volkhonka Street. As he drove off, Gabriel noticed with amusement the way he buzzed the window down and leant his head almost out of the cabin.

The smell *was* bad, though.

Before leaving the dacha, Gabriel had pissed on the old military greatcoat and dumped half a bottle of whisky over it, then rubbed some of the chef's kitchen waste into its stiff skirts for good measure.

It, and he, stank.

He'd also rubbed mud from the forest floor into his face and hands. Having scraped and buffed his skin with old rags, he now had a patchy complexion of blackish-brown, his own pale skin showing through in smeared stripes here and there.

In addition to the greatcoat, which was hot and heavy as well as noisome, he wore a military cap with the ear flaps down, scruffy trousers and fingerless gloves, all purchased the previous day by one of Max's men on his instructions.

He walked – weaved, rather – along Lenivka Street, then turned right into Volkhonka Street. Number Seventeen turned out to be a smart townhouse of three-storeys, brick-built and guarded outside by two potted bay trees, trimmed into pom-poms, and two less attractive but more dangerous figures in black jeans and bomber jackets. Their shaved skulls revealed curly, translucent wires running from ear-pieces down into their overtight shirt collars.

Keeping to the other side of the street, Gabriel leaned back against the wall and eased his legs out from beneath him, settling to the pavement. From his righthand coat pocket, he brought out a battered Starbucks cup and set it in front of him. From the left he removed a battered square of cardboard on which, in black marker pen, he'd scrawled, in Cyrillic and English:

Голодный ветеран.
Пожалуйста помогите.

Hungry veteran.
Please help.

And then he waited.

50

By making himself inconspicuous, tucking himself well back into a shallow gap between two buildings, Gabriel essentially disappeared from view. The wealthy Muscovites walking along the wide pavement either didn't see him or didn't care to. Either way, he was content.

After an hour and a half, judging from the passage of the sun overhead, bathed in sweat, he saw what he had been waiting for. One of the doormen outside Byko's house touched his earpiece, nodded, spoke a few words into his wrist, then turned to his colleague. They stood a touch straighter, glancing up and down the street.

A few moments later, the front door swung inwards and a man appeared, framed in the dark rectangle as if for a portrait: blond, clean-shaven, a jut to his jaw. Byko stood there for a second as if waiting for acknowledgement. Not particularly tall, but stocky, he was attired in tight-fitting jeans and a white jacket made of some kind of shiny fabric. He placed sunglasses on his nose, said something to the doormen then walked up the street towards Red Square. He had a boxer's grace, Gabriel noticed, looking light on

ANDY MASLEN

his feet as he walked, with the two doormen-cum-bodyguards falling
into step behind him.

* * *

Max owned various properties in Central Moscow, and he'd given
Gabriel the key to a one-bedroom flat in an old Soviet tower-block
several kilometres from Byko's address. Where the buildings on
Volkhonka Street were either old-school classical, with pediments,
porticoes and columns, or architect-designed modern, all right-
angles, smoked glass and exposed steel, those on Sovkhoznaya Street
were simple brick, concrete and glass high-rise blocks.

At five, after a day shuffling about on Volkhonka Street and a
few of its offshoots, he returned to the flat, stripped off his
disgusting outer casing, showered and changed. He prepared a
quick meal from some stuff he'd bought in a minimart then watched
Russian TV – soap operas and a current affairs show – for the rest
of the evening.

He was back on duty on Volkhonka Street at 8.00 a.m. the
following day, the forest mud replaced with city dirt. And again the
morning after that. And again. And again. The lurk wasn't bad.
He'd been on plenty a lot worse. Sitting half-submerged in a tropical
swamp, being eaten alive by leeches below the waterline and
mosquitos above, shitting into plastic bags, eating C-rations for a
fortnight, had been one of the highlights of his military career.
Apart from a warm flat to return to each evening, on Volkhonka
Street he had Max's driver to thank for provision drops: posing as a
concerned citizen, the man, Lenko, offered Gabriel a wrapped
sandwich or a bar of chocolate, a coffee or a can of Coke as he
passed.

Byko's routine was unvarying. He emerged from the house at
10.30 a.m. on the dot, nodded to the two heavies, then made his
way northeast, towards Red Square.

* * *

On the fifth morning, Gabriel stationed himself at the entrance to a narrow alley between a hardware store and a closed-down Western Union outlet. The window behind him was shuttered with a perforated steel sheet, and the door had been plastered with club flyers and posters for rock bands. Gabriel wondered that the well-heeled residents of Volkhonka Street allowed such an eyesore to exist in their otherwise swanky environment, then reflected that in the new era of Russian wealth, perhaps they all thought it was somebody else's job to remove them.

Once upon a time, the State would have employed someone – a babushka perhaps, or ageing veteran – to keep everything spick and span. But then, in those days, Volkhonka Street wouldn't have been worth keeping clean anyway. And Stalin, the real Stalin that is, not his impersonator at Number Seventeen, would probably have rounded the residents up and shot them in the back of the head.

In a cracked and roughened working-class Moscow accent, he asked a passerby – a young blonde in Moschino-branded sneakers and soft, silky running gear – for the time. She wrinkled her nose as she looked down at him but answered him anyway, after checking her iPhone.

"Ten fifteen. God, why don't you have a shower or something? You stink of, like, death or whatever."

As she strutted off, head held high, Gabriel made ready. Wiping the gathering sweat from his eyes and trying to ignore the furious itching beneath his army cap, he pushed his Starbucks cup out a little further into the pavement and arranged his cardboard sign so it would be facing Little Stalin.

The street was busy. Useless for a covert assassination. Perfect for what Gabriel had planned. Mostly wealthy types off for a day's shopping plus the odd tourist and business executive on their way to a meeting. Hubbub. Random movement. Cover.

He looked down the street. Little Stalin had just emerged from his front door and set off. As usual, the two heavies were walking in lockstep two paces behind their boss. *Dumb formation. Should have one in front of you*, Gabriel thought, standing then bending to pick up his beggar's cup and sign.

Ten metres to contact. He shuffled a couple of paces out into the flow of pedestrians. They parted around him, faces averted, handkerchiefs whipped out and pressed to wrinkled noses.

Five metres. He stooped a little and shuffled down the street towards the oncoming trio. Adjusted his grip on the sign, and the object concealed behind it.

Two metres. He caught Little Stalin's eye.

"Hey, boss! Spare some change for a veteran. I fought for Mother Russia," he rasped.

One metre. Byko smiled and reached into his pocket. Behind him, the two heavies also slowed. Gabriel glanced at each of them in turn. They were watchful but he could see disdain, dismissal, even, in their glares. *You're not a problem*, the gazes said. *You're nothing*.

Together the four men made a little knot around which other people flowed like water round a rock. Byko withdrew his hand from his pocket clutching a fat wad of banknotes.

"Here you go, friend. I always like to support our boys," Byko said, peeling off a turquoise-and-green one-thousand-ruble note from the wad and dropping it into the Starbucks cup.

Gabriel glanced into the cup, eyes wide, then stared into Byko's eyes, beginning to tremble and sway slightly from side to side though holding Byko's gaze in an intense, unblinking stare.

"Oh, boss, you are a prince! Truly. I mean, such generosity. They call you Little Stalin but I call you Lord. A lord of plenty. Of such munificence. You didn't need to do that but you have and it's a gesture worthy of a play by our esteemed Tolstoy or Chekhov or Pushkin or Dostoyevsky and I thank you from the bottom of my veteran's wounded heart."

Gabriel held out his filthy right hand. Clearly flattered, and maybe even baffled by Gabriel's off-kilter speech of gratitude, Byko accepted Gabriel's outstretched hand and pumped it up and down. And Gabriel stepped in behind it.

If Byko realised Gabriel had penetrated his personal space and was now standing so close the bodyguards' view was completely obscured, he gave no sign. But then, those tricked by Yinshen fangshi – the Way of Stealth – never did know. That was the ancient art's point and its purpose. And the young Gabriel Wolfe had been an avid student as he stood before Master Zhao and practised, hour after hour after hour.

And then Byko's eyes rolled upwards in their sockets and his knees gave way. Gabriel stepped back, pulling Byko towards him and let him crumple to the ground.

"He's had a heart attack!" Gabriel yelled at the top of his voice, drawing stares from passersby and causing a handful of them to turn and stop, or hurry over to see what the fuss was about.

The two heavies, faces masks of panic, bent to their dying boss. Gabriel slid a hand back inside his greatcoat for a second.

"Call an ambulance!" one shouted, reaching for his phone.

"Yeah!" Gabriel bellowed. "Call one-oh-three! It's his heart! He's dying!"

In truth, Kasimir Byko aka Little Stalin was already dead. But Gabriel wasn't lying. His heart *was* the problem. Gabriel had just stabbed him with a stiletto. His thrust had driven the long, narrow blade into its left ventricle and severed the thoracic artery. Instead of transporting newly oxygenated blood down to the rest of his body, the thick tube of tissue simply allowed litre after litre to be expelled into Byko's thorax, surrounding the vital organs, filling the space between his lungs and his ribcage and flowing out of the five-millimetre hole in his chest wall, where it soaked into the fine poplin of his shirt.

People were crowding around the fallen gangster and his bodyguards, most holding phones aloft, but a few more public-spirited types actually using them to call the emergency services.

"Get that homeless guy!" one of the bodyguards shouted above the commotion.

What homeless guy? the crowd of onlookers might have asked. The filthy, stinking veteran had vanished. All that remained of him, trodden on and scuffed, was a stinking greatcoat and an army cap, its furry flaps lending it the appearance of an animal's head. The cardboard sign lay face up on the pavement, marked with footprints. The Starbucks cup, minus the one-thousand-ruble note, lay flattened beside it.

. . .

At the far end of the alleyway, wearing a black Adidas tracksuit and blue-and-orange Saucony running shoes, and wiping street grime from his face with a damp towel, Gabriel Wolfe jogged away, up Lebyazhiy Pereulok. A black Mercedes S-Class was waiting for him, engine idling. As he reached the rear door, it opened, and he slid into the welcoming embrace of its plush leather seats and air-conditioned interior.

"You stink worse than before," Lenko said, as he merged into the traffic. "Is it done?"

"Let's just say Moscow's veterans will be looking for a new benefactor from now on."

As Lenko piloted the big Mercedes northwest, back to the dacha, Gabriel stared out of the window. You could change a country only so much, he mused. Chuck out Communism, hail the new democratic freedoms, bring in designer brands, luxury car showrooms, five-hundred-quid-a-night hotels, businesspeople, the New Russians.

But take a scraper to that shiny surface, and you'd find the same old savagery. Gangsters in tailored suits trafficking kids halfway round the world so paedophiles could indulge their evil perversions. People like Max Novgorodsky, kidding themselves they were global tycoons when they were really just better-dressed versions of the mobsters they'd always been. A former KGB agent sitting in the Kremlin, sending private-enterprise hitmen out to eliminate his enemies, then claiming it was nothing to do with him.

He caught a whiff of the stench rising from his skin and fought down a wave of nausea.

51

They arrived at the dacha just before midday. Lenko rolled the car to a stop on the gravel parking area and practically leapt from the car. Inhaling deeply, he looked at Gabriel, though Gabriel could tell it was a look of respect, albeit mixed with disgust.

Lenko shook his head.

"Man, I tell you, that car is going to the valeter's first thing tomorrow morning. It smells like two skunks fucked themselves to death in there!"

Gabriel grinned and went inside.

Max greeted him in the hallway. He came towards him, arms wide, then, as he closed the distance between them to hugging range, stopped and let his arms fall by his sides.

"Gabrisha, did anyone tell you, you stink like —"

"Two skunks fucking? Yes. Lenko did. Sorry, boss. I'll go and get myself cleaned up."

"And is it done?"

"Mm-hmm. Turn on the news. I guess he was enough of a big noise in Moscow to make the lunchtime bulletins. Here. He gave me this."

Gabriel held out a one-thousand-ruble note, its turquoise-and-green surface now stained with Byko's blood so that the bell tower and onion-domed church on the reverse appeared to be submerged in a red sea.

Max took the bloody banknote and held it to his nose, sniffing deeply. He nodded appreciatively as if judging a fine wine.

"Let's watch together, Gabrisha. Come."

Then he laid a heavy arm across Gabriel's shoulders, clearly not letting the smell bother him, and led him into the lounge. A leather-and-chrome corner-unit and matching armchairs occupied most of the floorspace, a stark contrast to the rustic charm of the exterior. Russian landscape paintings hung on the walls, mostly oils but a few little watercolours as well. Max clearly fancied himself as an art collector.

"Where did that come from?" Gabriel asked, pointing to a long, curved sword, resting on steel brackets on one wall.

The weapon had no guard, leaving Gabriel to imagine the care its wielder would need to exercise to avoid cutting his own hand in two.

"That? From the Caucasus. It's a *shashka*. My ancestors were Cossacks. It reminds me of my roots. Now, sit. No, wait! Stay standing. I'm not having you ruining my upholstery."

He jabbed a remote at the vast flatscreen TV mounted on the wall, then sat back in a deep-blue sofa. Gabriel stood behind him and watched as the black screen blossomed with colour. A heavily made-up brunette newsreader wearing a scarlet blouse and a serious expression was speaking above a scrolling banner.

"—collapsed and died of a suspected heart attack in Volkhonka Street earlier today. A well-known Moscow businessman, Kasimir Byko was of Georgian descent, born in Gory, the hometown of Joseph Stalin. He—"

The picture snapped off. Max turned to look up at Gabriel, a wide smile on his face.

"Thank you. Welcome to Kuznitsa. We'll celebrate properly tonight. Nozh and Krasivyj are coming to meet you, and we'll seal the deal properly. The chef's doing Kobe beef. Japanese cows. They massage them every day, did you know that? Massage! But it's worth it. Best bloody meat you'll ever taste, I promise you. They'll be here at six. Now. Go and clean up. You smell more like *four* skunks fucking!"

After a long, scalding shower and liberal application of Max's guest-room toiletries, Gabriel reckoned he had removed ninety-nine percent of his previous alter ego. Re-dressed in jeans, T-shirt and boots, he went to find his host.

The ground floor seemed deserted. Gabriel left through the back door, wondering if Max was in the garden. Two grey-haired men were sitting in rattan chairs, tumblers of clear liquid – vodka, he assumed – by their elbows on a glass-topped table. They noticed his arrival and stood simultaneously, revealing at once the almost comical difference in their stature.

One was built like an ogre, well over six feet and with so much muscle cladding his frame his arms hung out from his sides. His face bore the obvious marks of battle: on the left side, a mess of burnt, pink skin, swirled like hot plastic; on the right, an ugly scar from a blade of some sort. The other, though shorter, was still muscular beneath his clothes; his biceps in particular were straining the fabric of his shirt.

"So," the shorter man said, offering his hand. "This must be the famous Gabriel Wolfe that Max has been bleating on about! Apparently we owe you a vote of thanks, is that right?"

His hand released from the older man's crushing grip, Gabriel smiled and nodded.

"If you mean Byko, yes. That was me."

"Impressive work. They're still saying it was his heart."

"It was. Just not in the way they said on the news."

"Ha! Very good. I'm Nozh. This is Krasivyj."

The other man stepped in and shook Gabriel by the hand.

"So, you and Max smoothed it over did you? Buried the hatchet?"

Gabriel nodded.

"Something like that."

Krasivyj pointed to the scabbed-over lettering on Gabriel's left forearm.

"He do that to you? Or was it Fedya?"

"Neither. I did it. To show my loyalty."

"You're really joining us, then?"

"If you'll have me. Like I told Max, I was making shit money working as a torpedo for the British Government and I reckon they were getting ready to throw me on the scrapheap anyway. Always younger, fitter guys coming along looking for a billet in black ops."

"Yeah? Well you'll have more fun with us and you'll be making serious money. Play your cards right, and you'll be able to quit at fifty and never work again."

"Forgive me, as the new boy, but you aren't going to see fifty again, and Max certainly isn't, so how come you're still working?"

Both men laughed and Nozh gestured with his glass of vodka, taking in the vast garden and the woods beyond.

"You call this working, my friend? Anyway, we're management. It's our business. You don't think Warren Buffet's ever going to retire, do you? Same with us. Kuznitsa's not a job for us. It's our life. It's Max's life. We've been together since the beginning."

"Did someone say my name?" Max called, striding across the grass towards them. "Ah, Gabrisha! I see you've met my two oldest friends."

"Hi, Max. I hope I smell better now."

Max bear-hugged him and inhaled theatrically.

"Sweet as a newly-washed whore! Now, come with me, I want to introduce you to a few of the other guys who work for me here. Forgive me, Nozh, Krasivyj. I'll see you later."

Max led Gabriel away from his two friends and round to the front of the house, where a couple of men cut from the same cloth as Little Stalin's heavies were standing guard, armed with Heckler & Koch MP5 submachine guns, fitted with integral suppressors.

"Donat, Anfim, this is Gabriel. He's one of us now. You'll be seeing him around."

"OK, boss," the heavies chorused.

They nodded at Gabriel but made no move to shake hands or introduce themselves further. He nodded back and allowed Max to lead him away, towards the front door.

"They don't say much, but then again, I don't pay them for their public speaking skills, eh?" Max said, pushing open the front door and gesturing for Gabriel to go in ahead of him.

Still being cautious, eh, Max? I don't blame you.

"Where now?" Gabriel asked.

"Come and meet the most important man in my life."

Max pointed to a door leading into a corridor, Gabriel went ahead, opening the door and walking down the narrow underlit hallway. At the far end was another door, punctuated by a circle of glass at head height. He peered in, then pushed through the door.

The kitchen wasn't huge, but it was still big enough to house a professional-looking range-cooker with six full-size gas burners, a pair of ovens, a double-doored fridge and matching freezer, both in brushed stainless steel finish, and a central island workstation with a stainless steel top.

On the far side of the workstation, a short, fat man in chef's whites was slicing into a thick joint of meat, marbled through with streaks of fat. He looked up as Gabriel entered the kitchen, frowned, then smiled as Max came in behind Gabriel.

"Here he is!" Max said, in an overloud voice, as though introducing a theatre act. "The best chef in all of Russia. Stefan Kubarev. How's tonight's dinner coming on Stepashka?"

The chef smiled, revealing a gold tooth, and wiped a shining forehead with a tea towel. He had twinkling brown eyes and a snub nose that gave him the appearance of a mischievous child.

"This beef is a very good batch, Max. The butcher on Simonovskiy Street only got it in this morning. Flown straight from Hyōgo Prefecture on Honshu. It's going to melt in your mouth. And who is this?" he asked, gesturing with the knife in his right hand.

"This is Gabrisha. He came to me via Red Dog."

"Oh, then I'd better cut him a thicker steak. He'll need feeding up before he's of any use to you."

"No worries on that score. He's already proved his worth to me."

"Well, I'm pleased to meet you, Gabrisha," the chef said, wiping his hands in his apron then offering his right.

"You too, chef."

"Call me Stepashka. You're family now."

The new member of the Kuznitsa family nodded, then left the chef to his work, mentally adding a dozen cook's knives and a steak tenderizing mallet to the tally of weapons he'd identified during his stay at the dacha.

52

"Is it OK if I take a walk before dinner, Max?" Gabriel asked when they were outside again. "It feels like a long time since I had good honest earth under my feet and not concrete. And maybe I could ask Stepashka to make me a sandwich to keep me going till dinner?"

"Of course! Tell you what. Why don't you take Pyotr with you? He likes it out there, and he knows the way back if you get lost."

Gabriel smiled, and nodded.

"OK, yes. I'd like that."

"Go get your sandwich, then come and find me in the garden. I'll get Pyotr for you when you're back."

Gabriel made his way back to the kitchen, grabbing a thin cotton bomber jacket from a hook in the hall. He pushed through the swing door as before. The chef looked up. Before him, four thick cuts of beef sat in a spreading pool of juices, trimmed of excess fat and looking so good Gabriel could imagine eating one raw.

"Hello, Gabrisha! Forget something?"

"I'm taking Pyotr for a walk in the woods. I was hoping I could get a sandwich to last me until dinner. Prison food wasn't up to much," he added, patting his stomach.

"Of course, of course! You want me to make it for you?"

Gabriel smiled and shook his head.

"No need. You carry on with preparing dinner. Just point me at the bread."

The chef smiled, drawing fans of crinkles in the outer corners of his eyes.

"Bread's over there in the enamel box," he said, pointing to one of the worktops round the edge of the kitchen. "Cold meat, cheese, pickles in the fridge, there." Another gesture. "You can work over there, out of my way. Don't want blood in your sandwich do you?"

Gabriel cut two thick slices of bread. The loaf, with its irregular shape and unevenly browned crust, was obviously homemade. He found ham and a hard, whitish cheese in the fridge and added a sliced gherkin, then slathered the top slice of bread with mayonnaise and mustard from brightly labelled jars in the fridge door.

"Any foil, Stepashka?" he asked over his shoulder, slicing the sandwich in half with a boning knife, which he then wiped on a cloth behind the sink.

"Third drawer down under the toaster."

With the sandwich wrapped, Gabriel moved towards the door.

"Thanks, chef!" he called, about to leave.

"Wait!" the chef said looking up from a chopping board covered in diced red onions.

Gabriel turned. *What now?*

"Did you say you were going into the woods?"

"Yes."

The little man grinned.

"Excellent! I can prepare a special treat for the boss. And you, of course," he added hurriedly. "Hold on a second."

He bustled over to a shelf laden with cookbooks and ran his finger along the spines with his oddly round head cocked to one side.

"Aha! Here you are."

He pulled out a battered book with a photograph of a basket of mushrooms on the front cover. He flipped through the pages until he came to a much-stained recipe opposite a photo of a fat-stemmed mushroom with a bulbous reddish-brown cap in a patch of leaf mould. He beckoned Gabriel.

Gabriel stood by the chef's side and looked at the photo.

"What's that?" he asked.

"That, my friend, is a *Russula xerampelina*, to give it its Latin name. We call them shrimps in this part of the world. Fried in butter with a little garlic, one taste and you'd think you'd gone to heaven."

"And they grow locally, is that it? Want me to look for some?"

"Yeah. They're a real delicacy. Plenty in the woods, especially near the ponds. Ideally, you'd want an expert mushroomer to guide you, but Pyotr'll probably lead you there. He likes to drink the water. Just one thing."

"What's that?"

"If they've got white flecks on the caps, leave them be. Those are *Amanita muscaria*, what we call *Mukhomor*. They can kill you if you eat them raw, but in any case, they taste horrible and send you tripping like you're on acid. OK?"

Gabriel nodded, the eager student.

"OK. Red cap with no white spots equals shrimp. Pick. Red caps *with* white spot equals *Mukhomor*. Don't pick."

"You got it. We'll make a mushroomer of you yet! Now, be off with you. Let me get on with my cooking."

Gabriel found Max deep in conversation with Nozh and Krasivyj by a pool covered with water lilies. Each man clutched a tumbler of vodka clinking with ice cubes. A bottle sat in an ice bucket on the grass, its silver sides beaded with condensation.

"Ah, here he is!" Max said loudly as Gabriel approached. "Provisioned for your trip, I see."

"Yeah. And chef's sending me mushroom-hunting. Special treat for tonight, apparently."

"Excellent! Did he tell you to look for shrimps?"

"Yes."

"God, I love that man. He'd make your mother weep with his

cooking, I tell you. Now, where's Pyotr?" Max turned away and raised his hands to his mouth. "Pyotr! Come!"

Gabriel counted, reaching five before the wolf hurtled round the side of the dacha, its paws kicking up dust as it skidded out of the corner then gaining traction as it reached the grass. It bounded up to Max, wagging its tail for all the world as though it were a retriever or a pointer, and not some oversized character from a Russian folktale. He scratched Pyotr under the chin, avoiding the drool that dripped from his maw and puddled in the dust under his head. Then he got down on one knee so he was face to face with the wolf.

He seized its massive head in his hands and shook it gently from side to side in time with his words.

"Now, you go with Gabrisha here for a nice long walk in the woods. Keep on the lookout, OK? And if anyone tries anything, you eat them. OK?"

Then he kissed the wolf on the tip of its nose and stood, knees popping.

"Dinner's at seven. Don't be late," he said to Gabriel. "Pyotr! Woods!"

He pointed towards the far corner of the garden and the wolf set off, presumably towards a gate. Gabriel followed at a jog.

* * *

Kuznitsa's ruling triumvirate watched as Gabriel left them with the wolf trotting a couple of metres ahead of him.

"Here you go," Nozh said, topping up Max's vodka.

"Thanks."

Max swallowed a quarter of the vodka and put the glass down.

"OK. He's gone out with Pyotr."

"You're not seriously recruiting him, are you?" Krasivyj asked. "All that bullshit with carving your name into his arm and doing Byko for you. That's just a smokescreen."

Max smiled. Krasivyj was his oldest friend. They'd grown up together. But he could, at times, be monumentally thick.

"Tell him, Nozh."

Nozh smiled at Max then turned in his chair so he was square on to Krasivyj.

"No, we're not recruiting Wolfe. He thinks he's tricked his way into our confidence, but he's alive for one reason and one reason only. To give us everything he knows about British counter-terror strategy, Special Forces training and operations, security protocols, tactics, hardware, software, intelligence techniques, personnel, command structures, all of that. Then, when we've bled him dry, Max'll give a signal and—"

"—we cut him to ribbons and send the bits back to 10 Downing Street by DH-fucking-L," Max finished, before picking up his glass and draining it.

Krasivyj frowned.

"But what if he runs off? In the woods, I mean?"

Max laughed.

"I put Fedya on his tail. Wolfe's coming back, all right. One way or another."

The light of understanding seeped across Krasivyj's features. The frown lifted, and his forehead smoothed out. He nodded and smiled.

"Ah, OK. That makes more sense. After we're done, I'll do the cutting, OK?"

"As you like, old friend," Max said. "As you like. Now," he clapped his hands together, "We've business to discuss before dinner. Let's go inside."

Casting a look over his shoulder, Max led the others towards the rear of the dacha.

53

Gabriel followed the wolf down a long, curving path through gradually thickening vegetation ripe with the smell of summer. The trees were all in full leaf: plenty of birch, some ash, sycamore, a few oaks, and some species he couldn't identify. The wolf's multicoloured coat made excellent camouflage and it disappeared for a few seconds at a time as the gradations of grey, tawny-brown and silver blended into the dappled sunlight filtering down through the trees.

Remembering the chef's pleas for shrimp, Gabriel looked around, searching out the red-capped fungi that Stepashka said were such a delicacy. Almost at once, he saw one and bent to pick it. Stepashka had said, "Where there's one, there's a family," and his words proved true. Within a square yard, Gabriel found two dozen more of the fat-stemmed mushrooms. He loaded up his basket and was about to stand up when another red-cap caught his eye. But this was no shrimp. This was a white-spotted *Mukhomor*. The poisonous mushroom he knew as *fly agaric*. He picked it, spotted six more, and added them to his haul. Then he walked on, listening for the sound of the wolf's paws crackling through the undergrowth. The path grew narrower and less well defined until it became little more than an animal track.

He picked up the distant sound of running water. The wolf was already moving faster, then broke into a run. Noting the precise path it had taken, Gabriel stopped. Crouched down. And listened.

Let me off the leash on my own, Max? I don't think so. I wouldn't, and I'm not the one running a global crime gang. It won't be Donat or Anfim, though. They're strictly open-air guys. Too big and too clumsy for surveillance. That leaves Fedya. So, my little friend, what are you carrying? Not the Dragunov. Too unwieldy in this undergrowth. And too much. Probably a pistol, and maybe your garotte or a knife as backup. Fine. Bring it on.

He inhaled deeply, then let it out through open mouth, soundless. He waited. Then Fedya made his presence known. It wasn't much of a noise. A faint crack then a swish. But it signified everything to Gabriel. A snapped twig and a branch being pushed aside. He turned left, heading deeper into the forest, off the track. Dead leaves carpeted the forest floor, and out of the drying rays of the sun they remained soft, damp – and noiseless. Employing a loose-limbed, sinuous technique taught to him by Zhao Xi, and refined by SAS jungle warfare instructors, Gabriel moved silently, deeper into the forest, before veering leftward.

Perhaps sensing he'd lost contact with his quarry, Fedya was making more noise. The cracks and swishes were louder and more frequent. *You're speeding up, my friend*, Gabriel thought. *Speeding up and getting careless. Anxious. That's bad. For you. Good for me.* After a few more minutes, Gabriel emerged back onto the path, a hundred metres closer to the house than his position when he'd let the wolf run ahead. He trotted along, keeping to its well-worn centre, which was free of twigs and dry vegetation.

Fedya had made no attempt to camouflage himself. Gabriel saw his white T-shirt flash between two birch trees twenty metres ahead, where the path disappeared and only the narrow animal-track remained. The midget was making heavy weather of the undergrowth, pushing through the stiff branches and crushing fallen twigs under his shiny black shoes with no regard for the noise he was making.

Are you more used to guarding your boss in the open, too?

Fedya had a pistol in his right hand. His left was curled round something. At this distance, Gabriel couldn't make it out, though he had a good idea. *Silence is golden*, he thought as he closed in. With just three metres separating them, he pulled out the little boning knife he'd slipped off the chopping board while making his sandwich.

The knife caught in the lining of his pocket and sliced into the fabric as it came free. Fedya whipped round at the short, sharp sound.

Gabriel leapt forwards and slashed at the midget's incoming gun arm, hitting him in the wrist and almost severing his hand. The pistol thumped into the leaf mould at their feet. Before Fedya had a chance to scream, Gabriel clamped his left hand over his mouth and pushed him over, throwing his weight behind the move but losing his knife as they slammed into the ground.

Even with his right hand out of action, and spraying them both with blood, Fedya was a skilful fighter. Writhing and bucking under Gabriel, he managed to get his left hand free. He punched Gabriel hard in the side of the head then flicked out his garotte and swung it. Gabriel saw the flash of piano wire as it whirled over his head. But he'd been expecting the move and shot out his right hand to block its progress. He grabbed the short wooden handle and wrenched the garotte out of Fedya's grasp.

With both handles now gripped in his fists, he jammed the murderously thin weapon down across Fedya's neck. The little man's eyes bulged and though his mouth worked, no sound emerged. The garotte had bitten deep, severing his windpipe. Over the whistle of escaping breath, Gabriel clenched his teeth and pushed down harder. The arteries went next, releasing a fan of scarlet blood into the air. Fedya's eyes widened further then glazed over as the life force left him. Gabriel leant down with all his weight, forcing the wire almost down to the spine before releasing it.

Panting, Gabriel crawled off the dead man and retrieved the pistol. Sticking it into his waistband, he stood and collected his knife. He strode off, following the path the wolf had taken, heading for the water. After a hundred metres or so, the vegetation opened out, and he found himself on the bank of a wide body of water maybe the size of a couple of tennis courts. *Some pond*, he thought. A stream fed it from one end, accounting for the sounds Gabriel had picked up earlier, before killing Fedya.

The trees on the far side were waving in the breeze and nearer to him, bulrushes swayed, their brown, furry, sausage-shaped heads nodding. As if summoned by an artist intent on creating the perfect scene, perhaps called *A Lake Outside Moscow*, a pair of fat-bodied, iridescent dragonflies buzzed low over the surface and described a tight circle round his head, so close he could hear the helicopter whirr of their wings, before ranging back out over the pond, searching for prey.

A slurping sound caught his attention and he turned to his left. The wolf was leaning forwards, snout in the water, lapping furiously as if he hadn't drunk for a week. Gabriel estimated the wolf to be nudging two metres from nose to tail. Maybe weighing as much as a full-grown man. And packing a lot of muscle beneath that shaggy coat.

He watched as the wolf raised its head from the water, a stream of droplets cascading from its half-open mouth. The animal must have sensed it was being scrutinised, and turned its head, slowly, to the right. A ray of sunlight hit it full in the face and it blinked lazily, its yellow eyes fixed on Gabriel.

The wolf growled deep in its throat. The low, saw-toothed rumble ignited a primal emotion in Gabriel's endocrine system and the hairs on the back of his neck erected as adrenaline started loading his bloodstream. Keeping his movements slow and even, he rotated about his hips before moving his left foot out so he was standing facing the huge wolf.

You know, don't you? he thought. *You can smell Fedya's blood on me.*

In any other situation, faced with a predator of this size and lethality, Gabriel would simply have shot it before it could attack. But that wasn't an option here. The gunshot would alert Max and his cronies. They'd either assume Fedya had killed Gabriel or the other way round. Either way, he'd lose the element of surprise.

Backing away from the water in a series of awkward shuffling steps, the wolf swung round to face him, head-on. The growling went on, unceasingly, without any obvious pause for breath. Slowly, its upper lip retracted, showing those long, curved fangs and a row of small incisors between them.

Gabriel bent his knees a little, reached into his left-hand pocket and retrieved the sandwich. He tossed the foil-wrapped snack towards the wolf with his left hand. The yellow eyes flicked downwards as it thumped into the leaf mould at its feet. Lowering its head so it could sniff the package, it kept its gaze locked onto Gabriel. With its head down, Gabriel could see the thick ruff of hackles standing straight up behind its head, a fuller version of the pared-down response happening on the nape of his own neck.

It sniffed the foil package twice, loudly. Then, looking down, it nipped at the foil with its front teeth, steadying it with one forepaw, before tugging it free and gobbling down the bread, meat and cheese inside.

Gabriel moved a step closer while the wolf was eating, flexing his right wrist and tilting up the boning knife's razor-sharp blade. His heart was cantering along like a horse ready for the big moment when it would be given its head and allowed to race towards the finish line.

Up jerked the wolf's head. It licked its lips with that long, pink tongue and resumed growling, lips fully retracted now so that top and bottom teeth were exposed.

Its haunches twitched as it settled its weight down over its hind quarters.

Gabriel crouched lower, bringing his face almost on a level with the wolf's bared teeth.

"Come on, then," he murmured. "Let's have you!"

With a sound somewhere between a bark and a roar, the huge wolf sprang forwards, getting airborne from the force of its massive thigh muscles.

Gabriel had time to notice the deep-pink interior of the wolf's mouth and the sharp blades of its carnassial teeth.

He fell back under the wolf and grabbed its lower jaw tight in his left fist, pushing up and to the left. With his right hand he jammed the boning knife up to the hilt in the base of its neck. Three more times he thrust, as the wolf strained to reach his throat with its teeth. Each blow of the blade brought forth a yelp from the wolf, and a freshet of blood that sprayed onto Gabriel's face and neck, but it kept powering down onto him, scrabbling its hind paws against the ground between Gabriel's legs as it strove for purchase.

Its hot breath stank, and Gabriel could feel the strength going in his left arm, allowing those long, yellow canines to move closer to the soft, exposed tissue of his throat.

"No!" he shouted, and thrust again, sawing the blade up and down deep inside the soft tissue of the wolf's neck.

Suddenly, a gout of hot blood spurted from the wound he had opened in its throat. Litres of the stuff jetted out, soaking his torso and covering his face. With a whimper, the wolf went limp and rolled sideways. Gabriel scrambled out from under it and got to his knees, panting for breath. He watched the light in those huge yellow eyes dim and then disappear altogether as a film appeared on the shining surface and they dulled in death.

"I honour your life," he said in a ragged gasp.

Then he got to work.

* * *

MP5 slung over his shoulder, Anfim wandered down to the very bottom of the garden to take a piss. Now that the two deputy bosses had arrived in their black Range Rover, he was feeling more relaxed. He liked knowing they were all inside. Though the walls looked as though they were constructed from rustic timber, he could visualise the half-inch-thick steel plating sandwiched between the planks, just one of the boss's precautions. The wolf was another. He'd watched it tear a man to pieces on more than one occasion at a simple verbal command from Max.

A crash from the underbrush beyond the garden boundary made him jerk upright, taking his eye off what he was doing and splashing a dribble of urine onto the front of his jeans.

"Fuck it!" he muttered, zipping up.

Then he saw a slender birch sapling bend and spring back with a swish. He unslung his submachine gun and yanked the charging lever back.

"Hey, is that you, Pyotr?" he called out. "Or is it you, newbie, playing some stupid trick? Come out or I might spray some lead in there. See if that makes you laugh, eh?"

Then he caught sight of the wolf's shaggy head, that oddly mottled mixture of grey, black and brown fur, moving through the dense foliage of the nearby bushes.

"Oh, it *is* you. You gave me a scare you stupid animal. Come out here where I can see you."

The wolf emerged from the trees and, in a single, flowing, *insane* movement, stood upright and yawned, its bloody, fanged mouth filled with a grinning human face.

As he tried to process the sight of a blood-smeared werewolf walking towards him, his normal reflexes shut down and his hands refused to obey his brain's command to aim and fire. The beast raised its right hand and he caught a glint of silver. His last thought as it came to within two metres of him was that werewolves were supposed to be killed by silver.

Then the werewolf rushed him, snarling lips pulled back from its teeth. The blade came up and then slashed in from his left, biting deep into his neck with a pain like nothing he had ever experienced.

He dropped his gun and clutched his spurting neck in a frantic attempt to stem the flow of his own, dear lifeblood, but it was no good. He knew it. The pain was fading, though, which was a good thing. And the light was dimming and his balance was going. And the werewolf was in front of him snarling with those white teeth like a grinning death's head in all that blood. As he fell backwards, his last sight was a translucent arc of his own blood spraying up into that beautiful, cloudless, Russian sky.

* * *

Gabriel bent to retrieve the MP5. He adjusted the knot on the pelt's front legs, which he'd tied round his neck, and pulled the upper jaw further down over his face. The teeth were scratching his forehead, but he was enjoying the pain.

He strode towards the front of the house, catching a glimpse of the backs of the three Kuznitsa bosses' heads silhouetted against the wall-mounted TV in the living room.

Out front, he saw the other guard Donat leaning against the bonnet of an all-black Range Rover rolling a cigarette.

Gabriel padded closer on silent feet – *Thank you, master Zhao!*

From an arm's length behind Donat he spoke in a jokey tone.

"Hey, Donat. Who do you reckon will win tonight, Spartak or Dynamo?"

The man turned, a smile on his face.

"No contest. Dynamo. I'll—"

He died with his eyes wide and his mouth half-forming the next word in his sentence, Gabriel's boning knife slashing his throat from left to right, releasing a hiss of air and a torrent of foamy blood.

Gabriel removed the magazine from the second MP5 and worked the charging lever to eject any unfired rounds in the action. None came. Donat had not been expecting trouble. He pushed the mag into his other back pocket and flung the empty submachine gun into the bushes. He turned and headed inside.

The passageway to the kitchen was dark, and as Gabriel reached the swing door he heard singing, a high, melodious voice with a melancholy edge declaring its owner's undying love to a girl named Valentina.

Gabriel pushed the door open and walked in.

The chef had his back to Gabriel. His left arm was cradling a copper bowl while his right was working a balloon whisk hard, its wires clicking and scratching against the sides of the bowl. Beside him, an almost-empty bottle of vodka stood beside a heap of empty eggshells, open bags of flour and sugar and a big pile of ground almonds, whose smell penetrated even beyond the bloody reek that had taken up residence in Gabriel's nostrils.

This is too easy, Gabriel thought. *Here we go again, Master. Time for a spot of the old hypnosis, eh? Oh, that's interesting, I've picked up Max's little verbal mannerism. Focus, focus, focus.*

He grasped a dangling paw and hooked his right thumb and little finger around the outer claws, then he stretched out a hand and tapped the drunk chef on his right shoulder.

The chef stopped singing mid-line.

"Come back to me, Valentina, the memory of your sweet smile—"

The chef stumbled as he turned, a smile on his lips, the eyes watery but still twinkling. Then his mouth dropped open.

"Wha—?"

Gabriel swayed and locked his gaze onto the chef's pupils. He began the ritual movements, synchronising his breathing with the chef, and flicking his eyes left to right, to left, to right. The chef blinked. *Drunks are too easy. No real challenge. A straight sequence of commands will send him down into the obedient place all subjects reach in the end.*

"Stepashka, listen to me. Are you listening to me?"

"Yes, but who?"

"I am your friend, am I your friend?"

"Yes, but, I mean you're—"

"Say after me, you are my friend."

"You are my friend."

"And I want to help you."

"And I want to help you."

"Tell me what to do."

"Tell me what to do."

Gabriel told him what to do.

The chef sliced the mushrooms and fried them in a little butter. While he took them through to the dining room, Gabriel set to work on the meat.

54

In the dining room, Max, Nozh and Krasivyj were sitting round one end of the long table. Max himself had laid out the cutlery, table linen and wine glasses and all three were engaged in a heated discussion – as Donat had expected to be – about the likely outcome of the football match that evening at Khimki Arena.

The chef entered bearing three plates of fried mushrooms.

Max looked up and smiled drunkenly.

"Hey, hey! Here he is, my darling Stepashka, the best chef in all the Russias. What've you got for us Stepashka? It smells like angels' breath."

"Your favourite, boss. Shrimp fried in butter."

Max placed his hands together at his sternum and bowed his head.

"For what we are about to receive may the Lord make us truly thankful. Amen."

Three clinks, three plates of heavenly-smelling wild mushrooms placed before three ravenous, drunk gangsters.

"Where's the new boy?" Nozh asked.

"You see him, Stepashka?" Max asked.

"He came back without Pyotr. Said he was going back out to look for him."

Max grunted.

"Stupid man. Pyotr knows the forest better than his mother's teats. He'll be back when he's good and ready. Probably doing a little hunting."

The chef nodded, executed an off-kilter about-turn and left them to their food.

Max placed a forkful of the mushrooms on his tongue and closed his mouth softly around the fungus, not wanting to rush things. These were, after all, the best the forest had to offer.

"Oh, my God, boys, taste them," he groaned.

"Good," Krasivyj mumbled through a mouthful.

"Good? Jesus, Krasivyj, what are you, some city-type who wouldn't know a shrimp from one of those anaemic little shop-bought things?"

"No, sorry, Max. I mean, they're delicious."

"So when do we start on the new boy?" Nozh asked, taking off his glasses and wiping them on a corner of his napkin.

"After dinner. We can work on him for a few hours, then get some sleep and start again in the morning. When we're done, we kill him. Then Pyotr gets a proper meal."

"But I thought you said we were going to send him to London in a box," Krasivyj said, frowning, wiping a piece of bread round his plate.

"A figure of speech, that's all. Don't worry Krasivyj, you can still do the wet work."

"Oh, OK. Thanks, Max," Krasivyj said, smiling again.

The door swung open and the chef appeared again, bearing an even larger tray than for the first course. Three big oval plates groaning with vast steaks, their upper surfaces criss-crossed with black lines from the bars of the griddle.

"Here you are. The best that Japan has to offer," the chef said, setting a plate before each man. "Enjoy!"

"Oh, we will, Stepashka, we will," Max said, slicing into his steak and revelling in the way the thin, pink meat juices ran out around the blade of his knife.

The three men ate in silence for a minute, then Krasivyj spoke up, his jaws working on a lump of the meat.

"Hey, Max? Not being funny or anything, but if this is the best the Japs have to offer, maybe we should go back to getting Russian beef. This is as tough as old boots. And it tastes like shit, too."

"What's yours like, Nozh?" Max asked, forcing down another gobbet of thoroughly-chewed but still fibrous meat, reluctant to acknowledge the truth of Krasivyj's judgement.

Nosh wrinkled his nose and shook his head.

"Got to agree with Krasivyj. I had better meat in the army."

Max put his knife and fork down.

"Mine, too. Hey, Stepashka!" he bellowed. "Get your drunken arse in here! If this is Kobe beef then I'm a fucking ballet dancer!"

* * *

The chef didn't respond to the yelled command. He lay dead in a curdled lake of blood and egg custard beneath his stainless steel workstation, surrounded by the tools of his trade. A single suppressed round from the MP5 to the back of the skull was as fast and as painless as Gabriel could make it.

Max's yell was the signal Gabriel had been waiting for. He took his ear away from the door and straightened up. He adjusted the wolf-mask, bringing the upper jaw a little lower over his brow. Checked the MP5's fire-selector switch was set to full-auto. Inhaled deeply. And opened the door.

55

In the dining room, Max, Nozh and Krasivyj are sitting round one end of the long table. The seating arrangement is perfect for his needs. Nozh and Krasivyj are facing Max across the table. They see the door opening. Max has his back to it. The angle means Max is out of the field of fire.

Nozh and Krasivyj begin to rise, their faces masks of terror and anger mixed. Sober, they might have had a fighting chance of at least diving for cover. This drunk, all they manage to achieve is to make themselves larger targets.

Gabriel shoots Krasivyj first. No special reason, although his obvious relish for torture made him Gabriel's least favourite of the two henchmen.

The burst hits him high in the chest. Red blossoms on his shirtfront.

Gabriel shoots him again, higher this time, exploding his skull.

Blood and brain tissue paints the wall behind him in a scarlet starburst.

The body topples sideways against Nozh, whose eyes are staring, wild.

Gabriel's second burst rips Nozh almost in half, tearing open his gut and spilling a slimy mess of intestines onto the table. The blood washes all the way across the polished surface and runs off the edge into Max's lap.

Max is half-turned round in his chair. If he notices the flood of wetness on his trousers, he gives no sign. His eyes are wide, whites visible all the way round the irises.

How many seconds have passed? Gabriel has no idea. Two? Three? Four? No more than five? Things move fast and slow when things get kinetic. The brain goes into overdrive, using every single nerve cell to keep its owner alive and focused at times like these.

He aims down and squeezes the trigger. The MP5's pistol rounds smash into Max's legs. He screams and grips the arms of his chair in an effort to avoid toppling out of it.

Gabriel watches the blood flowing from Max's shattered shins, over his shoes and onto the floor.

Keeping the MP5s smoking muzzle pointed at Max's face, Gabriel walks over and sits opposite him, shoving Nozh's corpse out of the way first.

Max's face is a rictus of pain. Leg wounds are rarely fatal, and nowhere near as painful as being gutshot, when stomach acid spews into the wound, but they still hurt plenty. Oh, yes. They still hurt. Max gasps as he takes in Gabriel's monstrous headgear and cape.

"Steak a little tough, was it, Max?" Gabriel asks, his voice flat, free of emotion, waiting for Max to make the connection.

"You, you – Pyotr! No!"

Max throws his head back and howls with pain and grief. Gabriel waits for the impotent moan to end.

"Ironic, isn't it? Not quite how Prokofiev imagined the story ending. The wolf alive and Peter dead. Think yourself lucky I didn't poison you with *Mukhomor* first. I only didn't because I realised they'd take too long."

"What do you want, Gabrisha?" Max gasps out, his face slick with sweat. "You can still be part of Kuznitsa. With them gone, I need a second in command. That could be you. I'll anoint you my successor."

Gabriel shakes his head.

"Shut up, Max! I was behind the door. I know what you had planned for me. Don't be sad. I would have done the same in your shoes. Now it's time for you to be quiet and listen. I'm going to tell you why you have to die. But I don't want you getting hungry as I tell you the story. Eat up!"

Max jerks back in his chair, shaking his head. His face is white. *Not only blood loss,* Gabriel thinks. *Shock, too.*

"What? You crazy fucking Englishman! No! No fucking way!"

Gabriel has been expecting this. He shrugs. Then he moves the MP5's fire-selector lever to semi-auto. He aims carefully and shoots Max through the left upper arm. A single round, carefully placed. The suppressor does a good job of quietening the explosion of the round leaving the muzzle, and Gabriel hears, or thinks he hears, the sound of Max's humerus shattering.

Max screams again and clutches his ruined arm with his right hand. Blood is leaking between his fingers.

"Funny thing, bullet wounds to the major skeletal bones," Gabriel says conversationally. "I learned this from a nurse back in England. According to Helen, there's a lot of fatty marrow inside them and when it escapes, it travels round the bloodstream. You can actually die of a fatty embolism if it reaches the brain or blocks a major blood vessel. Now EAT!" he roars. "Or I'll show you the true meaning of pain."

Moaning, eyes rolling like a stunned cow, Max picks up the half-eaten steak with his fingers and brings it to his lips. Opens his mouth. Bites. Chews. Swallows.

"Good," Gabriel says. "Keep going or I'll do your other arm and then we'll see about some of Krasivyj's wet work. You think this was some sort of soldier's grudge because you tried to have me killed, don't you? You're wrong. This is because you are a force of darkness, Max. You're one of them. The people who try to leach all happiness out of the world. I need a drink," he says suddenly, and grabs one of the glasses of wine, which, miraculously, have stayed upright, though their bowls are spattered with blood. He drains it in a single gulp and refills it. Drains that, too.

"Aah! That's better. I tell you what, Max. I have taken a shitload of drugs over the last few weeks. Not the kind you or you *biznes* partners trade in. I've been chugging antibiotics, painkillers, whatever they gave me in Red Dog. What did they call it? Oh, yes: Prison Brandy. Did you ever hear that phrase? Doesn't matter. Where was I? Oh, yes. Happiness. I don't expect much for myself. But this was someone who had a shot. You know? A real shot at happiness. Her name was Britta Falskog. Her middle name was Ingrid. Britta Ingrid Falskog. Hometown, Stockholm. Funny, clever, wickedly good sharpshooter. Rubbish with English slang."

A tear bulges in the corner of Gabriel's left eye and rolls down, clearing a pink path through the dark-red mess on his cheek. He ignores it, and the others that follow, and continues.

"Keep eating, Max. I meant what I said. I'll go to work on you with some of Stepashka's kitchen tools. You're thinking if I keep talking long enough, Donat and Anfim will come and save you. Good luck with that! They're both dead. Britta Ingrid Falskog. I proposed to her once, did you know that? No, of course not. Sorry. Then she broke it off. Said we couldn't be happy together. It cut me to the quick at the time, but she was right. Then, out of the blue, she comes to see me and tells me she's getting married. To a schoolteacher. He's a nice guy. Jarryd, his name is. Lives in Uppsala. They met at a *Midsommar* party. Now he's a widower before he was even married. He blames me. He hit me at her funeral. I don't blame him. But I don't blame myself, either. Because here's the thing, Max. I *know* I'm not perfect. Fuck, I'm about as far from perfect as it's possible to get and still be one of the good guys. But I try. You hear me? I try to be good. I try to forgive myself. Fariyah's always telling me that. She'd say, 'Did you pull the trigger, Gabriel?' And then I would say, 'No.' And she'd say, 'Exactly. The man who pulled the trigger is dead.' But who pulled *his* trigger, eh, Max? Who sent Nils Kristersson to kill me? Who murdered Britta Ingrid Falskog?"

Gabriel gets to his feet. The muzzle never wavers. It stays pointed at Max's undamaged arm. The Russian's head is wagging left and right. He has lost the power to speak and is keening quietly. His plate is empty. His chin is streaked with meat juice.

Gabriel moves to the wall. Slings the MP5 over his back. Takes down the shashka from its brackets.

He turns to face Max. Runs his thumb along the blade. Nods appreciatively. He moves behind Max. Using his left hand, he yanks the chair out before turning him around so Max's back is to the table. Then he takes a pace back and raises the sword above his head in a two-handed grip. Lowers it to his right side. Draws it back.

"Say her name," he whispers.

"What?"

"Say her name. Britta Ingrid Falskog. Say it and I'll make it quick."

Max tries to push himself upright with his good arm. Fails. He looks up at Gabriel. He opens his mouth. Inhales raggedly.

"Britta. Ingrid. Falskog."

The last part of her name is little more than a wisp of air that escapes the gangster's pale lips.

Gabriel puts everything he has into the blow. He whips the blade forward in a flat, whistling arc and fetches Max's head from his shoulders. It tumbles off the neck backwards and bumps to a stop on the table. The heart still has enough energy to send a jet or two of arterial blood squirting up towards the ceiling. Then the arcs diminish in height and volume. Max has lost a lot of blood already.

Gabriel reverses his grip on the sword so the point is downwards. Using both hands again he raises it high above his head then plunges it into the chest of the body that had once been Max Novgorodsky.

He leaves the room. Drops the MP5 and the shashka. Stumbles upstairs. Falls onto a bed. And sleeps.

56

Birdsong. The soughing of the wind through the trees beyond the garden's boundary. The smell of a summer morning out in the countryside.

Gabriel opened his eyes. Blinked at the brightness of the sunlight throwing bright white rectangles onto the wall opposite the open, uncurtained window.

He breathed in and retched immediately, so strong was the stink of dried blood – wolf and human – covering him from head to foot.

At some point in the night he must have woken long enough to untie the wolf pelt from around his shoulders and discard it. It lay on the floor to the right of the bed in a scraggy heap. He peeled himself away from the blood-hard sheets and wandered, half-dazed, into the bathroom, where he turned on the shower and stepped under the jets without waiting for the temperature to adjust.

He gasped as the ice-cold water hit the top of his head and ran over his skin, then yelped as it flashed to a few degrees from boiling, before settling down to a comfortable temperature. Staring down, he watched as the blood-red water swirled around his feet before spiralling away down the plughole. Minutes passed this way, the water lightening from deep, rose-pink, paler and paler, then running clear.

With a generous measure of shampoo in the palm of his hand, he started scrubbing at his hair, releasing a second torrent of red into the shower tray. After more shampoo, lime-scented shower gel, bar-soap and another fifteen minutes under increasingly hot jets, he stepped out, finally feeling clean.

Max had thoughtfully laid out shaving gear on the shelf above the sink, and Gabriel spent five minutes removing the last few days' stubble.

He dressed in chinos and a loose-fitting black polo shirt, then wandered downstairs. He was hungry, but there was something he wanted to do first.

* * *

The process of decay begins at the precise instant of death. In a cold climate, or in certain anaerobic conditions, the lack of heat and oxygen slows it down. In the warmth of the dacha, at the height of a Moscow summer, the conditions had had the opposite effect. The dining room had been transformed into a charnel house. Blood, viscera and brain matter spattered the walls and ceiling, and had run, dripped, fallen and pooled on the floor. The stink of putrefaction was enough to make Gabriel's eyes water. With one of the clean table napkins as an improvised bandanna, he strode over to the headless corpse of Max Novgorodsky.

He reached into the inside jacket pocket and removed the phone. He repeated the process with the other two bodies. Nozh's phone was smashed. A bullet had hit it dead-centre. Gabriel pocketed it just in case the techs back home could do something with it. Krasivyj's was intact. Breathing shallowly, he retreated to the fresher air beyond the door.

He went outside and pulled out the two working phones.

Now, Max. You were the boss. And the smart one. Yours will be locked. But Krasivyj. You were the idiot-friend who Max probably brought along for your good nature and willingness to do the jobs nobody else wanted to touch. A kopek to a ruble says yours is unprotected.

Gabriel pressed the home button and the screen lit up with an array of icons.

"Thanks, Handsome!" Gabriel said, happily reverting to speaking English.

He tapped in a number from memory. While he waited for the call to connect, he looked up. Buzzards were circling high above the dacha. He walked round to the front of the house to find a couple of the big, brown raptors hopping about and over Donat's corpse, darting their hooked beaks forward now and again to pull free a morsel of flesh.

The phone at the other end started ringing. Gabriel waited. Breathing steadily. In. Out. In. Waiting. Hoping everything would be OK.

The phone stopped ringing.

"Hello?" Unknown caller. The tone suspicious, wary. Who wouldn't be?

"Eli, it's me."

"Oh, my God, Gabriel. Where are you? Is everything OK?"

"Yeah. I'm OK. I'm fine. How's your Mum?"

She's doing well. They removed the bullets and she had some reconstructive surgery on her arm but she's OK. That was weeks ago, though. She's been at home getting physio and she's planning to return to work next week. I'm back in the UK now. What's been going on?"

Gabriel laughed. It was such a simple question, with such a complicated answer. He went for the simple version. Outcomes.

"They're all dead. Max, his two partners, everyone. It's over, Eli. I'm coming home."

"You sound tired. Was it hard this time?"

"It's always hard. But yeah, not the easiest of trips. I'll be fine. I just need to sleep in my own bed and eat some decent food for a while. Maybe go sailing with a beautiful Israeli girl. I don't suppose you know any, do you?"

"Cheeky bugger! You're obviously not doing too badly."

"Yeah, well, I miss you. I'm sorry I've been out of touch, especially with your mum being hurt. I—"

Hey! Enough. You did what you had to do. I only wish I could have been there with you. But Don's got me on what he calls a 'LETO' op here."

"LETO? That's a new one on me."

Eli laughed, and Gabriel's heart lifted at the sound.

"He was pretty pleased with it. It stands for Loose Ends Tying Off."

"OK. Have fun with it. Listen, I wish I could talk more, but there are things I need to do, and I should plan a way out of here. I'll see you soon, OK? A few days at the outside."

What Gabriel really craved was a huge plate of fried eggs, bacon, sausages and whatever else he could find to fry. But not wanting to stand at the hob with the splattered brains of the chef all over the front of the range cooker beside him, he grabbed a loaf of bread, some ham from the fridge and made a cup of instant coffee, then took the improvised meal out into the garden.

With the sun warming his face, he sat in one of the wicker chairs and ate.

"LETO," he said, and smiled.

He could imagine what that meant in reality.

57

LONDON

The intercom on Robert Finnie's desk buzzed.

"Robert, your eleven o'clock is here."

Even after three years, his secretary's cut-glass tones still sounded absurdly upper-class to his ears.

"Thanks, Caroline. Show her in, would you, please?

Finnie's latest client was ushered into his luxuriously appointed nineteenth floor office by a svelte secretary dressed in black, a double-row of pearls at her throat and a black velvet Alice band keeping her sleek, dark hair in check.

"Robert? This is Miss Myasnikova."

Finnie rose from his softly upholstered leather chair and came round the side of the desk to greet his visitor, an olive-skinned woman wearing a well-cut navy-blue trouser suit and carrying a slim, black briefcase. Large, circular sunglasses obscured her eyes. He'd found Russians liked such affectations. Musing that a name meaning "butcher's daughter" was singularly ill-suited to such an attractive woman, he held out his hand.

"Miss Myasnikova, a pleasure," he said, smiling warmly and

shaking her gloved hand, catching as he came closer, a whiff of lemon and sandalwood. "Please."

He gestured to a pair of armchairs positioned on each side of a tall, ornate fireplace, white marble streaked with black. A low table stood between them. She took the left-hand chair, the one with the light from the window behind it, and sat, crossing one leg over the other and smoothing her trouser leg down over her thigh. She ran a manicured hand through her bobbed, platinum-blond hair, then placed her case on the table.

"Thank you, Lord Robert," she said, in Russian-accented English.

Sitting down himself, he waved a hand.

"Please, call me Bob. These English titles are such a bore."

She smiled slightly, her frosted-pink lips parting fractionally.

"Bob. Then you must not call me Miss Myasnikova. Is too formal."

"Very well. What would you like me to call you?"

"Hmm." She removed her sunglasses and raised kohl-rimmed, grey-green eyes to the ceiling, then looked back at him. "How about," she paused, "Max?"

Finnie's pulse shot up.

"What?"

"Max! Is short for Maxine?"

"Oh, er, yes, of course. Sorry. Fine. Max."

Her brow furrowed.

"Everything is all right, Bob? You look like you see ghost."

He shook his head, willing himself to calm down. What just happened? The real Max hadn't made further contact, despite his having communicated the news to him. That was a good thing, wasn't it?

"No. I mean, everything's fine. Sorry. What do they say? A goose walked over my grave?"

The woman smiled.

"I have not heard before this expression."

Relaxing now, he managed a smile.

"It's an English saying. Like a premonition of death."

"Oh. That is, how would you say, morbid?"

He straightened in his chair and cleared his throat.

"Max, I have been remiss. Would you like some coffee? Or tea?"

She shook her head.

"No, thank you."

"Then, to business. How can I help you? You mentioned on the phone something about right to remain?"

She nodded.

"Yes. Is big problem."

"So, you're living here at the moment but only on a short-term visa?"

"No. I am living here permanently. With full approval of British Government."

Finnie frowned.

"Then forgive me, Max. I'm puzzled. If you already have permanent leave to remain, who are we talking about?"

She smiled.

"Why, Bob, you, of course!"

His frown deepened, as did a gnawing anxiety that this meeting wasn't playing out the way they normally did.

"I don't understand."

"Come and look at document I have. It makes everything plain."

Saying this, she opened the briefcase so that the lid obscured his view.

Wondering whether he was having his time wasted, he sighed, then got up, came round the table, and bent to peer at the contents of the briefcase. It held a single sheet of paper, face up. On it was typed a single word.

Traitor

Finnie tried to stand up but the woman's left hand shot out and grabbed him by the back of the neck. He struggled, but her grip was unyielding. Then he felt a sharp prick in the side of his throat,

ANDY MASLEN

which deepened into the kind of hard, focused, steely pain he associated with dental anaesthetics.

"What did you just do?" he croaked out, feeling his heart stutter in his chest.

"Killed you. Sixty seconds from now. Which is just long enough for me to tell you why. Sit down."

He staggered backwards and collapsed into his own chair, heart jumping and bouncing around in his chest like it was trying to escape. The woman fixed him with a hard stare.

"Robert Finnie, you betrayed your country to Max Novgorodsky. You—"

Finnie wondered what had happened to the accent. Shaking, and feeling sweat soaking into his shirt, he found the energy from somewhere to croak a response.

"I didn't—"

She continued as though he hadn't spoken.

"—provided intelligence, gained via a private investigator called Scott Randolph, whom we have interviewed, that my partner Gabriel Wolfe had not been killed by Novgorodsky's hired gun. Mr Finnie, like many before you, you chose the wrong side. As a result of your actions, your leave to remain on God's earth has just been revoked."

* * *

Eli waited the remaining fifteen seconds while the combination of Russian-manufactured carfentanyl (seized from a Russian agent the month before by MI5) and diazepam slowed, then stopped Finnie's heart.

She closed her briefcase, and left the office, running straight for the secretary's desk.

"You must call ambulance! Is Lord Robert. He is having heart attack!"

"Oh, my God!"

The secretary picked up her desk phone and punched in 0-9-9-9.

378

In the ensuing chaos, as a first-aider was called and people began rushing into the outer office, "Maxine Myasnikova" left the offices of Langham, Finnie, Hall and Robinson LLP, took a last look over her shoulder, smiled, then flagged down a black cab.

"Where to, miss?" the driver asked.

"Whitehall."

Shortly after pulling away, the cab driver swore and pulled over sharply, as an ambulance, blue lights flashing, sirens wailing, swerved round the wrong side of a traffic island, heading east.

58

MAX'S DACHA

His breakfast finished, Gabriel climbed out of the wicker chair and turned to go back inside. He planned on a final recce in Max's office, to collect and, if possible, transmit whatever files he could find, assuming the PC wasn't password protected. Then he planned to douse the dacha in petrol and torch the place. Leave no trace.

The familiar engine note of a Range Rover stopped him dead. For a split second, he imagined that somehow he hadn't killed Donat, and he'd managed to drive away for reinforcements. Then he pictured the Russian heavy staggering sideways before collapsing, blood spurting in thick, translucent jets from the rent in his throat and the buzzards feasting on his corpse.

Another Rangie then? And how come so many gangsters bought them? Did the company have some sort of special sales department targeting organised crime?

He ran towards the folding doors at the rear of the dacha then skidded to a stop as he saw an armed figure inside the sitting room, staring around him at the carnage. The man inside looked up, as though from some sixth sense, saw Gabriel, then turned his head to the left and yelled something. Gabriel couldn't hear anything through the glass. He didn't have to. Nobody yells if they're on their own.

He turned and sprinted for the end of the garden, aiming to lead – *Who? More Kuznitsa soldiers?* – away and then circle back to collect the MP5. Shit! Where had he left it? The hall? The dining room? The kitchen? He realised he couldn't remember. *First things first, Wolfe. Evasion.*

He heard more shouts from the front of the dacha. Spanish! Not the standard Castilian of a native-born Spaniard. This was South American Spanish. *Fuck! The Colombians.*

Not bothering to worry how they had tracked him here or even whether it was him they were after, Gabriel dodged through the little wooden gate and ran into the forest. From behind him, a burst of automatic fire fractured the air and he heard the bullets tearing through the foliage all around him. He ducked and ran down the path.

The Colombians were gaining on him, and he could make out at least two voices. They were coordinating.

"Vete a la izquierda. Voy a la derecha!" *Go left. I'll go right.*

More gunfire and this time, rounds smacked into the trunks of the trees ahead of him, throwing out sharp splinters.

Gabriel ran on. He dodged down the narrow path leading to the pond. After running round the edge for fifty metres, he turned left and began tracking back towards the dacha, this time taking care to make no noise.

More shouts from the Colombians.

"Por dónde se fue?" *Which way did he go?*

He heard them crash out of the underbrush and onto the pond's perimeter path. But no more gunfire and no more shouting. That meant they were all together and talking at normal volume.

He could see the side of the dacha and found an animal track just wide enough for a man. With silent strides, he headed back along it, remembering, with a quick and silent prayer of thanks, that he'd left the MP5 at the foot of the stairs, presumably dropping it there on his way upstairs.

From behind him, he could hear the Colombians again, shouting to each other and crashing through the forest back towards him. He pushed through the gate and dashed across the lawn, up towards the dacha. The plan was simple. Get in through the sliding doors, get to the stairs, grab the MP5, shoot the approaching enemy forces from cover. Preferably an upstairs window if he had time.

Then everything changed.

A dark-skinned man in black leather jacket and jeans stepped out from the side of the house, an assault rifle at his hip. *Colt M4*, Gabriel thought irrelevantly, unable, even in the heat of battle, to switch off his mental weapons identification system.

The Colombian grinned. The distance between them was well over forty metres. Gabriel was exposed in the middle of the lawn and the Colombian had all the time in the world to aim. He had tattoos on both cheeks. Even at this distance, Gabriel could see what they were: alligators.

The Colombian brought the rifle up to his shoulder.

And then his right arm spun away from his shoulder, two-metre jets of scarlet spurting sideways from the stump and painting the side of the dacha.

The gunman screamed as he dropped the M4 and half-turned. Then a long, narrow blade emerged from his side and just as quickly disappeared.

He fell forwards. Behind him, dressed in black from head to toe, stood a slender young woman, a long sword clasped in both hands. She wiped the sword, then swept it up and over her left shoulder, sheathing it in some sort of back-mounted scabbard. She brought round a short-barrelled Uzi submachine gun and yanked the charging lever with a snap audible over the distance between her and Gabriel.

She didn't shoot. So he completed his plan, running into the dining room and out through the far door to the hallway where the MP5 lay, just as he'd remembered. He checked the charging lever. It was ready to fire. Then he ran upstairs to the guest bedroom and took up a position beneath the window.

The other two Colombians had just reached the far edge of the garden and were running towards the house. Each man carried an M4. The leading man pointed at the back of the dacha, then sprinted off to Gabriel's left. His trajectory would bring him into the swordswoman's range.

Gabriel waited until his target was twenty metres from the back of the dacha then opened up with the MP5. The onrushing Colombian attempted to dodge sideways, then a round clipped his left leg, and he stumbled. The next burst took him in the head and he died as a welter of blood and brain matter exploded from his shattered skull. The MP5's magazine emptied with a final click.

Another burst of gunfire came from the edge of the dacha. Two weapons firing simultaneously. Gabriel couldn't see the action. He wasn't sure who he wanted to emerge from it. If anyone.

Then the shooting stopped. In the eerie silence that followed, he strained to hear a voice, even one calling out *in extremis* for its owner's God, or mother, just to help him identify whether he would be facing a Colombian or the mystery woman. But there was nothing.

Gabriel ran for the stairs. He reached the bottom and almost collided with the woman coming in the opposite direction. She aimed at the centre of his torso and he flinched, expecting the punch and the heat and the pain and the screaming and the darkness.

Up close he could see that she was at least part-Chinese. Her face was heart-shaped and her chin was pointed, almost elfin in its neatness. She stared at him with large, round, dark-brown eyes, a direct gaze he found impossible to read. She hadn't fired, so maybe there was hope. Her full, dark-red lips pursed, forming a cupid's bow. Those round eyes narrowed. She frowned, drawing lines in that otherwise flawless, high forehead.

His heart was pounding, and yet he didn't feel frightened of this woman with a submachine gun levelled at his guts. Not exactly. She spoke, in a clear, soft voice edged with suspicion. In Cantonese.

"Nǐ shì shéi?" *Who are you?*

"Méiyǒu tāmen de péngyǒu." *No friend of theirs*, he answered, jerking his head in the direction of the garden.

Her eyes widened, clearly surprised he could speak her language. "Hái yǒu tāmen?" *And them?* She jerked the gun barrel left, towards the dining room.

Gabriel shook his head.

"Wǒ shāle tāmen." *I killed them.*

She nodded. Touched the tip of her left index finger to her top lip.

Gabriel could feel his pulse settling. Was she still going to kill him? Or was she hesitating because he'd done her dirty work for her? If he could find a way to distract her, he had a chance at closing the gap between them. Inside the barrel length of the Uzi, he gave himself better-than-evens odds at killing her using his bare hands. The sword hilt protruded from its scabbard above her left shoulder, so she'd try to draw it. He'd have to get to it first or immobilise her sword arm.

She grinned at him, revealing small, even teeth, and took a step back, adjusting her grip on the Uzi. Shaking her head, she spoke.

"Ó, bù, nǐ méiyǒu!" *Oh, no you don't!*

Gabriel frowned. She was good. He didn't think he'd communicated his intentions, but maybe she was just highly trained. She must have been to deal so effectively with the Colombians.

She levelled the Uzi.

Gabriel tensed.

And again, that pause. She frowned. Held his gaze as seconds ticked by.

She shook her head again and pulled the trigger.

59

Gabriel fell, arms across his stomach, smacking the back of his head against the wooden floor. Chunks of plaster and wood rained down onto him from the ceiling, which was riddled with bullet holes. He coughed as he inhaled the fine white plaster dust, scrunching his eyes shut at the pain from the gritty particles.

He rolled onto his side and sat up, still clutching his midriff with his left hand. He waited for the pain. Gingerly felt around for a wound, alive to the imminent contact between fingertips and his own insides. But he was uninjured. His ears were ringing from the gunfire, and his nose stung from the sharp tang of burnt propellant.

Blinking rapidly, he gradually managed to open his eyes, struggling against the urge to rub them or try to pick out the debris that had virtually blinded him. He staggered down the passageway into the kitchen and groped his way to the sink, where he ran the cold water and leaned forwards until his head was in midstream and he could wash out the grit.

Finally able to see again, though with eyes still smarting, he ran back to the hallway and the front door. Outside, Donat's corpse, black and buzzing angrily with flies, lay beside the Range Rover.

Behind it, a second, this one in white, had been parked at an angle blocking in the black SUV.

The woman had vanished. He studied the ground. Two sets of tyre tracks only. Both from the Range Rovers. So either she'd come on foot or from the air. But she was gone. Frowning, and feeling as though he'd awoken from a dream, Gabriel returned to the dacha. It was time to leave. But not for England. Not quite yet. He had one last appointment in Russia.

* * *

Travelling by borrowed Range Rover, taxi, plane and hire car, Gabriel took two days to reach Tatyana's company headquarters in Saint Petersburg. The pink stone building on Admiralty Embankment overlooked the River Neva. From the ornate architecture, he guessed it dated from the nineteenth century.

After introducing himself at Reception, he took the lift to the fifth floor. Tatyana's office gave onto the river. They sat opposite each other in two Louis Quatorze armchairs, the gilt legs and purple velvet upholstery making Gabriel feel as though he were a courtier at the court of the French "Sun King" himself.

He explained to Tatyana that Kuznitsa was effectively finished. Yes, there might be a few local underbosses scattered around, maybe some foot soldiers. But without their leadership to direct them, pay their wages and provide the glue holding them together, they would eventually peel away to other gangs or set up in business for themselves.

She asked him about the Colombians, bringing up the question of the blackmail threat. After he told her the story of the three who'd turned up at Max's dacha, and their end at his hands and those of the mysterious Chinese assassin, she seemed visibly relieved.

"If only I could get those damned photos back," she said, "then I'd know the whole mess was truly behind me."

"I know this sounds like the long shot to end all long shots, Tanya, but if I ever hear of them, or even meet somebody who's heard of them, I'll find them and bring them back to you. I promise."

"Thank you, dear Gabriushka. I know you will, if you can. Now," she said, clapping her hands together, "What do you need for your trip back to England?"

"Just the things I left at your dacha. Then I can make my own way."

She had his things, from passport and wallet to clothes and toiletries driven down to his hotel by one of her staff the following day.

60

SHOREDITCH

On the ride into London from Heathrow, Gabriel's phone had buzzed and delivered a stream of emails and texts. One in particular made him smile.

Camaro ready for collection at Felixstowe. Please bring two forms of ID and shipping receipt.

As the black taxi clattered away down Haberdasher Street, Gabriel turned and walked up the short path to Eli's front door. He stood at the gate and looked up at the red-brick house. Eli's flat occupied the first and second floors. She'd planted scarlet geraniums in window boxes that glowed against the white-painted window frames. Closing the black wrought-iron gate behind him – *No squeak, efficient Eli!* – he walked up to the canary-yellow front door. He stretched out his right arm, finger poised to ring the bell, then hesitated.

Will she want me like this? That was about as far from a disciplined operation as it was possible to get. I think I lost it over there. Killing people just to worm my way into Max's confidence – a doomed mission, as it turned out, since he never trusted me. And I need Don's plastic surgeon again, only this time it's not to repair the damage caused by a state torturer, but my own crazy knifework. I—

The door swung inwards and Eli stood there.

"Eli. I'm back," he said.

She looked at a point somewhere above his eyes, frowning.

"What the fuck happened to your hair?"

Gabriel had forgotten his Moscow thug look altogether. He ran his fingers through it, realising that his hair had grown out from the super-short cut the Moscow Barber had given him. He could imagine it, half-brown and half-blond.

"You don't like it?" he deadpanned.

Her face broke into a huge smile and she threw her arms around him.

"Oh, God, I'm so glad to have you here with me again," she whispered fiercely into his ear.

He inhaled deeply, wanting to fill his lungs with her smell, desperate to dispel the stink of blood that had haunted him all the way from Max's dacha to Moscow. She led him inside, down the narrow hallway and into the kitchen. He glanced at the wall clock above the table: 7.45 p.m.

"Sit down and let me get you a glass of wine, then you can tell me what you've been up to," Eli said moving towards the fridge. "I put some Chablis in when you called."

"Actually, you know what I'd really like?"

"What? A beer? A gin and tonic?"

"A mug of tea. Large. English Breakfast if possible."

Eli laughed.

"I think we can run to that. We'll drink the wine later."

As Eli ran water into the kettle and spooned tea into the pot, Gabriel felt his shoulders relax and the tight band of tension around his chest loosen.

"How's your mum?" he asked.

Eli turned, her smile still wide.

"She's good. I spoke to her this morning. She's going back to work on Monday. Dad wanted her to take more time off, but she told me he's been driving her crazy, bringing her the morning paper, cups of tea, insisting she rests the whole time. 'Eliya, it's either go back to work or get a divorce,' she said to me! Poor Dad, I think it just shook him up."

"I'm glad. She's better, I mean. Not that he was shaken up."

Eli poured the water into the teapot and brought it to the table along with two mugs and a bottle of milk.

She took Gabriel's hands in hers and looked straight into his eyes.

"So. Tell me everything. Leave nothing out."

Gabriel looked at the ceiling for a moment, then back at Eli. Realised at that precise moment how much he loved her.

"After I got my hair dyed, I headbutted a Moscow cop," he began, enjoying the way Eli's eyes widened above a grin.

The next morning, Gabriel rose before Eli, and went for a run along the pre-commuter-quiet streets of Shoreditch. Back at 6.55 a.m., he made coffee and toast and took it up to Eli on a tray.

"Morning, sleepyhead," he said, as he prodded the bedroom door open with his toe. "Brought you breakfast."

All that was visible of Eli was a tousled mass of auburn hair on the pillow. The hair lifted from the pillow and turned through ninety-degrees to reveal its owner's sleep-smeared face.

"Morning," she said. "What time is it?"

"Just after seven. I'm due to debrief the boss at ten."

Eli hauled herself upright and pulled the duvet up to cover her breasts. Gabriel handed her a mug of coffee and a plate of toast, then sat on the edge of the bed and turned to face her.

"Eli?"

"Yes."

"While I was on the plane back from Saint Petersburg, I was thinking about us."

"Oh, yeah? Nothing bad, I hope?"

He smiled.

"No, only good things. And I just wondered, I mean I know how you hate this part of London, and The Department, well it's not known for its bureaucratic efficiency so it could be ages before they sort you out with somewhere else to live, and I just wondered—" He coughed, suddenly uncertain how to phrase what he wanted to say.

"What are you wittering on about?" she said, grinning. "You sound like a vicar asking for a blowjob!"

Gabriel burst out laughing.

"I just wondered if you want to have a holiday at mine?"

Eli looked at him with narrowed eyes.

"A holiday," she said, flatly.

"Yeah, you know. Maybe a long holiday. You could keep this place on, so, you, you know, you'd have a bolthole, but I'd just love it if you'd think about coming back to Aldeburgh with me. Even for a week. Just to, I mean, so you could—"

"Still hearing the vicar," she said, grinning. "Look, these last few months, you've been under a shitload of stress. I mean, even by our standards. I don't know how many pills you popped, or what the combination of uppers, downers and sidewaysers did to your brain, but you lost it a couple of times. Big time. So, yes, I'd love to come and stay for a bit. God knows, somebody has to try to keep you out of trouble. But let's take it slowly, OK? No need to rush into anything."

Gabriel didn't say anything at first. He tried to separate the thoughts and feelings that were tangling in his head. Keeping Eli safe. Not dragging her into the crosshairs. Wanting to be with her. Not wanting to go to a funeral in Israel. She was right about the drugs, too. Weapons-grade painkillers, antibiotics, horse tranquiliser, Usbayev's antidote, Prison Brandy and enough plain old hooch to float a battleship. *I need to get myself straight. I'll do that before she and I get in any deeper. She doesn't need my protection.*

"Sounds like a plan," he said, aiming for nonchalant and sounding more like couldn't-care-less.

"Fine," she said. "I'm going to get a shower and then pack some clothes and stuff. I'll come with you to see Don, and then we can go straight from Rothford to your place."

Gabriel felt his heart balloon inside his chest – a physical sensation of lightening that made him grin before taking Eli in his arms.

By using every last litre of storage space in Eli's Mini, including the boot, back seat, rear footwells and even the glove box, Gabriel and Eli managed to squeeze his bags and hers into the undersized car. Eli drove fast through the streets of East London, heading for the M11 and Essex.

Gabriel was silent. Worrying at the problem of how to have some sort of normal life with Eli and still do the only job he was fit for. Then he thought of Tatyana. How she'd lost first her honour, then her idiot of a first husband, much later, her son, and then her second husband. Yet she kept going. Never weakening, never giving in.

"Penny for them," Eli said, breaking into his thoughts.

"I was thinking about Tanya. She's had a tough life. Losing Grigori and then Genady like that. It takes its toll on a person."

"What doesn't kill me—"

"—makes me stronger. Yeah, I just hope Nietzsche was right."

"I think he was. Look at us. Look at my mum. Tanya's at least as tough as the life she's led. With friends like you in the world, and people like Oleg, she'll be fine."

They pulled up at MOD Rothford's main gate at 9.45 a.m. Eli turned off the Mini's engine, which spun down with a whine like a food mixer coming to a stop.

She climbed out and stretched, attracting an appreciative glance from the soldier on duty. Gabriel smiled, shaking his head. He wasn't sure if she knew the effect she had on men, especially, for some reason, those in uniform, but it was amusing to watch.

"Morning, Sarge," she said. "Schochat and Wolfe here to see Colonel Webster."

"Yes, miss. It's Eli, isn't it?"

"Well remembered," she said, flashing him a wide smile that had him grinning back.

"OK, let's just get you signed in and you can be on your way."

The formalities dealt with, Eli jumped back in, started the car and drove carefully over the traffic treadles, which clunked and clacked beneath the Mini's wheels.

"How do you do it?" Gabriel asked.

"Do what?"

"Turn battle-hardened sergeants into your slaves?"

Eli glanced at him, her face a mask of incomprehension.

"I have literally no idea what you mean."

Don welcomed them at the door to the admin block, holding his arms out wide to Eli who accepted the hug before stepping back. Don turned to Gabriel.

"Good to have you back, Old Sport," he said. "Don't worry, I'm not going to hug you," he added, extending a hand.

"How's your mother, Eli?" Don asked.

"She's fine, thanks, boss. Back at work on Monday."

"Good, good. Strong lady. I hope to meet her one day. Please understand, I want to debrief Gabriel on his own. Can you amuse yourself for a while? I called the armourer to let him know you might want to spend some time on the range. I believe he's got some new toys for you to play with."

In Don's office, Gabriel gave his boss a longer and more detailed version of the narrative he'd shared with Tatyana in her river-view office. When he finished, Don didn't speak immediately, instead resorting to the mannerism that he used, consciously or not, to give himself some thinking time.

"Hmm, mm-hmm. So, apart from the business with the Moscow Attorney General's office, no interference with the Russian state apparatus."

"No. I did my time at Red Dog with fake papers, and whatever

Max had over the governor or the Moscow prosecuting authorities would have been a criminal matter between Russian citizens."

"OK, good. That looks eminently containable. And obviously we're pleased that Kuznitsa's a busted flush. I spoke to my oppos at Five and Six yesterday. They're more than happy. Margot Stevens actually offered to buy me dinner, which was a first. Now, we need to have a think about what you're going to do next."

Gabriel frowned.

"What do you mean?"

Don sighed and steepled his fingers under his chin.

"Look here, Old Sport. The last few months have been, what shall we call them, more than usually testing, even by our standards? Even by *yours*. I want you to take some time off. Get that arm seen to. Maybe pay a visit to Fariyah. Maybe more than one."

Gabriel felt his pulse speeding up.

"No! I'm fine. I don't need to see her. I just need to take a day or two. I'll take the boat out. Get some sun. I'm fine, boss."

Don shook his head.

"I don't think you are. From what you just told me, there were at least half a dozen times when you were reckless beyond even your own," he frowned, "*relaxed* standards. That you're standing here and not dumped in a Russian landfill with a 7.62 in your brain has as much to do with luck as planning."

Gabriel wanted to contain the anger banking up inside him. But he couldn't. He could feel it swelling in his gut like black bile.

"I just took out an organised crime group on my own! I killed the people who murdered Britta! You and the Swedes, that fool Ekström, should be thanking me, not benching me."

Don's face hardened and he smacked an open palm down on his desk.

"That's enough, *Agent* Wolfe! Far from being a fool, Olof Ekström has been your staunchest supporter in all of your recent adventures. Once he learned what you were doing, and the progress you were making, he argued for leaving you in play. There were others – not me, I hasten to add – but powerful others, who wanted you extracted, forcibly if necessary. It was felt, and I quote, 'We simply can't have covert operatives running their own private revenge missions deep inside Russia.'" Don delivered this sentence in a lisping parody of a British public school accent.

Gabriel tried to control his breathing, folding his arms across his chest and staring at a point on the wall just behind and to the left of Don's head. Don hadn't finished.

"You need to watch your step, Old Sport," he said, in a fatherly tone. "You're one of my best people, and you know my personal feelings towards you, but this is a high-stakes game we play. The highest. Nothing comes before operational effectiveness, do you understand me? Nothing. I want you to take some time off. *Proper* time off. Six weeks. Do nothing. Go fishing. Sail your boat. Learn a musical instrument. At the end of that period, I want you to take a psych. eval. Fariyah can do it, or if you prefer to keep work and personal issues separate, I'll arrange for a Department shrink to do it. Understand?"

"Do I have a choice?"

"No."

"Then, yes, I understand."

Don pursed his lips.

"Look here, Gabriel. Try not to take this personally. If it were anyone else, Eli, Sam, Patch, Nick … any of them, I'd ask the same of them."

Gabriel stood.

"Thanks, boss," he said.

Outside, he found Eli leaning against the Mini, face tilted back. Her auburn hair flared red whenever the sun lit it, and it did so now. She pushed herself upright.

"How did it go?"

"He was so happy with my performance he just benched me."

"What?"

"Told me I had to take six weeks' leave and get a psych. eval. at the end of it."

Eli didn't answer immediately. Then she spoke.

"Get in. We'll talk on the way. It's easier."

Clear of the base and heading towards Aldeburgh on the A12, Eli spoke.

"You *have* been on edge recently. You know, not quite your normal self."

"As in—"

"As in coming to bed at some ungodly hour in the morning smelling of adrenaline like you'd been in a firefight. As in getting into it with those Swedish bikers. Maybe the boss has a point. Is a paid break really that bad an option?"

Gabriel shrugged, knowing she was right, and realising, as he reviewed the meeting with Don, that something uncontrollable had bubbled to the surface like gas escaping a toxic swamp.

"Maybe. I just thought he'd be more, you know, pleased."

"Oh, dear!" Eli stretched out her left hand and squeezed his thigh. "That sounds like you need his love, not his approval. Of course he's pleased. But you know Don. He's pretty stiff upper lip, eh, what?" she said, putting on a cod English accent like a World War One general. "No sense giving the chaps too much praise, turns them bally soft!"

It was just silly enough. Gabriel burst out laughing.

"Oh, God, Eli, you're right. *He's* right. It's just, I don't know, ever since that confrontation with the Chinese girl I've felt that something's wrong."

"Wrong how? With you?"

"No. Yes. I don't know. She could have killed me. She had an Uzi aimed at my head. Then she just emptied the mag into the ceiling. Why did she do that?"

"Maybe because you'd just helped her out with her targets. Is that so hard to believe?"

"Maybe. But is that what you or I would do? Wouldn't we want to clean up after ourselves? Leave no trace, all that? It's what I was in the middle of doing myself, until the Colombians arrived."

"Yeah, I guess I would. So what's your theory?"

"I don't have one."

"OK, look. Forget the mystery Chinese assassin. Forget Max Novgorodsky. Forget Don. You've got six weeks to enjoy yourself. Take advantage! Have some fun!"

"OK. I will. And I know exactly how to start."

Gabriel called the shipping company and arranged to collect Lucille, Vinnie Calder's black Camaro, the following morning.

* * *

Driving Lucille on American roads was one thing. Driving that same, fat-bodied muscle car on English B-roads from Felixstowe to Aldeburgh proved to be quite another. Having been almost run off the road by an oncoming metallic pink Honda Jazz occupying the centre of a hedgerow-lined lane, Gabriel drove the rest of the way straining to catch sight of another elderly Kamikaze pilot before she totalled herself, her economical hatchback, the Camaro and Gabriel.

He managed to find a couple of empty roads where he could let the 6.2-litre-engined car stretch its considerable legs, laughing aloud as the ridiculous bellow from the exhaust let most of Suffolk know he was coming.

Perhaps because it was half the size of Lucille, Eli's Mini gradually left him for dead, zipping round corners and shimmying through twisty S-bends. Although he could catch her on the straights, these were few and far between. Then, red lights flashing, a level-crossing started to close. Not even doubting what Eli would do, and fearing a chase would lead to something messy on the tracks, Gabriel braked the Camaro to a halt. Eli shot across the crossing, briefly leaving the ground and striking sparks from the underside of the car on the far side.

While he waited for the two-coach train to trundle into sight and cross in front of him, Gabriel watched as the Mini's metallic-blue behind disappeared around a distant bend.

He made it home to find Eli in the garden reading a magazine wearing a denim sundress that showed off her figure.

She looked up and raised her eyebrows.

"Hello! I thought we'd lost you."

"Haha! Very amusing. What're you reading?"

Eli held up the magazine, its pages flapping in a sudden gust of wind.

"It's a personality quiz. You know, 'What kind of job would make you truly happy?'"

"And?"

Eli's face was completely expressionless as she answered him.

"It says I would make an excellent driving instructor."

Gabriel's mouth dropped open.

Eli cracked first, throwing her head back and laughing.

"Gotcha!" she shrieked, tears streaming down her face. "Oh, you poor thing. Your face!"

Gabriel went to grab the magazine, and they ended up wrestling on the grass, much to the amusement of a family passing by.

After an early dinner at the Brudenell Hotel, Eli said she wanted to walk along the beach.

"To say goodbye," as she put it.

Gabriel left her to it, crossing the near-empty carpark and going inside. In his office, he removed a sheet of paper from the printer tray. Then he sat down, uncapped his pen, and began to write.

61

My vengeance for Britta's death is complete. Max Novgorodsky is dead. So are his two lieutenants, Nozh and Krasivyj. And his three bodyguards, Fedya, Anfim and Donat. His recruiting sergeant, Vlad the Impaler, is also dead. And his chef, Stepashka, who had the misfortune to be in the wrong place at the wrong time. I also killed, skinned and butchered his pet wolf, Pyotr, an act of which I am not proud. To ingratiate myself with Max, I killed another gangster who called himself Little Stalin. His nickname rang a bell. I did some research and found his inspiration. A 1931 gangster movie called Little Caesar, starring Edward G. Robinson.

In Max's dacha, I came face-to-face with a Chinese assassin. Was she there to kill Max, or was she tracking the three Colombian cartel members she and I killed? Presumably they were the ones who were heading for New Galaxy. She could have killed me. In fact, I think she wanted to. *Meant* to. Then something stopped her. I have no idea what.

My brains have been fried, scrambled and boiled over the last few weeks. I suspect I may have lost more than a little perspective while I was in Russia. Certainly, looking back on my time there, I distinguished myself not by the soldierly values of valour, restraint, clear thinking and military discipline, but by a ruthless, determined, single-minded and at times maddened desire to wipe out Kuznitsa and everything connected to it, whatever the cost. No quarter asked, or given.

This was always personal, despite the fig leaf of national security that Don offered me. He was accommodating, I suppose that's the right word. He knew what I'd want to do, and he made no attempt to stop me. But I hope I repaid his trust and forbearance with the intel I gathered at Max's dacha. Having one fewer organised crime group in the world can only be a good thing, so I suppose I have done her Majesty a favour by my actions. That's what makes Don's benching me really hurt.

At some point very soon, I need to go back to Sweden. To see Sixten and Ebba, and Freja and Karl. And Jarryd. To tell them I have avenged the death of the woman they all loved so much. The woman I loved, too, in my way.

The Russians have a word for a contract killer. Like the one they sent after me. The one who killed Britta. It's the same in English.

When Max pressed the fire button, he thought he was launching just one. He was wrong.

The End

COPYRIGHT

ACKNOWLEDGMENTS

As with every book I write, the finished story has been shaped by a team of talented and dedicated people whom I now have the opportunity to thank. My first readers, Simon Alphonso and Sandy Wallace. My editor, Michelle Lowery. My proofreader, John Lowery. My "sniper spotters": OJ "Yard Boy" Audet, Ann Finn, Yvonne Henderson, Vanessa Knowles, Nina Rip and Bill Wilson. My cover designer, Stuart Bache. My advanced readers. And, as always, my family.

I must also thank the serving and former soldiers, friends all, whose advice helps me to keep the military details accurate: Giles Bassett, Mark Budden, Mike Dempsey and Dickie Gittins. Any and all mistakes in this area are mine alone.

Andy Maslen
Salisbury, 2019

ABOUT THE AUTHOR

Andy Maslen was born in Nottingham, in the UK, home of legendary bowman Robin Hood. Andy once won a medal for archery, although he has never been locked up by the sheriff.

He has worked in a record shop, as a barman, as a door-to-door DIY products salesman and a cook in an Italian restaurant.

As well as the Stella Cole and Gabriel Wolfe thrillers, Andy has published five works of non-fiction, on copywriting and freelancing, with Marshall Cavendish and Kogan Page. They are all available online and in bookshops.

He lives in Wiltshire with his wife, two sons and a whippet named Merlin.

AFTERWORD

To keep up to date with news from Andy, join his Readers' Group at www.andymaslen.com.

Email Andy at andy@andymaslen.com.
Join Andy's Facebook group, The Wolfe Pack.

Printed in Great Britain
by Amazon

85358123R00242